## About the Authors

...t Wilson ... nd ... never stopped ... of ... *rley and the M*... , ... th names beg... avid ... , Scarlet star... every Enid Blyton book, ... on to the *Chalet School* series and many years ... er found Mills & Boon.

... ined and worked as a nurse and health visitor, ... currently works in public health. For her, finding ... l Romances was a match made in heaven. She ... ted to find herself among the authors she has ... ad for many years.

... lives on the West Coast of Scotland with her ... and their two sons.

... **Singh** lives outside of Boston, USA with her ... d, children, and a very rambunctious yorkie. ... r several years in the corporate world, she finally ... ed the advice of family and friends to 'give ... writing a go already'. She's oh-so-happy she did. ... n not at her keyboard, she likes to spend time on ... tennis court or golf course. Or immersed in a good ... d.

**...nna Neil** loves writing romance and has written ... re than sixty books for Mills & Boon. Before her ... iting career started she had a variety of jobs, which included being a telephonist, a clerk, as well as nursing ... d work in a hospital pharmacy. She was an infant teacher for a number of years before her love of writing took o... and ga...

# Love Islands: Summer Kisses

SCARLET WILSON

NINA SINGH

JOANNA NEIL

MILLS & BOON

First published in Great Britain 2019
by Mills & Boon, an imprint of HarperCollins*Publishers*
1 London Bridge Street, London, SE1 9GF



ISBN: 978-0-263-27553-7

# THE DOCTOR SHE LEFT BEHIND

SCARLET WILSON

For Cathy McAuliffe, Catherine Bain and Shirley Bain with lots of love for the women who manage to put up with all these Bain boys!

# CHAPTER ONE

'YOU REALLY THINK this is a good idea?' Nathan Banks shook his head. Nothing about this sounded like a good idea to him.

But Lewis nodded. 'I think it's a great idea. I need a doctor. You need a job.'

'But I already have a job.' He lifted his hands. 'At least I think I do. Is my contract not being renewed?'

His stomach turned over a little. Last night had been a particularly bad night in A & E. His medical skills were never in question but his temper had definitely been short. It hadn't been helped by hearing a car backfire on the walk home and automatically dropping to the ground as if it were gunfire. His last mission for Doctors Without Borders had been in a war zone. Dropping to the floor when you heard gunfire had become normal for him. But doing it in the streets of Melbourne? Not his proudest moment. Particularly when a kid on the way to school had asked him what was wrong.

Lewis smiled. The way he always did when he was being particularly persuasive. Nathan had learned to spot it over the years. 'The last few days in A & E have been tough. You came straight out of Doctors Without Borders after five years and started working here. You've never really had a holiday. Think of this as your lucky day.'

Nathan lifted the buff-coloured folders. 'But this isn't a holiday. This is a form of torture. My idea of a holiday is walking in the hills of Scotland somewhere, or surfing on Bondi Beach. Being stranded on an island with nine B-list celebrities? I'm the least celeb-orientated person on the planet. I couldn't care less about these people.'

Lewis nodded. 'Exactly. That's what makes you perfect. You can be objective. All you need to do is supervise the fake TV challenges and monitor these folk's medical conditions for the three weeks they're on the island. The rest of the time you'll get to sit around with your feet up.' He bent over next to Nathan and put one hand on his shoulder, waving the other around as if he were directing a movie. 'Think of it—the beautiful Whitsunday islands, the surrounding Coral Sea, luxury accommodation and perfect weather with only a few hours' work a day. What on earth could go wrong?'

Nathan flipped open the first folder. Everything about this seemed like a bad idea. It was just a pity that the viewing public seemed to think it was a great one. *Celebrity Island* had some of the best viewing figures on the planet. 'But some of these people shouldn't be going to a celebrity island, let alone doing any challenges. They have serious medical conditions.'

Lewis waved his hand. 'And they've all had million-dollar medicals for the insurance company. The TV company needs someone with A & E experience who can think on their feet.'

'I hardly think epidemic, natural disaster and armed conflict experience is what a TV crew needs.'

Lewis threw another folder towards him. 'Here. Read up on snake bites, spiders and venom. The camp will be checked every night but you can't be too careful.'

The expression on Lewis's face changed. The hard sell wasn't working and it was obvious he was getting desperate.

'Please, Nathan. I agreed to this contract before I knew Cara was pregnant. I need to find someone to replace me on the island. The last thing I want is to end up sued for breach of contract. You're the one person I trust enough to ask.'

Nathan took a long, slow breath. Working for a TV company was the last thing he wanted to do. But Lewis was right. He was close to burnout. And in some ways he was lucky his friend had recognised it. How bad could three weeks on an island in the Coral Sea be? The celebs might have to sleep by a campfire but the production crew were supposed to have luxury accommodation. He shook his head. 'Why didn't you just tell me this was about Cara's pregnancy?'

Lewis looked away for a second. 'There have been a few issues. A few complications—a few hiccups as we've got closer to the end. We didn't really want to tell anyone.' He slid something over the desk towards him. 'Here, the final sweetener. Look at the pay cheque.'

Nathan's eyes boggled. 'How much?' He shook his head again. 'It doesn't matter what the pay cheque is, if you'd told me this was about Cara I would have said yes right away.' He lifted his hands. 'I would have volunteered and done it for nothing. Sometimes you've got to be straight with people, Lewis.'

Lewis blinked, as if he was contemplating saying something else. Then he gave his head a little shake. 'Thank you, Nathan.' He walked around and touched Nathan's shoulder. 'I need a medic I can trust. You'll have back-up. Another doctor is flying out from Canberra to join the TV crew too. Last year I was there I worked twelve hours—tops—over three weeks. Trust me. This will be the easiest job you've ever had.'

Nathan nodded slowly. It still didn't appeal. He had a low tolerance to all things celebrity. But three weeks of easy paid work in a luxury location? He'd have to be a fool to say no. Plus, Lewis had helped him when he'd landed in Australia straight out of Doctors Without Borders and with no job. Of course he'd help. 'What happens when I get back?'

Lewis met his gaze. 'You're a great medic. We're lucky to have you. I'll give you another six-month contract for A & E—if you want it, of course.'

He hesitated only for a second. Lewis was one of his oldest friends and he knew they'd waited four years for Cara to fall pregnant. There was no way he could let him down. Even if it was the last place on this earth he wanted to go.

He picked up the pen. 'Tell Cara I'll be thinking about her. Okay, where do I sign?'

Rachel Johnson took a few final moments lying on the sun lounger at the pool. She couldn't believe for a second she was getting paid for this.

She'd been here two days and hadn't had to do a minute of work. Apparently her job started as soon as she hit the island. Which was fine by her. From what she'd seen of the nine celebrities taking part in *Celebrity Island,* she suspected they ranged from mildly whiny to difficult and impossible. Her old university friend Lewis Blake had persuaded her to take part and the fee was astronomical. But that wasn't why she was here.

She was here because her Hippocratic oath seemed to have her over a barrel. Her ex—an Australian soap star—was taking part. And she was one of the few that knew his real medical history. It seemed that one of his bargaining chips had been to ask for a doctor he could trust. And even though there was nothing between them, part of her felt obliged to help.

'Are you ready, Dr Johnson? The seaplane has just landed.'

Rachel jumped up from the comfortable lounger and grabbed her rucksack packed with her clothes. Two days staying in the luxury five-star resort had been bliss. All the medical supplies she would need had already been shipped. Apparently the other medic was already on the island. And since there was no way off the island for the next three weeks she hoped it was someone she could work with. Between the two of them, they would be on call twenty-four hours a day for three weeks. Lewis had assured her that apart from monitoring the challenges there really wasn't anything to do. But, as much as she loved him, Lewis had always been economical with the truth.

Rachel climbed into the seaplane that was bobbing on the blue ocean. She'd never been in one of these before and the ride was more than a little bumpy. But the view over the island worth it.

The pilot circled the island, letting her see the full geography. 'This is the beach where some of the celebrities will be dropped off. The beach on the other side is for the crew. It has umbrellas, sun loungers and a bar—so don't worry, you'll be well looked after.' As he crossed thc middle of the island the view changed to a thick jungle. 'Camp is in the middle,' he said. 'Don't tell anyone but they actually have a rain canopy they can pull overhead if we get one of the seasonal downpours. We didn't have it the first year and the whole camp got swept away in a torrent of water.'

Rachel shifted uncomfortably in her seat. That sounded a little rougher than she'd expected. 'Where will I be staying?'

He pointed to some grey rectangular buildings in the distance. 'The three big grey buildings are the technical huts and production gallery. You'll be staying in a portable cabin. The medical centre is right next to you.' He let out a laugh that sounded more like a pantomime witch's cackle. 'Just next to the swamp and the rope bridge. The celebrities love those.' He gave Rachel a nod. 'I won't tell you how many of them have fallen off that rope bridge.'

For a second her throat felt dry. Lewis's version of the truth was already starting to unravel. A portable cabin and a hotel were not the same thing. Her dreams of a luxury bed and state-of-the-art facilities had just vanished in the splutter of a seaplane's engines. There might be an ocean right next to her but there was no swimming pool, no facilities and definitely no room service. This was sounding less and less like three weeks in the sun and more and more like she would be wringing Lewis's neck the next time she saw him.

The seaplane slowed and bumped to a landing on the water, moving over to a wooden quay. A burly man in a grey T-shirt tinged with sweat grabbed the line so she could open the door and jump down.

'Doc Johnson?'

She nodded.

He rolled his eyes. 'I'm Ron. Welcome to paradise.'

The wooden quay gave a little sway as she landed on it.

They walked quickly along the beach and up a path towards the grey portable cabins. 'Kind of out of place for paradise?' she said.

Ron laughed. 'Is that how they got you out here? Told the same story to the other doc too. But he's been fine. Said he's used to sleeping in camp beds anyhow and it doesn't make any difference to him.'

A horrible shiver crept down Rachel's spine. She'd spent five years at university in London with Lewis and a group of other friends. Then another couple of years working in the surrounding London hospitals. Lewis knew everything about her. He knew everything about the guy she'd dated for five years back then. Lewis was the common denominator here. He wouldn't have done anything stupid, would he?

Ron showed her up to the three cabins sitting on an incline. 'The rest of the crew stay along the beach a little. You and the other doc are in here. Medical centre is right next to you. And the one next to that is the most popular cabin on the beach.'

'Showers?' she said hopefully.

'Nope. Catering,' he answered with a broad smile.

'Okay. Thanks, Ron.' She pushed open the door to the cabin and sent a silent prayer upwards.

The cabin was empty. There was a sitting area in the middle with a sofa. A bathroom with a shower of sorts, and two rooms at either end. It wasn't quite army camp beds. They were a little better than that. But the rooms were sparse, with only a small chest of drawers and a few hooks on the wall with clothes hangers on them.

Rachel dumped her rucksack and washed her face and hands, taking a few minutes to change her T-shirt and apply some more mosquito spray and sunscreen.

Her stomach was doing little flip-flops. It was pathetic really. Ron had only made one remark about a camp bed. It was nothing. It could apply to millions of guys the world over. But she had a bad feeling about this.

Lewis had been especially persuasive on the phone. He'd given her the whole 'my wife is pregnant' and 'one of the celebrities is being difficult' routine. When she'd heard who the celebrity was she hadn't been surprised. She'd met Darius under unusual circumstances. Both of them had been vulnerable. And he'd loved the thought that by dating a doctor he had an insider's view of treatments.

But dating Darius Cornell—Australia's resident soap opera hunk—had been an experience. They'd dated for just over a year. Just enough to get both of them through. She'd been relieved when the media attention had died down.

Her stomach flipped over one more time as she walked outside and reached for the door handle of the medical centre. It was strange to be here at his request. But Darius could be handled.

Her biggest fear was that the person behind this door probably couldn't.

He was dreaming. More likely he was having a nightmare. He pushed his hat a little further back on his head and blinked again.

No. She was still there.

Rachel Johnson. Brown hair tied in a ponytail, slightly suntanned skin and angry brown eyes set off by her pink T-shirt.

'Just when I thought this couldn't get any worse.' He pulled his feet off the desk.

Her lips tightened and her gaze narrowed. 'I'm going to kill Lewis Blake. I'm going to kill him with my bare hands. There's no way I'm getting stuck on this island with you for three weeks.' She folded her arms across her chest.

He pointed out at the sky. 'Too late, Rach. You just

missed your ride home.' The seaplane was heading off in the distance.

Her forehead creased into a deep frown. 'No way. There must be a boat. Another island nearby. How do they get supplies?'

Nathan shrugged. 'Not sure. I've only been here a day. And don't worry. I'm just as happy to see you. Particularly when I've just looked through the medical notes and saw your lovely ex is one of the celebs. No wonder you're here.'

He couldn't help it. When they'd split up years ago Rachel had come to Australia and a few months later been photographed by the press with her new boyfriend—an Australian soap star. It had been hard enough to get over the split, but seeing his ex all over the press when he'd been left behind to take care of his younger brother had just rubbed salt in the wounds. *She'd* gone to Australia. The place they'd planned to go to together.

'What exactly are you doing here, Nathan? You seem the last person who'd want a job like this.'

He raised his eyebrows. 'And what's that supposed to mean?'

She shrugged. 'I'd heard you were working for Doctors Without Borders. *Celebrity Island* seems a bit of a stretch of the imagination.'

He tried to ignore the little surge of pleasure that sparked; she'd been interested enough to find out where he worked. He'd never wanted to ask any of their mutual friends where Rachel was. Everyone knew that she'd gone to Australia without him and they were much too tactful to bring up her name.

He folded his arms across his chest. 'I think you know exactly why I'm here. At a guess I'd say he hoodwinked me just as much as he hoodwinked you.' He gave his hands a little rub together. 'But don't worry. I've got three weeks to think of what I'll do to him when I get back.'

She frowned again. 'How did he get in touch?'

Nathan's gaze met hers. 'I've been working with him.'

'In A & E?'

Nathan shrugged. 'Seemed the most logical place to work after five missions with Doctors Without Borders. He offered me the job as soon as my feet hit Australian soil.'

She gave a little nod. He could almost hear her brain ticking. He'd been the logical one and she'd been the emotional one. He'd thought they'd counterbalanced each other and worked well together. He'd been wrong.

'And don't think I've not noticed.'

Her cheeks were flooded with colour. 'Noticed what?' she snapped.

'That there's information missing from his medical file. What does your boyfriend have to hide?'

'Stop calling him that. He's not my boyfriend. Hasn't been for more than seven years. It might have escaped your notice but he's actually engaged to someone else. There's absolutely nothing between us.' She was getting angrier and angrier as she spoke. The colour was rushing up her face to the tips of her ears. He'd forgotten how mad she could get about things. Particularly when something mattered to her.

He lifted up the nearest folder. It took both hands. 'Look at this one.'

She frowned and placed her hands on her hips. 'Who does that belong to?'

'Diamond Dazzle. Model. Grand old age of twenty-two and look at the size of her medical records. I know every blood test, every X-ray and every piece of plastic surgery and Botox she's ever had. This one?' He held up Darius's records. Paper-thin. 'I know that Darius had an appendectomy at age eight. That's it.'

She folded her arms across her chest. 'And that's all you need to know. I know the rest.'

'No physician works like that, Rach.'

'You work like that every day, Nathan. You rarely know the history of the people who turn up in A & E, and I imagine on your missions you must have had patients from everywhere. They didn't come with medical files.'

He stood up. She was annoying every part of him now. It didn't matter that the angrier and more stubborn she got—the more her jaw was set—the more sensations sparked around his body. Rachel had always had this effect on him. He'd just expected it would have disappeared over time and with a whole host of bad memories. The rush of blood around his system was definitely unwelcome. 'So, you're going to look after one patient and I'll look after eight? Is that how we're going to work things?'

She shook her head fiercely, her eyes flashing. Rachel had always hated it when someone suggested she didn't pull her weight. After all these years he still knew what buttons to press.

'No, Nathan. I'll look after *all* the patients—just like you will—if required.'

But Nathan wouldn't be beaten. Not after all these years. He folded his own arms across his chest and matched Rachel's stance. He couldn't help but smile. It was like a stand-off. 'Well, I don't think I can do that if I don't have all the facts about the patient.'

The colour of her face practically matched her T-shirt now and he could see tiny beads of sweat on her brow. It was unquestionably hot on the island. But he was quite sure that wasn't why Rachel Johnson was sweating.

She shifted her feet. It was unusual to see her in khaki shorts, thick socks and heavy boots. She'd obviously been warned about the island paths. Rachel had spent her time as a student and junior doctor dressed smartly. Always in dresses and heels. This was a whole new look for her. Maybe her time in Australia had changed her outlook on life?

'Of course you can, Nathan. Stop being difficult. Three weeks. I can tell you'll be scoring off the days on the calendar just like I will.'

She turned to walk away. And it surprised him just how much he actually didn't want her to. If you'd asked him if he wanted to come face to face with Rachel Johnson again he'd have said, *Not in this lifetime*. But reality was sometimes stranger than fiction.

She stopped at the door. 'How's Charlie?'

The question caught him off guard and his answer was an automatic response. 'Charlie's fine. Not that you would care.'

She sighed. 'That's not fair, Nathan, and you know it.'

He shrugged. 'Why? You didn't want to hang around when I had to look after my little brother for a couple of years. Why bother now?'

She shook her head. He could see her biting her lip. She probably couldn't find the words for why she'd run out on them both. 'I always loved Charlie. He was great. Did he finish university?' A thought must have flickered across her mind. 'How was he when you were away?'

'Charlie was fine. He finished his engineering degree and got a job before I left for my last mission. He's married now with two young children.'

She gave a little nod of her head. 'Glad to hear it. Tell him I'm asking for him.'

She walked out of the door, letting it slam behind her. Nathan picked up the bottle of water on the table and downed it in one, wishing it was a beer. No matter how he tried to avoid it, his eyes had settled on her backside and legs as she'd walked out of the door. Eight years on and Rachel Johnson was as hot as ever.

And eight years later she still drove him crazy.

*I always loved Charlie.* The words echoed in his mind. 'Just as well you loved one of us,' he muttered.

She'd thought the cabin was hot but outside was even hotter and the high humidity was making the sweat trickle down her back already, probably turning her hair into a frizz bomb.

She stopped for a second to catch her breath, leaning against the metal bodywork and hoping to feel a little of the coolness on her body.

Trapped on an island with two exes. You couldn't make this up.

A little wave of nausea rolled over her. Nathan Banks. Eight years had done nothing to diminish the impact of seeing him again. Her hands were trembling and every hair on her arms stood on end. She'd never expected to come face-to-face with him again.

His blond hair was a little shorter. His build a bit more muscular. But his eyes were still the neon green they'd always been. They could stop any girl in her tracks—just like they'd done to her.

They were supposed to be continents apart. What on earth was he doing in Australia? She knew he'd spent five years working for Doctors Without Borders. He was still friends with a lot of the people they'd trained with.

And even though she'd pretended not to, she'd spent the last five years searching mutual social media sites with her heart in her mouth, hoping she wouldn't ever hear bad news about him. That was the trouble with working in humanitarian missions—sometimes they took you into places with armed conflict.

Trouble was, five minutes in Nathan's company could make her *mad*. No one else in her life had ever managed to spark that kind of reaction from her. But there was just something about Nathan and her alone in a room together. Sparks always flew. Sometimes good. Sometimes bad.

It was clear he still hadn't forgiven her for leaving. She couldn't blame him. But if she'd told him why she was really leaving he would have put his life—and Charlie's—on hold for her. She hadn't wanted that—she couldn't do that to them. They'd just lost their parents; they'd needed to focus on each other.

And if she told him now why she'd left, she would be betraying Darius's trust. Caught between the devil and the deep blue sea.

She stared out at the perfect blue Coral Sea. It was no wonder they'd picked one of the Whitsunday islands for this show. At any other time, with any other person, this would be perfect.

Too bad Nathan Banks was here to spoil it for her.

# CHAPTER TWO

'EXACTLY HOW LONG will this take?' The director was scowling at them both.

Nathan shrugged. He couldn't care less about the man's bad attitude. 'It'll take as long as it takes. We need to see every participant and have a quick chat about their medical history—then we'll be able to tell you if anyone is unsuitable for the challenge tomorrow.'

The director stomped out of the door, closing it with an exasperated bang.

Nathan smiled at Rachel. 'Now, where were we?'

Rachel lifted the printed list. 'Okay, we have nine celebrities and one backup that we'll need to assess if he arrives.' She frowned. 'This doesn't seem right. Aren't they all supposed to be filmed jumping from a plane and rowing or snorkelling their way here? What are they doing already on the island?'

Nathan shrugged. 'The magic of television. They arrived yesterday when I did. They plan to do the filming later on today, pretending they've just set foot on the island. But they haven't seen the camp yet. They spent last night in one of the cabins and you want to have heard the list of complaints.'

She shook her head as she looked over the list. 'More fool me. I had no idea they faked their arrival. Want to take a bet on how quickly one will bail?'

He held out his fist. Old habits died hard. He and Rachel used to do this all the time. She blinked as if she were having a little flash of memory, then held out her fist, bumping it against his. 'Six days.'

He shook his head. 'Oh, way too ambitious. Four days.'

She frowned. 'Really? But they're doing it for charity. Surely someone wouldn't give up that easy?'

He raised his eyebrows. 'You really think these people are doing it all just for charity?'

'Of course.' She looked confused and Nathan sighed and picked up the list.

'Let's see. Darius Cornell—actor—let's leave him for now. Diamond Dazzle—model—she's looking for a lingerie contract. Frank Cairns—sportsman—he's looking for a presenter's job somewhere. Molly Bates—comedienne—she needs the publicity for her upcoming tour. Tallie Turner—actress—she just needs a job. Pauline Wilding—politician—always likes to be in the papers. Fox—boy band pop star—he's hoping some teenagers remember his crazy name. Billy X—rapper—with his past history he's probably about to be arrested for something, and Rainbow Blossom—reality TV star. She probably doesn't want to fade from the spotlight. Are any of these people actually celebrities? Do any of them have a real name?'

He saw Rachel's lips press together and waited for her to immediately go on the offensive for her apparent ex. But she surprised him. She didn't.

'I didn't realise you were such a cynic.'

'I guess we really didn't know each other at all, did we?' he shot back.

The words hung in the air between them. He sounded bitter. And he was. But even he was surprised by how quickly the words had come out. They'd never had this conversation before. She'd just told him she was leaving and hotfooted it out of the hospital as if she were being chased by a bunch of killer zombies.

Five years of missions for Doctors Without Borders had loosened his tongue. He'd dealt with armed conflict, natural disasters and epidemics. He was less willing to placate and tolerate. Life was too short—he knew that now. He and his brother had lost their parents to an accident eight years ago, and he'd lost too many patients all over the world.

She flopped down into the chair next to him, letting her floral scent drift under his nose. That was new. Rachel didn't smell like that before. She'd always worn something lighter. This was stronger, more sultry, more like something a woman eight years on would wear. Why would he expect anything to stay the same?

'Actually, you're right,' she muttered, going back to the original conversation and completely ignoring his barb. 'Darius is probably the most well-known of them all. Five of them I don't recognise and three I've never even heard of.'

It was almost a relief that finally they could agree on something.

'How do you want to do this?' She pointed to the pile of notes. 'Do you want to go over each patient individually or do you just want to split them up?'

Splitting the pile would be easier and quicker. But Nathan wasn't about to let her off so easy. He needed to have another doctor he could rely on. Rachel had been a good doctor eight years ago—but he'd no idea how she was now. 'Let's do them together. That way, if either of us is on call we're familiar with all the patients. There's only nine—this won't take too long.'

He picked up the nearest set of notes and started flicking. 'Diamond Dazzle—real name Mandy Brooks. She's had liposuction, two breast enlargements, one skin biopsy, one irregular smear test and lots of Botox. She apparently had her lips done a week ago—so we'll need to keep an eye on her for any signs of infection.'

Rachel shook her head. 'Why would an already beautiful twenty-two-year-old think she needs all this?'

Nathan put the file back on the desk. 'Beats me.' He folded his arms across his chest. 'Do you think this makes her ineligible for the challenge? Having spiders or rats crawl over her body—and probably face too—will make her more vulnerable to infection.'

'I think just being in the jungle alone makes her at higher risk. Who would do that? Know that they're coming somewhere like this and go for a procedure less than a week before?'

Nathan smiled. He knew exactly where she was coming from but he also knew the answer. 'Someone who wants to be on TV.'

Rachel shook her head. Some of her hair was coming loose and the curls were starting to stray around her face. It was odd. She hadn't aged as much as he had. There were a few tiny lines around her eyes and her body had filled out a little. But nothing else. She was every bit as beautiful as he remembered.

His face and skin had been weathered by five years of on and off postings in countries around the world. The last had been the worst. The sand felt as if it would never wash off and the darkening of his skin—coupled with lots of lines—made him more weathered. It didn't help that he felt about a hundred years older.

'Shall we call her in?' He had to focus on work. That was what they were here to do. Lewis hadn't lied about everything. On the surface, this could be three weeks of paid vacation time. Supervising the challenges would only take a couple of hours each night. He could live with that.

Rachel stood up and walked to the door. 'I'll get her. They're down on the beach with the director. Apparently they're going to make it look like they had to row part way here.'

Nathan just rolled his eyes.

It didn't take long to chat to each celebrity and review their medical files. A few were taking medications that they'd still require in the camp. A few others had intermittent usage of medications for angina, migraines or asthma that Rachel and Nathan agreed they could still take into camp. None of that stuff would be shown on camera.

Eventually it was time to speak to Darius. As soon as the guy walked into the room Nathan bristled. He just didn't like him—would never like him. For some reason, the pictures of Darius and Rachel together were imprinted on his brain.

Rachel smiled nervously. 'Darius, this is Nathan, the other doctor on duty. We are having a chat with everyone about their medical file and requirements in the camp.'

Darius had that soap actor look. Clean tanned skin and straight white teeth. He looked as if on occasion he might work out at the gym and he also looked as if he needed to gain a little weight.

Nathan held up his file as Rachel shifted from foot to foot. 'There's not much in here, Darius. If I'm going to be the doctor looking after you I need to know a little more about your medical history.'

Darius's eyes shifted over to Rachel. He was a confident guy who was obviously used to things going his way. 'There's no need. Rachel knows my medical history. That's why she's here.'

Nathan leaned across the desk. 'But Rachel might not always be available. She's not on call twenty-four hours a day for the next three weeks, you know. And she'll have other patients to treat too. The rest of your campmates and the crew need doctor services too.'

Darius gave a fake smile as he glanced at Rachel. 'I'm sure she'll cope.'

Nathan's hand balled into a fist as he kept his voice deadly calm. 'Any allergies I should know about? Are you in good health right now? Do you require any medications or special diet requirements?'

Darius took a few seconds to reply, almost as if he was rehearsing his answer. 'No allergies. I'm in perfect health and I'm not taking any medication right now.'

Measured. That was the word that Nathan would use. Rachel, in comparison, looked like a cat on a hot tin roof. What on earth had happened between these two?

There was something in the air. But it wasn't like the spark Nathan had felt between him and her when Rachel had first walked in here. It was something different. Something easier—at least it seemed easier to Darius. He seemed cool and confident around Rachel. Assured.

Darius stood up and put a hand on Rachel's shoulder. 'Thanks for being here, Rach.' He glanced at Nathan. 'I hope it doesn't cause you too many problems.'

He disappeared out of the door to where the director was assembling the production crew.

Nathan folded his arms. 'Well, that was informative. What does he have on you, Rach?'

Her expression of relief changed quickly. It was amazing how quickly he could put her back up. 'What do you mean? Nothing. He has nothing on me. Why would you even think that? I've already told you I'll be looking after Darius. There's nothing you need to know.' She was getting angrier by the second and he knew he was right.

He moved around the desk, leaning back against it, only inches away from where she stood. Her perfume filled the air around him. 'Really? So what did he mean by "I'm not taking any medication *right now*"? When was he taking meds and what for?'

He could see the conflict flitting across her eyes. The rational part of her brain knew exactly why he was asking. His suspicion hadn't been misplaced. There was something to tell; that was the whole reason Rachel was here. But what was it? Three weeks of this would drive him crazy.

She stared him straight in the eye. 'This is ridiculous. I don't want to be here. You don't want to be here. Why doesn't one of us just leave?'

She was cutting straight to the chase but he hadn't missed the fact she'd just circumvented his question.

This was the closest he'd been to Rachel in eight long years. Her pink lips were pressed in a hard line and her hands were staunchly on her hips. He tried not to look down. He tried not to notice the way her breasts were straining against the thin pink T-shirt. He tried not to notice the little lines around her brown eyes. Or the faint tan on her unblemished skin.

But everything was there. Everything was right in front of him. He breathed in and her scent was like an assault on his senses. He bristled, the tiny hairs on his skin upright and the beat of his heart increasing in his chest. This was crazy. He wasn't interested in this woman. He wouldn't *let* himself be interested in this woman. She'd walked away. More accurately, she'd flown away when he and Charlie had needed her most.

Australia hadn't just been her dream. It had been *their* dream. They'd both planned on going there after they'd worked as senior house doctors for a year. It was easier for Rachel. Her mother was Australian and Rachel had dual nationality. But the application to work had been in both of their names and nothing had hurt more than when Rachel had just upped and left without him.

The words were on the tip of his tongue. *You leave.* But he couldn't bring himself to say them. And it drove him crazy. It should be easy. She deserved it. So why couldn't he say it?

He turned his back and sat back down. He had to get away from her smell, her stance, the look in her eyes. He could do without all these memories.

'I can't leave. I'm working with Lewis. Believe it or not, I'm doing this as a favour to him. Cara's near the end of her pregnancy and he needs to be there. When I go back he'll give me another six-month contract at the hospital.'

She frowned, wrinkling her nose. Rachel had always looked cute when she was frowning. 'He's blackmailing you into being here?' It sounded worse when she said it out loud.

He couldn't help the rueful smile on his face. 'Not really. He gave me "the look". You know—the one he always gives you when he needs his own way? Anyway, he really didn't want to be away from Cara and apparently I needed a holiday. A break. Some time off.'

Now she looked worried. 'He thought you needed some time off? Is something wrong? Did something happen?'

*You.* But he'd never say that word out loud. He hadn't realised how big an effect all this was having on him. And he didn't even want to acknowledge it. He'd spent the last eight years blanking Rachel out of his life. Forgetting about her. Locking her away in a box, along with all the unresolved feelings he had about her. It wasn't quite so easy to do that when she was standing in front of him.

He took the easy route. 'I spent five years working for Doctors Without Borders. I've been halfway around the world. I didn't really have a holiday when I finished my last tour. Just came to Australia, looked up Lewis and started working for him on a temporary contract.'

She hesitated, something flitting across her eyes. 'You never talked about going to Doctors Without Borders. What made you go?'

He couldn't bite back his natural response. 'We didn't talk about lots of things.'

She flinched, almost as if she'd been stung.

He took a deep breath. 'An old friend came back after working for them. When he told me about the work he'd been doing—the epidemics, the natural disasters and in areas of armed conflict—I was interested. Who wouldn't be? Lots of these people have absolutely no access to healthcare. Doctors Without Borders is their only hope. I felt as if I had to go. Charlie had finished university and got a job. The timing worked out. I was only going to do one mission in Africa for nine months. But one year turned into two, then three and eventually five.'

He paused. She was watching him carefully, almost holding her breath. 'It was good experience.' It seemed the best way to sum things up. Rachel didn't need to know what he'd seen or what he'd dealt with. She had a good enough imagination. He'd already told her more than he'd intended to.

But curiosity about her was getting the better of him. 'What's your speciality?'

For a second she seemed thrown. She bit her lip and fixed her eyes on a spot on the wall, her hand tugging nervously at her ear.

With Rach, it had always been a telltale sign. And his instant recognition came like a thunderbolt. He'd thought he'd known this woman so well. But he hadn't really known her at all. That was probably what stung the most.

'I took a little time off when I came to Australia.' Her eyes looked up to the left. 'Then I worked as a general medical physician for a while, dealing with a mix of diabetic, cardiac, respiratory and oncology patients.' Her feet shifted on the floor.

Her gaze meshed with his and something shot through him. A wave of recognition. She tugged at her ear. *She's going to change the subject.*

After all these years he still knew her little nuances. 'I thought you might have gone into surgery. That's what you were always interested in.'

She was right. He had talked about going into surgery. And he'd certainly had his fair share of surgical experience around the world. But even though he'd just acknowledged that he still knew her little nuances, he was annoyed that she thought she still knew things about him.

She'd walked away. She'd lost the right to know anything about him. She'd lost the right to have any insight into his life.

His voice was blunt. 'A surgical internship would have taken up too many hours. At least with A & E I had regular shifts without also being on call.'

The implication was clear. Looking after his brother had changed his career pathway. He didn't like to think about it. He didn't like to acknowledge it—especially not to someone who had turned and walked away. Maybe if Rachel had stayed he could still have chosen surgery as his path? It would have been easier to share the load between two people.

But Rachel didn't seem to be picking up his annoyance. 'You must have got a wide range of experience with Doctors Without Borders. Did you do some surgery?'

'Of course I did. It's all hands on deck out there, even though you're in the middle of the desert.' His eyes drifted off to the grey wall. If he closed his eyes right now he could almost hear the whump-whump of the incoming medevac helicopters. He could feel the sensation of the tiny hairs on his arms and at the back of his neck standing on end in nervous anticipation of the unknown.

Sometimes civilians—men, women and children—sometimes army, navy or air force personnel. You never knew what you were going to see when you pulled back the door on the medevac.

The medical services were some of the best in the world, but at times Nathan's surgical skills had been challenged.

The tick-tick of the clock on the wall brought him back into focus. A little shiver ran down his spine.

A warm hand touched his arm and he jolted. 'Nathan? Are you okay?'

A frown creased her brow. The concerned expression on her face made him angry. How dare she feel sorry for him?

He snatched his arm away. 'Of course I'm fine.' He crossed his arms over his chest and walked around to the files again. 'I'm going to write up some notes. Make a few recommendations to the director. Why don't you go over to the beach or something?'

It was dismissive. Maybe even a little derogatory. But he just wanted her out of here. Away from him.

For a second Rachel looked hurt, then her jaw tightened and the indignant look came back in her eyes. The Rachel he'd known would have stood her ground and torn him down a few pegs.

But this Rachel was different. This Rachel had changed. She nodded, almost sarcastically. 'Sure. That's exactly what I'll do.' She picked up one of the pagers from the desk, clipping it to her waist without even acknowledging the act. She walked away without a glance. 'They better make cocktails at that bar...'

The door closed behind her with a thud and he waited a few seconds before he collapsed back into the seat. One minute he was mad with her, the next he was being swamped with a whole host of memories.

One thing was for sure. This island wasn't big enough for the both of them.

# CHAPTER THREE

RACHEL WAS FURIOUS. She couldn't wait to put some distance between her and Nathan.

She rubbed the palm of her hand against her shorts. It was almost burning. The contact with his skin, the gentle feel of the hairs on his arms underneath her hand was something she hadn't been ready for.

It was hard enough being around him again. She felt catapulted into a situation she was unprepared for. In her distant daydreams, she'd been sure that if she'd ever met Nathan again she would have been ready. Mentally. And physically.

She'd be wearing her best clothes. Something smart. Something professional. Her hair would have been washed and her make-up freshly applied. She would have practised how to casually say hello. All her responses would be easy, nonchalant. Or at least rehearsed over and over again so they would seem that way.

She would have a five-minute conversation with him, wishing him well for the future, and then walk off into the distance with a little swing of her hips.

She would be composed, controlled. He would never guess that her heart was breaking all over again. He would have no idea at all.

But most of all there would be absolutely no touching. *No touching at all*. Because, in her head, that was the thing that would always break her.

And she'd been right.

Her hand started to shake. Rubbing it against her thigh was no use. No use at all.

Her footsteps quickened on the descending path. The beach was only a matter of minutes away. A few of the crew members were already on the beach, sitting on the chairs. But the truth was she couldn't stay here for long. In an hour's time the celebrities would be split into two teams and dropped into the middle of the ocean.

Their first challenge would be to row to the island. The winning team would be rewarded with better sleeping facilities and more edible food. The others would spend a night sleeping on the jungle floor. Just the thought of it made her shudder. The rangers had already pulled a few spiders as big as her hands from the 'camp' and a few snakes she had no intention of identifying. The book that Lewis had given her on poisonous creatures had photographs of them and then notes on antidotes, treatments and antivenoms. It wasn't exactly fun bedtime reading.

She climbed up onto one of the bar stools, which gave a little wobble. It seemed to be designed for people of an Amazonian stature. She looked down to the sandy matting beneath her.

'What'll it be?' asked the guy behind the bar. He didn't look like a traditional bartender. He looked like a guy running between about five different jobs. Most of the crew seemed to be doing more than one thing.

'Remind me not to get too drunk. I don't fancy falling off this bar stool. It's a long way down.'

The bartender smiled. 'It's okay. I know a handsome doc that will be able to patch you up.'

She shook her head. 'Absolutely not.' She held out her hand. 'Rachel Johnson. The other doc. And, believe me, he's the last person who'd be patching me up.'

'Len Kennedy. You don't like Nathan? I'm surprised.' He set a glass in front of her. 'Don't tell me. Diet soda or fruit juice?'

She nodded ruefully. 'You guessed it; I'll be on duty soon. A diet cola will be fine.' She watched as he poured and tossed in some ice, a slice of orange and a couple of straws.

He watched while she took a sip. 'Nathan seems like a good guy. What's the problem?' The bartender's voice was steady with a curious edge. But it felt as if he'd just drawn a line in the sand as to where his loyalties lay. Great. She couldn't even come to the bar for a drink.

She gave her shoulders a shrug and took a sip through her straw. 'Some might say it's ancient history.'

Her eyes met the guy in front of her. He was handsome, but a little rough around the edges. A scar snaked from his wrist to his elbow, he had a closely shorn head, a few days' worth of stubble and eyes that had seen things they shouldn't. She wondered what his story was.

He gave her a knowing kind of smile. 'Then maybe that's the best place to leave it. Sometimes history should be just that—history.'

She'd been wrong. He didn't seem like a crazy crew member. He was a typical bartender. The kind that seemed to be able to read your mind and tell you exactly what you didn't want to hear.

She looked out at the perfect ocean. This place might not have the luxury facilities she'd been promised. But it was an incredibly beautiful setting. The kind of place where you should relax and chill out. The kind of place that probably had the most gorgeous sunsets in the world. She gave a sigh. 'Sometimes history is too hard to let go of.'

Len put another glass on the bar and filled it with lemonade. He held it up to hers. She hesitated, then held up her glass and chinked it against his. He smiled. 'Maybe you should look at this a new way. Maybe it was fate that you both ended up here at the same time.'

Fate. More like an interfering friend. She arched her back, her hand instantly going to the skin there, tracing a line along her own scar. She hadn't thought for a second Nathan would be here. Her backpack had two bikinis that she'd never wear in front of him; they'd have to spend the next three weeks languishing at the bottom of her bag. She didn't want him asking any questions. She didn't want to explain her scar. It went hand in hand with her relationship with Darius. Things he didn't need to know about.

She didn't really want to consider fate. It didn't seem like her friend.

She smiled at Len. 'So what are your duties around here? I haven't had a chance to look around much yet.'

'Apparently I tend the bar, refill the drinks, supply ice and help the crew with setting up some of the tasks.' He took another sip of his drink. 'I've got experience in rock climbing. They said it would be useful for one of their tasks.'

Rachel's eyes widened. 'You might have experience rock climbing but I'm betting none of the celebrities have. How safe is it to make them do something like that?'

Len shook his head. 'I've no idea. I'm just the extra pair of hands. I'm assuming they'll have a safety briefing before they start. At least I hope they will.'

Rachel gave a sigh and looked out over the perfect

blue Coral Sea. This place really could be an island paradise. She rested her head on her hands. 'What on earth have I got myself into?'

Len laughed. He raised his glass again and gave her a worldly-wise gaze. 'Probably a whole load of trouble.'

She lifted her glass again and clinked it against his. She had a sinking feeling he could be right.

# CHAPTER FOUR

RACHEL WATCHED AS the celebrities rowed towards the island. At least that was what she thought they were trying to do.

'There's going to need to be some serious editing,' said the quiet voice behind her. 'This is really quite boring.'

She didn't turn. She didn't need to. She could actually feel his presence right behind her.

He was right. The journey to the island didn't seem like much of a journey. They'd been put into two boats and asked to row ashore as if they'd done it from the mainland. The truth was they were only a few hundred yards away. The boat with the sportsman Frank Cairns was already miles in front of the other. On a hot day his patience was obviously at an all-time low and he'd decided to do most of the rowing himself. His fellow celebs arrived onshore with big smiles on their faces.

The second boat arrived filled with long, grumpy faces and instant moans. 'My agent said I wouldn't have to do anything like this,' moaned Dazzle.

'Your agent lied,' muttered Pauline Wilding, the politician. 'Haven't you learned anything yet?'

The male and female TV presenters appeared, trying to placate the celebrities and keep the atmosphere light.

Rachel scanned her eyes over them all. One of the older women was limping already. The trek through the forest to the campsite wouldn't help.

Darius appeared comfortable. The row didn't seem to have bothered him in the slightest. It made her feel a little easier. Everywhere she looked she could see potential problems. Scratches and bites that could become infected. Lack of proper nutrition. Contaminants from the horrible toilet the celebrities would need to use. If Darius had asked her if this was a good idea—she would have told him to run a million miles away.

If any patient who'd just finished another dose of chemotherapy had asked if they should come here she would give a resounding no. A relaxing holiday in the Whitsunday islands on a luxury resort was one thing. Being dumped in a jungle to sleep for the next three weeks was another thing entirely.

She'd been lucky. She'd only had to take a year out of her medical career. A long, hard year involving surgery to remove her cancerous kidney; chemotherapy, radiotherapy and annual check-ups for five years.

Darius hadn't been so lucky. They'd met in the cancer centre, with her fighting renal cancer and him fighting non-Hodgkin's lymphoma. He'd relapsed twice since, each time becoming a little sicker than the last.

What the world didn't know was that Darius really hadn't been her lover. He'd been her friend. Her confidant in a place she'd just moved to without any real friends.

Nathan had no idea why she'd left. He'd just lost his parents and realised he needed to be his brother's guardian for the next two years. She hadn't mentioned any of the symptoms she'd had—the blood in her urine, the sick feeling and loss of appetite. They'd both been so busy in their first year as junior doctors that she'd barely had time to think much about her symptoms. A simple urine test dipstick on the ward had made her realise she needed to get some professional advice. But then Nathan's parents had been killed and they were both left stunned.

She'd held him while he'd sobbed and tried to arrange a joint funeral and sort out all the family finances. He'd just lost two people he loved. She'd nearly forgotten about her investigatory renal ultrasound. When her diagnosis had come she couldn't possibly tell him. She couldn't put him and Charlie through that. They needed time to recover. Time to find themselves. Charlie needed healthy people around him. Nathan needed to concentrate on getting his life back and learning how to be a parent to his brother.

Neither of them needed the uncertainty of someone with a cancer diagnosis. So she'd done the only thing that seemed right. She'd phoned her mother in Australia and made contact with the local cancer unit over there. Her notes transferred and her treatment planned, she'd bought her plane ticket and packed her case.

Australia had always been on the cards for Nathan and Rachel. They'd applied together. They'd meant to go together. But the death of Nathan's parents meant all those plans had to be shelved.

It was too risky to stay in England and be treated. Someone, somewhere, would have come across her and word would have got back to Nathan. She didn't want that. She loved him with her whole heart. He, and Charlie, had been through enough. She knew the risks of renal cell carcinoma. Not everyone survived. She couldn't take the risk of putting Nathan and Charlie through that.

And she knew Nathan better than he knew himself. At the time of his parents' death he'd tried so hard to be composed, to keep on top of things. This would have been the final push. Nathan would have stood by her—of that she had absolutely no doubt. No matter how hard she tried to push him away, he would have been by her side every step of the way.

In a way, she hadn't felt strong enough to be brave for herself and for Nathan too. She had to be selfish. She had to put herself first.

So that was what she'd done. She'd bought her ticket and gone to the ward where Nathan was working to let him know she was leaving.

It was the hardest thing she'd ever done. She'd been flippant, matter-of-fact. A job opportunity had arisen in Australia that was too good to give up. She didn't want to cause a scene so she hadn't warned him.

He'd be fine. Charlie would be fine. They'd been together too long. They both needed some space apart. She'd wished him and Charlie well for the future.

Her legs had been shaking as she'd made that final walk down the corridor, knowing that every single word that had come from her mouth had been a lie.

Horrible heartless lies that had hurt the person she loved.

No wonder Nathan couldn't bear to be around her.

No wonder at all.

Nathan was watching the celebrities crossing the swinging bridge made of rope and planks of wood suspended sixty feet above the jungle canopy. Any minute now…

Right on cue, one of them vomited over the bridge, clinging on for all she was worth. He couldn't stifle the laugh. He shouldn't really find it funny. But it was ridiculous. None of them had expressed a fear of heights.

It took nearly an hour for all nine celebrities to cross the bridge. It reminded him of the hysteria he'd witnessed as a student doctor at a school immunisation session when one teenage girl after another had a panic attack in the waiting room. The celebrities' legs seemed to have turned to jelly and even some of the guys made a meal of it.

Darius wasn't one of them. Neither was the sportsman. Both walked over the bridge as if they were crossing the street. Darius was beginning to pique Nathan's curiosity. What had Rachel seen in the guy? And why was he so stoic? He didn't seem fazed by the jungle—or the potential challenges. It was as if he had so much more to worry about.

There was a yell behind him and he spun around. A few other shouts followed and his legs moved automatically, crashing a path through the jungle towards the noise.

It only took him a few seconds to reach a scene of chaos. Some of the crew had obviously been transporting equipment and a whole pile of barrels that had previously been in a tower were spilled all over the ground.

'What's wrong? Is someone hurt?'

'It's Jack,' yelled one of the burlier men as he grabbed hold of one of the barrels and tried to move it aside. 'He's caught underneath.'

Nathan didn't hesitate. First priority—get to the patient. There was no way to see or assess how Jack was right now, so he used his muscle power to grab an end of one of the barrels to try and throw them out of the way. The weight of each of the barrels was extreme. 'What on earth is in these?' he grunted.

'Sand.'

'What? Why on earth do we have barrels filled with sand?'

The muscles in his arms were starting to burn as he kept pace with the others grabbing barrels and moving them away from the site.

'For one of the challenges,' shouted the crew guy.

There was a flash of pink near to him, then a figure shot past him and wriggled in between some of the barrels. 'Stop!' came a yell.

He moved forward, crouching down. 'Rachel, what on earth are you doing?'

He could only see the soles of her boots as she continued to wiggle forward, her slim body and hips pushing sideways through the barrels. None of the rest of the crew could have fitted.

Her voice seemed to echo quietly back to him, reverberating off the curved sides of the barrels. 'I've got him. He's unconscious. Give me a second.'

The site director appeared next to Nathan, talking incessantly in his ear. *Health and Safety...not safe...insurance...liability...*

'Shut up,' said Nathan sharply, tuning the man out. 'Rachel. How are you doing in there?'

There was a creak above him and several of the crew ran forward with their hands above their heads. 'Watch out, Doc. Some of these are going to go.'

Of course. They'd been so close they couldn't see the bigger picture. They'd been so quick to think about getting to Jack they hadn't considered the swaying semi-collapsed tower.

Rachel gave a little squeak. 'He's breathing. But he's unconscious,' she shouted. 'Definite sign of a head injury with a head lac, and a possible fractured ulna and radius.'

'Any other injuries?'

'Give me a sec. I can't see his legs but I can feel his pelvis and abdomen.' Nathan held his breath. His brain was trying to calculate how long it would take to medevac someone out of here. A few seconds later she shouted again. 'His pelvis seems intact and his abdomen is soft. But there's a few barrels right above us that look ready to come crashing down. Do you have anything we can use to keep us safe?'

Nathan started shouting to the crew. 'We need something to put over Jack and the doc. What do we have?'

A few members of the crew pointed to some piles of wood. But there was no chance of squeezing those in amongst the barrels. Nathan's brain was working frantically. Yesterday, he'd read a list of the challenges that the celebrities would do over the next few weeks. It sparked something in his brain. 'Wait a minute. What about the inflatables for the water challenge later—anyone know where those are?'

He hadn't even seen them but, from what he could remember about the challenge, they might help.

Ron's eyes lit up. 'Yes! They'll be perfect!' He turned on his heel and ran towards one of the equipment storage cabins.

Nathan's black medical bag thumped down beside him. He didn't even know who'd brought it. He just stuck his hand inside and pulled out a stethoscope. He ran forward and threw the stethoscope inside. 'Rach, can you sound his chest?'

There was a muffled response. Ron and the others were still running around. The feeling of camaraderie struck him. When something happened, all hands were on deck. He didn't know most of these people. He could count on one hand how many names he knew. But it didn't matter; everyone was working towards one purpose and that he could understand. It had been the way of his life for five years in Doctors Without Borders.

Ron stopped next to him, clearly out of breath—he'd need to remember to check him over later. 'We've got them—almost like giant sausages. They're thin enough when they're deflated to wiggle them through next to the doc.'

'How do you inflate them?' His brain was starting to see where this could go.

'With a pressure machine.'

'How quickly can they go up?'

'Within ten seconds.'

He ran his fingers through his hair. 'When that inflates will it push all those barrels outwards?' How on earth could he keep Rachel and Jack safe?

He turned to the technician next to him. His logical brain was trying to calculate how to do this. 'Put one on either side. They stay in the middle. That way, all the barrels will fall outwards.' At least he hoped and prayed they would. He glanced at the anxious face next to him. 'What do you think?'

Ron gave a small nod. 'I think you're a genius, Doc. Let's get to work, guys.'

They moved quickly, trying to get things in position.

Nathan took a deep breath and moved forward. 'Rach?'

Her voice echoed towards him. She sounded stressed. Climbing in amongst the barrels was probably starting to feel like a bad idea. 'It's harder than I thought. Chest clear and inflating on one side, but I can't get access to the other—he's lying on that side.' There was a definite waver in her voice. What he really wanted to do was crawl in beside her. But unless that space got about two foot wider there was no physical possibility of that—not without putting the already teetering pile at further risk.

He signalled to Ron. 'How soon will you be ready?'

Ron's facc was rcd and swcating. Hc gestured towards the other guys. It might look like chaos around them but everyone seemed to know exactly what they were doing. They all had a purpose. 'Two minutes.'

Nathan crouched down, pushing himself as close to the entrance as he could. 'Good. Rach, listen to me. We need to get you and Jack out of there. The barrels aren't safe; they could fall at any minute. But we think we've got something that could help.'

'What is it?'

'Ron and the guys are going to manoeuvre some inflatables in beside you. They're rolled up like sausages and should squeeze through the gap. One will be in front of you and Jack, and the other behind. I'll give you a signal and we'll flick the switch to inflate them. It's quick. It only takes ten seconds, and once they inflate they should push all the surrounding barrels outwards. You need to keep your head down. Are you okay with that?'

'Is there any other option?' Her voice sounded shaky.

Nathan bit his lip. He was trying to make it sound as if this was perfectly planned when they both knew it wasn't. 'This is the quickest and safest option. You'll be out of there soon.' He switched back to doctor mode. 'How's the patient?'

He tried to shut out all the outside noise and just focus on her. How was she feeling in there? Any minute now the whole pile could come crashing down on top of her. He didn't even want to give that head space. He *couldn't* give that head space. Because it might actually make his hands shake. It didn't matter that he hadn't seen her in years. It didn't matter he had all this pent-up frustration and rage wrapped up in memories of her. This was Rachel.

He didn't want her to come to any harm. No matter what else went on in this world. He couldn't push aside his protective impulses towards her. He didn't dare to think about anything happening to her.

He'd just managed to see her for the first time in eight years. And, no matter how he felt about anything, he wasn't ready for that to be over.

Her bravado was obviously starting to crash. 'He's still unconscious. We'll be able to assess him better when we get out.'

Ron tapped him on the shoulder, standing in position with the bright yellow, tightly coiled inflatables in the crew's hands.

'Rach, hold on. Ron's ready. Get yourself in position.'

He couldn't imagine what it must be like in there with the heavy barrels stacked all around. It took a good ten minutes for Ron and the rest of the crew to slowly edge the giant sausage-like inflatables into position and connect them to the air pressure machines.

It was the first time in his life Nathan had ever cursed his muscular frame. He should be the one in there. Not her.

He spoke in a low voice. 'Are you sure the rest of the barrels will fall outwards? None are going to land on them?'

Ron met his gaze; there was a flicker of doubt in his eyes. 'I'm as sure as you are.'

Nathan glanced towards the crew member standing with his hand on the air pressure machine. 'Get back,' he yelled to the rest of the crew members, who scattered like leaves on a blustery day.

Nathan couldn't help himself. He rushed forward as he signalled to the crew guy. 'Now, Rach,' he shouted. 'Get your head down!'

Strong arms pulled him backwards just as the switches on the machine were thrown. It was only ten seconds. But it felt like so much longer.

The giant sausages started to inflate, pushing everything around them outwards. The barrels teetering at the top started to rumble and fall, cascading like a champagne tower. Nathan couldn't breathe. It was almost as if everything was happening in slow motion.

One blue barrel after another thudded heavily to the ground, some landing on their side and rolling forwards, gathering momentum as the crew dived out of their path. From beneath the pile the thick yellow PVC was emerging, continuing to throw the blue barrels outwards as the air gathered inside.

Relief. He didn't even want to consider what might have happened. As the last barrel rolled past, Nathan sprinted towards the yellow PVC, crossing the ground quickly. He could hear the thuds behind him and knew that the rest of the crew were on his heels but it didn't stop him bounding over the thick inflatable.

Rachel was still crouched behind it; her body over the top of Jack's, protecting him from any falling debris. Her head was leaning over his, with her hands over the top of her head. The other yellow inflatable had protected them from behind, creating the shelter that Nathan had hoped it would.

Nathan landed beside her with a thud, dropping to his knees and gently touching her arms. 'Rachel? Are you okay?' He couldn't stop the concern lacing his voice.

Her arms were trembling and she lifted her head slowly, licking her dry lips. Her eyes flicked from side to side. 'It's done?'

The wave of relief in her eyes was obvious. He had to hold back. He had to really hold back. It would be so easy just to wrap his arms around her and give her a quick hug of comfort and reassurance. But this was Rachel. This was *Rachel.*

He'd already experienced the briefest contact with her skin and he'd no intention of doing it again. No matter how relieved he was to see she was okay.

His black bag thumped down next to him again—the black bag he should have been carrying in his hand. Something shot through him. His first thought should have been for the patient but it hadn't been. His first thought had been Rachel.

She was still looking at him. Staring at him with those big brown eyes. As if she were still in shock after what had just happened.

He had to focus. One of them had to do their job.

He grabbed the stethoscope from her hands and bent over to sound Jack's chest. Now that the barrels were out of the way he could get access quite easily. It only took a few minutes to hear the air entry in each lung. He pulled a pen torch from his back pocket and checked both of Jack's pupils. Both reacted, although one was slightly sluggish. He grimaced. 'We really need to get some neuro obs started on this guy.'

His voice seemed to snap Rachel to attention. She jumped to her feet and held out her hands towards the crew members who were handing a stretcher towards them. It only took a few seconds to load Jack onto the stretcher, with plenty of willing hands to help them carry him back to the medical centre.

If this accident had happened in the city Nathan would have a full A & E department at his disposal, with a whole host of other doctors. Here, on this island there was only him and Rachel. She'd always been a good, competent doctor. He hoped that nothing had changed.

He didn't even glance behind the stretcher as he walked alongside the patient. His brain was spinning furiously, trying to remember where all the emergency equipment was in the medical centre.

Medical centre. It could barely even be called that. It had the basics, but was better designed for general consultations than emergency medicine. He'd expected to treat a few bites and stomach aches. Not a full scale head injury.

The crew members carried Jack inside and helped Nathan slide him across onto one of the trolleys. He did the basics and hooked Jack up to the cardiac monitor and BP cuff; at least they had one of those.

Rachel seemed to have gathered herself and was pulling Jack's notes from the filing cabinet. 'No significant medical history,' she shouted as Nathan pulled an oxygen mask over Jack's face and quickly inserted an IV cannula.

'Do we have any Glasgow Coma Scales?' It was unlikely. The Glasgow Coma Scale was used the world over to monitor unconscious patients. Rachel pulled open a few admin drawers and shook her head, passing him a recording sheet for pulse and BP, then taking a blank sheet of paper and making some quick scribbles.

She walked over and handed it to him as she slid the pen torch from his back pocket as though she did it every day, lifting Jack's eyelids and checking his pupils.

Nathan glanced at the paper. It was Rachel's attempt at an impromptu Glasgow Coma Scale. It had captured the basics—eye response, verbal response and motor response. Both of their heads snapped up as the monitor started alarming.

He ran his fingers down Jack's obviously broken arm. The colour of his fingertips was changing. They were beginning to look a little dusky, meaning that the blood supply was compromised. He swapped the oxygen saturation probe over to the other hand and watched as it came back up to ninety-eight per cent.

He looked up and his gaze meshed with Rachel's. He didn't even need to speak; she could see the same things he could.

'Nathan, do you have keys to the medicine fridge?' He nodded and tossed them in her direction. For a doctor who didn't routinely work in emergency medicine, she'd certainly remembered the basics. He finished his assessment of Jack, recording all the responses while she drew up some basic pain medication.

Even though Jack wasn't awake they were going to have to straighten and splint his broken arm to try and re-establish the blood supply. No doctor could assume an unconscious patient couldn't feel pain. It didn't matter that Jack hadn't responded to the painful stimuli that Nathan had tried as part of the assessment. His breathing wasn't compromised so they had to administer some general pain relief before they started.

His arm fracture was obvious, with the bones displaced. Thankfully, they hadn't broken the skin so the risk of infection would be small.

Rachel spun the ampoule she'd just drawn into the syringe around towards Nathan so he could double-check the medicine and the dose. He gave a little nod of his head while she administered it.

He couldn't help but give a little smile as she positioned herself at Jack's shoulder. 'Do you remember how to do this?'

She shook her head. 'Of course not. Why do you think I'm in the anchor position? The responsibility for the displaced bones and blood supply is yours.'

Of course she was right. It would have been years since she'd been involved in repositioning bones. He'd done it three times in the last month.

It only took a few minutes to reposition the bones and put a splint underneath the arm. The most promising thing was the grunt that came from Jack.

'Can you patch that head wound?' he asked. 'I'm going to arrange to medevac Jack back to the mainland.'

Rachel opened the nearest cupboard and found some antiseptic to clean the wound, some paper stitches and a non-adhesive dressing. She worked quickly while he made the call. She waited until he replaced the receiver and gave him a nervous smile. 'I haven't sutured in a while so I've left it for the professionals.'

He nodded. It was good she wasn't trying to do things she wasn't confident with. She'd just been thrown in at the deep end and coped better than he'd expected. If the shoe was on the other foot and he'd found himself in the middle of a medical unit, how well would he do?

He might be able to diagnose and treat chest infections, some basic cardiac conditions and diagnose a new diabetic but would he really know how to treat any blood disorders or oncology conditions off the top of his head? Absolutely not.

Nathan picked up the phone and dialled through to the emergency number. Thank goodness he'd checked all these yesterday when he arrived. It didn't matter that Lewis had told him nothing would happen. Working for Doctors Without Borders had taught him to be prepared.

The call was answered straight away and arrangements made for the dispatch of the medevac. 'It's coming from Proserpine Airport. We're in luck; they were already there.'

Her sigh of relief was audible and he joined her back at the trolley. Jack still hadn't regained consciousness. Nathan took a few more minutes to redo the neuro obs and stimuli.

'Do you know where the medevac will land?'

He gave a nod of his head. 'Can you go outside and find Ron? We'll need some help transporting Jack down to the beach. They've probably cleared the landing spot already.'

She disappeared quickly and he sucked in a breath. This was a whole new experience for him. They'd trained together at university and spent their first year working as junior doctors in the same general hospital. But they'd never actually done a shift together. She'd done her six months medical rotation first while he'd done his surgical placement. They'd swapped over six months later.

He'd already known he wanted to specialise in surgery at that point, whereas Rachel had expressed a preference for medicine. They'd applied to the same hospital in Melbourne and been accepted to work there. But he'd been unable to take up his job and had a frantic scramble to find another in England. He'd always assumed that Rachel had just carried on without him. Now he wasn't so sure.

Ron's sweaty face appeared at the door. He'd really need to check him over at some point. ''Copter should be here in a few minutes. Once it's down, there are four guys outside to help you carry the stretcher.' His brow creased as he glanced at Jack. 'How is he?'

Nathan gave a little nod. 'We've patched him up as best we could but he's still unconscious. Hopefully, he'll wake up soon.'

Ron disappeared and ten minutes later the thwump-thwump of the helicopter could be heard overhead. A wave of familiarity swept over him. For a few seconds he was back in the sand, war all around, his stomach twisting at the thought of what throwing back the medevac door would reveal. But then Rachel rushed back in and the moment vanished. He finished another blood pressure reading and pupil check, then disconnected the monitor.

He pulled the blanket over Jack's face to protect him from the downdraught and any flying sand but it actually wasn't quite as bad as he'd expected. Helicopters didn't faze him at all. He'd spent the best part of five years travelling in them and pulling patients from them. But Rachel looked terrified.

She ducked as they approached the helicopter even though the spinning blades were high above her head. Several of the crew members did the same. The paramedic flung open the door and jumped down.

The handover only took a few seconds. 'Jack Baker, twenty-four. A few tons of sand-filled barrels landed on him. Suspected broken ulna and radius, blood supply looked compromised so it's been realigned. Unconscious since the accident. GCS six with recent response to pain. His right pupil has been sluggish. No problems with airway. Breath sounds equal and abdomen soft.' He handed over the charts he'd made, along with a prescription chart and Jack's notes. 'He's had five of diamorphine.'

The paramedic nodded as he anchored the stretcher inside and started connecting Jack to his equipment. His eyes met Nathan's. 'Our control centre will give you a call and keep you updated.'

Nathan pulled the door closed and backed off towards the trees next to the beach. The water rippled as the blades quickened and the helicopter lifted off. After a few minutes the members of the crew started to disperse, mumbling under their breath as they headed back towards the accident site. It would take hours to clean up. It would take even longer to write the report for the insurers.

Nathan started to roll up his khaki shirtsleeves. Report writing could wait. He'd rather be involved in the clean-up and get a better idea of the general set-up. Health and Safety might not be his direct responsibility but, as one of the doctors on the island, he didn't want to have to deal with something like that again.

Something caught his eye in the foliage next to the beach—a little flash of pink. It wasn't the tropical flowers that he'd spotted earlier; they'd been yellow, orange and red. This wasn't fauna. This was man-made.

Rachel was sitting on the edge of the beach, just as it merged with the dark green foliage. Her pink cotton T-shirt stood out. She hadn't even noticed him, her knees pulled up to her chest and her eyes fixed on the sky above.

He bit his lip. He couldn't leave her there like that. She wasn't used to trauma. She wasn't used to accidents. This was totally out of left field for her.

Part of him wanted to walk in the other direction. The Nathan of eight years ago wanted to leave her sitting there alone. But the Doctors Without Borders medic wouldn't let him. In his five years he'd never once left a colleague alone after a traumatic incident. He wasn't about to start now.

His legs moved before his brain started to function. They were on automatic pilot. He didn't even think. He just plopped down on the sand next to her and put his arm around her shoulders.

'Okay?'

She didn't speak, but she didn't pull away either—not like earlier. Her breathing was shaky and her shoulders gave the slightest quiver beneath his arm. He moved closer, pulling her to him and speaking quietly. 'You did good, Rach. Emergency medicine doesn't come easily to some folks. You acted as though it was second nature.'

'I just acted on instinct.' Her voice wavered.

'Did that include when you dived amongst those barrels that could have pounded you to pieces?' He still couldn't believe she'd done that. He still couldn't believe he hadn't been quick enough to stop her.

Her head sagged onto his shoulder. She stared out at the sea. 'I don't know why I did that.'

He smiled. 'Probably because you're headstrong, stubborn and don't listen to anyone around you.'

She gave a little laugh. 'I guess some things don't change at all.'

He felt himself tense a little. Part of him didn't want to offer comfort to her. Part of him didn't want to reassure and support her. He could feel his body reacting to hers. The familiarity of her underneath his arm, leaning against him as if they still fitted together—even after all this time.

His breath was caught somewhere in his throat. He wanted to tell her that everything changed. Things changed in the blink of an eye and the world you thought you had just slipped through your fingers.

But he couldn't let the words out.

He'd been down this road himself—acting on instinct

in places where it could get you into trouble. But he'd been lucky. He'd always been surrounded by supportive colleagues. Doctors Without Borders was like that.

He didn't even want to touch on his natural instinct to the car backfiring in Melbourne that ended with him crouched in a ball on the street. Working in war zones did that to you. And it was hard to shake it off.

And, because of that, he took a deep breath and stayed where he was. Sometimes—even for a few minutes—a colleague just needed some support. He'd had colleagues who'd supported him. Now, it was his job to return the favour. No matter what else was going on in his head.

Right now it was just them. Just the two of them for the first time in eight years, sitting together on a beach.

He pushed everything else away. Three weeks on an island with Rachel?

There would be plenty of time for repercussions. But, for now, he would just wait.

# CHAPTER FIVE

THE SHOWER WAS distinctly dodgy, spouting an uneven trickle of water. With thick hair like Rachel's, rinsing the shampoo out was a challenge. She pulled on a plain pink button-down shirt and another pair of khaki shorts and her hiking boots again. The smell of breakfast was wafting around. Ron had been right; the catering cabin was definitely the most popular place on the island.

Part of her felt bad for the celebrities who had spent their first night in camp, half of them lying on the equivalent of yoga mats on the jungle floor. If it had been her she would have stuck her head in the sleeping bag, pulled the tie at the top and not come out again until morning. But, then again, she wasn't here to entertain the audience.

Last night in the cabin had been hard enough. Knowing that across the simple sitting area and through the thin walls Nathan was lying in another bed made her skin tingle.

She'd spent years trying not to think about Nathan. Guilt always ensued when she thought about him. For the first year she'd had to concentrate on her own treatment and recovery. The support from Darius had actually helped; he'd been a welcome distraction. He liked to be the centre of attention in his own little world—

even if he was keeping it secret. Sometimes it had felt as if Rachel was his only confidante and that could be a bit overwhelming—especially when she had her own recovery to consider.

Last night had been pretty sleepless. She tried to rationalise. She was on the Whitsundays—beautiful islands in the Coral Sea with a whole host of wildlife around her. The nightlife sounds were always going to be a little different. But that wasn't what had kept her awake.

If she closed her eyes really tightly she could almost imagine that she could hear Nathan breathing in the other room. It brought back a whole host of memories she just wasn't ready for. Her hand on his skin, watching the rise and fall of his chest and feeling the murmur of his heart beneath her palm. The soft noises he made while he slept. The fact that in their five years together, he'd never ever turned his back when they'd slept together. His arms had always been around her.

The feelings of comfort and security swept over her—things she'd missed beyond measure these last few years. And that didn't even begin to touch on the passion. The warmth. The love.

Getting up and heading for the shower to try and scrub off the feeling of his arm around her shoulders had been all she could do. Nothing could change what had happened between them. Nothing could change the look in his eyes when he'd first seen her.

She'd felt the buzz yesterday. She'd heard the concern in his voice when she dived in amongst those barrels. She still wasn't quite sure why she'd done that. It seemed like a good idea at the time—she was the only person small enough to get through the gap and to the patient.

But once she'd been in there she was scared. Hearing

Nathan's voice was not only reassuring but it also bathed her in comfort, knowing that he was concerned about her. She shouldn't read anything into it. She shouldn't. She knew him. Or at least she used to know him. Nathan would have been concerned for any colleague.

Had five years working for Doctors Without Borders changed him? Had her walking away from him changed him? She hoped not. She hoped his good heart was still there. Even if he only showed it to her in a moment of crisis.

She followed the smell of eggs and bacon. Most of the crew were already eating at the variety of tables. Nathan was in the corner, having a heated discussion with one of the directors.

Rachel filled her plate with toast, bacon, eggs and coffee, then walked over, putting her tray on the table. 'Anything I should know about, guys?'

The angry words instantly dissipated as both sets of eyes looked at her in surprise. The hidden similarities between a television crew and a hospital was amazing. Rachel had spent too many years working amongst people with big egos to be thrown by anything she came across.

'Is this a medical matter or a technical matter?' she asked as she sat down and spread butter on her toast.

Nathan blinked. He still seemed surprised at her frankness. 'It's a mixture of both. Bill just presented me with a revised list of the challenges. I think some of the changes could impact on the health and safety of the contestants. He's telling me that's not our concern.'

'Really?' Rachel raised her eyebrows and bit into her toast. She chewed for a few seconds while she regarded Bill carefully. On this island, he obviously thought his word was law. To the rest of the production crew it probably was. But he hadn't met Rachel or Nathan before. No matter how at odds they were with each other, he was about to find out just how formidable they could be as a combined force.

She gave Bill her best stare. 'So, just out of interest, what would the insurance company say if both your doctors bailed?'

A slow smile started to spread over Nathan's face. He knew exactly what she was doing.

'What do you mean?' snapped Bill.

She shrugged and started cutting up her bacon and eggs. 'I'm just asking a question, Bill. I'm pretty sure you can't have this production without your medical team in place. After yesterday, I think you'll find Nathan and I aren't prepared to negotiate on anything.' She popped a piece of bacon in her mouth. 'You either listen to us or you don't.'

She was so matter-of-fact about it. Probably because she wasn't prepared to negotiate. Employees, including herself, had been put at risk yesterday. They'd already identified a few celebrities who couldn't take part in certain challenges. She didn't even know the schedule for today. But, no matter how many years had passed, if Nathan knew enough to get angry about it, that was good enough for her.

Bill stood up abruptly, knocking the table and sloshing some of her coffee over the side of the cup. 'Fine. I'll change it back to the original plan.'

Nathan watched Bill as he stormed across the large cabin and slammed the door behind him. None of the crew even batted an eyelid. This obviously wasn't news to them.

Rachel mopped up her coffee with a napkin. Now it was just the two of them her earlier bravado was vanishing. She was thinking about his arm on her shoulders last night and the way he'd just sat and held her until she'd composed herself. When she'd finally taken a deep breath and felt calm, he'd just given a little nod and stood up and strolled off into the sunset.

She'd no idea where he'd gone. But it had given her a chance to go back to the shared cabin, have a quick wash and change and hide in her room. She'd lain there for hours until she'd eventually heard the click of the door.

But she was a fool. He hadn't come to speak to her. And she should be grateful. Her initial reaction to him earlier had been pure and utter shock. She'd more or less said she couldn't work with him, which wasn't true. He'd just been the last person she'd expected to see.

Nathan's breakfast plate was empty, as was his coffee cup, and he picked them up. 'I've heard that filming last night varied from boring to very boring. I think they were trying to spice things up today at one of the challenges and I'm not sure I trust Bill not to still try. Are you happy to come along to the filming?'

She nodded as she glanced at the now congealed egg on her plate. Her appetite had definitely left her.

He stood up. 'I've also put up a notice saying we'll have a surgery every morning for an hour for the crew. Anyone with any difficulties. I take it you don't have a problem with that?'

She gulped. She was an experienced medical physician. Why did the thought of general practice fill her with fear? 'That should be fine.' No way did she want to express any concerns around Nathan. He'd already seen her wobble last night. That was already once too many.

'Good,' he said. 'We start in ten minutes.'

He walked out ahead of her as she scrambled to pick up her tray and she felt a flash of annoyance. Ratbag.

This was something they actually should have sat down and discussed together. He wasn't senior to her. They were both here as doctors. She could almost bet if she were any other person he would have discussed this with her first.

A few of the crew were waiting when she arrived. Thankfully, there was nothing too difficult to diagnose. A few chesty crackles, another inhaler for someone and an emergency supply of blood pressure tablets for someone who'd misplaced their own.

An hour later, Ron arrived in a Jeep to pick up her and Nathan and take them to the first challenge on the other side of the island.

'Challenge has been changed,' were Ron's first words.

'What a surprise,' said Nathan. 'What to?'

'The underground scramble.' Ron kept driving while Rachel exchanged a glance with Nathan. The underground scramble was not a challenge she'd want to do. She searched her brain. Several of the celebrities suffered from claustrophobia and would have to be exempt from scrambling through the dark underground tunnels filled with a variety of creatures.

'What about Diamond?' she asked. 'I think there's too big a risk of infection.'

'I agree. I'll tell the producer she's ineligible.'

'Shouldn't that have been decided before the public voted?'

Ron looked over his shoulder. 'Don't worry about it. Vote's already decided that Darius will be doing the challenge. Diamond's safe.'

Nathan's eyes fixed hard on her as her stomach flipped over. A man who'd just undergone a bout of chemotherapy shouldn't be dragging himself through dirty, water-filled tunnels with a variety of biting creatures and insects. But she already knew what he'd say.

'I'll need to speak to Darius before he starts,' she murmured.

Ron laughed. 'Don't think you'll have a chance. They'll announce live on TV it's him and do the challenge immediately afterwards. You won't have time to talk.'

'But I need time. He'll get a safety briefing, won't he? I'll make time then.'

Nathan's gaze narrowed. 'What's wrong? Doesn't he like the dark? If he can't do a challenge shouldn't I know about it?'

She pushed back her retort. Nathan was right. It was already a bugbear that Darius was her ex. The fact that his medical details hadn't been released to Nathan was obviously annoying him. It wasn't her fault. It wasn't her choice.

But she was being paid to do a job. And she wouldn't be doing a good job if she didn't warn Darius of the risks to his health—whether he listened or not.

'He can do the challenge—and I'm sure he will. I just need to discuss some underlying issues with him.'

Nathan folded his arms across his chest and fixed his gaze back on the road ahead. The jungle foliage was beginning to thin as they reached the hollowed out tunnels at the other side of the island.

All of the celebrities were perched on a bench, talking to the hosts. Rachel jumped from the Jeep and made her way quickly to the entrance of the caves. 'How deep are they and what's in them?' she asked one of the nearby crew.

He guided her over to the side, where some TV screens were set up, showing the cameras with infrared filters that were positioned in the man-made tunnels. She grimaced at the sight of scampering creatures. 'Anything that bites and could break the skin?'

One of the rangers nodded. 'Just about everything.'

Rachel squeezed her eyes closed and pushed her way past the hosts, grabbing hold of Darius's arm. She was making an executive decision. This whole thing was fake anyway. She was pretty sure the only thing that was real was the viewers' votes.

'What's wrong, Rachel?' Darius's brow creased as he glanced to make sure no one could overhear them.

'I don't think you should do this challenge,' she said quickly. 'There's a strong possibility of getting cuts, bites or scrapes. Any break to the skin is a risk of infection and your immunity will already be low right now. There's no telling what the infection risks are from the unknown creatures or the dirty water.'

Darius shot her his famous soap star smile as he realised what her words meant. 'Lighten up, Rach. I've won the public vote? Fantastic.' He shook his head. 'I'm not worried about the tunnels. Why should you be?' He glanced over her shoulder. She could already tell that Nathan had closed in and was listening to their conversation. 'You can check me over for broken skin when I come out.' Darius gave her a wink and walked back to the bench with the other celebrities.

The producer hurried over to her, hissing in her ear. 'What are you doing? You'll spoil everything. This is supposed to be a surprise.'

She spun around. 'My job. That's what I'm doing. And what are you worried about—didn't you know Darius is one of the most famous soap stars in Australia? I'm sure he can act surprised.'

She stomped away back to the television screens.

Darius was more concerned about his screen time and popularity than his health. It was maddening.

Nathan appeared at her side. 'Are you going to tell me what's going on?'

She gritted her teeth. 'I can't.'

He turned without another word and walked away.

After shooting her a few glares, the TV hosts smiled right on cue for their live broadcast. Darius was suitably surprised when he found out he'd been voted for the challenge. He smiled all through the televised safety briefing, then dived head first into the tunnels. Some of them were a tight fit. There was no way the sportsman could have forced his way through these tunnels. If Darius had been at his normal weight he probably wouldn't have fitted either. He must have lost a little weight during chemotherapy. In the end he completed the challenge in a few minutes and emerged wet and muddy with his rewards in his hands. There was a large gash on one leg and a few nips on the other from some baby alligators.

She waited impatiently for the filming to finish. 'In the Jeep,' she said as the cameras stopped.

Darius flinched and rubbed at the open wound. 'I think we're supposed to go back directly to camp.'

Nathan appeared at his back. 'Do what the good lady says. You won't like her when she's angry.'

There it was. That little hint to Darius that he actually knew her a whole lot better than Darius did. She could see the instant recognition on Darius's face as they eyed each other suspiciously. It was ridiculous—like pistols at dawn. She was irritated enough already and this wasn't helping.

Ron appeared, sweating as always, and smiling. 'Back to the medical centre then, folks?'

All three climbed wordlessly into the Jeep. The journey back seemed so much longer. Ron talked merrily as if he hadn't noticed the atmosphere in the car, dropping them all at the path leading down to the medical centre.

Rachel strode ahead, flinging open the door and pulling things from cupboards. She gestured towards the examination trolley. 'Climb up there.'

She was so angry with them both right now she couldn't even look at them. Darius for being so stupid and Nathan for being so stubborn. Part of her knew that Nathan was right. Any other doctor would want to know the patient's history too.

But any other doctor wouldn't get under her skin and grate like Nathan could.

He was like a permanent itch. Part of her still felt guilty around him. Part of her felt angry. Irrational? Yes, of course. She was the one who had walked away. She had left him and Charlie and put herself first.

Even if she could turn back the clock she wouldn't change that—no matter how much it had hurt them both. Her outcome could have been so different. She was one of the lucky ones; she knew that. She'd had her treatment and reached the five-year magic survival milestone. That was good; that was positive.

But this whole place had just thrown her into turmoil. She'd distanced herself from Darius these last few years. He needed to find others to rely on. Coming here had been a mistake.

As for the sizzle in the air whenever she and Nathan were in the same room? She really couldn't have predicted it. If anyone had asked her, she would have sworn it would never exist again. But it did exist. Every time she looked at him her skin tingled. Every time he stood close enough, all the little hairs on her body stood on end, almost willing him to come into contact. She couldn't control her body's responses. And it was driving her nuts.

She washed her hands and opened the sterile dressing pack. Nathan had angled a lamp over Darius's leg, even though he hadn't touched it. He seemed to sense it was wise to stay out of her way.

She slipped on her gloves and leaned over to get a good look at the wound. It was around four inches long and ragged, with a few tiny pieces of debris. She took a deep breath and irrigated with saline, removing the debris with tweezers. 'It's not deep enough to stitch. I'll close it with paper stitches. But it does give a route of entry for infection. Who knows what was in that mud or those tunnels? You're going to need this dressed and observed every day.'

Darius sighed. 'That seems like overkill. This place is miles away from the campsite. I don't want to have to come here every day. The rest of the celebrities will think I'm getting special treatment—either that or they'll think something is wrong.'

Nathan cleared his throat loudly. 'Actually, Darius, Rachel's right. And it isn't overkill. Since Rachel has highlighted you're susceptible to infection, I think it would be wise to put you on antibiotics. It's pretty much a given you're going to get some kind of infection in that wound.'

Rachel was surprised to hear Nathan back her so quickly. She finished cleaning the wound and applied some antiseptic cream and a dressing.

'It might be easier all round if either I or Rachel come up to the campsite every day to dress the wound. We can bring supplies with us and it should only take a few minutes. That way, it's pretty obvious why you're being seen. It's not special treatment. It's wound care.'

Darius nodded. He seemed oblivious to the fact she was mad at him. But of course the world revolved around Darius. At least his world did. What made her more curious was the way Nathan was actually giving him some leeway. She hadn't expected it. Hadn't expected it at all.

'That sounds great. Thanks for that.' He slid his legs from the examination couch while she got rid of the waste and Nathan dispensed some antibiotics. He held them out for Darius. 'You do realise I'll tell the producer you can't be eligible for tomorrow's challenge?'

'What?' He had Darius's instant attention. 'But it sounds like one of the best ones!'

'You can't go swimming and diving with a potentially infected leg. No way.'

Nathan was still holding onto the antibiotics. All credit to him. He knew exactly how to deal with Darius.

'But it'll look as if I'm using it as an excuse not to take part.'

Nathan shrugged. 'The producer and director have to abide by our recommendations. Feel free to say on camera that the docs have refused to let you take part. Feel free to let the world know you've got a potentially life-threatening infection in your leg.'

Rachel could almost see the headlines running through Darius's head. He gave a little nod. 'Thanks for this.' He took the antibiotics and a bottle of water from Nathan. 'I'll see you both tomorrow.'

He exited the medical centre and disappeared down the path to where Ron was waiting to drive him back to camp.

Rachel folded her arms and leaned against the wall. She could tell Nathan knew she was watching him. He started opening the filing cabinet and flicking through notes.

'That was very kind of you. What's going on?'

He glanced upwards. 'I have no idea what you mean.'

'Yeah, right. We both know you don't like Darius. Why are you being so obliging?'

Nathan sat down behind the desk. 'How much weight has he lost recently?'

She blinked. It wasn't the response she'd expected.

She shook her head. 'I'm not sure. He lost weight a few months ago. I just presumed he hasn't put it back on again yet. He is looking a little gaunt, but I'm sure once his time in camp has passed he'll be fine. All the celebrities lose some weight in camp.'

Nathan looked thoughtful. 'I don't care that you're not telling me his medical history. I just don't like the look of him.' His mouth curled upwards for a second. There was a definite glint in his eye. 'In more ways than one.' He looked serious again. 'I think there could be something else going on with Darius Cornell.'

She took a deep breath. She was having a professional conversation with Nathan Banks. It was just so weird. She'd been so wrapped up in Darius's history of non-Hodgkin's and keeping it confidential she hadn't really thought about anything else. Sometimes you needed someone else to help you look at the big picture.

She bit the inside of her lip and gave a little sigh of recognition. 'This way we get to keep a direct eye on him every day?'

Nathan smiled. 'You got it.'

So this was what working with Nathan Banks could be like. She'd waited over eight years to find out. She'd never really expected it to happen. Even though they'd attended the same university, they'd never actually worked on a ward together. Once they'd qualified, choosing different specialities meant that it was unlikely to ever happen. This had been totally unexpected.

She watched as he flicked through a few files. His hair was so short she had an urge to run her palm over his head and feel the little bristle beneath her skin. He must have got used to wearing it in the buzz-cut style while he was working away.

The first thing she'd noticed was the little lines around his eyes. He'd aged. But, like most men, he'd done it in a good way. He'd lost the fresh face of youth and replaced it with something much more lived in and a whole lot more worldly-wise.

Nathan had always managed to take her breath away. Before, it had been with his good nature, laughter and sex appeal. Now, it was something entirely different. The man in front of her made her suck her breath between her teeth and just hold it there. He had so much presence. His bulkier frame filled the room. But it was whatever was hidden behind his eyes that made her unable to release the breath screaming in her lungs.

It could be a whole variety of things. The loss of his parents. His time over the world for Doctors Without Borders. Did Nathan have a medical history she didn't know about? Why had he changed his career pathway? It could even be the fact that his brother had now settled down with a family before him. But she doubted that very much.

She wanted to peel back the layers. She wanted a diary of the missing years. But she wanted it all about Nathan, without revealing anything of herself.

Pathetic, really.

But she just wasn't ready to go there.

His head lifted and their gazes meshed. 'Is there anyone else you're worried about?' he asked.

Her brain scrambled. *You. Me.* She bit back the obvious replies.

'Ron,' she said quickly. 'I don't know if he just has a sweating disorder but I'd like to check him over.'

Nathan nodded. 'Me too. We'll get him in soon.'

He stood up and walked over to the door. 'I'm going to go for a run along the beach before we need to supervise the diving challenge.'

Rachel bit her lip. An empty beach and the open ocean sounded like a great idea. Somewhere to clear her head. Somewhere to get her thoughts together. But if Nathan was going to be there it was too crowded already.

She stood up. 'I'm going to go and talk to the production crew about the diving challenge. I'll talk to you later.'

As she stepped outside the medical centre she took a few gulps of air. This island seemed to be getting smaller by the second…

## CHAPTER SIX

RACHEL STRETCHED OUT on the sun lounger and wiggled her toes, the only part of her currently in the sun. The last few days had been odd. After the hiccup on the first day and Darius's minor injuries on the challenge, things had pretty much been how Lewis had promised. A few hours' work every day followed by hours and hours to kill. That would be fine if they were staying at a luxury resort, or in the middle of a city. Instead, they were on an island with a distinct lack of facilities and where the only entertainment was the Z-list celebrities. The days seemed longer than ever.

The challenges had been going well. Frank, the sportsman, had aced the diving challenge around the coral reef without managing to do himself any damage. The next challenge had been to scale a thirty-foot tree to reach a fake bird's-nest. Billy X, the rapper, had proved surprisingly agile but Darius had obviously been annoyed that he'd not been voted for by the public.

His wound was gradually healing and the antibiotics seemed to have warded off any sign of infection. He still wasn't looking any better though and Rachel had started to wonder if they should be monitoring his weight. The celebrities had to prepare and cook their own food over a campfire and, even though there weren't excessive amounts of food, there was still enough to keep them sustained. Maybe Nathan was right—maybe there was something else to worry about?

She shifted uncomfortably on the sun lounger. If Darius's non-Hodgkin's relapsed he would be in big trouble. He had already relapsed twice. Each treatment plan had been more intense than the one before. She knew first-hand exactly what these treatment plans involved. He wouldn't be able to keep his illness a secret much longer.

She heard muffled voices up in the trees around her. The crew were gossiping again. She smiled. They were a great bunch but sometimes it was like being trapped on an island with a bunch of teenage girls.

Thankfully, no one seemed to have picked up on the tension between her and Nathan. Or, if they had, she hadn't heard anyone mention it.

Ron caught her eye as he walked slowly towards the medical centre. Rachel had asked him to come in twice in as many days and she was glad he'd finally showed up. Nathan was on duty and would check him over.

As he reached out his hand towards the door he winced. His face was bright red. He almost looked as though he could burst.

She hesitated for a few seconds. Nathan was an experienced A & E doctor. He could handle this—she knew he could. If she went in now, he might be resentful of her interference.

But the expression on Ron's face couldn't let her sit there much longer. She sat up and dug her toes into the sand for a second as she reached underneath the lounger for her sandals. She wasn't getting much of a tan anyway. She was too worried that if she took her sundress off and just wore her bikini people might ask questions about her scar.

She wasn't normally self-conscious and if Nathan hadn't been on the island she would have worn her bikini without a second thought. But suddenly she was wishing she had a schoolgirl-style swimsuit in her backpack—one that covered all parts of her back and front. It might not be stylish but would stop any awkward questions.

She shook the sand from her feet and pushed them into her sandals. Ron. That was who she needed to concentrate on now. It was time to stop fretting about the future and put her professional head back into place.

Nathan was feeling restless. The last few nights he hadn't been able to sleep. Lying in a cabin with only two thin walls separating him and Rachel was driving him crazy. Every time he heard the shower running he imagined her soaping her smooth skin under the spluttering water. He imagined the water running in rivulets down her straight spine, in long lines down to her painted pink toes.

The pink toes had been haunting him. It was practically the only part of her skin that could freely be seen. Unlike the rest of the crew on the island, Rachel had kept herself well covered up. T-shirts and long shorts coupled with socks and hiking boots were the flavour of the day. Even in the evening she wore long pants and long-sleeved T-shirts. The only part visible were her toes.

All his memories of nights with Rachel had revolved around short satin nightdresses and shoestring straps. There certainly hadn't been a lack of skin.

And it certainly wasn't helping his male libido. His imagination was currently working overtime. He needed to find himself a distraction, a hobby. But finding something else to do on this island was proving harder than he'd thought.

He'd put a call through to Len to see what his plans

were for later. Maybe a hike around the island would help him think about other things.

Nathan was just replacing his phone when the door opened. Ron walked in, panting heavily, with a strange expression on his face and his signature sweat marks on his grey T-shirt.

He really didn't look great. His face was highly coloured with beads of sweat on his brow. Nathan stood up quickly and helped him over to the examination trolley, lifting his legs up onto it and helping him to rest back.

He could hear Ron rasping for breath so he switched on the monitoring equipment, connected it and pulled an oxygen mask over Ron's face.

'How long have you been feeling unwell?'

'Just…today,' Ron wheezed.

The blood pressure cuff started to inflate. 'Ron, are you having any chest pain?'

Ron frowned. 'Not really. Well…maybe a little.'

Great. He'd suspected Ron wasn't feeling great but he hadn't responded to any of Nathan's invitations to be checked over. Right now, he had heart attack written all over him.

Nathan looked at the reading on the monitor and opened the drug cabinet, taking out an aspirin. First line treatment for an MI. Actually—the only treatment they had on this island. Not ideal. Still, it was better to be safe than sorry. 'Here, take this.' He handed Ron the tablet and a glass of water.

'Not really pain…' Ron continued. 'Just indigestion.'

'Indigestion? How often?'

Ron thumped the glass of water back down; even taking a sip had been an effort. 'Every day,' he gasped.

Nathan raised his eyebrows. 'Ever had problems with your blood pressure?'

Ron gave a nod.

'Does your indigestion come on when you're working?'

Another nod.

'Does it ever go down your arm?'

Ron's high colour started to pale. The oxygen was finally getting into his system and his heart rate was starting to steady.

'How bad is your indigestion today?'

'B…bad.'

'Feels like something is pressing on your chest?'

Nathan stood at the side of the examination trolley. He watched the monitor closely. It gave a clear tracing of Ron's heart rate. The PQRS waves were all visible. No ST elevation. 'The good news is you're not having a heart attack. The bad news is you've probably got angina—and had it for quite a while. I'm going to give you a spray under your tongue to see if that eases the tightness across your chest.'

It only took a second to administer the spray and another few minutes for it to take effect. Nathan frowned. In a way it was a relief that angina was Ron's problem but on an island this would be difficult. Uncontrolled angina could easily lead to a heart attack. Ron really needed to be reviewed by a cardiologist. Chances were, an angiogram would reveal blocked arteries that would need to be stented and cleared. He could just imagine how Ron would take the news. But keeping him here would be dangerous. They didn't have the equipment that would be needed if Ron did have a heart attack. Apart from aspirin, they didn't have any clot-busting drugs.

'Ron, I think you probably know this isn't indigestion you've been having. It looks like angina. You need a twelve-lead ECG, a cardiac echo and an angiogram—none of which we can do here.'

Ron waved his hand. 'I can get all that when we get back to the mainland. I'll be fine until then.'

Nathan sat down next to the examination trolley. 'It's too big a risk. Tell the truth, Ron; you're having angina every time you exert yourself.' He nodded at the monitor. 'Your blood pressure is too high and you're constantly out of breath. Your heart is working too hard because the blood vessels aren't clear. You need to see a cardiologist.'

Ron shook his head. 'Forget it. I'll be fine.'

'No, you won't.' Nathan turned at the voice. Rachel was standing at the doorway, wearing her trademark pink. This time it wasn't a T-shirt and long shorts. This time it was a pink summer dress. She must have been down on the beach. His eyes went immediately to her painted toenails, visible in her flat jewelled sandals.

She walked over next to the trolley and put her hand in Ron's. He met her gaze immediately. Rachel had the people-person touch. In A & E you rarely got a chance to form any kind of a relationship with your patients. Medical physicians were different. They frequently saw their patients year on year.

'Ron, it's time to look after yourself. This really can't wait. Tell me honestly—how long have you been having these symptoms?'

Ron hesitated. His breathing had gradually improved. 'A few months.'

'Have you seen anyone about this?'

He shook his head. 'I've just kept taking my blood pressure tablets.' He gave a rueful smile. 'I did think it was indigestion.' He pulled a pack of a well-known brand of antacids from his pocket. 'I've been going through half a packet of these a day.'

Nathan could tell that Rachel was hiding a wince behind her smile. 'If your symptoms have been getting worse then it's definitely time for some investigations. We don't need to call a medevac to get you off the island, but we can arrange for you to go back by seaplane. We can arrange that for tomorrow. In the meantime I'll give you a spray and some instructions on how to use it. I don't want you going back to work. I want you to rest.'

Nathan watched carefully. For some reason Ron seemed to relate better to Rachel's instructions than his. She had a gift for talking to patients. Her tone was firm but friendly. He liked it.

His time working for Doctors Without Borders had been fraught. There had hardly been any time for conversations like this. As soon as he finished patching one patient—he was on to the next. There was barely time to think, let alone speak.

He sucked in a breath for a second. Something else had just struck him. He'd spent five years working with people, but not getting close—never staying in one place long enough to form true relationships. That thought started to chip away at his brain as he watched Rachel empathise and relate to Ron.

Rachel squeezed Ron's hand. 'Stay here for the next few hours, then I'll take you down to the canteen for dinner. We can have a further talk about things then.'

It was almost as if a giant weight had been lifted from Ron's shoulders. He sighed and rested back on the examination trolley, letting his eyes close. 'Dinner with a beautiful woman,' he muttered. 'I'd be a fool to say no.'

Rachel shot Nathan a smile—a smile that sent a little jolt all the way down his body. Maybe it was her humanity that was drawing him in. Even though he knew better, he'd spent the last few years labelling Rachel as heartless in his head. It had been easier to do that—because he'd never been able to get his head around the way she'd walked away and left him and Charlie.

He'd known her for seven years. The first few years of university they hadn't dated—just casually flirted. The five years after that, they'd been inseparable. Rachel had never seemed heartless to him. That just wasn't her. That wasn't how she worked. No one could spend five years with someone and not know them. It just wasn't possible to put on a good enough act to hide all your flaws and character traits for that long. He did know her. Or at least he *had* known her.

So why had she done something so out of character? What on earth had happened?

Their eyes locked. Chocolate-brown, framed with dark lashes, her eyes had always been one of his favourite parts of her. Her tan was deepening slightly after a few days on the island. Her dark hair was pulled up at either side of her face and tied in a rumpled kind of knot, the rest sitting on her shoulders. And the pink sundress covered everything, just giving enough of a hint of the soft curves that lay underneath. *Pretty as a picture.* Those were the words he'd always used for Rachel in his head. And no matter how angry he'd been with her—still was with her—some things were just buried too deep. The underlying frustration and resentment was still there.

No one had hurt him like Rachel had. What she'd done was unforgivable. But now he was in her company again he kept having little flashes of the good stuff. The way she tilted back her head and laughed when she was joking with some of the crew. The way she frequently reached out and touched someone when she was talking to them. The way that every now and then she drifted off, thinking about something else. All sparked waves of memories for Nathan. Memories of good times…memories of better times. Five years of shared memories.

Why had she walked away?

She wiggled her toes, the sand from the beach obviously caught between them. He dragged his eyes away from her painted toes and stood up. 'I'll stay with Ron for the next few hours. Come back and take over at dinner time.'

She gave a nod and glanced around the cabin. 'I promised Tallie I'd get her some petroleum jelly for her dry skin. She's trying to ward off an eczema flare-up. Do you know where it is?'

He looked up from Ron's notes and pushed the stool towards her. 'There's not enough storage in here. I think it's at the top of the cupboard over there.'

'Great, thanks.' She dragged the stool over to the counter and climbed on top to open the cupboards. Nathan glanced at Ron. Thankfully, his eyes were still closed and he wasn't watching Nathan fix on Rachel's bare legs and backside as she rummaged through the cupboard. The corners of his mouth turned upwards. Most of the prescribed medicines were easily accessible but the more routine things had to be packed away wherever there was space.

After a few minutes she finally found what she was looking for. 'Here it is.' She bent down and placed the container on the counter at her feet, ready to jump back down. But her rummaging had dislodged a few of the precariously stacked items in the cupboard and, as she looked back up, a few packages of bandages tumbled from the cupboard, bouncing all around her. It was pure instinct. As the items started to fall, Rachel lifted her hands, crouched down and curled into a ball.

The movement made her dress ride up, and not just a little. She was wearing a bikini under her dress—pink, of course. He'd already noticed the straps tied around her neck. But this time he got a flash of something else. The bright pink bikini bottoms covered some, but not all, parts of her. She was quick to grab at her dress and pull it back down, colour flooding into her cheeks.

She spun around as he got to his feet to come over and help. She lifted her hands quickly. 'Oops. Bit of a disaster.' She couldn't meet his gaze as she jumped down from the stool and made a grab for the wrapped bandages that had landed all around her. He bent to help, their hands brushing.

He saw her gulp as for a split second he caught her gaze. 'Just as well you've seen it all before,' she said quickly.

He didn't reply. He couldn't. He was still crouching down as she grabbed some of the bandages and set them on the counter. 'I'll let you get the rest. I'll take this to Tallie and be back in a few hours.'

She rushed towards the door, still talking nervously as she made a quick exit. Nathan still hadn't moved. He sucked in a deep breath as he reached for the last few bandages.

He couldn't be sure—he just couldn't be sure. But he'd seen more than enough battle scars in his time. He'd definitely seen something. But what it was he just couldn't fathom.

He'd seen Rachel's bare body a thousand times. He knew every contour of her body, every blemish, every mark. What he didn't know was the flash of a surgical scar just above her right hip. He'd no idea how far it went; she'd pulled her dress back down much too quickly. And it had only been the tiniest flash. Maybe he was wrong. Maybe he was reading too much into something.

He closed his eyes for a second, trying to visualise what he'd just seen. It wasn't ragged; it was clean. It couldn't be from an accident. It had to be deliberate. It had to be surgical.

Rachel had always been in perfect health. She still looked in perfect health today. So where on earth had the scar come from and what was it?

## CHAPTER SEVEN

NATHAN SAT ON the sidelines while Rachel had dinner with Ron. It was clear she was onto the health promotion part. She was pointing at his plate and obviously talking about food choices. Next she swapped his soda for a diet one. Then she persuaded him to have some salad with his steak.

Ron wasn't eating much but the flushed colour of his cheeks had faded. Next, Rachel held his GTN spray for angina in her hands and talked him through how and when to use it.

'Earth to Planet Nathan. Are you home?'

Len was grinning at him from the other side of the table.

'What is it?'

Len gestured with his fork. 'You haven't taken your eyes off her for the last ten minutes. I keep expecting you to make an excuse to go on over there.'

'What? No way.' He speared a bit of his steak.

Len raised his eyebrows. 'I know.'

'Know what?'

'That you two have history.'

He almost dropped his fork. 'What do you mean?' He shot a quick wayward glance in her direction again. He'd love to say that Len was far too observant for his own good. But Len was one of the crew members he had a rapport with. He hoped Len would be on his side.

Rachel reached across the table and put her hand over Ron's, obviously offering some words of comfort.

Just as well he knew there was absolutely nothing in it, otherwise he was pretty sure his stomach would be twisting right now.

Len had started eating again. 'I knew it when I talked to her down at the bar. She mentioned you then.'

'She did?' All of a sudden Len had his instant attention. 'What did she say?'

Len laughed. 'Oh, nothing good. I take it you didn't leave things on the best of terms?'

Nathan started toying with his food. His gaze drifted back to Rachel. Her dark hair had fallen in waves over her shoulders and she'd put a pink wrap around her shoulders.

Rachel liked pink. She always had—at least seventy per cent of her wardrobe was pink. But what she probably didn't realise was just how good she looked in the colour; it didn't matter what the shade was. It seemed to make her lightly tanned skin glow and her dark hair and eyes shine.

He hesitated. It was obvious Len was waiting for an answer. 'We've not been on the best of terms for eight years.' The words kind of stuck in his throat. 'Before that, we were good together…' he paused '…really good.'

As he said the words out loud he realised how much they hurt. How little he understood about what had happened in his own life. Charlie was settled now. He'd grown up before his time and was married with a family. If his parents hadn't died that was pretty much where he'd expected him and Rachel to end up. Married with a family, probably here in Australia.

But he'd lost all that. He'd lost not just the woman, but also his dreams and aspirations. The life he'd been supposed to live. The career pathway he'd had all plotted out in his head without even knowing if he could be a decent surgeon. He'd barely had the chance to hold a surgical scalpel.

The resentment had flowed through his blood for years. He'd resented her for walking away and leaving him. He'd resented her for carrying on with her career. He'd resented the fact she'd had a life whilst he felt as if he'd been stuck in limbo.

His training in London hadn't fulfilled him; it hadn't captured his passion and enthusiasm and he'd wondered if he would ever get that back.

Joining Doctors Without Borders was his way out. It was his way of trying to live again. Trying to feel useful. He'd saved lives. He knew he had. And knowing that had helped in a way. He might not have been able to save his parents, but he had been able to save others. And for five years he had. In lots of different ways. He still felt a little numb. Some days that had been the only way to survive out there, to just block out certain things so you could continue to function. But the camaraderie with the other staff had been amazing. He'd felt valued—an essential part of the team. He'd worked hard to make others feel that way too and do the absolute best job that he could.

And he'd made friends—good friends that he would have for life.

But the truth was that everyone burned out over there. He had too.

And once you'd burned out it was time to leave. The bosses at Doctors Without Borders often recognised it before the staff did.

Australia had always been the aspiration. Now, it was a reality. But it wasn't working out quite how he had thought. Lewis was a good colleague. And the hospital he'd been working in was fine. But, the truth was, when he woke up in the morning his job wasn't the first thing on his mind.

He'd changed. Life had changed. And as he glanced across the canteen he wondered how life had changed for Rachel too.

Len cleared his throat, then took a drink of his beer. He was off duty tonight. Officially, Nathan was off duty too. But even a couple of beers didn't appeal.

'Well, maybe it's time.'

Nathan frowned. 'Time to do what?'

'Time to find out if eight years' worth of bad feeling is worth it.' He winked at Nathan. 'I've got a nice bottle of chilled Barramundi behind the bar.' He nodded towards the wall that had the shooting schedule on it. 'There's nothing scheduled for tonight. Nothing will happen, apart from the celebrities fighting over whose turn it is to empty the dunny. Why don't you take a seat down at the beach with the fine lady and have a chat? I hear the sunsets around here are to die for.'

'Not a chance.' The words were out of his mouth immediately. He hadn't even given it a moment's consideration in his head.

Because it was more than a little tempting.

Len stood up. 'Well, if you change your mind I'll leave the bottle in some ice at the bar. Up to you, buddy. I'll see you tomorrow at the cliffs. Let's see how fast you can climb.'

Rachel and Ron had stood up and were clearing their trays. Len picked up his and walked over to the kitchen doors, exchanging a few words with them on the way.

Nathan stared down at his steak. The food here had been surprisingly good. He'd heard from the crew that television jobs were often judged on the catering and, if *Celebrity Island* was anything to go by, people would be fighting to get a job here. But his appetite had left him.

The seed that had planted in his brain earlier was beginning to bloom and grow. The more he was around Rachel, the more he realised just how much he'd done to try and avoid being in the same position again—the position where Rachel walking away had hurt more than any physical pain he'd experienced.

He'd spent eight years never really forming true relationships. He still had a good relationship with his brother, Charlie, and a few good friends from university. But other than that? The experience of losing his parents and Rachel so soon after seemed to have affected him more than he'd realised. Trusting someone with his heart again just seemed like a step too far. It was much easier to totally absorb himself in work and other issues. Trouble was, this island didn't have enough work to keep him fully occupied, leaving him with far too much thinking time.

He cleared his tray and murmured a few words of greeting to some of the other crew members. He didn't feel like socialising tonight, but on an island as small as this—with some parts out of bounds for filming—it could be difficult to find some space. The atmosphere in the cabin was becoming claustrophobic. And he was sure it was all him. Rachel seemed relaxed and at ease. She'd obviously got over the whole thing years ago. It wasn't giving her sleepless nights.

He kicked off his trainers and wandered down to the beach. The path was only lit with a few dull lights and the insects were buzzing furiously around him. The waves around this island were a disappointment. Nathan had counted on spending a few hours in the surf every day but it wasn't to be. As a result, he hadn't spent much time on the beach.

He saw her as soon as his feet touched the cool sand. Saw the pink wrap around her, rippling in the night-time breeze.

Len had obviously whispered in her ear. A silver wine cooler was on the sand next to the sun lounger she was sitting on, a glass of wine already in her hand.

He should leave her in peace. She was probably trying to escape, just like he was.

Or he could join her. He could ask her about Ron. It was a pathetic excuse. Even he knew that. But from a fellow medic it was a reasonable question. He stuck his hands deep into his shorts pockets as he moved across the sand towards her.

She was silhouetted against the warm setting sun, which sent a peachy glow across her skin. The condensation was visible on her wine glass as she took a sip.

'Don't spoil this, Nathan.'

Her words almost stopped him in his tracks. He paused for a second, his toes curling against the sand. He knew exactly what she meant. But somehow he still didn't want to go there with her.

'Don't worry. Wine's not really my thing. I prefer a beer.' He missed out the obvious remark. *Remember?*

It was flippant, completely circumventing the whole issue. She didn't turn at his voice, just kept her gaze fixed on the horizon and let out a sigh.

She sipped at her wine. 'I'm tired, Nathan. I'm tired of all this.'

It seemed as if the barriers were finally down. Rachel

was saying what had been on her mind since she'd first set foot in the medical cabin and caught sight of him.

If she'd said those words a few days ago his temper would have flared. How dare she be the one to be tired of the atmosphere between them when it was just as much her fault as his?

But the last few days had made his head spin. He couldn't work out how he really felt about her.

He'd felt it all. Searing jealousy when Darius had appeared. A whole host of sensations when his skin had come into contact with hers. Confusion and rage for the first few days. Flares of passion. His gaze couldn't help but linger on her when he thought she wouldn't notice. Certain glances, nuances, would make his heartbeat quicken and send his blood racing around his body. All sensations he wanted to deny, to ignore.

He hadn't expected to see Rachel again. And he certainly hadn't expected to feel like this around her. Feeling was the problem. It was interfering with everything and because they were virtually stranded on an island together, that seemed to amplify it all.

He stepped forward—it felt like crossing a line—and bumped down on the sun lounger beside her. Her barriers were down. Maybe it was time for some home truths.

She shuffled over a little to make room for him. He reached over and took the glass from her hand, taking a sip of the chilled wine and handing it back. His eyes were focused entirely on the orange setting sun. It seemed easier. Like sitting in a movie theatre together.

The sharp wine hit the back of his throat.

'I didn't expect to see you again, Rach.' He let the words hang in the air between them.

When she finally spoke she didn't sound quite so exasperated. 'I didn't expect to see you again either.'

She turned her head towards him. Her voice had changed; it wasn't so strong. There was the tiniest waver. 'I don't know how to be around you. I don't know how to act. I don't know what's normal for us any more. I don't think things can ever feel normal for us again.'

She was right. She was saying everything that was running through his head. They'd gone from normal to nothing. One day she'd been there—the next she had gone. With a fifteen-minute fraught and tearful conversation tacked on the end.

This situation was alien to them both.

After spending a couple of years at university together with flirtation and attraction, he'd finally acted on instinct and asked her out. They'd been together for five years—through finals, through placements as medical students and then out into the world together as junior doctors, and then senior house officers.

Their relationship had been good. There had been passion and mutual respect in equal measures with only the occasional cross word. She'd been his best friend. Losing her had devastated him at a time when he'd needed her most.

In a way it was a relief that she was struggling with this too. He'd always thought he'd been instantly replaced by Darius Cornell. He'd never understood how she could just walk away from their relationship without a backward glance. And it made him doubt himself—doubt his own ability to read people. He'd questioned that he'd ever known her at all.

She turned her body towards his. 'Would it help if I said sorry? I'm sorry that I left?'

'It would help if you told me why you left.' It came out without any censorship. Without any thought. After eight years, he had to say the thing that was truly on his mind. He needed an explanation. He *deserved* an explanation.

She paused, obviously searching her brain for the right words. 'I had to go.' The words were measured—deliberate. 'It was the right thing for me. It was the right thing for you. It was the right thing for Charlie.'

The mention of his brother made his temper flare. 'Don't you dare tell me that was the right thing for my brother. You weren't there. You didn't see. You *chose* to not see. In a world of madness you were the one thing to give him a sense of normality. You never even told him you were going. Have you any idea how hurt he was? He'd just lost his mum and dad. He didn't need to lose someone else who'd been a permanent fixture in his life for five years.'

A tear rolled down her cheek. She reached over and touched his arm, the cold fingers from the wine glass causing him to flinch. 'I know that. Don't you think I know that? And I'm sorry. It broke my heart; it really did. But I had to. I just had to.' She was shaking her head, oh, so slowly. As if she'd had no choice. But that was rubbish. There was always a choice.

It was words. It was just words. There was no explanation. No rational reason to explain what she'd done. But it was just the two of them sitting alone on this sun lounger on the beach in the glow of the setting sun. And she was confusing him all over again. How could she still do that after eight years?

He could see the sincerity in her eyes. He could hear the emotion in her voice. She wasn't lying to him; she meant every word—even if she wouldn't explain them.

Frustration was simmering in his chest. All he wanted was an explanation. A reason. Something he could make sense of in his head. 'Why, Rach? Why can't you tell me now? It's been eight years. Surely whatever mattered then is in the past?'

Her lips were quivering, her fingertips still on his arm. He could feel the tension in the air between them, hanging like the fireflies above their heads. But there was more than that. There was the buzz, the electricity that still sparked between them.

All he wanted to do was reach up and catch the tear that was rolling down her cheek and wipe it away.

But she moved first. Something flitted across her eyes and she leaned forward, crossing the gap between them. Her perfume surrounded his senses, invading every part of him. He stopped breathing as her lips touched his. It was gentle, coaxing. Her fingertips moved from his arm to the side of his cheek.

His first reaction was to pull back. He'd thought about this from the first second he'd seen her. But he hadn't actually imagined it would happen. He hadn't even let his mind go that far.

But his body had other ideas. His hand tangled through her long hair, settling at the back of her head and pulling her closer to him.

He couldn't think straight. But he could kiss.

And Rachel was kissing him right back.

Her fingers brushed against his tightly shorn hair, sending tingles down his spine as the kiss intensified.

Eight long years he'd waited to do this again. Eight long years to feel her familiar lips against his. They fitted, just the way they always had. Memories of kissing Rachel swamped him.

In their student accommodation…in one of the on-call rooms in the hospital…at one of the hospital balls… and on the street one night in the pouring rain when they just couldn't wait to get home.

All of those memories raced around his head. This was too tempting. *She* was too tempting. Her hair was softer than cashmere, the skin around her neck and shoulders smoother than silk.

His hands slid down her back, feeling the contours of her spine and the curve of her hips. He paused. This was where he thought he'd glimpsed a scar. But now his brain felt as if it were playing tricks on him.

Every pore in his body wanted to move closer, to lie backwards on the sun lounger and pull her body against his. To feel the warm curves underneath her sundress press against the hard angles of his body. But the beach was too exposed. Any minute now some of the crew could appear. Anything that happened between him and Rachel was private—not for public consumption.

Then he felt it—the tear brush against his cheek. Was it the one that was already there? Or was she still crying?

He sucked in a breath. She gently pulled her lips from his, not breaking contact, leaving her forehead resting against his while she gave a few little gasps.

He had so many unanswered questions. So many things he wanted to say.

But she lifted her finger and placed it against his lips before he had a chance to speak. She gave the tiniest shake of her head. As if she was still trying to stay in the moment. Not trying to face up to the past, the present or the future.

His hand lifted and stroked her cheek. It was wet with tears. 'Rach?' he murmured.

She pulled back, her cheeks glistening. 'I'm sorry,' she whispered. 'I really am. But I just can't talk about it. I can't give us that time back. I just can't.' Her voice cracked and she stumbled to her feet, making a grab for her wrap. 'I'm sorry. This was a mistake. I need to go.'

She was off in a flash, running towards the path away from the beach and back to the cabins. Nathan didn't move. His heart was thudding against his chest. The caveman instinct in him wanted to run after her. But he could hardly get his head around what had just happened. Why had she kissed him?

He'd wanted to kiss her…but Rachel? Making the first move? It left him stunned.

Then his legs moved before he had a chance to think any more.

No. No, he wouldn't let her do this. He wouldn't let her disappear out of his life without explaining what had just happened. He pounded across the sand after her, catching up easily and grabbing her hand, spinning her around until she was back in his arms. His heart was thudding and his breathing rapid.

'No, Rach. Don't do this. This is it. This is the chance to clear the air between us. You have to tell me. Don't you think after all this time I deserve to know?'

Her face was wet with tears now. He hated that. He hated to think he had anything to do with that.

But he couldn't let this go. He just couldn't. It was time for the truth.

His voice was rich with emotion. 'Tell me.'

It was the thing that she'd always dreaded. The thing she'd never thought she would have to explain.

A thousand variations of the truth spun around in her head. Everything about it swamped her. The words she didn't want to say out loud just came to her lips. It was almost involuntary, but she'd been holding it in so long it just had to come out.

'I had renal cancer,' she whispered. Her voice could barely be heard above the quiet waves. The final rays of the sun had vanished now. The beach was in complete darkness, with only the occasional twinkling star.

Every part of Nathan's body stiffened. He turned towards her. He couldn't hide the horror written across his face. 'What? When? Why didn't you tell me? Why didn't anyone tell me?' He stiffened. It was as if something in his brain had just clicked. 'That's what the scar is on your back? You had your kidney removed?'

Her heart squeezed. It was obvious he was totally and utterly stunned.

The tears spilled down her cheeks and she nodded. 'No one knew. I didn't tell anyone.' Her voice broke.

His arms moved from her shoulders. This time he put both his hands on the tops of her arms. He shook his head. 'But why, Rachel? Why would you go through something like that alone? Why wouldn't you tell me?'

Anger flared inside her. Years of pent-up frustration at having to do what she'd thought was right. 'How could I? You and Charlie had just lost your parents. You were barely holding it together. I almost didn't go for the tests. I knew something wasn't quite right, but I'd pushed all that to one side while I'd helped you plan the funeral.'

'You ignored your symptoms because of me? Because of Charlie?' He looked horrified. He kept shaking his head. 'But when did you find out? When did you get the results?'

Her voice was shaking. 'Just before I left. I arranged to get my treatment in Australia.'

'That's why you left? That's why you left me?' He was furious now. The ire in his voice was only vaguely clouded by disbelief.

She shook his hands off her arms. 'Yes, that's why I left. Why did you think I left? Because I didn't love you any more?' She was shouting now; she couldn't help it.

'Why? Why would I do that? Do you know what the statistics are for renal cancer? Do you know how it's graded? You think I should have stayed? I should have stayed and put you and Charlie under even more pressure, even more stress? You were broken, Nathan—you both were. Can you imagine getting through your parents' funeral and spending the next year trying to support a girlfriend who might die? What would that have done to you? What would that have done to Charlie? Why on earth would I do that to two people that I loved?'

She was almost spitting the words out now, all the years of pent-up frustration firing through her veins. All the anger. All the bitterness of being on her own and not being supported by the people that she'd loved. She'd had her mother, but their relationship had been different. She hadn't lived with her for more than seven years—since she'd gone to the UK and started university. It wasn't the same as having the people she'd grown to love beside her. It wasn't just Nathan and Charlie she'd walked away from—she'd also left her father. He'd tried to understand, he really had, but it had changed their relationship too.

Nathan stood up and paced the beach with his hands on his hips, his head constantly shaking. 'I can't believe it. I can't believe that's why you left. You didn't trust me? You didn't trust me enough to tell me about the cancer? You didn't think I would support you through it? You didn't think I could handle it?'

He was angry but she felt even angrier. If she could stamp her feet on the soft sand that was exactly what she'd be doing.

'That's just it. I *knew* you would support me through it. And I knew Charlie would too. But in a year's time you might have ended up organising another funeral.

I couldn't do that to you. I couldn't put you both in that position.'

'That wasn't your choice to make!' he spat out. 'We were together. We were a partnership. I thought we meant something to each other. I loved you, Rachel.'

'And I loved you. That's why I left!'

Their faces were inches apart. He was furious at her, and she was equally furious with him. How dare he think she'd just upped and walked away without a second thought? She hadn't even realised that she'd been angry with him too. Angry that he didn't come after her. Angry that he didn't jump on a plane to Australia to find her.

Of course she knew that hadn't been a possibility. She knew that he'd had Charlie to look after, but it still made her feel as if he hadn't loved her enough.

Not as much as she loved him.

*Wow.* The thought muddled around in her brain. She wasn't thinking about the past. She was thinking about the present. No matter what had happened between them, she still loved Nathan Banks. She'd never stopped. Her legs wobbled a little.

'I can't believe you didn't trust me, Rachel. I can't believe you didn't trust me enough to let me be by your side when you were sick.' The anger had left his voice. Now, it was just disbelief. It was obvious he'd been blindsided by this. He looked as if she'd torn his heart out and left it thrown on the beach.

'I've always trusted you, Nathan,' she said quietly. She couldn't look at him right now, with the tears falling down her cheeks. 'I thought I was doing what was best for both of us. If things had gone the other way we wouldn't be standing here having this conversation. You've no idea how many of the people I met at that treatment centre aren't here any more. I was lucky. I beat the odds. I just couldn't guarantee that. I didn't want you to have to bury someone else that you loved.'

He stepped forward, his finger brushing a tear from her cheek. 'I didn't need guarantees from you, Rachel. I just needed you.' His voice cracked and she shook her head.

'I'm sorry, Nathan. I'm sorry I didn't stay and help with Charlie. I'm sorry you had to change your speciality. But even if I had stayed, I couldn't have helped. I was too sick, too weak to have been of any use. There was no way I wanted to be a burden to you. You wouldn't have been able to stand the strain of working long hours, looking after Charlie and looking after me. No one would.'

'You can't say that! You don't know. You didn't give us the chance to find out.' Pure frustration was written all over his face.

She pressed her hand to her heart and closed her eyes. These were selfish words but she had to say them. There was no other way. She had to try and make him understand just a little. 'But what about me, Nathan? I had to concentrate on getting better. I had to concentrate on getting well. I couldn't afford to worry about you and Charlie too. I barely had enough energy to open my eyes in the morning let alone think about anyone else. I wouldn't have been a help. I would have been a hindrance, a drain.' She shook her head again. 'You didn't need that.'

Nathan didn't hesitate for a second. He stepped forward and gripped her arm. 'You had no right. No right to make that decision for me. You had no right to make that decision for Charlie. You were our family. You were all we had left.'

His words took the air right out of her. In every scenario she'd imagined over the last few years she'd always believed that what she'd done had been for the best. But the force of his reaction was wiping her out. She'd always felt guilty but she'd never really considered this. He'd been grief-stricken—already feeling abandoned by his family. But hearing his words now made her feel sick.

Yes, her actions had been sclfish. But she'd thought she'd done it out of love. Now, she was beginning to wonder if playing the martyr had been the most selfish thing that she could have done.

Her legs wobbled underneath her and she collapsed back down onto the blanket, putting her head in her hands. Everything was going so wrong.

Minutes ago she'd been in Nathan's arms—the place she truly wanted to be. Minutes ago he'd been kissing her and now, with one sweep of his fingertips and the touch of a scar, there was just a world of recriminations. Exactly what she'd dreaded.

She'd expected Nathan to storm off and not talk to her any more. But he hadn't.

He stepped forward and took her hands in his. Pain was etched on his face. 'I'm sorry. I'm sorry you had renal cancer. I'm sorry you thought you had to go to the other side of the world alone to be treated. But you should have never done that, Rachel. You should have never walked away—no matter how well-intentioned you thought it was. This was about trust. This was about you and me. You didn't trust me enough to stay.' He dropped her hands. 'I just don't think I can get past this.'

He stepped back and she felt a wave of panic come over her. 'I did love you, Nathan. Really, I did.' Her voice dropped as she realised how painful it must be to hear those words.

He spun back around and glared at her. 'Really? Well,

you replaced me as soon as you got to Australia. With Darius.' He almost spat the words at her.

It was pure frustration and she knew it. 'You decided you trusted him enough to help you through your surgery and treatment. Someone you barely even knew. So don't give me that, Rachel. Don't lie to me. I've had just about as much as I can take.'

He turned on his heel and strode across the beach, never once looking back.

She crumpled to the ground and started to sob. The night was ruined. Everything about this was wrong. She'd always been sure about her decision—so sure that she'd done the right thing. Now, her brain was spinning. Her thoughts were jumbled. For the first time in her life she wondered if she might have been wrong.

It was pathetic. She was pathetic. But all she'd wanted to do was kiss him. So she had. No rational thought behind it. She'd acted purely on selfish instinct.

It was just too hard. It was too hard to be this close to him again and not touch him. In the past when she'd been with Nathan she'd spent most of her time in his arms. He'd completed her. He'd given her confidence when she'd doubted her abilities and strength when she'd struggled with the long hours of being a junior doctor.

She'd loved being with him. She'd loved being part of his family. Her own mother and father had split years before, her father staying in England and her mother settling in Australia. And although they loved her and she loved them, it had been a disjointed kind of upbringing.

When Nathan and Charlie's parents had died it had broken her. She'd wanted to be strong for them both. And she'd managed it right up until she'd found out about her diagnosis.

It had been the final straw.

And all of this was flooding back. For too long she'd kept it in a box—far out of reach, somewhere it couldn't affect her emotions. She couldn't concentrate on what her leaving had done to Nathan and Charlie. She'd been so focused on getting well and getting through her treatment that she hadn't allowed herself space to think about any of this. When her treatment was over, she'd focused on her career, trying to get things back on track after taking a year out.

But she'd never got over the guilt attached to leaving Nathan. She'd never got over the fact she didn't have the guts to say goodbye to Charlie; one tear from him would have been the end of her and she would never have made it onto that plane.

She was lucky. She'd had a good outcome and for that she was so grateful. But it hadn't been guaranteed. The prospect of deteriorating and forcing Nathan and Charlie to be by her side had been unthinkable.

And, even though she had a barrel-load of regrets, if she had her time over she would still get on that plane. She would still walk away to face the cancer on her own.

Except she hadn't really been on her own. She'd had her mum in Australia and then, even though it wasn't what people thought, she'd had Darius too.

It could barely be called a romance. There might have been a few kisses exchanged but it had been entirely different from the relationship she'd had with Nathan. There had never been the passion, the deep underlying attraction. It had almost been like a mutual support society. At times he had been a shoulder to cry on. And during her surgery and renal cancer treatment that was exactly what she'd needed.

Nathan hated her. It didn't matter that he'd kissed her back. Every time he looked at her she could see it in his eyes. If only she could have just five minutes when he looked at her like he'd used to. Just five minutes.

But the world was full of people with 'if only's. It was too late to be one of those. She wasn't here to re-examine her faulty love life. She'd never managed to sustain a decent relationship since the break-up with Nathan. At first she'd had no time or energy for it. No one quite seemed to live up to the man she'd left behind.

But this Nathan was different. He wasn't the same person she'd loved. She could see the changes behind his eyes. In the weathered lines on his face—textured in the eight years she hadn't known him. Who had he loved in that time?

What had she just done? If she'd thought this island was claustrophobic before, she'd just made the situation ten times worse.

She'd been so careful. After her initial exchange of words with Nathan she'd tried to be so cool about things. She understood his resentment. Nathan must hate her.

But it couldn't stop all the feelings he was reviving in her—all the memories. She'd dealt with her renal cancer the best way she felt she could. But it didn't stop her regretting her actions every time she looked at him.

Part of her was resentful too. How would life have turned out if the renal cancer hadn't happened? Would they have come to Australia together and settled here? Would they both have stuck at their chosen specialities? She already knew that Nathan had changed his plans—would that have happened if they'd still been together?

Something coiled inside her. Her life could have been so different.

His life could have been so different.

*Their* lives could have been so different.

# CHAPTER EIGHT

NATHAN WAS PACING. He hated waiting.

The crew were all standing around watching him. Did they know about last night—or was he just being paranoid? Sometimes this island was just far too small.

Rachel. He hadn't had a chance to speak to her since last night and he wasn't quite sure what he wanted to say.

He could still feel the sensation of her lips on his. He could still feel the tremble in his body when she'd run the palm of her hand over his bristled hair. He could still remember the dampness on her cheek…

There was a murmur around him as he saw her approach. His eyes automatically went to the ground. He wanted to have a conversation with Rachel—but not like this. Not when cameras and twenty members of the crew were around them.

He gave a nod to Len, one of the safety instructors for this challenge, and stepped into his harness, pulling on his gloves and fastening his helmet.

Focus. That was what he needed to do right now. The time for conversations was later.

To say the atmosphere was awkward would be putting it mildly.

Neither of them could look at each other. Rachel

hadn't emerged from her room this morning until she'd heard Nathan get up and use the shower and then the cabin front door banging shut.

When the director had told her that she and Nathan were responsible for checking out the safety of the challenge together this morning she'd thought of a hundred and one excuses.

But this was work. Rachel Johnson had her professional pride. And a stubborn streak a mile wide. Part of her felt responsible. *She'd* kissed him last night. She'd been the one to set the wheels in motion. Not Nathan.

Trust. The word was burning in her brain, and it had done for most of the night. The look of hurt in his eyes had been gut-churning.

Up here, on the top edge of the cliff, with the sea winds swirling around her, trust was certainly an issue.

'There is absolutely no way I'm going down there.'

The director sighed. 'You both have to inspect all challenge sites. You can't do that from here.'

Nathan still hadn't made eye contact with her. It was apparent he'd already had this conversation because he was standing with a harness around him, gloves on his hands, receiving special instructions from Len, one of the crew members who would be overseeing their descent.

A boat bobbed on the water at the bottom of the cliff face. It was a *long* way down.

'I can do this myself, Rach, if you'd prefer.'

Nathan's low voice carried on the wind towards her. It sparked fury in her stomach. There was no way she was letting him think she was scared. She wouldn't give him the satisfaction.

She ignored him completely and stalked over to where Len was holding out the harness for her to step into. His safety briefing was thorough. She would be held safely in place; all she had to do was feed the line slowly through the carabiner. She clipped her helmet into place, then swapped her boots for the rock climbing shoes supplied by Len to ensure her grip on the rock face and pulled the gloves on to protect her hands. Lewis had never mentioned *this* in the hard sell of *Celebrity Island*.

It wasn't that she was particularly afraid of heights. She just didn't really want to step off a cliff edge into oblivion and dangle from a piece of rope.

From the corner of her eye she saw Nathan get himself into position and step backwards, easing his way down the cliff face like Spider-Man. Typical.

She turned and faced the cliff edge.

'Not that way,' joked Len as he turned her around so her back was facing the sea.

She gulped. She knew everything she was supposed to be doing. But leaning back, letting the rope take the strain of her weight and stepping into nowhere wasn't really appealing.

Len stood in front of her, talking steadily and smoothly, but the words all seemed to run into one. She'd stopped listening. Right now, she was concentrating on her breathing. Trying to stop the hysterical beat of her heart. How on earth would the celebrities manage this without having a whole bunch of heart attacks?

Len put both hands on her shoulders, edging her back. He stopped for a second and spoke again. She was pretty sure that she must resemble a ghost.

Everyone in the crew was looking at her. Watching to see what her next move would be. It was embarrassing. And it gave her the kick up the backside that she needed.

She leaned back, keeping her eyes firmly on Len as he nodded encouragingly. Her heart was in her mouth.

As she took the step backwards it felt like stepping into mid-air. She was almost over the edge when she felt a hand on her backside. She was already midway. It was too late to stop.

There was only one person who could have their hand there.

Things were in motion now. Her rubber-soled shoes connected with the white cliff as she leaned back and let the rope take her whole weight. After a second, the hand moved. Nathan was right next to her.

'Are you sure about this?'

She glared at him. 'Oh, I've never been more sure.'

The edges of Nathan's mouth turned upwards. If she hadn't been holding onto the rope for dear life she could have cheerfully punched him.

'Do we know which celebs have been picked for the challenge?'

He nodded. 'It's Diamond Dazzle and Fox, the pop star. I guess a boys against girls kind of thing.'

Rachel groaned. 'Did they really get voted for the challenge?'

Nathan shrugged. 'Who knows?'

She took a moment to look around. The view from here across the Coral Sea was nothing short of spectacular. It would be even better if she didn't have a helmet stuck on her head. It gave her a real bird's eye view of the other islands dotted around them. In any other life, this might actually be a place where she could spend some holiday time. Provided, of course, that there was something resembling a hotel with proper beds.

Her descent was slow. Len's instructions had been spot-on and easy to follow.

She frowned. 'What happens with the celebs? Does someone come down alongside them?'

Nathan nodded. 'No way are they being left to come down on their own. Len will be with them every step of the way. One of us will have to be there too. I'm assuming you'll be okay if I do that? If there are any problems I'm right on hand to fix them. You'll be in the boat in casc there are any problems at the bottom.'

It was so odd. Hanging from a cliff, having a conversation with someone you'd kissed the night before. Neither of you saying what you should be saying.

She nodded. 'Fine with me.' She didn't even care that the boat was being buffeted by the waves below them. She'd much rather be in the boat than on the cliff.

'Great.' Nathan bounced down the cliff a bit—just bent his knees and jumped back, letting his rope out easily. Anyone would think he'd done this professionally in a past life.

Rachel wouldn't be bouncing anywhere. She eked out her rope slowly, taking tentative corresponding steps down the cliff face. Up above she could see nothing—just her rope. It was currently looking like a strand of thread. Could that really keep holding her?

Nathan, in the meantime, was driving her crazy. He'd bounced, and now he bounded. There were different coloured flags at various points on the cliff face. The celebrities were supposed to race down the cliff later and collect as many as they could. He was moving sideways and checking the little ledges they were positioned on, making sure it was easy to reach each one.

She'd only passed two. Both seemed to mock her on her careful descent. Thank goodness she wasn't doing this against the clock. She would fail miserably.

He bounced next to her and she could hear his heavy breathing. 'If you'd told me a few weeks ago I'd be abseiling down a cliff in the Whitsundays I wouldn't have believed you.'

His movement and voice distracted her, startled her. Her hands faltered as she eased the rope through, her feet coming up against the crumbling part of the cliff face. As the rocks loosened beneath her feet she lost her concentration. For a second she was falling into oblivion.

But it was only for a spilt second before the rope locked into place and she was left dangling in mid-air, scrambling to find her feet again.

She saw something out of the corner of her eye. It was Nathan. He'd moved sideways across the rock face and he was above her in an instant, leaning all the way back, holding his hand out to hers.

'Rach, take my hand!' He looked nervous.

As she dangled from the rope, things moved all around her, disorientating her and making her lose her sense of focus. The only one consistent thing she could see was Nathan's hand.

Her own gripped hard onto her harness. One foot connected roughly with the cliff, only for the rocks to crumble again. Panic was starting to grip her.

'Rachel, take my hand!' he shouted again. She could hear something in his voice. It was echoing the panicked reactions of her own body.

His hand brushed against her hair. He was trying to make a grab for her.

She was spinning now on the rope, her own body weight causing the momentum. If she didn't stop she'd be sick.

After last night, no part of her wanted to touch Nathan Banks again. Not when she knew the reaction it caused to her system. Not when she knew the havoc it caused.

*Trust.* The word echoed through her head. He'd

accused her of not trusting him enough. At the time, she'd thought the opposite was true. She'd trusted him too much to stay. Too much—because she knew what he would give up for her.

'Rachel!' Now he sounded angry.

Her body acted instantly; it was pure instinct. She thrust out her hand.

There were a few seconds of scramble. Skin touching but not quite grabbing, then his hand closed over hers and he pulled her straight, yanking her towards his body.

It took another few seconds for her head to stop spinning. To gain some equilibrium again.

'Rach, are you okay?' He had her anchored against his hip, his warm breath hitting the side of her cheek.

The rubber soles of her shoes planted against the cliff. Now she'd straightened, the strain of her rope held her harness firmly in place. Her hands moved, going automatically to the carabiner.

Her breath was starting to come a little easier, but her heart was still thudding in her chest. She wasn't quite sure if that was due to the shock of what had just happened or the feel of Nathan's body next to hers.

She glanced down between her legs. It wasn't quite such a long way down now. For the first time, she thought she might actually make it.

'Rachel, are you okay?'

She still hadn't answered. She took a deep breath, securing her hands on the rope and moving sideways to steady herself on the rocks.

Nathan fixed her with his gaze. There was so much they should be saying to each other right now.

But it was almost as if they were still shell-shocked from the night before. And this was hardly the time, or the place.

She nodded. ‘I’m fine.’ A few seconds later she added, ‘Thank you.’

He hadn’t moved. He just stayed next to her. His eyes were serious.

‘What do you think?’

Her heart thudded again. ‘About what?’ The sea wind was whipping around them, her hair blowing across her face and her shirt plastered against her body.

‘About the challenge?’

The challenge. Of course. Ever the professional, Nathan was thinking about the job.

He wasn’t thinking about last night. At least—she didn’t think so.

She sucked in her breath. ‘I think it was my own fault I slipped. I lost concentration. Part of the cliff is crumbling. But I have to assume that all cliffs are like that.’

*This challenge is crazy* was what she wanted to say. But she didn’t want to seem weak, to seem scared. Especially not in front of Nathan.

He gave a little nod. ‘Okay, then. Are you ready to continue down to the boat?’

She looked at the boat bobbing beneath them. The sea seemed quite calm. It almost seemed reachable.

She gave a nod. Nathan knees were bent and he was bouncing on his rope again, ready to make the final part of the journey. She just wished she was.

‘Let’s go then.’

She watched as he started down, controlling his descent with confidence. She glanced at the rope in her hands. *Slow and steady wins the race.* A distant memory of her father’s voice echoed in her head.

*I’m not sure I want to win any race against Nathan.*

He looked up. ‘Come on,’ he shouted.

The harness was starting to pinch around her waist

and hips. The tension on her rope was almost as much as the tension between them.

Would it ever be resolved?

'You're going to do the challenge in that?' Rachel couldn't hide the disdain in her voice. Diamond Dazzle was wearing the tiniest white sequin bikini known to man. Hanging from a cliff with cameras underneath? Definitely not family viewing.

But Diamond was too busy climbing into the harness. 'Do I have to wear this?' she whined, wincing as they fastened the clips.

Rachel sighed. 'I'm off down to the quay. I'll see you at the bottom.' But Diamond wasn't listening. She was too busy admiring her reflection in a mirror that one of the production crew had handed her. The celebrities weren't supposed to bring beauty products onto the island with them. But Diamond had a whole beauty counter—and made no secret about it.

Yesterday, she'd spent most of the day 'washing' herself in an equally tiny orange bikini. Rachel could only imagine she'd made most of the red-top front pages this morning. There really wasn't much to do in camp. She only hoped Diamond listened to the safety briefing at the top.

It took ten minutes for the boat to reach the bottom of the cliff face. From here, it looked a long way up—and a long way down.

She was glad Nathan had volunteered to stay at the top. The last thing she wanted to do was abseil again. Being in the boat was bad enough; the currents were a lot stronger than they looked out here.

One of the crew nudged her as Len appeared over

the top of the cliff face. The challenges were normally filmed later in the day, but as this one was on the cliff it was essential it was completed in daylight.

Fox quickly followed. It seemed the pop star was a natural. He appeared comfortable in his holding position at the top of the cliff, gloves and helmet with camera attached in place, waiting to start.

Diamond was a whole other story. After twenty minutes Rachel picked up the radio. 'Nathan?' It crackled loudly. 'Anything I should know about?'

'Give me a sec,' was the sharp reply.

She rolled her eyes at the nearest crew member. 'I guess we wait then.'

After another few minutes, Diamond's perfectly tanned legs and barely clad bottom appeared over the edge of the cliff. 'Look away, guys,' muttered one of the crew members.

It was clear Diamond was making a meal of it. Rachel had no idea what the camera was capturing but she was sure that by tonight, she would be able to watch every second. She did have the tiniest bit of sympathy. Standing at the top of that cliff had terrified her. How was Diamond feeling?

After a few seconds Nathan's voice came over the radio. This time it was low. He let out a sigh. 'To be honest, I'm not happy.'

'What's wrong? Did she have a panic attack?'

'That's just it. She was making a fuss, but it all seemed put-on. She did complain of some abdominal pain earlier but she said that she was due her period and she always has some abdominal pain. I gave her some analgesia.'

Rachel kept her eyes on Diamond's descent. It was very stuttered. Had hers looked like this? Len was right alongside her, obviously giving her instructions and talking her down. In the meantime, Fox had waited gallantly until Diamond was in position and then taken off at a rate of knots, bouncing down the cliff face, gathering flags as he went. The other boat had already moved position ready to pick him up once he reached the water.

It happened so quickly. The tiniest flash of white. Arms waving. Legs flapping, a slight body tumbling, still inside the harness, and a helmet coming into contact with the cliff face.

Len was over to her instantly, talking into his radio. 'Diamond—talk to me. Guys, I might need some assistance. Give me a second.'

'What happened?' Nathan's voice cut across the radio.

'She lost control of the descent, her hands slipped and the autoblock came into play. She lost her foothold on the cliff.'

Rachel was looking up from the bottom, conscious of the fact Nathan couldn't see what she could. She knew exactly how Diamond felt. At least Rachel hadn't hit her head on the cliff.

'Is she conscious, Len?'

Even as she said the words she could hear Diamond's hysterical voice coming through Len's mike. 'I'm dying out here! I feel sick. I'm dizzy. Oh, my stomach, this harness is killing me.'

Len's voice was steady. 'Diamond, stay calm. You're absolutely fine. I'm right beside you. You're quite safe. Your harness will hold you in position. Take some deep breaths.'

'I'm not fine. I'm dangling from a cliff!'

Rachel grimaced. This was going to be a nightmare.

'Len? Do you need some assistance down there?'

She could picture Nathan stepping into his harness already.

Len made a quick assessment. 'I think it would be better if you and I helped Diamond back down the cliff face to the boat.'

Within a few seconds she saw Nathan come over the edge of the cliff and descend easily to Diamond and Len's position. It was clear this challenge was over. Poor Fox. He wouldn't even get his five minutes of glory. Tonight's television would be all about Diamond.

She waited patiently while Diamond continued to have a panic attack dangling in mid-air and flapping her arms and legs between Len and Nathan.

It was difficult to tell if it was all real or all fake. She hated being cynical, she really did.

After a few minutes Nathan spoke. 'There's no head injury, just a few small grazes on her legs and arms. We'll just take things slowly.'

She let out a long breath. They'd already had drama on the first day and then again with Ron. They really didn't need anything else.

The descent was slow. Rachel could hear the whole thing through the radio she had pressed against her ears. Nathan had the patience of a saint. He'd always been like that in doctor mode—calm, rational, reasonable. Even if he wasn't too sure what he was dealing with. How was he feeling about doing this twice in one day?

After a while the crew started to get restless. 'Can someone give me a hand with this?' The cameraman's arms were obviously burning under the strain of constantly trying to focus on the figures on the cliff face while being buffeted around in a boat. Several of the other crew members moved to assist with a lot of general grumbling.

After a painstaking half hour, Nathan, Len and Diamond finally reached the bottom of the cliff and were assisted into the boat. Diamond glanced around her and sank to the bottom of the boat curled in a ball. For a second Rachel wondered if she'd spotted the camera behind her.

Len looked exasperated and he leaned over to release her harness.

'Don't touch me!' she screamed.

Rachel flinched and dropped to her knees. 'Let me loosen your harness.' She didn't wait for agreement, just moved swiftly and unclipped it. Len and Nathan were having a quick discussion.

If Diamond hadn't had Botox it was quite possible her face would be scrunched in a deep frown. Rachel ran her eyes over Diamond's skin. There were no abrasions or redness on her abdomen. It couldn't be the harness that was causing her problems.

She shot Nathan a glance. 'Diamond, would you like to sit up?'

Diamond groaned and clutched her arms around her stomach. 'No. I can't. This is agony.'

The boat was rocking fiercely on the waves as they made their way back to the quay. She placed a hand over Diamond's and saw her flinch. 'When we get onshore I'll take you up to the medical centre and we'll have a look at you.' Her eyes flickered over to Joe, the cameraman. 'And there will be *no* cameras.'

She wasn't quite sure if she said it for her own reassurance or for Diamond's. In any case, she wanted a chance to take a closer look.

The boat pulled in and one of the crew jumped out and ran to get a stretcher. Nathan was biting his lip. She knew he was still suspicious—wondering whether Diamond's pain was genuine or not.

She watched as he walked over and murmured in the cameraman's ear, putting his hand over the front of the camera. The guy nodded and pulled it down from his shoulder.

It only took a few minutes to get Diamond onto the stretcher and up to the medical cabin. It was probably the biggest strength of the production crew—they never hesitated to assist.

Rachel helped Diamond over onto the examination trolley and waited until everyone had left the room and Nathan had closed the door.

She switched on the angle lamp. It gave a much better view of Diamond's colour, which was distinctly pale. She quickly fastened a BP cuff around her arm and pressed the button to start the reading, then walked to the sink to wash her hands.

Nathan gave her a little nod. He was obviously happy to let her take the lead on this, which was a little strange—given that he was the emergency doctor.

She waited a few seconds for the reading. It was a little below average but not worryingly so. 'Diamond, I'm going to put my hands on your stomach. Is that okay?'

The model's eyes widened. 'Do you have to?'

She nodded. 'Nathan told me earlier today you complained of period pain. Is that normal for you?'

Diamond nodded. 'I always get it. Just cramps—and that's what it was like this morning. But this is much worse. The painkillers haven't touched it.'

'Any other symptoms? Have you been going to the toilet frequently?'

Diamond wrinkled her nose. 'Maybe.'

'What about your bowels? Are they moving normally?'

'*Eeoow.* Don't ask about things like that.'

Rachel smiled. 'I have to. It's part of being a doctor.'

Diamond winced again. 'No problems then.'

She flinched as Rachel gently laid her hands on her stomach.

'Can you tell me where the worst of the pain is? In your front or around your back?' She pressed very gently. Diamond seemed to wince at every movement, then she pulled her knees up quickly.

'*Yaoow!* It's definitely worse on that side.'

Rachel lifted her hands. 'Have you been eating? Feeling sick, nauseous?'

'I've felt sick most of the day. But I haven't actually been sick.'

Rachel bit her lip. Diamond's pain was on the opposite side from her appendix. 'Do you think you could give me a urine sample? I'd like to dipstick it for any sign of infection.'

Diamond groaned. 'You want me to get up?'

Rachel nodded. 'We don't exactly have a lot of equipment here. I'll help you to the bathroom. It's only a few steps.'

She gently swung Diamond's legs to the edge of the trolley and helped her limp over to the bathroom, handing her a collection bottle.

Rachel and Nathan waited outside the door. He glanced at her, mouthing the words, 'What do you think? UTI or ectopic?'

She lifted her shoulders. 'Could be either.'

After a few minutes Diamond opened the door and handed her specimen container over with shaky hands.

'Your colour's not too good. Let me help you back over.' Nathan didn't wait. He picked her up in his arms and carried her over to the trolley.

Rachel took the specimen over to the countertop and dipsticked it with a multistick for blood and protein, and dropped some onto a pregnancy test. It would take at least a minute until it showed.

She took a few steps nearer Diamond. 'I know that you said your period is due, but can you tell me how long it is since your last one?'

Diamond screwed up her face, her arms still across her belly. 'I'm not that regular. Probably around six weeks. I always get cramp—but not usually as bad as this. I feel as if it could come any minute.'

Nathan wound the BP cuff back around her arm. 'I'm just going to check this again.' He pressed the button. 'This will get quite tight.'

Rachel glanced over towards the tests on the bench. A positive pregnancy test and some blood in her urine. She swallowed. 'Diamond, is there any chance you could be pregnant?'

Diamond's eyes opened quickly. It was almost as if she were trying to rationalise the possibility.

Rachel reached for her hand. 'I don't think the pain you're experiencing is normal period pain. I think it's something else.'

Nathan moved closer. 'Diamond, we don't have all the facilities here that we need.' His voice was sympathetic. 'Your urine shows a positive pregnancy test, but it also had some blood in it—even though you might not have noticed. Your blood pressure is on the low side and with the pain you have in your side—it could be that you're having an ectopic pregnancy.'

Diamond looked stunned. She started shaking her head. 'I can't be pregnant. I can't be.'

Rachel squeezed her hand. 'Have you had unprotected sex in the last six weeks?'

Her pale cheeks flushed. 'Well… yes.'

'Have you had any bleeding at all?'

She glanced between Rachel and Nathan. 'I had a tiny bit of spotting yesterday. I just thought my period was starting.'

Nathan nodded. 'Do you know much about ectopic pregnancy, Diamond?'

She shook her head quickly. 'Nothing.' There was something about Diamond's wide-eyed reaction that made him slow down.

He glanced towards Rachel. He was surprising her—which was ridiculous, as Nathan had always been a compassionate doctor. The truth was they'd both had doubts about Diamond's symptoms.

He spoke slowly. It was obvious he was trying to make things as clear as possible, whilst he knew he was dealing with a highly sensitive issue.

'In an ectopic pregnancy the embryo doesn't implant and grow in the womb as it should. It gets stuck somewhere along the fallopian tube and the embryo starts to grow there. That would be why you're having pain. There isn't room for the embryo to grow.'

She looked scared. 'So what happens now?'

He spoke carefully. 'In an ideal world, we'd do an ultrasound to confirm our diagnosis. But we don't have ultrasound equipment here, so we just need to go on your symptoms and the fact you've had a positive pregnancy test. We class this as an emergency. Your fallopian tube can rupture and cause internal bleeding. Because of that, we'll arrange a medevac to take you off the island and to a hospital on the mainland where it's likely you'll need to go for surgery.'

'I need to leave the show?'

It wasn't the response Rachel was expecting to hear. But Diamond just looked stunned.

'You definitely need to leave the show.'

She nodded. 'Okay. Can someone phone my agent?'

Rachel and Nathan exchanged glances. Diamond seemed to have switched into professional mode.

Rachel walked over and took her hand. 'No problem. Nathan will get someone to do that.' He gave a quick nod. Rachel walked over to the medicine cabinet and quickly drew up some analgesia. 'I'm going to give you something for the pain meantime'

Rachel leaned forward and kept talking as she administered the injection, 'This is an emergency, Diamond. I don't want to scare you, but if your fallopian tube ruptures it will cause more pain and the bleeding can be serious. You need to be in a place that can deal with that kind of emergency.' She held out her hands and looked around. 'And that's certainly not here.'

Nathan nodded in agreement. 'We don't have any medication that we can give you here to try and stop the embryo growing. You have to go to a specialist hospital.'

Diamond winced as she tried to sit up. Her eyes widened and she fixed them on Rachel. 'I'm pregnant? I'm really pregnant?' The look of disbelief on her face was obvious. It seemed things were just starting to sink in.

Rachel walked back over to Diamond and started the BP monitor again. Diamond looked completely shocked.

'I'm pregnant?' she asked again.

Rachel chose her words carefully. If a pregnancy was ectopic there was no hope for the growing embryo. Diamond's reactions earlier had been odd—almost as if she wasn't taking in what they'd been saying to her. Maybe the truth was just hitting her now.

Nathan appeared at the other side of the trolley. It was as if he sensed how she might react.

Something squeezed inside Rachel. This was a horrible experience for any woman. She'd never been in this position. Chances were, after the treatment she'd received for her renal cancer, she might never be in the position to be pregnant.

Although they'd been junior doctors, she and Nathan had never been afraid to talk about the future. They'd been so sure that their future would be together. They'd talked about eventually getting married and having children together, Nathan as a surgeon and Rachel probably working as a GP at that point. Looking back, it had been a strange conversation for two young, ambitious, career-orientated people to have. But both had loved the idea of having a family together. As doctors, they both knew they would need support with their children. Nathan had been adamant that he, as well as Rachel, should only work four days a week. That way, both would have a day at home with the kids, with Nathan's parents or Rachel's dad helping on the other days.

She flinched. More hopes and dreams that had disappeared in the blink of an eye. Destroyed by a car crash and a cancer diagnosis.

Had she really taken on board how big an impact these things had had on both their lives?

She lifted her head. Nathan's gaze interlocked with hers, his green eyes holding her steady. She swallowed. There was pain etched on his face. It was almost as if all the same thoughts were going through his head. Did he remember the conversations they used to have about family?

Rachel took a deep breath and turned her attention back to her patient. 'You had a positive pregnancy test and the symptoms you're showing suggest you have an ectopic pregnancy. Nathan explained earlier that the embryo is growing in your fallopian tube instead of in your womb. That's why you're in so much pain.' She squeezed Diamond's hand. 'I'm really sorry, Diamond. But what this means is that this pregnancy isn't viable. This pregnancy could never result in a baby for you.'

She hated saying those words out loud because she already knew the impact it would have on their patient.

Diamond shook her head as a tear slid down her cheek. 'But I always thought I couldn't get pregnant.'

'Why did you think that?' Nathan's voice cut in before Rachel had a chance to reply.

'They told me my tubes were scarred. They told me if I ever wanted to get pregnant I'd probably need to use IVF.' She was shaking her head in disbelief.

Scarred tubes—exactly the kind of place an embryo could implant. It made the diagnosis of ectopic pregnancy even more likely.

Nathan checked her BP reading. Low, but steady. 'You saw an ob-gyn?'

Diamond's face flushed a little. 'I had an infection a few years ago. She did some follow-up tests.'

He'd read her medical notes; this hadn't been in them. She clearly wanted to keep it secret.

He nodded sympathetically. 'It makes the chances of this being an ectopic pregnancy even more likely, but we can't tell you for sure. They'll need to scan you once you reach the mainland. How is your pain? Is it any better since Rachel gave you the injection?'

Diamond gave a little nod just as there was a knock at the door. 'Five minutes, docs,' came the shout.

Rachel still wasn't entirely sure about Diamond. 'How do you feel about transferring in the medevac?'

There was no getting away from it. The medevac could be terrifying. The noise and buffeting from the air currents could make it a bumpy trip. Rachel wasn't certain that she'd like to be the one going.

Diamond nodded slowly. 'I really can't come back?' Her voice was quiet, almost whispered.

'Absolutely not.' Nathan didn't hesitate. 'You need to be in a place where you can be taken care of and get the support that you need. The island isn't the place for that.'

Her eyes were downcast and Rachel wondered if the true nature of what had happened was now sinking in. 'Is there someone you'd like me to phone for you?' She wasn't sure if Diamond had a partner or a boyfriend. She didn't really keep track of celebrity relationships. Being in the spotlight herself for a few months had been bad enough. Whether the pregnancy had been planned or not, losing a baby could be a big shock to any couple.

Diamond shook her head. The tears were flowing freely now. 'I think that's a phone call I need to make myself.' Her voice was shaking now and Rachel could feel tears springing to her own eyes.

Nathan walked over and put his arm around Diamond's shoulders. 'I'm really sorry, Diamond. I'm really sorry about your baby and I'm really sorry it happened here.' He glanced at Rachel. 'We're going to give you something else for the flight. It can be a little bumpy and I want to make sure your pain is under control and you're as relaxed as possible.'

He walked over and unlocked the medicine cupboard, taking out another vial and turning it for Rachel to double-check. She nodded as she dialled the number and spoke urgently into the phone, giving the medevac all the details they would need.

Nathan administered the medicine quickly.

Rachel nodded as she left the cabin. 'I'll get the crew to prepare for the medevac and I'll let the producer know what is happening.'

Thank goodness they were out of earshot because Phil, one of the producers, nearly blew a gasket when she told him she'd arranged a medevac for Diamond.

'What? You've got to be joking. We need her for the viewing figures. This will affect our ratings.'

'And if she doesn't get appropriate treatment this could affect her life,' she said sharply. She was getting tired of this—tired of how some people didn't seem to care about the actual individuals—just the figures.

In fact, she was getting tired of everything. Tired of being trapped on an island with Nathan. Tired of the way they tiptoed around each other constantly. Tired of her conflicting emotions around him. And the fact that on an island like this there was no privacy, no escape.

Next time she saw Lewis Blake she was going to kill him with her bare hands. It didn't matter what the salary was here—he'd got more than his money's worth.

By the time she'd finished with Phil, she received a message to say the medevac had arrived. The crew, as always, were only too happy to assist.

As they headed down to the beach the downdraught from the helicopter swooshed around them and Diamond started to shake. Nathan kept his arm around her the whole time. It only took five minutes to do the handover and get her loaded on board. The paramedic winked at them both. It was the same guy who'd picked up Jack. 'This is getting to be a habit. Here's hoping I don't hear from you two again.'

Nathan pulled the door closed and retreated to the trees, watching the helicopter take off before heading back to the cabin. They could hear Phil somewhere in the complex, shouting at the top of his voice.

Nathan gave Rachel an ironic smile. 'So much for working twelve hours in three weeks.'

Her eyebrows lifted. 'Lewis used that line on you too?'

'Oh, yes.'

Their smiles locked for a few seconds. She felt the buzz. It was hanging in the air between them. Familiar. Sparking lots of warm, passionate memories.

Something washed over her. More than regret. More than sadness. The awareness of what might have been. The loss of the life they could have had together.

She couldn't help it. It brought instant tears to her eyes. Nathan had been her soulmate, the person she'd thought she would grow old with.

And in two fell swoops everything had changed.

A driver's momentary distraction on a country road, and the view of cancer cells under the microscope.

Where would they have been in the life they should have lived? Married? Probably. With children? She certainly hoped so. It didn't matter that this parallel universe didn't exist. It didn't matter that this was all a figment of her imagination.

At times, during her treatment, it had been the only thing that had kept her going. Imagining that Nathan had built a new life for himself, met someone else and moved on had been just too much for her. It didn't matter that she'd told herself that was what she wanted for him. A long lifetime of happiness.

Her own heart told her differently.

'Rachel?' His voice was quiet and he stepped closer to her. 'Are you okay?'

He must have noticed the tears glistening in her eyes. It would be so easy to make an excuse—to say it was the sand thrown up by the helicopter blades, to say it was the sea breeze in her eyes. But she didn't want to. She didn't want to tell lies. She was so tired of it all. Keeping her guard up continually around Nathan was wearing her down.

She fixed on his neon green eyes. She'd always loved looking into Nathan's eyes. She'd spent the last week virtually avoiding them, skirting past them whenever she could for fear of the memories they might stir up.

'No,' was all she replied.

He blinked and waited a few seconds, his gaze never wavering from hers. 'Me neither.' His words were low. So low she wondered if she'd even heard them.

He reached over and touched her arm. She froze, her breath stuck in her throat.

'Rachel, do you want to have dinner tonight—just you and me?'

She nodded.

He didn't smile. 'We both have a few things to do. And we can't talk in the canteen. I'll meet you back here at seven and arrange some food for us.'

The filming for the day was already done. By seven the sun would almost be setting and the beach should be quieter.

'Sounds fine. I'll see you then.' She turned and walked away, her heart thudding in her chest.

Dinner.

It sounded so simple. But it wouldn't just be dinner. They both knew that. It would be so much more. It was time to put the past to rest.

## CHAPTER NINE

NATHAN LOOKED DOWN at the hamper one of the chefs had given him. It should be perfect. It was packed with all the kind of foods that he enjoyed—and the ones that he remembered Rachel liked.

Stuffed in next to the food were two bottles of wine and a couple of glasses nabbed from behind the bar.

Would he even be able to eat anything? His stomach turned over. There was no doubt the attraction between him and Rachel was still there. The attraction had never been in doubt. It was the history that was the problem.

He couldn't act on his instincts around her. Every time he looked at her he felt his self-protection barriers fall into place. Guys didn't admit to being hurt. Guys didn't admit to being broken-hearted.

But he'd felt both when Rachel had left.

Eight years on, he hadn't moved past that and it was crippling him. He hadn't really formed a proper relationship since then. Initially he'd been too busy watching out for Charlie, then he'd been too busy working.

For the last five years he'd been trying to save the world. He hadn't been able to save his parents—they'd been left trapped in their twisted car for the best part of an hour before anyone had found them. By then, both of them had been unconscious. His mother had never made it to the hospital. His father had barely survived the journey and had died before Nathan was notified about the accident. At least with Doctors Without Borders he knew his work counted. He knew he could look back on the lives he'd saved—the difference he'd made. And in a tiny way it had helped patch his heart back together.

But recognition was dawning slowly—he'd spent so much time trying to save other people and not enough time trying to save himself.

Seeing Rachel had brought everything to the forefront again. There were things—feelings—that he couldn't deny. At some point in his life he was going to have to move on. He'd just never expected that moving on with Rachel might even be a remote possibility. He still wasn't entirely sure it was. But tonight it was time to find out.

All he felt right this minute was hideous guilt. Rachel had told him she'd had renal cancer. And, instead of asking her all the questions he should have, he'd been so overcome with anger that he'd forgotten all the important stuff. He'd forgotten to ask her all the medical questions that had been spinning around in his brain ever since. Her treatment—and the outcome. The future. What kind of guy was he? What kind of friend was he?

He hated this. He hated all of this.

He walked down to the beach. There were a few people around, chatting and talking at the bar.

He didn't want to join in. He was already too wound up. Chances were, they'd meet and be fighting within five minutes. But fighting wasn't what he wanted to do with Rachel.

His fingers were itching to touch her. He wanted to run them through her shiny hair; he wanted to stroke them across her perfect skin. He wanted to touch the place where she had that scar. He wanted to kiss it.

He wanted to let her know that the renal cancer didn't change how he felt about her. Wouldn't *ever* change how he felt about her. More than anything, he wanted her lips to surrender to his. It was bad enough his dreams at night were haunted by her. He'd started to daydream about her too.

He couldn't go on like this. He couldn't function. Things just had to come to a head. Who knew where it would lead?

But the electricity in the air between them could light up this whole island. It was time to find out if she agreed.

Rachel stared in the mirror. She'd showered and her hair was washed and dried. She'd put on some bronzer, mascara and lipstick. She should be ready. She *could* be ready. If only she could decide what to wear.

Maybe it was delaying tactics. Maybe it was because her stomach was churning and she wondered if the nerves could make her sick. Or maybe it was because, deep down, she wanted to look perfect for Nathan.

Her rucksack was upended on the bed. Three pink sundresses, four pink shirts and three T-shirts all seemed to mock her. Nothing was right. Nothing *felt* right. And she wasn't sure why it was so important.

She rummaged around the bottom of the rucksack to see if she'd missed anything. Her hand slithered over some material and she pulled it out. A pink sequin bikini. She'd thrown it back inside as soon as she'd realised Nathan was here—her scar would have raised too many questions she didn't want to answer.

But now Nathan knew. Now, there was nothing to hide.

Except how he felt about what she'd done. Except the whole reality of her non-relationship with Darius. It was time to come clean about that. It was time to clear the air between them. Could that even be done?

Her stomach twisted. She was going to a beach. The night air was still warm. There were lots of reasons why her bikini was the perfect outfit.

Her black sheer kaftan with silver embroidery was hanging on the other side of the room. She walked over and grabbed it.

More than anything, she wanted Nathan to stop looking at her the way he did. With recriminations. With an undercurrent of anger. She wanted Nathan to look at her the way he'd used to. With love. With passion—even devotion. Just the way she'd looked at him too.

She'd almost seen it the other night before she'd ruined everything by telling him about the renal cancer. Maybe that was all he wanted to do tonight—ask her more questions about the cancer. Maybe she was getting herself all worked up over an attraction that wasn't even there.

She glanced at her watch—it was after seven. Nathan would be wondering where she was. She pulled on the bikini and kaftan before she changed her mind and slipped her feet into some sandals. There was no need for anything else. There was no time to think about anything else.

Her initial quick steps slowed as she reached the beach. She was nervous. After eight years, the thought of spending time alone with Nathan made her stomach flip over. In good ways and in bad.

Part of her couldn't wait for this to start and part of her couldn't wait for this to be over. She wanted to be with Nathan. She wanted to spend time in his company. She wanted to get past the bitterness, past the recriminations. She wanted to find out how Nathan really was.

How he'd spent the last eight years and, most importantly, if anyone had touched his heart. She wanted to acknowledge the buzz between them, the attraction. She wanted to know if she could trust her instincts and that, no matter what had happened between them, he wanted to act on them as much as she did.

Nothing in her head was certain right now.

She walked down the path. To her right, several members of the crew were at the bar, laughing and joking together. To her left were the sun loungers. All were empty except one. Nathan was sitting staring at the ocean with a basket at his feet.

The corners of his lips turned upwards as she walked towards him. He was so handsome when he smiled. It made her skin tingle and her heart melt—it was a pity he didn't do it more often. He didn't even hide the fact he was looking at her bare legs. He was dressed casually too, in shorts and a T-shirt. If he was surprised at her lack of clothes he didn't mention it. He just continued with the appreciative looks. It made her whole body shiver with anticipation.

He stood up as she approached and lifted the basket. Her stomach flip-flopped. She was even more nervous than she'd expected.

He gave a little nod. 'Let's get away from everyone. There's another beach just around the corner, set in a cove of its own.'

*Let's get away from everyone.* He had no idea what those words were doing to her heart rate and her adrenalin levels.

'Really? I had no idea.' She was trying so hard to appear casual but her smile had spread from ear to ear. Why hide it?

He grinned and raised his eyebrows. 'Neither did I.

Len told me when he caught me raiding the bar.' He picked up a blanket from the lounger and took a few steps down the beach.

'What did you get from the bar?'

'Some wine. Rosé.' His footsteps hesitated. 'It's still your favourite, isn't it?'

Even her insides were smiling now. He'd remembered. He'd remembered her favourite drink.

'Yes. It's still my favourite,' she said quietly.

'Good.'

There was a gentle breeze as they walked along the beach together. The orange sunset reflected across the undulating waves and the muted burnished rays across the water gave a remarkable sense of calm. As they walked, behind them, in amongst the trees, the insect life was rustling and chirping.

But the beach was quiet, the only noise the rippling waves on the sand.

As the voices behind them drifted further and further away Rachel felt herself relax a little. The lights from the bar area faded and as they rounded the bay towards the other beach the only light was the orange setting sun.

Nathan shook out the blanket and set it down on the sand. She hesitated as he opened the basket and took out the wine and some glasses. 'Aren't you going to sit?' he asked as he unscrewed the bottle.

How close should she sit? The blanket wasn't too big and as she lowered herself down her bare legs brushed against his.

It was like an electric jolt and his head lifted sharply, their gazes meshing. He handed her a glass without saying a word. Something fired inside her. All of a sudden this felt immediate. She didn't want to wait. She didn't want to think about this any longer. Words could get in the way of what she really wanted to do. She glanced over her shoulder. They were definitely alone and undisturbed.

When she reached for the glass she was slow, deliberate. Her fingers brushed over his.

His gaze was fixed on hers. It was almost as if he couldn't tear it away. Almost as if this was the moment they had been waiting for.

'How are you, Rachel?' he asked. She felt as if something had blown away in the gentle breeze. It was almost as if they hadn't seen each other before this. There was no guilt or recrimination. This was a new start.

It was time for complete honesty. 'Pretty rubbish,' she whispered.

This was it. This was where the doors were finally opened. This was the point of no return.

Nathan reached his hand over and touched hers. She didn't flinch. She didn't pull it away. 'Let me start,' he said slowly. 'I have to apologise.'

'What for?'

He took a deep breath. 'I didn't even ask you.' He fixed his eyes on the horizon. He couldn't even look at her right now. He was still angry with himself for not asking the questions he should have.

'Ask me what?'

He ran his hand over his short hair. 'What stage cancer you had—what treatment you had. You never even told me how you discovered it.' He shook his head. 'I should have asked—I'm sorry. When you told me that night I was shocked. I just needed a bit of space to get my head around it.'

She bit her lip. He could tell she didn't really know where to start.

'I was tired.' It seemed the simplest explanation and, as a medic, he knew it was probably the truest. 'My symptoms were mild. Fatigue, a bit of weight loss, just generally feeling unwell. I couldn't sleep very well—and that was even before your parents' accident. So I couldn't put it down to that. I had a few unexplained temperatures. Then, one day, I dipsticked my urine in the ward. Once I realised I had blood in it and not a simple infection I started to piece everything together.' She shook her head. 'I didn't like what I found. But my appointment for investigation came just a few weeks after the funeral. We'd had too much else to deal with—too much else to think about and I almost never went.'

His stomach turned over. Was he ready for this? Was he ready to hear that she'd been so worried about him she hadn't been thinking about herself? 'What stage were you at?'

She took a sip of wine. 'I had stage three. The tumour was bigger than seven centimetres and had spread through the outer covering of the kidney to the adrenal gland. I needed a total nephrectomy and some radiotherapy and chemotherapy.'

He nodded his head slowly while his insides cringed, twisting and turning at the thought of cancer invading the body of someone he loved. He knew exactly how serious her cancer had been and how invasive the treatment would have been. Every doctor knew about the staging of cancers.

He put his head in his hands. What if she'd ignored it? What if she'd been so busy with him and Charlie that her renal cancer had got even worse? The thought made him feel sick to his stomach.

He waited a few seconds then spoke, his voice steady.

'Would you have told me? If my parents hadn't died—would you have told me then?'

He heard her suck in a breath. She took a few seconds to answer the question. 'Of course I would, Nathan.'

He squeezed his eyes shut. He was trying not to be frustrated but the truth was he wanted to scream and shout. He shook his head. After a few seconds some strangulated words came from his throat. 'Everything—everything changed. When my parents died, everything I'd planned just changed in an instant.'

He turned to face her, still shaking his head. He couldn't contain anything that was inside any more. Eight years' worth of grief and frustration came bubbling to the surface. 'You. You left. You wouldn't have if my parents had been alive. You would have told me you were ill. I could have supported you. If they'd still been there I wouldn't have changed my speciality—I wouldn't have needed to; Charlie would have been fine. I could still have been a surgeon.' His fists were clenched and his jaw tight. 'I mean, what's the point?' It was as if now the words had started he just couldn't stop. 'What's the point of being a doctor if you can't save the people that you love? One second—one second on one road on one night—changed everything about my life. I lost you. I lost my career. I lost them.'

He'd never felt so angry. Eight years ago he'd never been prone to temper flares or angry outbursts. Even when his parents had died he'd been quiet, obviously upset, but subdued. She shrank back a little.

He stood up and started pacing. 'They were trapped in their car for an hour. If they'd had medical assistance they might have lived. Where were we that night? We were at the cinema. What if I'd been with them in the car? What if I could have helped?'

She stood up and stepped in front of him. 'What if you'd been killed too? I hate to say it, Nathan, but the car was crumpled. If you'd been in the back you wouldn't have stood a chance. Charlie would have lost you all.' Her anxious voice quietened. 'I would have lost you all.'

He responded immediately, his bright green eyes locking with hers, the anger dissipating from his voice. This time it was quiet. 'But you lost us all anyway, Rachel. Or we lost you.'

The two of them stood in silence and looked at each other. She could see every weathered line on his face. She understood now. She understood his complete frustration. That was why he'd stayed with Doctors Without Borders. Nathan was all about saving people. He hadn't been able to save the people he'd loved the most—so he tried to make up for it by saving others. And she felt as if she'd compounded it all by walking away when she was ill.

And he was still handsome. He would still turn any woman's head. But he was worn out. He'd reached the end of his emotional tether.

Something curled inside her. What if she hadn't left? What if she'd told him about her renal cancer and stayed with him? How would Nathan have reacted if he hadn't been able to save her either?

She'd spent most of last night tossing and turning, wondering if she'd done the wrong thing. Maybe she should have told Nathan? Maybe she should have stayed to help out with Charlie? It was so easy to have regrets now. She'd lived. She was a cancer survivor and had come out the other side. Because she had the gift of life again, she could easily spend the rest of her time asking *What if?*

But eight years ago she hadn't known that. She hadn't been able to take that chance. Would her treatment in the UK have been as successful as her treatment in Australia? She would never know that.

Even though she'd only been there for a little while, she'd hoped she'd helped Nathan and Charlie deal with their parents' death. Now, she was beginning to realise just how wrong she'd been. None of it was over for Nathan. He'd spent the last eight years consumed by guilt because he hadn't been able to save the people he loved.

He'd spent the last eight years trying to save everyone else.

A horrible feeling crept over her. Just how broken would Nathan have been if he couldn't have saved her either? She shifted uncomfortably and swallowed. She reached for his hand, giving it a little squeeze. She was full of regrets—full of emotion she couldn't even begin to fathom. 'We lost each other,' she said sadly.

Her breath came out in a little shudder. She needed to step away from Nathan again. It didn't matter that he looked muscular and strong. Now, she was realising that, with her strong and smart Nathan, appearances were deceptive.

A wave of fear came over her. In the back of her mind she'd had the tiniest flicker of hope. Hope that something could rekindle between them. Hope that she could feel a little of the magic she'd felt before with Nathan. It could be so perfect if she could just capture that again.

But her insides were turning over. She felt sick. All of a sudden she could see how damaged and worn down the guy she loved had become. With every tiny line and crease on his face she could see his pain, see how much he'd tried to patch himself back together. And in a way she'd contributed to all this.

Five years. She'd passed the golden five-year point for being cancer-free. But somehow it would always hang over her head. There would always be the possibility, however remote, that it could come back. What if she formed a relationship with Nathan again and had a recurrence?

It had always been in the back of her mind. But she'd tried to be so positive, tried to be so focused on recovery that she hadn't allowed any room in her mind for those kind of thoughts.

But as she stood in front of Nathan now she felt herself unravelling. She wasn't just going to have to walk away from Nathan once; she was going to have to do it twice.

What if, for one minute, he was the person she loved—the way that she had always loved Nathan? The way that he might still love her?

She couldn't do it. She hadn't been able to do it before. And she couldn't do it now.

She couldn't take the tiniest chance that her cancer might return and she could destroy the man she loved.

Before, she hadn't been afraid. She'd been on her own. Any future relationship that might develop would be based on the foundation that she was a cancer survivor.

Now, standing in front of Nathan, she was terrified.

She wanted to love him. She wanted to hold him. She wanted his big strong arms wrapped around her with the feel of his skin next to hers. She wanted to run the palms of her hands over his short hair. She wanted to feel his breath on her neck, the beating of his heart against her own.

But the realisation of how he'd suffered over the last few years was too hard. He'd spent the last five years trying to save the world. It couldn't be done. It could never be done. But it seemed, for Nathan, that was the only thing that healed him. His only redemption.

She reached out and touched his face, letting her fingertips come into contact with his cheek. 'I had no idea,' she whispered. 'I had no idea that's how you felt.' She spoke softly. 'Your parents had a horrible, hideous accident. There was nothing you could have done, Nathan. There was nothing anyone could have done.' Her fingers moved gently down his cheek. 'I'm so sorry I couldn't stay to help you work through this.' Her voice was shaking now. 'But look at the work you've done. Look at the lives you've saved, Nathan.' She gave her head a shake as tears sprang to her eyes. 'It's a horrible thing to say, but if your parents hadn't died—if I hadn't had the cancer diagnosis—things would have been different. We both know that. But who would have saved those lives, Nathan? Who would have made a difference to the kids you've helped through Doctors Without Borders?' As the tears slid down her cheeks she let herself smile. 'Maybe you've saved the next Louis Pasteur or Edward Jenner? Maybe, if you hadn't been there, they wouldn't have been saved?'

She pulled her hand back. It was too tempting. It was too tempting just to step forward and wrap her arms around his neck. To turn her lips towards his.

But she couldn't. She couldn't dare risk that.

He was shaking his head, his green eyes fixed on her. As she breathed he licked his lips and his pupils dilated a little.

She took a tiny step back. 'I have no idea about fate, Nathan. But I have to believe that things happen for a reason. Otherwise, I would be lost in the fact that too many good people are taken much too soon. I have to believe that you went to the places you were supposed to, and saved the people that you should.'

He looked so confused. It was almost as if a little scattering of lights had switched on behind his eyes. He was finally starting to realise how he'd been living. 'But what about you? What about us? What did we do that meant we had to be apart?'

She could almost feel a fist inside her chest grip her heart and squeeze it tight. 'I don't know,' she whispered. Her feet edged back further.

She could so easily slip. She could so easily tell him how she'd never stopped loving him and wanted to try again. She could so easily tell him that she'd thought about him every day for the last eight years.

But now the cancer seemed like a black cloud above her. If Nathan loved and lost her again, what would that do to him?

It was best to keep things platonic. No matter what her brain and body said about that. She could almost feel the little portcullis slide down in her brain—cutting off her emotions from the rest of her. It took her to a safe place and stopped her from thinking about the things that could break her heart.

She straightened her back and wiped a tear from her cheek.

'What happened when you got to Australia?' he asked. 'What happened with you and Darius?'

Her head dropped. He hadn't put the pieces together yet. He would at some point. But she'd passed the point of keeping secrets from Nathan.

She could trust him. She knew that now beyond a shadow of a doubt. This wasn't about her and Darius. This had never been about her and Darius.

'Ask me how I met him,' she said steadily.

Nathan moved. He set his glass down on the sand and held his hand out towards her. She put her palm in his, letting herself revel in the delicious sensations tingling up towards her shoulder. Her glass was still in her hand as she stepped forward, pressing the whole of her body up against his and wrapping her arm holding the glass around the back of his neck. His hands settled on her hips. The tension in the air between them was palpable.

It was as if they'd waited eight years to have this conversation. It was as if they'd waited eight years to finally be in this place, at this time.

'Rach, how did you meet him?' There was the tiniest tremor in his voice.

The tears flowed. 'I met Darius at the cancer treatment centre,' she whispered.

He froze, his fingers tightening around her waist. For a few seconds their eyes were just locked together in the darkening light. She could see everything on his face. The realisation. The acknowledgement. The recognition.

She could read everything he was thinking—the secrets, the paper-thin medical file.

'Is Darius well? Should he even be here?'

It was the doctor in him. He'd gone from seeing Darius as a rival to seeing him as a patient.

'He had non-Hodgkin's lymphoma. He's relapsed twice over the last few years. As far as I know, he's well right now.'

She could sense him start to relax a little. She licked her lips. 'Darius was never really my boyfriend. We leaned on each other while we were undergoing treatment. I was his sounding board. I knew how to keep a secret. I've never betrayed his trust. That's why he wanted me here. That's the only reason he wanted me here.'

He nodded and reached up, brushing the tears from

one cheek, then the other. He didn't ask her any questions. He seemed to instantly respect her explanation.

His anger towards Darius seemed to disappear in the sea winds. It was easy now he knew why she'd been keeping secrets from him. Now, it seemed his only focus was on her.

'Rachel?' he whispered. His fingers ran up her arm to her shoulder and he cradled her cheek in the palm of his hand. 'What next?'

Her blood was warming every part of her skin. This was exactly what she remembered. Exactly what she'd dreamed of. She remembered every part of him. His muscles had changed slightly; they were a bit more defined and a bit more angular. But her body still melded against his the way it always had done. They fitted together. That was how it was with a soulmate. That was the way it was supposed to be.

No one had ever felt as perfect next to her.

She let out a little sob as his hands brushed over her skin. She'd waited for this moment for eight years. She'd spent days and nights dreaming about this.

Dreaming about the moment she would be in Nathan's arms again and she could act on instinct.

He knew now. He knew everything. And although he'd initially been angry, now he had the full picture it seemed he felt exactly the same way she did. They might have been separated by continents, years, accidents and disease but their spark had never died. Their attraction had never died.

His hands were busy, reacquainting themselves with her body. It was like butterflies dancing on her skin. 'This could get wet,' he whispered as her hand slipped and a splash of wine landed on his shoulder. She laughed and stepped back, unwinding her arm and finishing what was left of the wine.

The sea was dark, with a few burnished orange beams from the setting sun scattering across it. This time of night it would be cold. But her skin was so heated she didn't care.

All she felt right now was relief. Relief that she could finally reconnect with the man she'd always wanted.

'Fancy getting completely wet?' she taunted. She set the wine glass down on the sand and held out her hand towards him as his eyes widened.

He didn't hesitate; he put his hand in hers and pulled her towards the water. Nathan wasn't shy. His T-shirt was pulled over his head in seconds and his shorts dropped on the beach. Rachel didn't need to do that. Her bikini was in place and she left the sheer kaftan covering her hips.

The water chilled her thighs as they strode out into the dark sea. Once they'd reached waist height Nathan turned around and grabbed her. She didn't wait for a second. Talking wasn't what she wanted to do right now.

The chilled water hadn't stilled the thudding of her heartbeat. As Nathan's hands pulled her closer the buoyancy of the water let her wrap her legs around his waist.

His lips came into contact with hers. It was what she'd been waiting for. Since they'd kissed yesterday. Since she'd walked away eight years ago.

And the promise of his lips hadn't changed. He didn't just kiss her. He devoured her. It was everything she remembered. It was everything that had haunted her dreams for the last eight years.

Nathan's lips had been made for hers. And she remembered exactly why they'd been so good together. Her hands curled around his head, brushing his buzz cut, feeling the bristles under her palm. His hands ran through her hair; one hand anchored her head in place whilst his lips worked his way around her neck and shoulders and his other hand was held against her bottom.

The waves continued to buffet them, pulling them one way, then the other. Every current pulled them even closer together, his hard muscles against her softer curves.

Now his hands moved lower, swiftly grabbing the bottom of her kaftan and pulling it over her head. It disappeared into the waves.

His hands were back on her bare skin, cradling her and pulling her tighter towards him. The chilled water did nothing to hide his response to her.

She leaned back a little and ran her palms up the planes of his chest. His years in Doctors Without Borders had left him leaner, more muscular. It was understandable. The places where he'd served would have required long hours and hard labour. Nathan wouldn't have shirked any of that.

Something pinged. The snap on her bikini top sprang apart and the cold water rushed underneath the pink Lycra. It billowed between them and was swallowed by the sea as his fingers brushed against her nipple.

Even in the dark she could see his green eyes on hers. Her teeth grazed the nape of his neck as she kissed even harder. He started walking, striding back towards the beach with her legs still wound around his waist. 'Let's take this back to land,' he said.

This time his hands fitted firmly around her waist, anchoring her in place. This time the pads of his fingers came in contract with the curved scar on her back. This time she had no cover. The bikini top and kaftan were lost amongst the waves. He inhaled sharply.

It was a jarring reminder of the gulf between them.

He fixed her with a stare she hadn't seen before—one of wariness—as he set her down. Then he didn't speak. He just moved her gently to one side, pushing her onto one hip.

She was holding her breath as he gently traced his finger down the curve of her scar. Her chest was hurting, struggling under the strain of little oxygen. Her stomach churned. She had no idea what he would do, what he would say.

But, as she let the breath whoosh out from her chest, he took it away all over again. He bent and gently brushed his lips against her scar.

His voice was husky. 'You should have told me, Rach. You should always have told me.'

His voice was cracking. She could see his emotions written on his face. It was breaking her heart all over again.

She hadn't stayed around the last time to witness this. Last time around she'd witnessed his shock, disbelief and then a little bit of anger. She knew exactly what she'd done to him. She just hadn't waited around for the fallout.

This time it was right in front of her. The hurt, the confusion, the sadness. This was why she hadn't stayed. She couldn't have stood this. She just wasn't strong enough for this.

Her voice was cracking. 'I always think I messed up. But I did the best thing in the circumstances. Even though I regret it every single day.'

Suddenly she felt swamped. Swamped by what had just happened between them, and confused by it even more.

She'd been so caught up in the fantasy of this. For a few moments, the beautiful setting and the man in front of her had just swept her away. But his lips connecting with her scar brought her back to the harsh reality of life and the decisions that she'd made.

She'd wished for this for the last eight years. But now it was right in front of her she couldn't let herself go. She couldn't lose herself in the moment with Nathan because of the multitude of fears she still had. The rational parts of her brain were telling her to move on. She was past the five-year cancer-free mark.

Now was the time to think about a new relationship and maybe even see if she could revive her dream of having a family.

But some part of her heart just couldn't let her take that final step.

The hurt on his face had been a painful reminder of what she'd already put him through. She didn't want to take the chance of hurting Nathan more than she already had.

Everything had happened too soon for her. Her brain really hadn't had time to process how she felt about all this. She needed some time. She needed some space.

Above all, right now, she felt as if she needed to get away. Needed to get away from the man she still loved with her whole heart.

She jumped up and made a grab for his T-shirt that was lying on the sand. 'I'm sorry, Nathan. I can't. I just can't.'

Confusion racked his face. 'What? What are you talking about?'

She waved her hand. 'This. It's all just too much, too soon. I need some time to think about things.' Her feet were already moving across the sand. Back towards the cabin. Back towards safety.

'Rachel, wait!' He jumped to his feet as if to come after her but she put up her hand.

'No, Nathan. If you care about me at all, you'll give me some space. We haven't seen each other in eight years. *Eight years, Nathan.* There's so much unfinished business between us. I can't straighten out how I feel about everything.'

She was still walking.

'Do you love me, Rachel?'

His voice cut through the sea wind and stopped her cold.

She turned again, but the words were stuck in her throat. Of course she loved him—she'd never stopped. She just wasn't ready to say that yet. She could never guarantee that she'd be healthy. She could never guarantee her cancer wouldn't come back. Was she brave enough to expose him to that? Was she brave enough to expose *them* to that? It was all about trust again. Could she trust their potential relationship to see them through anything? She just wasn't sure.

'Because I love you, Rachel. I'll always love you. I've spent so much time being bitter. I've spent so much time being angry about my parents dying. I've never stepped back to see how much it impacted on my life—on Charlie's life.' He gave a little laugh. 'It turns out my little brother is more of a man than I ever thought. He's got past it—he's moved on. He's found love. He's got a family. And I envy him every single day.' He emphasised those words as he stepped towards her.

But he didn't reach out and touch her. He kept his

hands by his sides. 'You've had cancer, Rachel. It's time for you to move on too. It's time for both of us to move on.' He took a deep breath. 'But I'll give you time. I'll give you space. You need to get to the same place as me. The one where you can say that you're ready to love me again.'

He let the words hang in the air between them.

The sky was dark. She was too far away to see the expression on his face. All she could feel was an invisible weight pressing down on her chest.

Her head was so jammed full of thoughts that she just needed to get away. So, before he could say anything else, she turned on her heel and ran.

Ran as fast as she could along the beach and back to the cabin, slamming the door behind her and heading straight to her bed.

She had to make a decision. She had to try and find a way to think straight.

Because right now she just couldn't.

# CHAPTER TEN

'HOW MANY TIMES has he refilled that water bottle?'

Nathan was watching the monitor that was fixed on the camp. Camp life was boring. There was no getting away from it. The director had spent most of the day trying to stage a fight between two of the celebrities.

And Nathan had spent the last two days trying to avoid Rachel.

Part of him thought that giving into the undeniable chemistry between them might have diminished the tension between them. He couldn't have been more wrong.

There was nothing like being stranded on an island with your ex for increasing tension to epic proportions—particularly after what had just happened between them.

Part of him felt sick. Rachel—*his Rachel*—had suffered from renal cancer.

His brain couldn't get past the part that she hadn't told him.

But now... *Now* he had a reason why she'd left. And the lack of trust was hard to stomach. But with a bit more thinking time and a bit more reason he could almost understand why she'd thought she was doing the right thing.

He still believed she had been wrong. The thought of Rachel having cancer might burn a hole inside him, but now the fact that she *hadn't* walked away because she didn't love him—as crazy as it sounded—that part was almost a relief.

That part had preyed on his mind constantly. He'd always wondered why she'd done it. Now there was a reason. She said she'd loved him too much. She said she'd walked away *because* she loved him. He still couldn't quite get his head around that.

The other night had been an epiphany for him. He'd stood on the beach and known that, no matter how he felt or how angry he'd been, he would always love her. Always. He'd always want her in his life.

The feelings were so overwhelming that he'd understood when she'd said she needed time. Now he'd found Rachel again, he didn't want her to slip through his fingers. Not again.

Parts of his heart still squirmed, his self-defence mechanism wanting to kick into place and stop him from being vulnerable. How on earth would he feel if Rachel walked away from him again? It was almost unthinkable.

But it could happen. And if he considered it too much he would simply turn and walk away himself. Eight years was a long time. They'd both changed so much. Niggling doubts were creeping in because Rachel hadn't been able to look him in the eye and say for sure what she wanted. He was taking a huge risk.

He'd survived her walking away once—but what about twice?

He took a deep breath and focused on the screen in front of him. He was here to do a job. Other parts of his life would have to wait. He asked the question again. 'How many times has he refilled that water bottle?'

The technician looked up from the monitor and

frowned, breaking him from his thoughts. 'Three—maybe four times? He spends most of his day in the dunny too.' He paused. 'Or sleeping.'

Nathan ran his fingers over his buzz cut. The dunny—the Australian equivalent of a toilet. He'd even used the word himself thc other day. Darius was drinking too much and peeing frequently. Something was wrong. He was in doctor mode now. He had to stop focusing on Rachel. His gut instinct told him that something wasn't right here. It didn't help that now he knew Darius's medical history he was even more worried. There was no getting away from the fact the guy just didn't *look* well.

He hated to admit it, but Darius was generally a good-looking guy—well-built, with dark hair, tanned skin and a movie star smile. He was kind of surprised the guy had stayed in a soap opera in Australia and not tried to hit Hollywood.

He watched as Darius tugged at his shorts, pulling them up. His weight loss had been evident the first time Nathan had seen him. Now, it was even more marked. And if the clothes he'd brought with him were falling off—it was time to act.

Nathan walked over to the director's chair. 'Darius Cornell. Get him out of there. I want to check him over.'

The director looked up. 'What are you talking about? Darius is fine. He hasn't complained about anything.' He looked at the rest of the people in the cabin. 'Has he?'

The ones that were listening shook their heads. The director held up his hands. 'See?'

Nathan leaned on the desk and pointed at the screen. 'Does that guy look well to you?'

The director glanced back at the screen and hesitated. 'He has been going to the dunny a lot. Maybe he has one of those parasitic bugs? Maybe he's picked up something in the jungle?' Unconsciously, the director started to scratch his skin.

Nathan put his hand on the man's shoulder. 'Leave the diagnosing to me. Can you send someone to get him out of there for a quick check over?' He looked around. There was no getting away from it—he couldn't avoid her for ever. 'And could someone find Dr Johnson and ask her to report to the medical cabin?'

He didn't wait for an answer, just walked back to the medical centre and tried to keep everything in his head in check.

Rachel and Darius in a room together. For the first time since he'd got here he couldn't care less. Now he knew Darius's history, he was worried about him—really worried. If the guy was having a third recurrence of his non-Hodgkin's it couldn't possibly be good.

It only took a few minutes for Darius to arrive and he was less than happy to see Nathan. 'What are you doing here? I thought I made it clear I'd only deal with Rachel.'

Nathan held up Darius's empty medical file. 'Rachel will be along soon. I'm worried about you, Darius. You don't look well. You can't possibly feel well. How much weight do you think you've lost?'

Darius scowled at him as he sat down in a chair and started scratching at his skin.

But Nathan wasn't going to let this go. He wasn't about to betray what Rachel had revealed to him but he had to get to the bottom of what was wrong. 'Darius, let's not play games. What I need to know right now is what your symptoms are. I'm worried about you.'

Darius blinked—as if a whole host of thoughts had just flooded his brain—and Nathan heard a sharp intake of breath behind him. Rachel.

'What's going on?' She walked straight in. 'Darius? Is something wrong?'

Darius, who normally spent his time trying to charm everyone around him, was unusually bad-tempered. 'Don't ask me—ask him. It was him that pulled me out of thc jungle.'

'With good reason,' cut in Nathan.

'What have you told him, Rach?' Darius looked mad.

Nathan's eyes fell on the water canister that Darius still held in his hands. He hadn't even put it down when he'd been called to the medical cabin. He obviously had a raging thirst. The question was—why?

Nathan took a deep breath and leaned against the desk. He tried not to fixate on Rachel in her unusual get-up of pink sundress, thick socks and hiking boots. He'd no idea where she'd been. But he could almost feel her brown eyes burrowing into the side of his head.

She paused at the doorway, taking in the situation in front of her. In the unflinching bright lights of the medical centre it was obvious that Darius was unwell. She walked towards him. 'I haven't told Nathan anything—but I'm just about to.' Her eyes met Nathan's, a silent thank you for not exposing what she'd already revealed. 'He's the doctor on duty and he needs the full facts. Darius and I met when we both had cancer treatment. I had renal cancer and Darius had non-Hodgkin's lymphoma. He's relapsed twice since.'

Darius glared at Rachel and gritted his teeth. But he didn't speak.

Nathan tried again. 'Darius, tell me honestly—how are you feeling? Because, to be frank—you look like crap.'

Rachel's eyebrows shot upwards and Darius almost

growled at him. He stood back up and pushed himself into Nathan's face. 'Who do you think you're talking to?'

And with that simple act Nathan's suspicions were confirmed. Darius's breath smelled of pear drops—something Nathan hadn't tasted since he was a child. It was a classic sign of diabetes and that, combined with all the other signs, probably meant that he was in ketoacidosis. Onset could be really rapid. He put his hand gently on Darius's arm and steered him back towards the chair, walking over to the cupboard and pulling out a glucometer. Rachel's eyes widened for a second and he could almost see the jigsaw pieces falling into place for her.

'Darius, I need to do a little test on you. It's just a finger prick; I'll squeeze out a little blood and we'll know what we need to know in ten seconds.'

'No.' Darius's aggression wasn't lessening but it wasn't him; it was his condition.

Nathan sat down opposite while Rachel moved over and kneeled in front of Darius. She put her hand on Darius's water canister. 'How much have you been drinking?'

He automatically took a swig from the bottle. 'I'm just thirsty.'

She nodded. 'And have you been going to the toilet a lot?'

'Well, I would. I'm drinking a lot.' He was snappy.

She reached over and took the glucometer from Nathan's hands. 'You've lost weight, Darius. More than we would have expected in the jungle. I think you might be suffering from diabetes. Let me do this little test.'

She was quick. He barely had a chance to reply before she'd done the little finger prick. The machine counted down rapidly and she grimaced and turned it to face Nathan.

She put her arm behind Darius and stood him up, leading him over to the examination trolley. 'We're going to set up a drip. Your body is dehydrated. Do you know what diabetes is?'

He scowled. 'Of course I do. My mum had it, remember?'

Nathan could see the flicker across Rachel's face. She remembered now. And diabetes could be hereditary. He should be feeling a little more relaxed. They had a diagnosis for Darius. Nathan looked through the drawers and pulled out a cannula and an IV giving set. It only took a few seconds to find a drip stand and a bag of saline. Rachel was an experienced medical physician. She must have looked after plenty of newly diagnosed diabetics. The condition was becoming more prevalent across the world. He'd certainly diagnosed it often in his time with Doctors Without Borders.

He walked around the other side of Darius and quickly inserted the cannula while Rachel was still talking.

'This is serious, Darius. We don't have a lot of facilities here. I'd like to transfer you to a hospital. That's the best place for you to be right now. We need to get some insulin into you and stabilise your condition. Once you're stabilised you'll feel a lot better. It only takes a couple of days.'

'I'm not going to hospital.' The words were sharp.

He saw her take a deep breath. Being unreasonable was right in there with the rest of the symptoms for diabetes, along with weight loss, drinking too much, peeing frequently and the acidotic breath.

He pulled out his stethoscope and tried to place it on Darius's chest but he batted his hand away. Nathan didn't even blink. He just calmly put his fingers on Darius's wrist, checking his pulse rate.

Rachel fixed her eyes on his. He spoke clearly. 'Only slightly tachycardic. Let's check his blood pressure.' He was trying to determine just how near to crisis Darius was.

'Do we have any insulin?'

Nathan nodded. 'There are a few varieties in the drug fridge. But we don't have an insulin pump.'

She gave a little nod and walked quickly to the fridge, unlocking the door and examining the contents. She looked over at Darius. 'You should be in hospital. You need your bloods taken and a few other assessments. You should be on a continuous pump and your blood sugar constantly monitored until we get you stabilised.'

Shc was saying everything she was supposed to be saying. But Nathan had the strangest feeling this wasn't going to go the way it should. Darius seemed strangely determined.

Darius was looking at her. 'If I go to a regular hospital they'll want to know my medical history. Can't you just give me insulin here and look after me? You do this stuff all the time.'

She shook her head. 'I do this stuff all the time in a general hospital with staff to assist me. I don't have the equipment I need. I can't even do a blood panel on you right now. I would class this as a medical emergency. I think we should call the medevac again.'

Nathan could see the mild panic in her eyes. Part of him understood and part of him didn't. Yes, this was a diabetic crisis. But, as an experienced physician, Rachel could administer the approximate dose of insulin and monitor Darius herself. With the IV in situ to correct his dehydration, it wasn't an ideal situation but it could be managed. There was no question Darius would have to be referred to a diabetic specialist but, in the immediate future, this could be controlled. He'd stabilised lots of newly diagnosed diabetics with far less equipment than they had here. Nowadays, for most patients, they tried to avoid admission to hospital unless they were at crisis point and instead had them attend a day care centre.

Nathan took a deep breath. Things were still raw between them both. And padding round about Rachel's ex wouldn't help. But he was rational enough to know that Darius was a patient. He had a right to make requests about his treatment.

It was time to get down to basics. He turned to face Darius. 'Why is it you don't want to go to a hospital? Is it because of your medical history—or because of the show?'

'The show,' Darius said without hesitation. 'It's in the contract that if I leave early—medical condition or not—I won't get my full salary. I promised Lynn she'd get her dream wedding. If I don't stay, I won't be able to do that.' He still sounded angry. He was still agitated. The condition was impacting every part of his body.

Nathan glanced at Rachel. She'd told him Darius was engaged to someone else but this was the first time he'd heard Darius mention his fiancée.

Rachel was still frowning. 'We need a set of scales.' She was moving out of panic mode and into doctor mode.

Nathan found the scales and brought them around to the side of the trolley where the drip was. He helped Darius stand up for a few seconds and took a note. He gestured towards the medical file. 'Do we have his weight when he first arrived?'

She flicked through a few pages. 'We have one—from the insurance medical.' She looked at the records.

'It was done just over a month ago. According to the scales now he's lost ten pounds.'

Nathan nodded and touched Darius's arm. 'Do you know what kind of diabetes your mother had?'

'She had it from childhood and was always on insulin. That's Type One, isn't it?'

He nodded. 'From your symptoms, it's likely that's what you have too.' He glanced at Rachel. 'Agree?'

She nodded as she dialled up the dosage on an insulin pen. 'We'll need a GAD test for confirmation but that's the way we'll treat it right now. We need to get your blood glucose levels down.'

Darius leaned back against the pillow on the trolley. 'I want to speak to the director. I want to go back into camp. But—' he closed his eyes for a second '—can I sleep for a bit first?'

Rachel gave a little tap at his abdomen. 'Pull up your shirt. I'm going to give you the first shot of insulin. Then I'm going to take some bloods and see if we can find a way to get them onshore. We need to keep doing the finger prick tests. Feel free to try and sleep through them.'

She gave him the insulin, then spent two minutes taking blood from inside his elbow. Nathan picked up the phone and spoke for a few minutes to one of the crew. He gave her a nod. 'The supply boat is due in an hour. They'll make special arrangements for the bloods.' He took the vials and stuck them in a transport container.

He hesitated and looked over as she scribbled some notes. Darius already looked as if he was sleeping. 'I'll grab us some coffee and we can have a chat about how best to handle this outside.'

Rachel's stomach was in knots. Everything that could go wrong had gone wrong. She couldn't believe it when she'd got the call about Darius and now she was kicking herself that she hadn't investigated sooner.

When she'd walked in, she'd thought he'd had a relapse. Seeing him in the bright lights of the medical cabin rather than the shaded canopy of the jungle had been a shock to the system. His skin pallor was terrible, the dehydration obvious and the weight loss evident on his face.

But knowing that it was diabetes and not a recurrence of his non-Hodgkin's lymphoma was a relief.

Diabetes she could manage. Nathan was right. She was an experienced physician—as was he. As long as she had insulin and glucose monitoring equipment they could stabilise him in a few days. His long-term care would have to be monitored by a diabetes specialist but there was no reason she couldn't manage his immediate care.

She'd just gone into shock when she'd first realised something was wrong. It had taken her a few minutes to calm down and be rational. She gave a little smile. Darius did have his good points. It was sweet that he wanted to see out his contract in order to give Lynn her dream wedding. He wasn't as self-obsessed as some might think. And the nice part was that she knew if Lynn heard that he'd done this she'd be furious in case he'd put himself at risk. They really were a devoted couple.

Nathan walked up and handed her a mug. The coffee aroma swept around her, along with something else. Hazelnut. Somewhere on this island Nathan had found her favourite drink—a hazelnut latte. He didn't even wait for her to speak. 'We have a patient to look after.'

She was surprised—surprised that he hadn't even mentioned what had happened a few nights ago. He'd said he'd give her space, and he had. She just wasn't sure that she'd entirely believed him that night. But Nathan had been true to his word. She'd never seen him alone since.

And now it felt as if he'd been avoiding her. Her stomach curled. She was sure he must regret saying those words to her. Telling her that he still loved her—that he'd always loved her. She hadn't reciprocated, even though she'd wanted to. It must have felt like a slap to the face. What would happen when he found out what her plans were? She didn't even want to go there.

She lifted her head. 'Yes. Darius…'

His shoulders set and there was a flicker along his jawline. 'How do you want to handle this?'

Work. She could talk about work. She could talk about a diabetes plan for Darius. 'I'll stay with him for the next few hours, monitoring his blood sugar. If he needs more insulin I'll talk him through doing an injection. I've no idea what his consultant's plan will be for him, but he's got to start somewhere. Might as well be here.'

Nathan nodded and placed his hands on his hips. At least he was being professional—at least he was being courteous. Then his green eyes looked right at her and she felt a jolt right through her system. 'What do you want me to do?'

*What do you want me to do?* She could answer that question and give him a dozen different variables that were nothing to do with diabetes.

But she was trying not to think about Nathan Banks, the man. She was trying only to think of Nathan Banks, the fellow health professional.

She tried to clear her head and be rational. 'I'd appreciate it if you could speak to the director and work out a plan so Darius can go back into camp for a few hours every day. Just for the camera. The director will need to tell the other campmates what's happened. And he'll need to agree to one of us being there.'

Nathan gave a sharp nod. 'I can do that. What about you? Do you want me to take over at some point? We'll still need to supervise the other challenges.'

She hesitated. She already knew that Darius wouldn't like it. But she had to be realistic. She could probably wake every few hours and monitor Darius's blood sugar, but she couldn't keep doing that for ever. It made more sense to spread the load.

'I want to try and get him back to normal as much as we can. How about we assess him later and, if he's up to it, he could walk to the canteen with you for dinner?'

He tried his best to hide the tiny grimace that she could see flicker across his face. 'Fine. I'll speak to the director and be back around six.'

He turned on his heel and walked away as she leaned against the doorjamb. She still had the coffee cup clenched in one hand and it crumpled beneath her fingers, sending the remainder of the coffee spilling down her pink dress.

She wanted to cry again. She wanted to go into her room, get into her bed, curl up in a ball and just cry.

Everything just felt like too much. Just being on this island felt like too much. The fact that Darius was sick. The fact that, after all these years, she could see the damage that had been done to Nathan—the man she still loved.

That tore at her heart most of all. Her barriers were breaking, her walls were crumbling. At work, if things got tough, you could always retreat to the sanctity of your own home. But there was nowhere to retreat to on this island.

There would always be someone there—a crew member or a camera to make you realise how little space there was. And now, with all the emotions—and the secrets she was trying to keep—there wasn't even room for her own thoughts.

All of a sudden she couldn't wait to get away from this place. It might be an island paradise for some, but for her it had turned into something entirely different.

How many more days could she try to avoid the man she had to work with? How many more days would she have to push aside everything she felt for him? This place was rapidly becoming unbearable.

For a tiny second she even considered phoning Lewis and telling him he had to get his butt out here so she could leave.

But she couldn't do that. His wife would be anxious enough waiting for her baby without her husband disappearing at short notice.

There was a cough behind her and she spun around. Darius was rubbing his eyes and sitting up a little.

'How are you feeling?' She dumped the crumpled cup in the bin and walked over to him.

His brow creased and he pointed at her stained dress. 'How long have I been asleep and what have you been doing?'

She shook her head. 'Nothing. Nothing at all. Now, let's get your blood sugar tested again and see if we can start to make you feel better.' She adjusted the flow rate on the drip and reached for the glucometer.

Doctor business. She could do this. She'd always been good at her job and at least if she was thinking about Darius she wasn't thinking about anyone else.

She quickly pricked his finger and waited ten seconds to see the result. She pasted a smile on her face.

'It's coming down slowly. What say I get some insulin and teach you how to do the next injection?'

She straightened her back. She had to start thinking about herself. 'Then we need to have a chat. I've made a decision I need to tell you about.'

## CHAPTER ELEVEN

It was more than a little awkward. Nathan didn't want to be there any more than Darius wanted him to be.

But they'd walked slowly down to the canteen together and were now sitting across from each other while Darius stirred his soup round and round.

There was no getting away from the fact the guy looked bad. His face was gaunt and there were big dark circles under his eyes. If he had any idea how he looked he'd probably be shouting for a mirror and make-up.

But Nathan could tell that Darius was just too tired. It was all part and parcel of the diagnosis of diabetes. The extreme fatigue would lift in a few days and his muscles would start to rebuild. Within a month he should look normal again. He still had an excessive thirst—he'd drunk three glasses of water since they'd sat down—but his appetite had obviously left him.

Nathan took a deep breath and let his professional head stay in place. 'You going to eat that? You've just taken another shot. You don't want to end up the other way and let your blood sugar go too low.'

Darius let out something equivalent to a growl and finally lifted the spoon to his lips. His eyes were fixed firmly on Nathan. There was clearly a mixture of resentment and curiosity in them. It seemed these feelings worked both ways.

'So, you're the famous Nathan Banks,' he finally said.

Nathan felt an uncomfortable prickle down his spine. He tried his best to be calm. 'I don't know what you mean.'

Darius lifted his eyelids just a touch. 'It took me a while to realise exactly who you were. You were her favourite topic of conversation.'

He was? The thought of Rachel and her then new boyfriend discussing him didn't sit well.

'I would have thought I was the last thing you'd want to talk about.'

Darius sat back and folded his arms across his chest. It was apparent he wanted to direct this conversation. 'You're not as good-looking as I thought you'd be.'

Nathan didn't know whether to laugh or punch him. This clearly wasn't a doctor-patient conversation any more.

He set his fork down. It was clear they wouldn't be eating any time soon. 'Really.' It wasn't a question; it was a statement of fact.

Darius shook his head. 'No. I saw a picture of you once. Rachel kept it in her bag.' He gave a little half-smile. 'Time obviously hasn't been kind to you.'

Nathan shook his head. On any other day of the week, in any other set of circumstances he'd probably knock Darius out cold. But this guy was clearly trying to play him. And he had no idea why. The thought that Rachel had kept a picture of him in her bag was sending strange pulses through his body. But this wasn't the time to get all nostalgic.

He countered. 'Botox has clearly been kind to you.'

He couldn't help it. Even though he hated to admit it,

Darius was normally a good-looking guy, with tanned skin and perfectly straight white teeth. Nathan was quite sure that with his weather-beaten skin and lines around his eyes he'd come up short in comparison.

He just couldn't help the fact that everything about this guy annoyed him. His hair, his skin, his teeth—even the way he ate. If Darius Cornell had been your average soap star Nathan wouldn't have cared less. But Darius Cornell was the soap star who had dated Rachel and that made his insides feel as if they were curling up and dying inside and gave him a completely irrational hatred of the guy.

He was trying so hard to put Darius in the 'patient' box in his head. That would help him try to keep everything professional. But then he'd go and say something about Rachel and all rational thoughts went out of the window.

*He knew.* He knew why they'd been friends. He just hadn't managed to push all the ideas that had fixated in his head over the years out of the way yet.

Because in his mind Rachel Johnson was still his.

In his mind, Rachel would always be his.

The other night he'd acted on instinct; he'd put his heart before his head and just told her that he still loved her. So many things she'd said had set off little pulses of recognition in his brain.

He *had* spent the last five years trying to save the world. Even if he hadn't realised it at the time. No one could do that. No one. All his pent-up frustration about his mum and dad had been channelled into his job. In that respect, it was time for change. It was time to re-evaluate and decide where he wanted to be. There was a tiny idea flickering in the back of his mind.

But, in other respects, things were exactly the same. Eight years on, nothing had changed.

Eight years on, he still loved Rachel Johnson.

Darius was still studying him as the feeling started to fully form in his brain.

'I always wondered what you were like,' Darius said. His tone was verging on disparaging.

'Why should you care what I was like? I was in England. You were the one in Australia—with her.'

For a few seconds Darius's gaze was still locked on his. It must be the actor in him. The overwhelming confidence. But Nathan wouldn't break the stare. It was almost like marking his line in the sand.

He didn't want anyone else to have any claim on Rachel.

Darius sucked in a deep breath. 'But Rachel was never really with me,' he muttered quietly. 'You were the one she was always thinking of.' His shoulders sagged as if all the wind had gone out of his sails. Maybe he was tired? Maybe he needed to find him something else to eat?

Darius looked up from under his heavy lids, his expression a little glazed. 'Rachel… She was never mine. You were always the person in her head.' He gave a little laugh. 'It does wonders for the confidence. And you're about to lose her all over again.'

The words made his head shoot up and focus. 'What did you say?'

What on earth did Darius mean? He wanted to give the guy a shake, but as he looked at Darius he realised that right now there was only room for doctor mode. His eyes were glassy. He reached into his back pocket and pulled out the glucometer, not even waiting for

Darius's permission. 'You haven't eaten enough. What do you want?'

'Toast.' A one-word answer from someone who obviously wasn't feeling great. Nathan strode across the canteen and walked straight into the kitchen, bypassing the baffled chef. He grabbed a few slices of bread, putting them in the toaster and opening the fridge for some butter and jam.

The chef lifted his eyebrows. 'Help yourself.'

Nathan patted him on the shoulder. 'Sorry, Stan. Darius isn't feeling too well. Just want to get some food into him.'

Stan nodded. 'No worries.' He carried on with his dinner preparations.

After a minute the toast popped and Nathan spread the butter and jam, pouring a glass of milk too. He walked back across the canteen, ignoring the curious stares around him, putting the plate and glass in front of Darius.

He needed this guy to feel well again—he needed to ask him what he'd meant about Rachel.

Darius didn't even look up—he just automatically started eating. After five minutes the glazed expression left him and he sat back in the chair, looking at the empty plate in front of him. His gaze narrowed and he folded his arms across his chest and glanced over his shoulder to check if anyone else was listening. When he was satisfied that the rest of the crew were more interested in their food than listening to anyone else's conversation, he turned back around.

'Do you feel better?'

Darius gave a brief nod. His look was still a little belligerent. But Nathan wasn't prepared to wait a second longer.

He leaned across the table. 'What did you mean about Rachel?'

Darius scowled. 'I was a bit foggy there. I might have said something I didn't mean to.'

'Lots of diabetics say odd things when their blood sugar goes a bit low. But you said something about Rachel. You said I was about to lose her all over again. What did you mean?'

Darius shook his head. 'It's private. Anyway, we should only be discussing doctor stuff.'

Nathan fixed his gaze on Darius and sucked in a deep breath, trying to keep professional. 'We should really discuss how you felt when your blood sugar went down. You need to be able to recognise the signs.' He turned the glucometer around. 'Normal blood sugar is between four and seven. But you've been running much higher in the last few weeks. Your blood sugar was ten. That's obviously the point you start to feel unwell. All that will change, but we need to keep notes.'

There was complete silence for a few seconds.

After a minute Darius stood up and picked up the glucometer. 'I'm feeling a bit better now. I think I'd prefer to discuss the diabetes stuff with Rachel.' He glared at Nathan. 'While I've still got the chance, that is.'

Nathan stood up too. 'You're not going anywhere until you tell me what you mean.'

Darius snapped at him, 'It's all your fault. She's supposed to stay on the island the whole time I'm here. But she's not. She's leaving. She's getting on the next supply boat that arrives the day after tomorrow. And she's doing that to get away from you!'

He turned on his heel and stalked out of the canteen as the bottom fell out of Nathan's world.

No. She couldn't. She couldn't leave him again.

Not Rachel. Not when he finally felt as if there was a real chance of a future together.

He just couldn't let it happen.

## CHAPTER TWELVE

THE TV PRODUCER and director had finally listened to reason. Nathan had been surprisingly persuasive. If she hadn't known better, she might have thought that he and Darius were friends.

They'd reached a compromise. Darius was hydrated enough to be off his IV fluids. They'd had his blood results sent back and spoken to a diabetic specialist about a treatment regime. Rachel would start his treatment, then, as soon as filming was finished, Darius would fly back to the mainland for a proper consultation.

He'd been quietly amenable. The background information he already knew about diabetes had been helpful. But treatments and plans had changed a lot since his mother had been diagnosed and Rachel was keen to make sure he got the best information.

The trickiest part had been the other celebrities. The phrase 'special treatment' had been readily bandied about. Nathan had ended up in the middle of the camp telling them straight how crucial it was for Darius to be monitored during these first few days. He would only be back in camp for a few hours each day for filming. The rest of the time he'd be monitored and recuperating in the crew area. Tallie Turner, the actress, had been the most disgruntled. The thought of someone else sleeping on anything other than a lumpy camp bed, away from the spiders and bugs, was obviously too much for her.

The rest of the celebrities had spent most of the day talking about it. Frank Cairns, the sportsman, was proving the public's obvious favourite. He didn't get involved in griping, rarely tolerated tantrums and had a real, self-deprecating sense of humour. Most of the votes in the last few days had been for him. Billy X, the rapper, was the second most popular. He'd done well in the challenges and had started a heavy flirtation with Rainbow Blossom, the reality TV star. Rachel was quite sure it was a calculated move for popularity but she wouldn't dream of saying so. There was only one more day to go. Tomorrow she would be on the supply boat and away from Nathan completely. She still couldn't figure out if that was what she really wanted.

She'd stayed at the medical centre last night with Darius but they'd both agreed that Darius should be allowed to bunk in with some of the crew tonight. One of them would go and wake him to check his blood sugar a few times in the middle of the night, but getting him back to normal as soon as possible was important. If he'd been diagnosed in the city he would maybe have had a one or two nights' stay in hospital if he was close to crisis to stabilise him, then he'd spend the next couple of days with a few hours at day care. All his other follow-ups would be done as an outpatient.

It was time to get things back to normal.

Normal? What was that? Because she didn't know.

Was it normal to wake up every morning and feel sick? Was it normal not to be able to sleep at night because of all the thoughts tumbling around in your brain? Was it normal not to be able to think straight and have a conversation with your colleague?

Normal didn't seem to exist for Rachel Johnson any more. Not since Nathan Banks had reappeared in her life.

Footsteps sounded on the path outside the cabin and her body tensed. She could even recognise his steps now. It was going from bad to worse. Her bed was currently covered with the contents of her wardrobe as she tried to cram them back into her rucksack. What would he say when he noticed? She still hadn't told him she planned to leave.

As she lifted up yet another carefully folded T-shirt she stopped to take a breath. Why had it taken her so long to pack? If she was really desperate to leave the island she should have just shoved everything into her rucksack. Instead, she'd been carefully folding everything, rolling up dresses and skirts. It was almost as if her head had made one decision and her heart another.

Was running away really the answer?

As the footsteps grew closer she squeezed her eyes closed for a second. *This* was what she needed to do. *This* was the conversation she needed to have—no matter how hard. She couldn't walk away from him again without talking to him first.

It wasn't fair to her. It wasn't fair to him.

Eight years ago she'd run away.

Eight years later, it was time to face things head-on.

'Hey, Rach?'

His happy tone took her by surprise. They'd spent the last day tiptoeing around each other and barely making eye contact.

She turned around. He had a bottle in his hand and two champagne glasses. She stood up, forgetting that she was only wearing her short pink satin nightdress. Nathan strode across the cabin and put the bottle on the table.

He didn't mention the clothes spread everywhere. 'Look what Lewis sent us. It just arrived on the supply boat.'

Her eyes widened as she spun the bottle around. Pink champagne from the man she planned to kill. It was kind of ironic. Then her brain clicked into gear.

'They've had the baby?'

Nathan was beaming. 'They've had the baby—a happy, healthy eight-pound girl.' He reached over and gave her a spontaneous hug. 'You know he'd been really worried, don't you? Every other female in his wife's family had developed pre-eclampsia while they were pregnant. I think Lewis spent the whole pregnancy holding his breath.'

He was still holding her and she was trying to pretend her body wasn't responding to his touch as his male pheromones flooded around her. The stubble on his chin grazed her shoulder and every tiny hair on her body stood on end. She'd always loved Nathan with stubble.

'No,' she whispered. 'I didn't know that.'

He was holding her gaze, his good mood still evident. This was the Nathan she remembered. This was the Nathan who'd kept her buoyed and supported through six years of hard study and work. This was the guy who made her laugh. This was the guy who she had always trusted, the person she trusted with her heart. Why couldn't she have him back? It was almost as if the little shadows behind his eyes had fallen away. He seemed more relaxed. He seemed at ease with the world around him. And whilst the tension emanating from him had diminished, the pheromones were sparking like fireworks.

He hadn't let her go. And she didn't really want him to.

Maybe for five minutes she could pretend that she'd never had cancer? She could pretend that she'd never left and he'd spent the last five years trying to save the world. Maybe for the next five minutes they could try being happy with each other. She wanted that so badly.

'What's the baby's name?' she asked.

His nose wrinkled. 'Gilberta.'

She pulled back a little. 'What?'

He shrugged. 'Apparently it's a family name.' He glanced over at the champagne on the table. 'What do you say, Rach? Wanna drink some champagne with me?'

His arms released her as he reached over to grab the bottle and she felt the air go out of her with a little whoosh. Nathan didn't notice. He was too busy popping the cork and pouring the bubbling liquid into glasses.

No. She couldn't do this. She couldn't keep living this life. If you'd asked her a few weeks ago about Nathan Banks, her heart would have given a little twist in her chest and she'd have said kind of sadly that he was an old friend. Then she would have spent the rest of the day miserable, wondering where he was and if he was happy.

She'd never met anyone else like Nathan Banks. She'd never met anyone who'd pushed her, inspired her, challenged her and loved her like Nathan Banks.

Her life had seemed so settled. Her career plan had been in place. She had a nice place to stay and good work colleagues. But it wasn't enough. It would never be enough.

She'd met lots of nice guys. But no one she wanted to grow old with. No one she could still picture holding her hand when they were both grey-haired and wrinkled. That was how she'd always felt about Nathan. As if they were a perfect fit. As if they could last for ever. No one else would do.

Meeting Nathan again had made her realise just how much she was missing out. She craved him. Mentally, physically, spiritually. Being in the same room as him and not being able to have him was painful.

Why did she have to have cancer? Why did those horrible little cells have to replicate and cause damage in her body?

She winced. This was making her become a terrible person. The kind of person who wished cancer on someone else. She didn't want to be like that. She couldn't let herself be like that.

'Rachel?' Nathan was standing in front of her, holding the glass out towards her. His brow was creased as if he could see that something was wrong. The bubbles in the champagne tickled her nose. 'Are we going to toast the baby?' he asked, a little more warily.

She met his gaze full-on. Everything had just fallen into place for her. She couldn't be this person any more. 'No.'

He started and pulled the glass back, setting them both down on the table.

She braced herself to be hit by the wave of questions. Questions she had no idea how she would even begin to answer. But Nathan didn't ask any questions. He stepped forward and put his hands on her hips. She could feel the warmth of his fingers through the thin satin of her nightdress. His body was up against hers.

She was going to leave. She wanted to get away. So why did Nathan's body feel like an anchor against hers?

'Enough.' His voice was husky. 'Enough of this, Rachel. Eight years is too long. Eight years is far too long.' He reached up and gently stroked her cheek. 'I've missed you. I've felt lost without you. I need you to be with me. I need you to trust me again and know that I'll be here for you. I'm sorry you faced cancer alone.' He closed his eyes for a second. 'I'm sorry that for a whole host of mixed-up reasons you ended up on one side of the planet whilst I was on the other.' He gave his head a shake. 'I didn't know and I didn't understand.' His eyes fixed on hers. 'I now know about Darius. I don't know everything, and I don't need to know. But I do know why you have that tie to him. I feel as if I've spent the last eight years waiting for this moment—I just didn't know it. I need to move on. *We* need to move on. We don't get those eight years back again. I need to let things go, and so do you.' He slid his fingers through her hair. 'Otherwise,' he said throatily, 'we'll never get this. We'll spend the rest of our lives just drifting—not really living.' He pressed his head against hers. 'There's no way I'm letting you get on that boat without me. Not again, Rachel. Don't walk away from me again.'

*He knew.* He knew she planned to leave. But he hadn't come to shout at her. He'd held back. He'd given her some space. Had she really wanted to leave?

Her breath was stuck in her throat as she tried to strangle her sobs. She lifted her hands and placed them on his chest as she moved forward, letting her head rest on his shoulder. She could feel the beat of his heart beneath her palm. It was so familiar. It felt *so* right.

When they'd used to lie in bed together that was always how she would fall asleep—with her hand on his heart. It gave her comfort and reassurance and feeling it now was sending a wave of pulses throughout her body.

She couldn't lift her head. She couldn't look at him as she spoke. 'I love you,' she whispered. 'I've always loved you and I'll never stop.' Her hand moved upwards, along his jaw line with the day-old stubble she loved so much. She took a deep breath and lifted her head. 'I don't know why we ended up here together. Maybe it was some kind of twisted fate. I've been so confused these last few days, and there's only one thing I know for certain. I can't be the one to break you. I might have passed the five-year cancer-free mark. But it's not a guarantee. It's always there—always hanging over my head. I don't want to be sick around you, Nathan. I don't want you to have to nurse me. I don't want you to have to look after me.' She pressed her hand against her chest. 'And it's not because *I* would be sick. It's because of what it would do to *you*. I couldn't bear to see you like that. I couldn't watch you suffer.'

'And that's a reason? That's a reason not to have a chance to live our life together? That's a reason to run away again? Haven't you learned anything, Rach?' There was an edge to his voice, but he wasn't angry. He was incredulous.

'So you're going to spend the rest of your life hiding away? From life?' He threw up his hands. 'What if you never get cancer again, Rachel? What if the worst-case scenario just doesn't happen? Are you going to be sitting on your rocking chair wondering why you let life slip through your fingers?'

He stepped forward, his face right in front of hers. 'What if I get sick? What if *I* develop cancer? Would you walk away from me? Should I walk away from you because I don't want to see you upset? Don't you see how ridiculous that sounds?'

He put his hands on her shoulders. 'People take this leap every day, Rachel. When people commit to each other there's no guarantee of a happy ever after. You have to just take what life throws at you, and hope that you're strong enough to see each other through it.'

He put his hand on his chest. 'I believe we are, Rach. I believe we can be. I believe we should get our happy ever after. We've waited eight years for it. I don't want to wait a second longer.'

She was shaking. Her whole body was shaking now as the enormity of his words set in. This was what it felt like. This was what it felt like to have someone declare they would face anything for you. This was what she would have given anything to hear eight years ago—but she hadn't given him the chance.

He ran his hands down her arms. 'Don't walk away from this, Rach. Don't walk away again. That's the one thing that I can't take. Anything else I can face. Anything else I can face—with you by my side.'

She lifted her head as the tears streamed down her cheeks. He was smiling at her and she drank in every part of him. The weathered little lines around his eyes and mouth, the dark line of his stubble and the sincerity in his bright green eyes. She could spend an eternity looking at his face.

Her breathing was stuttering but her heartbeat felt steady. 'You've no idea how much I want this. I'm just so afraid.' Her voice was shaking. It felt like stepping off the side of a cliff into an abyss. There could be so much out there if you were willing to take the leap.

But Nathan had enough confidence for both of them. His smile widened and he held out his hand towards her. 'You don't have to be afraid, Rach. We're in this together. Every step of the way.'

His hand closed around hers. Warm, solid and reassuring. It sent a wave of heat up her arm.

'But what about everything else? Where will we stay? What about jobs? What will we do?'

He pulled her hard and fast against him. 'Let's take it one step at a time. The rest we'll figure out together.' One hand snaked through her hair and the other followed the curve of her satin nightdress. He whispered in her ear, his voice low, throaty and packed with emotion. 'What say we start at the very beginning and get a little reacquainted?'

His bright green eyes were sparkling. It was like stepping back in time. And that look in his eyes sent the same quiver of anticipation down her spine that it always had.

Her lips danced across the skin on his shoulders, ending at the sensitive nape of his neck. Some things didn't change. 'I would very much like to get reacquainted with you, Dr Banks.'

He stepped back towards his bedroom and held out his hand towards her. It was the first time she'd felt certainty in eight long years. She reached out and grabbed it and let him lead her to her happy ever after—no matter what it contained.

# EPILOGUE

*One year later*

RACHEL WAS PACING. Her nerves were jangling and her heart was thudding in her chest, the swoosh of her cream wedding gown the only noise in the quiet bathroom.

Nathan reached over and grabbed her hand, pulling her towards him. He smiled as he settled one hand on her lace-covered waist and lifted the other to touch one of the little brown curls of her carefully coiffed hair.

'Anyone would think you were nervous,' he said, clearly feeling no nerves.

'Of course I'm nervous. I feel sick.' She looked back towards the sink. 'What time is it?'

He shook his head. 'Be patient, Rachel. We have all the time in the world for this.' He gestured his head towards the door. 'Our guests will think I'm in here trying to talk my bride out of her cold feet.'

Rachel sucked in a deep breath. 'Oh, no.' Her hand flew up to the sweetheart neckline of her dress. 'That is what they'll think, isn't it?' She broke from his grasp for a few seconds as she paced again, then stepped over and placed her hands on his chest, her sincere brown eyes fixing on his. 'You know I'd never get cold feet about marrying you. This is the surest I've ever been about anything in my entire life.'

He leaned forward and dropped a soft kiss on her pink lips. 'I know that,' he said. He looked over her shoulder. 'If the celebrant catches me kissing the bride before we say "I do" we might be in trouble.'

She nodded nervously. 'Is it time yet? Is it time?'

He glanced at his watch again, then took her hand in his. 'You know, I don't want you to be disappointed if it's not what you hoped. I'm marrying the woman that I love. I want our day to be about you and me and the fact we're committing to a life together.'

'I know that, I know that. But I just can't help thinking that there has to be another reason for my late period. It can't just be the stress of the wedding.'

He laughed. 'I don't think a wedding car driver has ever had to stop for a pregnancy test before. You nearly gave him a heart attack.'

She squeezed her eyes shut for a second. 'You look—I can't.'

Her head was spinning. They'd planned their wedding in the space of a few months. In less than two weeks they would be back in the UK, both in new jobs nearer to Charlie, Nathan's brother. She was to start training as a GP, and Nathan to start his training as a surgeon. He was already cracking jokes about being the oldest surgeon in town.

She'd always worried that her cancer treatment would have affected her fertility. Nathan had known that when he'd asked her to marry him. *Families can be made up in many ways.* Those had been his words. He was more concerned about not missing out on another eight years with the woman he loved.

Nathan took a step forward and glanced at the white stick.

She clenched her fists. She couldn't bear the waiting. 'One line or two?'

His eyes widened and his face broke into a smile as he grabbed her and lifted her up, spinning her around in the cramped bathroom at the courthouse. 'Two.'

'What?' She couldn't believe it. Not today.

He was still spinning her and she put her hands around his neck as he gently lowered her to the floor. 'So, are you ready? Are you ready to make me the happiest man on the planet, Mrs Banks?'

She rested her head on his shoulder as things started to sink in. 'Mrs Banks. Oh, wow. This day can't get any better, can it?'

There was a twinkle in his green eyes. 'Oh, I think it can.' He picked up her bouquet of pink roses that had been abandoned next to the sink and handed them to her. 'Let's settle our guests' nerves. They'll think we're not coming back out.'

There was a knock on the door and Charlie stuck his head in. 'Are you two okay? Freddie has already dropped the rings off that cushion twice. If he does it again you can find them.'

Charlie's little girl, Matilda, was their pink-gowned flower girl and Freddie, his little boy, was their pageboy.

Nathan gave Rachel a wink. 'Sorry, Charlie, it seems we've got some news.' He intertwined his fingers with hers. 'It seems that two are about to become three.'

It took a few seconds for the news to click, then Charlie's eyes widened. 'What?' He crossed the bathroom in two strides, enveloping Rachel in a bear hug. 'Fabulous.

I can't wait to meet my new niece or nephew.' He stepped back. 'Wait—is this a secret; can we tell anyone?'

They glanced at each other, Rachel's hand automatically going to her stomach. 'We need to wait, don't we? We need to get it confirmed?'

Nathan picked up the pregnancy test. 'We've already done that. Let's tell the world, Rachel. Let's tell them just how good life's about to get.' He winked. 'We'll just get married first.'

She nodded and took a deep breath.

Charlie led her over to the door. 'Now, let's get this show on the road. I've still to make you my sister-in-law.' He gave her a kiss on the cheek as he disappeared outside.

Nathan turned to face her. 'Your dad will be having a heart attack out there. Are you ready?'

She nodded. 'I've never been more ready.' She smoothed down the front of her dress and took a quick check in the mirror to straighten her veil. She'd embraced the whole pink theme for her wedding. Her cream satin and lace dress had a deep pink sash in the middle, matching her bouquet and the few scattered roses in her hair. Nathan had obligingly worn a pink shirt and tie and had the same coloured rose in his lapel. All for her.

Nathan walked out first and she joined her nervous-looking father. He'd been so happy when he'd found out she and Nathan were moving back to London. It had been an easy decision to make. They'd stayed and worked in Australia for another ten months before talking about plans for the future. Both of them agreed they'd like to be closer to Charlie, and she'd been over the moon when Nathan had proposed to her at Darius's wedding a few months before. They'd decided both things at once—to find jobs back in England and plan their wedding.

Her dad held out his arm. 'Everything okay?'

She gave him her widest smile. 'Everything's perfect, Dad, and it's going to get even more so.'

His brow furrowed curiously as he glanced towards the doors of the courthouse just as they were opened by the staff. Nathan and Charlie went in first.

She smiled and her stomach gave a little flip-flop. Eight years ago she'd thought her life was about to end—now, it was just beginning.

As the sun streamed through the windows Rachel walked in on her father's arm to join the man that she loved.

Her husband. Her baby's father.

Her fate.

* * * * *

# MISS PRIM AND THE MAVERICK MILLIONAIRE

**NINA SINGH**

For my wonderful husband and children.
Thank you for all the patience, faith, and support.
Not to mention, the many very needed nudges.
And for the best group of fellow writer friends
I could have ever hoped for.

# CHAPTER ONE

THIS DEFINITELY WASN'T in her job description.

Jenna Townsend glanced at her watch, not actually noting the time. Then glanced at it again. A car should be picking him up from the airport right at this moment. Which meant he would be here at her office within the hour. She took a too-large swig of coffee and gasped as it burned her tongue and throat. Why was she so nervous? Babysitting the CEO of Jordan's Fine Jewelry for the next several days shouldn't warrant this much anxiety.

Cabe Jordan, CEO extraordinaire, was on his way back to Boston. The man who'd taken the small business his parents started in the historic North End and made it one of the most profitable national corporations of the last decade.

Hard to believe they'd grown up together in the same small town just outside Boston. Two years ahead of her in school, Cabe had been her older brother's bane of existence, besting Sam at everything. Her brother had not been happy when she'd taken the position of regional manager and started working for his nemesis. But opportunities like this weren't ones to be passed up, not for someone like her.

The job had been everything she could have hoped for and more. Until the email in her inbox the other day "requesting" her assistance in escorting Mr. Jordan as he revisited the flagship Boston site. For some reason, he'd specifically requested that she be his local liaison on this trip. Jenna shook her head.

Why did he need one anyway?

She'd felt like she'd been sent to the principal's office, unable to shake the feeling that he was really here to check up on *her*. Had she done something wrong? Let something crucial slip through the cracks? Or had he woken up one day and realized he'd hired a small-town hick with no real-world experience. Maybe he was looking to replace her with some hotshot MBA from a real business school and he wanted to tell her in person. Maybe Sam had been right all these years and Cabe Jordan really was an elitist who had always looked down his nose at people like her.

Heavens, she had to get a grip. And try to stay positive. There could very well be a good reason for Cabe's visit. Hadn't she just come across an internal email regarding an opening in upper-level management? Perhaps he was here to tell her she was being promoted. It was possible. After all, her numbers spoke for themselves.

Did she dare to hope? Her job here meant so much for both her future and everyone who depended on her.

A quick knock on the door preceded the abrupt entrance of her assistant carrying a gleaming silver tray laden with pastries, a coffeepot and two brand-new porcelain mugs. Nothing but the best for Mr. Jordan.

"Thanks, Nora," Jenna said as she set the tray down on a side bureau.

"You got it. Do we know his ETA yet?"

"Won't be much longer now."

Nora put her hand over her heart, a dreamy, faraway expression on her face. "I wonder if he'll have Carmen with him."

"Carmen?"

"You know, that Spanish model he was photographed with recently."

Jenna shrugged. "I wouldn't know."

"Oh, come on. You have to be as curious as the rest of us. He's been spotted out and about with at least three different beauties in the last month alone."

Jenna merely smiled. If she was curious about anything, it was the reason for this whole trip to begin with. "Mr. Jordan's personal affairs are none of my concern. I simply work for the man."

"And what a dreamy man he is." Despite being a happily married grandmother of a newly born infant, Nora was unabashed in her appreciation of handsome men.

"Be that as it may…" Jenna brushed an imaginary piece of lint off her right shoulder. This conversation was making her uncomfortable. Cabe had always been an endless source of gossip around here. She understood the curiosity—of course she did. Handsome, successful, mysterious. Cabe had really made a name for himself in the retail jewelry business. But endless speculation about the man wouldn't get her a regular paycheck.

"I should probably get back to work on this presentation I set up for him." She glanced at the graphic on her screen. She'd worked all night on it, taking the initiative to put together a slide presentation for Cabe's review. Even though she didn't know the exact reason for his visit, she figured presenting him with some specifics on the current business numbers wouldn't hurt.

"I'm sure you'll impress him, dear. Please don't fret."

Nora, of all people, knew how much Jenna needed this job. Her school loans alone were enough to keep her in debt for a good portion of her adult life. But as far as assurances went, Jenna wasn't convinced.

"It can't hurt to be prepared."

"Of course, dear." Taking the hint, Nora walked out of the office, gently shutting the door behind her. As much as she wanted to relax about all this, Jenna couldn't seem to heed Nora's advice not to "fret."

She had to face it. Whatever his reasons, for the next several days, she would have to be Cabe Jordan's glorified and overqualified chaperone. If only she could figure out why he needed one.

The only thing draped on Cabe's arm when he walked in was his suit jacket. Not that she'd really thought he'd have a date with him when he came into the office. Though if the gossip websites were to be believed, he didn't travel far without female companionship. Jenna stood as she eyed him in the reception area, chatting with Nora.

She watched as he walked over to the doorway of her office. Dressed in a well-tailored suit that fit him like a glove, he looked impeccable. Tall, still fit. Jenna drew in a deep breath. Those websites hadn't done him justice. She'd refused to acknowledge it since receiving that email, but the truth was absolutely impossible to ignore now. The silly schoolgirl crush she'd had on him as a kid hadn't abated one iota.

Well, if he was out of reach then, he was downright

unattainable now. Still, like Nora, she could certainly appreciate his…pure masculinity.

*Snap out of it.*

He was waiting for her to invite him in as she stood there with her mouth gaping open. Staring at him. How utterly unprofessional. So much for coming across as the dynamic, invaluable employee Cabe's company couldn't do without.

"Mr. Jordan. So nice to see you here. Come in. Please."

Wow, now she was positively dazzling him with her talent for witty conversation. He strode into the room and gave her a warm smile that sent electric volts down to her toes.

"Jenna. We've known each other a long time. Please call me Cabe."

He spoke the words cordially enough, but she couldn't shake the feeling that she sensed some subtle undertone, some kind of underlying message. Or maybe that was just her silly attraction to him that she'd thought she had gotten over eons ago. She'd been so wrong about that.

Definitely not the time to realize it.

She gave her head a brisk shake to clear it. She could not blow this initial meeting. She had the distinct impression the future of her livelihood depended on it.

"Would you like a cup of coffee? Cabe."

His smile grew wider. "That's more like it. And I'd love some coffee. But only if you'll join me."

She nodded and moved to the serving tray. Cabe held up a hand to stop her. "Please, let me."

Really? *He* was going to serve *her*?

"How do you take it?"

"Just cream, please."

He poured with a steady hand, doctored it with the small pitcher of creamer and handed her the cup. He poured a cup straight black for himself before sitting down across from her desk. In the smaller chair.

Was it her or was Cabe going out of his way to make her feel less of his employee and more of his equal?

Jenna cleared her throat. "So, what brings you here?"

He shrugged. "Just figured it's about time I visit the flagship Boston site. Now that the Manhattan store is thriving, I can devote some attention to other areas. This is where it all began, after all. Feel I may have been neglecting it over the years."

Did he mean it would have fared better if he'd been more involved? But the regional New England stores were doing fine with her at the helm. Sales had grown progressively over the years. Not at an astronomical pace but pretty steady, despite the slow economy. Heavens, why such paranoia?

"I see."

"Just for a few days."

"Well, I think you'll be pleased with the overall numbers. Here, let me show you." She walked over to the other side of the desk to face her laptop and motioned for him to follow.

Mistake. She hadn't thought to pull over another chair facing the computer. They had no choice but to stand side by side. He smelled of pine and sandalwood.

She pushed herself to go through each slide, hardly aware of content. She stammered on every other sentence. Hopefully, she was at least coherent.

Cabe nodded at all the right points, so that was at least encouraging. He also asked some pertinent questions that Jenna was blessedly prepared for. Still, when she finished with her presentation, she felt as if she'd just trekked the full length of the Freedom Trail. And felt just as out of breath.

If Cabe noticed, he was too much of a gentleman to let on. "Very impressive," he said, still staring at the upward slope of the graph on the last slide.

"Thank you."

"Both the performance numbers and your presentation."

"Thank you." Again with the witty conversation.

"I'm not surprised. You're a very capable regional manager."

*Don't you dare say "thank you" again.* She simply nodded, tried not to duck her head at the praise. The burning in her cheeks crept clear up to her scalp. She resisted the urge to fan herself like an old-fashioned Southern belle.

He did seem genuinely impressed. Maybe she'd been wrong to be so nervous. Perhaps he really was here to talk to her about a promotion. Stranger things had happened.

She decided to take a chance. "Oh. Well, then. Excuse me, Mr. Jordan—"

He interrupted her. "Cabe."

She smiled politely. "I mean Cabe. If you don't mind my asking… Why are you really here? After all this time. What aren't you telling me?"

Cabe's response died on his lips as the older secretary entered Jenna's office. "Excuse me, Mr. Jordan. There's a call on the office phone for you, from Corporate."

He fished his cell out of his pocket, realizing he'd left it in airplane mode after his flight. "Thanks, Nora." Sure enough, the phone started buzzing as soon as he changed the setting. A naughty text from Carmen popped up. He tried not to groan out loud. The woman could be draining. He would have to do something about that pretty soon. She had her sights on something that wasn't going to happen. He'd have to find a way to let her down gently. No doubt it would cost him a pretty penny.

Then there were numerous messages from his assistant in New York, no doubt about the Caribbean expansion deal. Nothing about the project so far had run smoothly.

And so it began.

The interruption was just as well. He wasn't sure how much he could share with Jenna Townsend just yet. Sharp as she was, she'd surmised that something else had prompted his visit.

He wanted to believe there'd been some kind of mistake, that she had no involvement. But it wouldn't be the first time he'd misjudged someone.

"Would you mind if I take this, Jenna?"

She shook her head. "Of course not." She walked toward the door. "I'll give you some privacy."

"There's no need for that." But she'd already left by the time he reached for her desk phone.

Cabe hung up the phone several minutes later and tried not to curse in frustration. He'd been right. There were indeed yet more complications on the resort island where he planned to open a new high-end retail jewelry store, this time to do with zoning issues.

He would have to fly down there. The sooner the better. Which meant he had to wrap up here in Boston as quickly as he could. He had to address the real purpose of this visit. Of all the reasons to have to come back, a thieving employee. He shook his head at the utter surprise of it. There was absolutely no reason for an employee to steal from him. The company paid well and provided numerous benefits. The only reason had to be greed.

His head of security assured Cabe that such thefts were usually inside jobs, almost always involving the store manager, who in this case was Jenna Townsend. The timing couldn't have been worse—Jenna had been on track for a major promotion before the theft came to light.

As soon as he'd heard the name, he'd wanted to deal with the matter himself. He'd hired Jenna personally. His parents had always been quite fond of her. They'd asked him to give Jenna a chance when she'd graduated top of her class from business school two years ago. Despite what the town had thought about the Townsend family and its troubled history over the years, his parents had insisted that Jenna was cut from a different cloth and that she just needed a chance to prove it. His mom and dad were all about giving people a chance. He liked to think that had served them well, at least as far as their son was concerned.

Cabe's original plan was to spend a few days with her. Maybe even find some evidence. So he'd asked for her specifically to be his assistant on this trip. But now he had forty-eight hours at the most before he had to fly to the Caribbean to deal with the other pressing matter. That left him with only one choice. He had to come right out and ask her what, if anything, she knew about the missing jewelry.

He could be quite persuasive when he had to be. Besides, he didn't have the time to dwell on this. He had to get to the bottom of it all and move on to business as usual.

No one stole from Cabe Jordan and got away with it.

When Jenna returned to her office, Nora ran fast on her heels. "Is there anything else I can do for you, Mr. Jordan?" the older woman asked as she cleared the tray of mugs and coffee pitcher.

Cabe turned and flashed them both a smile that made Jenna's knees go weak. "As a matter of fact, you can, Nora," he replied. "Please clear Jenna's calendar for the next two hours or so and cancel her appointments."

What? Why?

To her shock and horror, he added, "I'd like to take my regional manager to lunch."

Oh, no. She had to nip this in the bud right now. She did not want to sit across a table from this man, just the two of them. She was absolutely no good at small talk. And her presentation earlier had covered all the business details she could possibly bring up. Whatever he had to tell her, he could do so right here in this office. "I'm afraid I just can't do that, Mr. Jord—"

"Cabe."

She took a steadying breath. "I can't steal away for lunch today, Cabe." She glanced at Nora, willing her to help. Instead, Nora threw her overboard.

"Nonsense. Of course she can. There's nothing pressing on her calendar this afternoon. And she hardly ever eats a real lunch. Usually a granola bar at her desk as she continues to work."

Cabe's smile dripped with satisfaction. "It's settled, then. Do you have a preference where to eat, Jenna?"

She could only shake her head.

He led her gently to the door. "How about Nawlin's, that sidewalk café on Newbury, then? It's a pleasant enough day to eat outside and I've missed their sandwiches."

Like it mattered. As if she'd be able to taste anything. She'd be lucky if she could keep it down.

"That's fine." Only it wasn't fine at all, and her stomach did another little flip to prove it.

The queasiness hadn't subsided at all ten minutes later when Cabe pulled a chair out for her at the quaint outdoor café on one of Boston's swankiest streets. The lunch crowd milled and bustled around them. Two food trucks parked nearby had lines several feet long. All in all, a perfect day to enjoy a leisurely meal outside. If only she could enjoy it.

Their food came out in no time. She was picking at her Caesar salad when things went from bad to catastrophic. Cabe was going to try to make small talk. And his first choice of topic: the absolute last thing in the world she wanted to get into right now.

"So, Jenna. If I recall, you have an older brother."

She had to discuss her broken, dysfunctional family, with none other than Cabe Jordan.

"Yes. Sam. You two must have been in a few of the same classes."

"It was just the two of you and your mom, right? How is she, by the way? Do I recall she hadn't been feeling well for a while?"

Jenna's blood froze in her veins and she lost her grip on her fork. It fell to her plate with a clatter so loud the sound echoed through the air. Of course he must have heard rumblings over the years. Stories about Amanda tended to get around.

Cabe stopped eating and stared at her.

She stammered for a response. There was no good way to talk about her mother. "Yes. Yes, she's doing better." Such a lie.

Cabe stopped eating. "I'm so sorry, Jenna. I hope it isn't anything too serious."

She so didn't want to go down this path. Any topic but her mother. Anything but discussing Amanda and her problems in front of this perfect man who grew up with the perfect family in his perfect home. But what choice did she have? He waited for an answer, staring at her expectantly.

"Uh…she actually is ill. In a way." She took a deep breath. "My mother's been having a hard time the past few years. Trying to kick a drug and alcohol problem."

Cabe blinked at her. Clearly, he hadn't seen that coming.

"She's trying really hard," Jenna added. Another lie.

In fact, her mother had just shown up at her door last night, asking for money for "groceries." When Jenna had insisted on taking her to the market herself, Amanda had grown violent, shattering a vase on her hardwood floor before storming out. She'd wanted groceries of the more liquid variety. It had been the last thing Jenna had needed as she'd been trying to finish up her presentation for today. Thanks to Amanda's visit, she'd been up most of the night due to the upsetting interruption.

"I'm sorry to hear that," Cabe said in a gentle and soothing voice.

"I'm sure you're a tremendous source of support for your mother," he continued. "She's lucky to have you."

Though her mother didn't see it that way. In Amanda's

eyes, Jenna always came up short. Even though if Jenna hadn't stepped in on numerous occasions, Amanda would no doubt be in jail. Or worse.

"I'm doing what I can to help her."

Cabe cleared his throat. The look he gave her was so understanding, so gentle that it made her breath catch. "It's quite admirable that you're trying to help your mother."

Oh, heavens. What could she say to that? She didn't have a choice but to help her mother. Otherwise, she and her brother would be left to deal with the cleanup.

"Thanks."

Several moments passed in awkward silence. So awkward that she wanted to give the waitress a hug when she interrupted to fill their glasses.

Jenna watched her leave before hesitantly turning her gaze back to Cabe. He gave her an unreadable look. Curiosity? Admiration?

She didn't and couldn't care. What did it matter what Cabe Jordan thought of her or her broken family? In a few days, he'd be gone from Boston and hopefully he wouldn't return for another three to four years. He would just go back to being nothing more than an electronic signature at the bottom of her office emails.

But for now, she still had to get through this godforsaken lunch with him sitting right across from her.

He'd never understand, Jenna thought as she pretended to eat. Even under the best of circumstances, she'd never be in league with people like Cabe or even his parents, who had always been so sweet to her. Cabe had probably never had to hide from a drunken tirade or had to clean up after a parent who'd barreled in at three in the morning then promptly gotten sick all over the carpet.

She and Cabe Jordan may have grown up in the same town, but they were from two different worlds.

## CHAPTER TWO

CABE PUSHED HIS plate away with half his sandwich still untouched. He'd lost his appetite. Clearly, Jenna had none, either, since she did nothing more than move lettuce around her plate.

He couldn't help but wonder. Maybe Jenna indeed did have some involvement in the jewelry theft. Was her mother in that much trouble that Jenna may have needed a large supply of cash to help her? Cabe didn't want to believe the worst, but his manager of security had been adamant that Jenna may indeed know something.

Damn. That would change things. Though wrong and criminal, if Jenna was guilty, she hadn't done it for herself but for her mother. She'd practically just admitted that she would do whatever she could to help her parent.

He'd decided back at the office that he wouldn't ask her about it there. Not in front of her friends and colleagues. So he'd taken her to lunch instead.

Now he just wanted to know the truth. He wanted to tell her he could help. That in turn she could get her mother some help.

After all, he and Jenna Townsend were not that different under the surface. His life could have easily turned out as difficult as hers if not for the random hand of fate all those years ago. Pure luck so often determined the entirety of one's life. He knew how lucky he'd been.

"Listen, Jenna," he began, not sure exactly where to start. Business school didn't prepare you for every scenario. "About my visit to Boston. There's something I came here specifically to see you about."

"Yes?" Her question was barely a whisper.

"I want you to know that I can be a friend as well as your corporate CEO."

Was she trembling? "You can be straight with me," he added. "I hope you realize that."

She gave her head a quick shake. "I'm afraid I don't understand."

"You really don't have anything you might want to talk about? Regarding the store, perhaps?"

"No. Not really." She swallowed. "Have I done something wrong?"

Cabe leaned back in his chair. If she did know anything, then she had the acting skills of a Hollywood-caliber actress. "Huh. You really have no idea what I might be talking about?"

"Not a clue."

Cabe tried to regroup. Damn. This conversation was becoming way too messy. "Allow me to explain. A routine inventory check last week by security resulted in a troubling discovery."

She sucked her bottom lip, and heaven help him, he lost his focus for a split second. "Why wasn't I made aware of this? As the regional manager of that store?"

"It's our policy to keep such matters quiet until a thorough investigation."

She gave her head a quick shake. "Investigation? What exactly was this troubling discovery?"

"One of the more valuable pieces seems to be missing. A bracelet."

Cabe watched as understanding dawned. Jenna sucked in a breath and grew as pale as the white linen tablecloth. "Oh, my God. You think I took it."

Whoa. He hadn't expected her to go there quite so soon. "Jenna, wait just a second—"

Her cheeks suddenly grew cherry red. "That's why you came down here yourself. You think I stole from my own store. You think I stole from *you*!"

It came so fast he didn't have time to react. Before he knew it, he wore the rest of his sandwich on his lap and his shirt was drenched in iced tea.

As he watched her storm away, Cabe came to three distinct conclusions. One, Jenna Townsend moved as fast as a prizefighter ducking a punch. Second, judging by her confusion and the vehemence of her reaction, she was most definitely innocent.

And third, if he didn't get to the bottom of it all real soon, he was likely to lose a damn talented regional manager.

Stupid. Stupid. Stupid. She would never learn.

Jenna bypassed the elevator and ran up the three flights of stairs to get to the floor that housed her office. She didn't want to risk running into anyone. How would she explain the tears?

To think, for a while there she'd believed Cabe Jordan might actually be in town to promote her! What a laugh. Instead, he'd accused her of stealing from him.

People like her weren't promoted to corporate-level positions. They were suspected of thievery. They were the first ones investigated when valuable jewelry went missing.

People like her dumped food on others' laps.

She tried to take a deep breath. She probably shouldn't have done that. It was reckless and impulsive. Rather than calmly and reasonably defending herself, she'd let her emotions take over. She'd succumbed to the urge to lash out.

Just as her mother would have done.

And she was her mother's daughter. The apple and the tree and all that. Why did she ever think she could escape that simple truth? The rest of the world wouldn't ever let her forget that fact.

It didn't matter how hard she worked, or how many hours she put in. All the years of studying and working her butt off didn't mean a thing to people like Cabe Jordan. The only thing they saw when they looked at her was where she'd come from.

She'd been fooling herself.

Well, if Cabe hadn't intended to fire her right there on the spot, there was no doubt he would now. She'd dumped his lunch in his lap! Never mind that she'd never actually stolen anything. She wouldn't even get a chance to defend her innocence now.

She no doubt should have handled it better. But she'd been barely functioning given what little sleep she'd gotten and the stress of being prepared for Cabe's visit.

How could he have even suggested such a thing?

She didn't realize she'd asked the question out loud until a voice across the room responded.

"Trust me, it wasn't easy."

Jenna's head snapped up. Cabe stood in her office

doorway, pants stained and shirt wet. She resisted the urge to cover her mouth in horror.

She pulled her planner out of the desk drawer. "I was just leaving."

"Could you recommend a good dry cleaner first?"

He had the nerve to joke at her predicament? God help her, if the coffee tray were still here she might have very well dumped more on him.

"Jenna, listen—"

"What?" she interrupted. "What could you possibly say to me? Do you want me to confess?"

He stepped into the room and shut the door gently behind him. "I simply want to talk."

"About how I stole from you?"

"I was given the information from my head of security. About a theft at the Boston store."

She crossed her arms in front of her chest. "Right. And then you decided that if something had been stolen, it must have been that no-good Jenna Townsend. She must have had a hand in the whole mess. It only makes sense. She comes from bad stock. She's never had much to begin with and she can't be trusted."

"Jenna, stop. That's not how this all came to be."

She merely glared at him. How dare he deny it?

He walked up to where she stood and gestured to the chair. "Please sit."

"Why? Would you like to accuse me some more? Should I call an attorney?" Now that she'd said it, she had the frightening thought that she may actually need one.

Her vision grew dark. This couldn't be happening. After today she may very well have no job. And no hope of finding one if word got out that she couldn't be trusted.

Despite all the years of hard work and sacrifice, she was going to end up penniless on the street. Exactly what she'd feared all along.

To think, the cause of her nightmare would be none other than Cabe Jordan, the man of her teenage daydreams. Who would have thought?

"Jenna, let's try to talk this out."

She lifted her bag. "Perhaps you want to go through this. Maybe pat me down before you let me go."

He blinked. "Pat you down? No. Of course not. I just want to clear all this up." He leaned over with both palms on the desk between them. "About a week ago my head of security requested an urgent meeting. Apparently, someone realized that a piece of rare jewelry at the Boston store had been switched out during a routine security department inventory. The real piece had been replaced with a cheap replica that looked exactly like the original."

"And you assumed I did it. Because you know where I come from and what I might be capable of."

He held one hand up. "Hold on. That's not what happened. The management team is always considered under such circumstances. It's just routine."

At her silence, he continued. "Additionally, there's an electronic log of anyone who's used their key to access that particular case, the one with the higher-end items. Your key was the one used."

Her blood went cold. But that just couldn't be. "Who says?"

"My head of security up at headquarters. He's always been very good at his job. I had no reason to distrust him."

Of course he didn't. "But you had every reason to distrust me."

Something shifted in his eyes. "Listen, Jenna. The only reason I came here personally was because it was you. I wanted to get to the bottom of it myself, do some investigating. But there's a sudden matter that needs my attention with a store opening in the Caribbean. I have to get down there. In my haste, I handled it very badly. I see that now."

People tended to do that with her, rush to judgment. She couldn't expect to be granted the benefit of the doubt, not given where she came from. Cabe may claim objectivity by saying he came to look into the matter personally, but it hardly mattered. No, she would have to find a way to fully clear her name, in such a way that there would never be any more doubt.

"There has to be some kind of mistake," she muttered, trying to think. There had to be an explanation, a way to prove her innocence. But how? She suddenly felt deflated. How could this be happening? Pulling out her desk chair, she plopped herself into it.

A sudden, encouraging thought occurred to her. She looked up at him. "The video? There has to be video footage. We have cameras all over the store."

He gave her a sympathetic look. "The video surveillance system was conveniently disengaged for a forty-eight-hour period on the fifteenth and sixteenth of last month. We believe that's when the theft occurred."

Oh, God. His words knocked the wind right out of her. If there was no video to exonerate her, she had no other ideas. Her eyes began to sting. There was nothing she could do, no way to clear her name. She had no job. She had no real family. She'd probably end up with a criminal record. Despite everything, all the years of busting her behind to get ahead, she'd end up like her mom after all.

Cabe Jordan would always question whether she was a no-good thief.

Wait a minute.

She snapped her head up. "Wait. What date did you just say? The fifteenth of March?"

He nodded. "Yes, that's correct."

"You're certain?"

"That's what I was told."

She knew it! Hopeful relief surged in her chest. "Cabe, I wasn't even in town the week of the fifteenth. I was away at a jewelry designers' expo in San Diego."

He quirked an eyebrow. "And?"

"And my keys were safely locked up in the main vault right here in this building. Including the one that would have opened that particular case. I have proof."

He didn't want to examine why he was so relieved. For some reason, Cabe had been hopeful all along that Jenna was completely innocent. And apparently she could prove it. "Proof? You have a way to prove your key was locked up?"

She nodded triumphantly. "Yes. The security officer on call the day before I left signed off on the paperwork. All my keys were locked up in the main vault before I left. Safe and secure."

"That's the correct protocol. Where is this security officer now?"

She shrugged. "I don't know. I'm not the one in charge of hiring and managing security."

Cabe pinched the bridge of his nose. "I have a sneaking suspicion he's no longer working for us. And that he has a very valuable piece of jewelry in his possession."

Jenna stood staring at him with satisfaction, clearly enjoying the upper hand. So she was indeed innocent. Just as he'd hoped. Heaven help him, he had to resist the urge to go and hug her. Not that she would have it.

"Guess your security head isn't as thorough as you would like to think," she said.

"In his defense, he's going through a rough patch personally. Clearly, it's affected his professional duties. I'll have a word with him."

She rolled her eyes at him and muttered something under her breath. He thought he heard the words "That's rich."

"Jenna, I know an apology isn't nearly enough. But it's all I have. My only excuse is that I've been swamped with various small projects as well as a major international expansion. I rushed and acted on something that I should have taken the time to examine more closely. I'm deeply, resolutely sorry."

Her face softened, and the effect nearly knocked him off his feet. "Thank you for that," she said simply, genuinely. "And I'm sorry for…you know." She pointed to his drenched clothing.

"Nah, don't mention it. I daresay I deserved a good food toss." He was also admittedly relieved. He didn't have to fire a dedicated and competent employee after all. That left only one problem. Things were extremely awkward now with a star employee who deserved better treatment than he'd just doled out. He had a major mea culpa on his hands. As usual, he had rushed to judgment, merely to save some time. Once again, he'd acted without fully thinking through the issue. Not a good attribute in a CEO, yet another character trait he had to work on.

First thing first. Somehow, someway, he had to make this all up to Jenna.

He was getting ready to say so when her assistant knocked and entered her office.

Nora stopped in her tracks when she saw the state of Cabe's clothing. "I'm sorry," she began. "Am I interrupting?"

"That's okay, Nora. What is it?" Jenna behaved like the consummate professional, addressing her admin as if nothing was wrong.

"The Wellesley store just called. They're panicked about their staffing shortage," Nora told her, her gaze still leveled at Cabe.

"I made two very strong offers this morning," Jenna said. "I have no doubt both candidates will take the job. Is that all?"

"One more thing," Nora continued. "The store manager at the Burlington site called again complaining about the lack of shelf space."

Jenna nodded. "Real Estate just called this morning about the sewing shop next door. It's finally shutting down, so we can take the space over. We'll sign the lease within the week."

Cabe watched in admiration. *Damn.* She really was good. Given her background and her hardships growing up, she couldn't have gotten this far in life without being smart and disciplined. Would he have fared as well? He had to wonder. If fate hadn't stepped in and turned his life in a different direction, would he have figured out a way to pull himself up the way Jenna Townsend had? All on his own, like her? Or would he have ended up on the streets? Or locked up in a cell somewhere? Or worse.

Jordan's Fine Jewelry absolutely could not lose someone like Jenna. Not for any reason, the least of which being his stupidity. If only he had someone like her in charge of the Caribbean project.

There it was.

The idea made perfect sense. Before this whole theft fiasco, Jenna's name had come up several times whenever a high-level position opened up at Corporate. She was already due for a promotion.

Perhaps he had a way to salvage the mess he'd made of this whole visit. And possibly even help himself in the process. He was about to make a very strong offer, too. One he hoped Jenna could not refuse. First, he had to get her to listen to him. And forget about what he'd almost just accused her of.

As soon as Nora left, Jenna stood and glared at him. "Well, now what, Mr. Jordan. Am I still under investigation?"

He reached out to gently take her by the arm. "Absolutely not. On the contrary, I need to show you how sorry I am."

She looked down at his hand, then back with clearly puzzled eyes. "Show me?"

"I assumed my security head knew what he was doing, Jenna. Please understand."

She stood silent, clearly not ready to cut him any slack. And why should she? He deserved her derision. How could he have let this happen? He hated looking misinformed. Or worse, appearing incompetent. Mistakes were a luxury he wouldn't allow himself in his position.

"You're one of the best regional managers we have at Jordan's Fine Jewelry," he continued. "I should have handled this differently. And I don't want to lose you over some…misunderstanding."

She visibly bristled. He really wasn't very good at saying sorry, not having had much experience. She had no idea how hard he was trying.

"This was more than a mere misunderstanding."

He nodded. "I realize that. I think I can make it up to you."

She pulled her arm free. But she was clearly listening. "How?"

"I could use the services of a competent and experienced regional manager to help me with a project."

Her chin lifted. "What kind of project?"

"I'm sure you know we're trying to expand internationally, starting with the opening of a new store in the Caribbean."

"Yes, I know."

"You should also know that so far it hasn't gone at all smoothly. In fact, I need to be there within two days to put out the latest fire."

She narrowed her gaze on him. "What does that have to do with me?"

"Come with me, Jenna."

It took a moment to process Cabe's words. "Are you offering me another job?"

He nodded. "One that comes with a higher title. And the adequate adjustment in pay, obviously."

Jenna's head spun. Within the span of a few minutes, she'd gone from decrying the loss of her next paycheck to being offered a promotion. If she examined the matter too closely, Cabe's offer might very well be construed as a bribe.

But it was also an opportunity of a lifetime. A very tempting one.

Cabe motioned to her desk chair. "Please have a seat. Let's discuss this."

Her pride pushed her to turn her back and walk away, slam the door on her way out. Her business-school-trained brain had other ideas.

Begrudgingly, she pulled out her chair and sat down. "What exactly did you have in mind?"

The look of relief on his face sent an odd shiver down her spine. She didn't dare read too much into it.

"I'm tired of trying to get this new site up and running by myself. I've been meaning to hire someone. You're perfect for the job."

"Cabe, you can't just expect me to forget that you were ready to believe I may be capable of theft."

"But that's exactly what I'm asking you to do," he said with the confidence of a successful tycoon who's used to getting his own way. "Rather than spend inordinate time on an extensive talent search, I'd like to offer you the position. You've been considered for several corporate positions recently, but none seemed to be the right fit for you. Until now."

"This is not how I imagined being promoted."

"That makes two of us. This is definitely not how I imagined doing the promoting. One way to look at it would be to say that we're going to start fresh," he added.

Maybe he had a point. But she wasn't about to let him know that. Why let him off easy? Clearly, Cabe Jordan was used to having things handed to him merely because he asked. Unlike someone such as her who'd had to work hard all her life for every accomplishment.

A small part of her nagged that resisting might indeed be a mistake. She still needed this job, pride or not. What if he called her bluff? Her pride won out. "You have to understand, Cabe. I'm no longer sure how I feel about working for you. Given our past history as friends, and that you've known me for decades, I would have appreciated it if you'd come to me right from the start." Oh, heavens. She nearly choked on the words. For all her bravado, she had to acknowledge that he'd genuinely and wholly hurt her. She'd been foolish to expect any more from the Jordan CEO, regardless of past friendship.

But then Cabe held both hands up in surrender and she had a split second of panic. For all her bravado, she really would prefer to be gainfully employed as she looked for another position. Her breath held while he spoke.

"Let's compromise. You just help me on this one overseas project. We'll start from there."

"And then what?"

"Then we revisit the situation and the matter of your employment."

She gave her head a small shake. "You're going to have to be more specific."

"I just mean that I don't think you should make any lasting decisions right now, in the heat of the moment."

Jenna's phone rang but she ignored it, unable to tear her eyes away from Cabe's intense, steel-blue gaze. "We don't want to be impulsive."

She decided to give in just a little. "Perhaps we don't."

Cabe pounced, assuming success. "Do you have a

valid passport? If not, we can request rush processing and you can meet me there once it arrives."

She raised an eyebrow. "Cabe?"

"Yes?"

"Do you actually know the definition of *impulsive*?"

Her question gave him pause, and then he laughed. "I see your point. Nevertheless."

"I have a current passport."

"Great. It's settled, then."

She stood, met him eye to eye. "Not so fast, Cabe."

Was that a smile still on his lips? He couldn't be enjoying this. "Before I say yes, I have a stipulation."

"What's that?"

"Once the new site is opened, upon completion of this project, I want a glowing recommendation from you. In case I decide to look for a position elsewhere."

"I hardly think that will be ne—"

She cut him off. "It's nonnegotiable. I want your word that you will assist me if I decide to leave Jordan's Fine Jewelry." It was the least he could do. After all the long hours of blood, sweat and tears that she'd put into this company. After the way he'd just treated her. And for all the work she was about to put in on this project. He owed her at least that much.

He merely nodded. "If, at the end, a recommendation is still what you want then I will give you one."

"It will be."

He crossed his arms in front of his chest and gave her a wide smile, the kind of smile that would have had her swooning if they were still in high school. Even now, her knees grew weak.

"Not if I change your mind."

# CHAPTER THREE

JENNA TOWNSEND HAD clearly never been on a private jet before. Cabe guided her into the cabin and tried not to react to *her* reaction, though he had a comical urge to gently nudge her mouth closed. Instead, he patiently waited as she took small, hesitant steps up the stairs and into the aisle.

Unfortunately, there remained an awkward tension between them. In the interest of business, he chose to ignore it. She thought she might be looking for another job after the Caribbean project when it was completed. He had other ideas.

Well, he'd deal with that scenario if it happened. He'd been watching Jenna in action since he'd arrived in Boston and he had very different plans for her. He was not about to let her go anytime soon.

Now she stood in front of him, taking in her surroundings as they entered the aircraft. Cabe let her take her time.

As far as private planes went, his wasn't terribly extravagant. Pretty much standard issue. Leather seats, a mahogany table so that he could get some work done. In fact, his only indulgence had been the fully stocked bar.

"Jenna, please, have a seat." Cabe gently guided her

toward one of the leather chairs and waited until she was seated before sitting down himself.

She immediately clicked on her seat belt and tightened it. She appeared to be more than merely awed. She seemed apprehensive, downright uncomfortable.

"Are you okay with flying, Jenna?" He knew she'd been on business trips before. So what was making her so jittery now?

The smile she gave him was strained, almost shy. "Mostly. I have to admit, flying is a bit of a new experience for me. We didn't travel much when I was a child." She glanced around at her surroundings. "And as far as flying in something like this…"

"It's just more convenient than flying commercial, that's all."

She let out a small laugh. "Right. Convenient."

Something he couldn't name tingled inside him. In so many ways, Jenna's reaction to his aircraft was refreshing. How many countless women had flown with him privately over the years? None of them had even seemed to notice the lavishness around them. Every one of them had taken for granted that they'd be arriving at their destination in the lap of luxury.

Ironically, rather than making him feel smug, her genuine awed reaction made him feel petty. Hadn't he been taking it all for granted himself? But he knew better than anyone that money couldn't fix everything.

He cleared his throat somewhat awkwardly as they both settled into their seats.

The flight attendant appeared momentarily. Cabe almost groaned out loud. This particular one could be quite the flirt. Normally, he let it slide and tolerated her suggestive comments. For some reason, he really wasn't in the mood to deal with it today. Not with Jenna here.

"Mr. Jordan. So nice to see you again," she said, her smile wide and inviting. She barely spared a glance at Jenna. He couldn't quite remember, but thought she had been the one to slip him her personal phone number after one flight.

Why did it bother him that she would flirt again this time? What was happening to him?

He had to remind himself this was nothing more than an ordinary business trip. He was way too focused on the woman—rather, the employee—accompanying him. That would have to change. And soon.

"Is there anything I can get for you, Mr. Jordan? Anything at all?" the woman asked, her emphasis on the repeated word impossible to miss.

He turned to find Jenna staring out the window, her cheeks stained slightly pink. Dressed in a smart navy pantsuit, her hair up in another impossibly tight style. Not one tendril drifting anywhere near her face. How in the world did she get all that hair to behave? He had a crazy image of unclipping the pin that held it all together, running his fingers through her long, thick tresses. He shook it off.

"Jenna? Is there something you'd like? Some wine, perhaps?"

Jenna shook her head. "No, thank you. I don't dare drink wine. I'll fall asleep."

"Are you sure?" He glanced at his watch. "We'll be in flight for a while. You definitely have time to take a nap."

Her eyes grew wide. You'd think he'd just suggested that she fall asleep on the job. Which in a way, he guessed he had. He laughed at her shock. “Jenna, it’s all right. You’ll be much more productive if you’re well rested.”

“Why do I get the feeling that’s like the pot calling the kettle black?”

He laughed and dismissed the attendant with a polite nod. The woman hesitated, clearly disappointed, before finally stepping away.

“We’ll even have some time to enjoy the sights while we’re out there,” he added.

She gave him a small smile that sent an inexplicable surge of pleasure through his chest. “That would be nice. I’ve never been to the Caribbean.”

“Do you like the beach?”

“Yes, of course.”

“What about fireworks?”

Her eyebrows drew together. “I love fireworks. What do the two have to do with each other?”

“The resort where we’re staying, the one I’m trying to establish the retail store on, has a beach party every Thursday night. Live band, plenty of food and drinks. And fireworks.”

“Sounds like quite a fete.”

“Today’s Thursday. We should go tonight. It would be a good way to introduce you to the island’s characteristic atmosphere.”

She chewed her bottom lip. He watched it swell and redden and redden. *Focus.* “Cabe, I’m not sure that’s such a good idea.”

“Why not?”

“I feel that it would just be better if we solely stuck to the business at hand.”

Cabe shifted in the chair. Jenna appeared so tense, so anxious. He wanted to help her loosen up somehow.

But he was her boss. He had to tread carefully. Given her upbringing, it was no wonder Jenna seemed unable to relax and just enjoy life once in a while.

He couldn't blame her. Maybe he was the flip side of the same coin.

He wanted to tell her there was no reason to be so uptight around him. He wanted to show her how to relax. His motives were pure and simple. Perhaps that would make her rethink her decision to eventually leave the company. She didn't have to constantly toil to get ahead. He wanted her to see that.

Work hard. Play hard. She definitely seemed to have the first part down. He knew for a fact she'd stayed very late at the office last night finishing up last-minute details she didn't want to delegate before leaving.

"I get the sense you don't take many vacations."

"Well, I told you about that jewelry designers' conference in San Diego."

"That was a business trip, Jenna. On behalf of the company."

She shrugged. "Sure. But I made time to visit the zoo one afternoon."

So maybe there was hope for her yet. She was a tough cookie, tougher to crack than any woman he'd ever dealt with. He couldn't help but think how pleasurable it would be to see her enjoy herself. She was one of those rare people who truly deserved it. Though she clearly didn't believe so. He found himself both curious and intrigued. What kind of personality would this highly accomplished, intelligent woman have developed if she'd had even the simplest of breaks in life? How much more dynamic and spirited would she be?

"I'm afraid you will have to do some social mingling while we're there," he told her.

She pursed her lips. Clearly she didn't like that concept. "How so?"

"Opening a new site requires much more than pushing paper around in an office. Much of it requires networking. The resort employees are very friendly and outgoing people; you'll be working with most of them. You don't want to appear to be the standoffish stiff suit from Corporate."

Sure, it was a bit of an exaggeration, but not exactly a lie. It *would* help to have her get to know the resort employees and the regular guests. Though pushing the matter could be very dangerous ground he was treading. He couldn't seem to help himself.

"Like going to this island party, you mean?"

"Parties are considered by most people to be fun, Jenna."

"I've never had much time for them." She tilted her head in his direction: her implication was clear. *Unlike yourself.*

He was quite aware how well-documented his social life was. "Believe it or not, most of those galas I'm photographed at have some type of business angle. Nine times out of ten, I'm not there because I want to be." And lately, each party had been more tiresome than the last. It was becoming harder and harder every time to feign a level of interest he simply didn't feel.

She raised an eyebrow. "Yes, you looked downright pained in that latest photo. The one on the yacht where you're popping open the bottle of champagne, surrounded by bikini-clad socialites. How do you stand it?" Her tone held such mock seriousness he couldn't help but laugh. Surprisingly, his laughter earned a small chuckle from her as well.

"Those photos aren't always what they seem," he responded.

Her mouth tightened into a thin line. "Well, most of the parties I've attended, I wasn't there to enjoy myself. I was there to work, serving or to clean up afterward."

"Is that how you helped pay for your education? Working at social events?" he asked. No wonder she didn't associate social events with anything remotely pleasurable. And no doubt she'd watched her mother cross the line far too many times with all sorts of partying. Jenna Townsend had never been afforded the opportunity to simply have fun and enjoy life, not even as a child.

She nodded. "One of the ways. I did all sorts of odd jobs. Mostly waitressing. The catered parties paid better than, say, waitressing at the diner." She turned back to him as the aircraft began to taxi down the runway. "Your parents were particularly generous. I worked some of those swanky backyard barbecues your mom and dad were known for. I think you were off at college by then."

Had she? She'd never been at any of the ones he'd been present at. He wouldn't have missed her.

"I would have noticed if you were there," she said, surprising him.

"You would?"

The red stain of her cheeks grew deeper. "Of course. You were a minor celebrity in school. Big man on campus."

"I guess I was a bit driven, even back then."

"That's an understatement."

"Yeah, well. It's not like I was doing it for me."

She studied him with interest. "Who else?"

Cabe shrugged. "My parents were very busy people. I figured out at a very young age that I could either get their attention by rebelling and getting into trouble. Or I could try and excel at everything. I chose the latter."

Funny, he'd never admitted that to anyone before. But he wanted Jenna to understand that what outsiders saw of his life as a teen wasn't the complete picture.

"Did you so much as ever get detention?" she asked with a sly smile.

"I think once. It wasn't my fault. I was merely at the wrong place at the wrong time."

"That happened to me a lot," she responded.

"Getting detention?"

She shook her head. "No, being at the wrong place at the wrong time."

Cabe was about to ask her to explain, but Jenna turned and looked out the window as if she'd prefer the conversation to be over.

Perhaps she was right—sometimes the past was better off left to stay there. Though he remembered those years well—all the parties his parents held that Jenna had referred to. Including memories of the first corporate outdoor luncheon he was allowed to attend. He must have been around age fifteen or so. He'd been so nervous, making sure to say all the right things and behave in all the right ways.

The Jordan Golden Boy.

He'd acquired the moniker right around that time as well, due to his stellar grades and lightning-fast skills on the basketball and tennis courts. Accomplishments he worked his behind off to achieve. All to make himself worthy of the Jordan family.

When he'd first found out that he was a Jordan in name only.

What had she gotten herself into?

Mistake. This whole trip had been a mistake. She'd been a fool to take on this assignment. She'd been a fool to think she could play in Cabe Jordan's league on her own terms.

She was only going on this trip and working on this project in order to get the achievement on her résumé. Not for some kind of working vacation. Cabe had to realize she wasn't the type to do island-wide parties.

As if traveling in his private jet weren't enough, she might have to accompany him to a lavish tropical extravaganza. With fireworks! How was she supposed to act distant and unaffected? How was she supposed to avoid falling under Cabe Jordan's spell? He was charming enough under the most innocuous of circumstances.

By the time their jet landed, Jenna still hadn't figured it out.

Cabe stood and offered her his hand. "Ready?"

Of course not. But she simply nodded and let him guide her out of the aircraft, his hand placed gently at the small of her back. She knew he was just being courteous. But his touch wreaked havoc on her senses. The man had absolutely no idea of the effect of his presence. Didn't he see how women around him practically swooned at his feet? The flight attendant being a perfect example.

Yet somehow she was supposed to ignore the way his hand on her back sent a tingle clear down to her toes. Or how he so casually vowed to "show her a good time" while here.

She nearly tripped over the last step as they disembarked.

"Are you all right?" Cabe said behind her.

"Yes, I'm fine. It's just much hotter than I'd anticipated." That was no exaggeration. A wall of heat and humidity enveloped her as they walked toward the small stucco building that housed the island's airport. Her smart, fitted suit jacket instantly clung to her skin.

"It'll get better," Cabe assured her. "The airport is always ten to fifteen degrees hotter. You'll feel more comfortable once we're closer to the beach with an ocean breeze to temper the heat."

And what was going to temper her reaction to Cabe Jordan? She'd said too much on the flight over, drifting dangerously close to "pity me" territory—something she'd sworn never to do over the years. She wasn't about to start now. Not even if Cabe's significant charm had her tongue loosening.

And what was his story? All those things he said about having to prove himself growing up. His accomplishments had seemed to come so easy to him when they were kids. Maybe that had all been an illusion. Not that it was really any of her business. Cabe was her boss.

A sleek town car awaited them outside once they were through with customs. The driver was a pleasant tall man with skin the color of mocha coffee. He kept up a steady stream of conversation with Cabe as he maneuvered the busy streets. Based on the familiarity, Jenna guessed he was Cabe's regular driver on the island.

Jenna found herself too distracted by the scenery outside to focus on their conversation. Among lush, green mountains and the majestic sight of the ocean, the roadside sat peppered with run-down, decrepit shacks. Such poverty among such beauty. On a much smaller scale, it reminded her of the way she'd grown up—the days when they weren't sure they'd be able to eat while just a few miles away stood the glamorous, ritzy grandeur of downtown Boston. Well, she'd fought tooth and nail to climb out of that bleak existence. And she was proud of it. She'd done it on her own, through hard work and discipline. Unlike her mother, who still to this day waited for the right man to come along and save her—a rich, powerful man. Well, that idea hadn't really worked out for any of them. Jenna knew better than to fall for such fantasy.

Within forty-five minutes they arrived at the resort. After the striking displays of poverty on the roads they'd just passed through, it was like entering a different world.

A guard outside a tall, metal gate pushed a button to let them through.

"You have a few minutes to freshen up," Cabe told her. "Then I'd like to show you around, particularly the shopping center attached to the resort. You can see where the new store is to be built."

"I won't need that much time," she answered, grabbing her things off the seat. "I'd like to get started as soon as we can."

He lifted his head and stared at her, as if studying some unfamiliar object. "I know we're in a bit of a time crunch but there's no need to be quite so rushed, Jenna."

She shrugged. "I'm just anxious to get going, that's all."

"Well, we're on island time now. Things always move slower down here. You may as well relax."

As if that was possible, Jenna thought, watching him remove his jacket as the car came to a stop outside the entrance. His shoulders strained against his well-fitting tailored silk shirt. Deft fingers removed his cuff links and he rolled up his sleeves to reveal toned, tanned arms. His days on the Caribbean had certainly given him a good dose of color.

She tore her gaze away. None of this was at all conducive to relaxing in any way. The driver helped her out of the car and she emerged to the light sounds of steel-drum music in the air. The aroma of exotic flowers hit her as she stepped out. They were surrounded by lush plants and thick greenery. And large colorful flowers like she'd never before seen. She wanted to run up and inhale the scent of every single one.

A tall, statuesque woman with a thick braid down her back approached them. "Mr. Jordan. So nice to have you back," she said to Cabe with a glowing smile.

"Glad to be back, Seema," he answered. "Though I wish it were for a more pleasant reason."

Her smile wavered. "More snags?"

"I'm afraid so." He gestured toward Jenna to join them. "But this time I have some help. Meet Jenna."

Jenna put her hand out to greet the woman but she had other ideas. Jenna found herself gripped in a tight hug.

"Welcome to the Paraiso Resort. So glad to have you here, Miss Jenna."

"Please. It's just Jenna. And I'm very glad to be here." It surprised her how much she meant it. The woman's friendly warmth magnetically drew her in.

"May I show you to your rooms?" she asked them both while a bellman grabbed their bags.

"We're right behind you," Cabe said.

Jenna tried to take in her surroundings as they were led away. Paradise. She had entered paradise. A piece of pure heaven. She could hear the gentle waves in the distance. The clear crisp air refreshed her despite the muggy heat. She loved her hometown city of Boston but this was an entirely different world.

A world full of beauty. To think, she'd almost turned down the opportunity to come.

She had to admit it to herself. Cabe was right to bring her here.

Cabe let himself fall slightly behind as they walked through the resort to the hotel room area. Seema was giving Jenna a raving summary of all the resort's amenities and attractions while Jenna listened carefully. He took a deep breath, finally allowing himself to relax. The scent of the ocean, the crystal-blue sky and the characteristic local friendliness worked their usual magic and he felt the tightness in his shoulders give way little by little.

He could hear the gentle crashing of waves and the sounds of laughter coming from the beach. A small salamander darted out and ran in front of them on the path. Jenna shrieked and jumped back, clutching her chest. In the process, she barreled right into Cabe. Realizing the intruder was a small lizard, her panicked expression turned to one of amusement. She laughed out loud, prompting him to laugh with her.

Instinctively, his arms went protectively around her

middle. “Close call,” he said against her ear. “But you’re safe.”

“You didn’t tell me I might be ambushed by small green creatures on this island,” she admonished with a chuckle.

“I was just hoping for a chance to rescue you.”

“I hardly needed rescuing,” she countered. “I was just startled, that’s all.”

He smiled at her. “Right.”

Seema gave them a curious look. With hesitation, he finally let Jenna go and they continued walking.

Life could be so simple in the Caribbean.

They were finally here. After his colossal mistake in Boston, he wasn’t so sure he could pull it off. Getting Jenna here was one thing. Now he had to get the project off the ground with her help, all the while trying to convince her to stay in his employ afterward. Employees like Jenna were hard to come by. And if she left, he’d have no one but himself to blame.

She couldn’t leave the company. He didn’t want to have to explain her loss to his parents.

His mom and dad put a lot of faith in him, their only child. So far, he liked to think he’d done well by them and made them proud. What he’d told Jenna on the flight here was the truth. He’d had two choices as an adolescent growing up. He could gain attention through rebellion or through accomplishment. Otherwise, his parents barely seemed to know he existed. Their grief had been encompassing and powerful, as it still was to this day. He chose to be an achiever because he realized at a young age just how lucky he was.

In his position, mistakes were out of the question. He couldn’t afford the luxury of making any.

He watched as Jenna rubbed the back of her neck and nodded at something Seema told her, her face squinted in concentration. Even from this distance, Cabe could tell she was processing all the information about the resort, making mental notes. She really was one of a kind.

No matter what it took, he wasn't about to lose Jenna Townsend.

## CHAPTER FOUR

"WOULD YOU LIKE to walk the rest of the way along the beach?" Seema asked her with a pleasant smile.

Jenna turned to Cabe, who gave a small shrug. "It's up to you. Though you should know, your shoes will definitely get sandy," he said, pointing to her smart navy pumps.

As if she cared. Right now, Jenna could think of nothing better than to feel soft, Caribbean sand between her toes.

"Why not?"

They took a right and the pathway led them through a network of buildings, bungalow-style structures with wooden steps spiraling up to tall doorways. The sounds of the ocean grew gradually louder and soon she could see the gentle lapping of the crystal-blue water and the golden silky sand that framed it.

She felt like she was in a travel catalog, each page a new and wondrous scene of bright, colorful images. Why had she never traveled here before? Money was always tight and her student loans were the top priority, but surely she could have scrounged and scraped and somehow over time pulled it off. How had she allowed herself to miss this part of the world for her whole adult life?

Without a cloud in the sky, the sea gleamed like liquid jewelry. She wanted so badly to run in and dive under the water, fully clothed. The image made her smile. She dared a glance at Cabe. Dear Lord, he'd undone a couple of his top shirt buttons and it took all her will to look away and not stare at the revealed patch of tanned golden skin.

Seema suddenly stopped, forcing Jenna to look around her at the reason. A procession of well-dressed men and women followed a small girl in a white lace smock toward an elaborately decorated archway on the beach.

A wedding. The scene took Jenna's breath away. A small band played reggae music next to rows of wooden chairs. Four bridesmaids dressed in calf-length, silky maroon gowns made their way down the path in front of them. Instead of shoes, their feet were adorned with golden chains and sparkly gemstone jewelry. The effect was both exotic and bohemian.

Jenna couldn't help but let a small "ooh" escape her lips. The women were all so lovely.

"Would you like to stay a moment and watch?" Seema asked her.

As much as she wanted to maintain the air of the unaffected professional, she couldn't tear herself away from the scene. She glanced at Cabe, who gave her a small nod.

"Yes, please."

Right behind them came a line of four handsome, strapping young men dressed in light gray suits. Hands clasped in front of them, they walked over to the bridesmaids' sides. The band switched to a rhythmic, reggae version of "Here Comes the Bride."

Jenna's breath caught when the bride emerged from a canopy off to the side. She was downright stunning. In a long silky white dress, she moved like a surreal vision. A tiara of colorful flowers sat on the crown of her head. A collective sigh sounded from the bridal party and those in attendance as she walked down the aisle, escorted by an older gentleman with gleaming silver hair. He looked both teary-eyed and happy.

Jenna found her eyes had moistened as well. How silly of her. Why in the world was she so moved by a beachfront wedding?

It made no sense whatsoever. None.

"Jenna? Are you all right?" Cabe materialized in her line of vision. Great. Just great. She was a sniffling fool who couldn't handle the sentimentality of watching two strangers get married.

"I'm fine." She thought about lying, claiming that sand had blown in her eyes and irritated them. But something told her he would see through that. Though they'd barely known each other growing up and though he'd only been a signature at the bottom of her memos for the past few years, Cabe Jordan seemed to be able to read her very well.

"It's just that she's so beautiful. And the scene is so touching," she admitted instead. "You wouldn't understand," she added. How could he? He'd grown up with the best that life had to offer. Two parents who were still together and who took good care of him.

He looked away. "You'd be surprised."

Jenna studied him. What could that possibly mean? Why did she want so badly to find out?

Seema patted her arm. "We have a well-earned reputation for planning the most romantic and unforgettable weddings."

"They seem so in love," Jenna said, staring at the laughing couple. "So lucky to have found each other."

"Luck is a mysterious thing," she heard Cabe say.

"Do you have something against weddings?" she asked him, then felt foolish for doing so. What a nonsense question to ask your boss.

"I don't really give them a whole lot of thought" was his reply as he turned back to them. "But they're certainly good for business. The resort caters to families as well as couples," he told her. "I've heard stories of couples traveling here to get engaged. Then returning for their wedding. And several years later, coming back with their toddlers in tow." She detected a hint of sadness in his voice. But that was silly. Surely she'd imagined it.

"And don't forget," Seema added. "When they marry here, the honeymoon immediately follows."

That was the most wonderful thing Jenna had ever heard.

"That's what this place is all about," Cabe said. "Love and family." His tone held an unmistakable tinge of something she couldn't place. Longing, perhaps? Again, just a silly thought. Cabe Jordan surely couldn't have wanted for much in his full and privileged life.

Boisterous applause from the wedding party suddenly erupted and she turned to see the bride and groom kiss each other in front of a smiling clergyman.

A profound sense of sadness overcame her as she watched the couple embrace. Everyone cheered them on. Friends, family. They were all so happy for these two people.

She could never hope to have such a happy ceremony in her own future, even if she met someone. She had no real family—only her brother, who was struggling just to get by as she was. She'd long ago given up on the hope that her mother might one day clean herself up and become the kind of woman who'd be able to help her daughter plan a wedding. That was a downright laughable thought.

She had no father figure to walk her down the aisle and tear up as he gave her away.

What did it matter? She had her life planned out. She had only herself and her brother. And that was fine. Her goals were set and clear. None of those goals included finding a mate and settling down. She'd be perfectly content with a fulfilling job and financial security. Even if she never met Mr. Right.

Her gaze traveled in Cabe's direction and she had to snap herself back. Thinking about Cabe in such a way was a slippery slope she did not want to find herself tumbling down.

Not that he was ever likely to see *her* in any kind of romantic light. She was no supermodel or high-profile actress, his usual type.

She shook off the useless thoughts. Nothing would be gained from them. She was here to do a job, not fantasize.

Still, it was hard not to imagine herself standing in front of a crystal clear ocean, under the bright blue sky, as the love of her life looked her in the eyes. Once more, an unbidden image of Cabe standing before her popped into her head and she nearly gasped out loud.

Now she had passed the boundary from fantasy into foolishness. As if.

On top of everything else, the man was a notorious womanizer.

She took a steadying breath and turned to Seema, avoiding Cabe's eyes at all costs. "That was lovely. You certainly know what you're doing in the wedding planning department."

"Thank you. We pay attention to details and try to make sure everything is perfect."

It certainly appeared that way to her. "I'd love to see the rooms. Something tells me those will not disappoint either."

Seema tilted her head and gestured with her hand for them to follow her. "We always reserve the best rooms for Mr. Jordan and any of his guests."

And how many "guests" had he previously traveled here with? Again, a wayward thought that didn't matter.

Jenna turned to catch one last glimpse of the fairytale wedding. The dancing had begun, right on the beach, in the sand. The flower girl seemed to be particularly enjoying the music. She and an older woman were happily dancing in the water as waves splashed at their feet.

Jenna made herself look away. She was happy for the unknown couple. She really was. They truly did appear to be an example of the lucky few who were fortunate enough to find their soul mate. But one never knew for sure. How often had her mother been convinced she'd found "the one," only to have the whole thing fall apart and send her into another downward spiral? Too often to keep track of. Each of Amanda's relapses being usually much worse than the last.

The sounds of bottle corks popping and joyful laughter followed them as they left.

Cabe watched Jenna as they opened the door to their suite. She inhaled sharply upon stepping inside.

The resort had provided his regular suite—he'd made certain of it. Jenna would be in the adjoining room and they'd share the center living area where they could work and go over the planning and budgeting of the new store.

Seema showed Jenna to her room as Cabe took the time to sign onto the Wi-Fi and check his messages. It was clear from the snippets of conversation he could hear that the two women were becoming fast friends. He wasn't surprised. Jenna seemed to be one of those rare authentic and open people who drew others in. She didn't even realize she was doing it.

When Seema bade them both goodbye several minutes later, Jenna wasted no time in getting to work. She hadn't even slipped off her shoes.

"Do you want to go over the project plan?" she asked.

"Why don't you freshen up first? Can I pour you a glass of wine? Then maybe we can grab a bite. The Hibachi restaurant on the premises is world-renowned."

She seemed perplexed by the question. He really had to figure out a way to get her to loosen up. People so often accused him of being a workaholic. Jenna Townsend could give him a run for his money any day.

He really wanted to change that. But he really didn't want to examine why.

"Wine? Now? With you?"

From the look on her face and the incredulous voice, you'd think he'd asked her to go streaking through Boston Common in the middle of a Saturday afternoon. "Or we could have soda. Or some juice."

She shook her head. "I'm not thirsty."

"Jenna, that's a lie. How can you not be thirsty? Or hungry? We've been traveling all day."

She swallowed. "If it's all the same to you, I'd rather just go over some of the to-do items for this trip and then call it a day."

Disappointment washed over him. The soft, affected woman who'd gone teary-eyed watching the beach wedding was nowhere in sight now. He couldn't help but feel it had something to do with him. Jenna Townsend turned into the stony, consummate professional whenever they were alone.

He pointed to the clock above the mantel. "It's five-thirty. We gained an hour due to the time change. There's still hours of daylight left. You'll be miserable if you don't fight through the jet lag and adjust to the new time."

Silence.

He sighed. "Jenna, look. It's been a tiring day. I don't know how productive we're going to be on an empty stomach after such a long trip. Sure, we can go over some paperwork. I think that's a great idea. But I'm going to have a glass of the resort's house Cabernet while we do so. I'd highly recommend it—it's spicy yet smooth with a hint of citrus. But of course, you can drink whatever you'd like. After which, I'd like to grab a bite of dinner, preferably at the Hibachi restaurant. I'd love for you to join me."

"It hardly sounds productive."

"You can't be productive if you're starving."

She pursed her lips. Most things with her seemed to

require a fight but he couldn't help but admire her tenacity. "This is no different than a working dinner that we may have had back in Boston. How about after dinner, we tour the mall where the new store is supposed to go. It's in an adjacent building to the restaurant. Everything is connected here."

She lifted her chin. "I suppose that makes sense. But…"

At least she was giving it some thought. Cabe realized he was holding his breath. He'd been on this resort countless times, both with and without companionship. Carmen had joined him just last month, lounging by the pool or on the beach during the day and then joining him for an evening meal and entertainment afterward.

But he'd also dined alone here on numerous occasions. The friendly staff being so accommodating and social, eating by himself had never bothered him.

Yet he found he really didn't want a solitary meal tonight. He wanted Jenna's company. He wanted to ask her how hard it had been to go to business school given all her responsibilities and lack of support. He wanted to talk to her about why she was so hesitant to let her guard down. He wanted to ask her about her brother. How hard had it been to put herself through school? He wanted to learn so much more about her. It would probably be the most interesting conversation he'd had with someone in ages.

Maybe it was all those years growing up that he'd had to eat his dinners alone, his parents either too busy or preferring to eat an "adult meal" by themselves. Maybe it was all catching up with him for some reason.

"But you have a different idea, I'm guessing," he said.

She lifted an eyebrow. "As a matter of fact, I do."

He waited.

"We go over the files while I have a cup of tea. And then we visit the mall. Before dinner. So that while we eat you can familiarize me with the logistics and the details."

He groaned and rubbed his stomach with mock exaggeration. She visibly fought hard to control it but an amused smile touched her lips. "As much as my hungry stomach protests..." He stood and extended his hand. "Deal."

Her smile turned to one of satisfaction and she reached for his hand to shake it. Her hand felt small in his, her skin soft. Cabe found himself not wanting to let go, silly as the notion was. Was her skin that soft, that smooth all over?

"Great. You grab a tea bag while I pour myself some wine," he said, finally dropping her hand. What in the world had come over him?

She turned to do so. Her smart, sensible pumps clicking on the tile.

Three hours later, after a tour of the mall and a very entertaining dinner, they made their way back toward their suite by way of the beach. The picnic tables were already filling up for the evening's festivities. Buffet tables lined with desserts, fruit and beverages framed the sitting area. All of it faced a makeshift dance floor with large speakers on either side.

"This is the big party?" Jenna asked, slowing her stride.

Cabe nodded. "Takes them a while to set up. I can drop you off back at the room and come back once it's in full swing."

Though the thought of coming back alone didn't exactly appeal to him. The last one of these he'd attended, Carmen had accompanied him. His feet hurt just thinking about it. The woman had an insatiable desire to dance the night away; no amount of partying seemed to be enough. He'd barely gotten a chance to sit all evening.

He wanted to experience the party through Jenna's fresh eyes. No doubt she'd be impressed if she just gave it a chance.

He was debating the wisdom of asking her again when they were interrupted by the sound of feminine laughter. Seema ran up to them, flashing a delighted smile.

"Jenna! I'm so glad you've come to our grand gala," she exclaimed and gave Jenna's shoulders a squeeze.

"Oh, I'm not—" The woman didn't give Jenna a chance to complete the protest. She took her by the elbow and guided her toward the middle of the action, closer to the speakers and dance floor. Jenna had changed into a flowing summery dress that clung to her in all the right places. But with her hair still up in that tight ponytail, she hadn't lost the look of the serious professional. Though at the moment she looked quite uncertain.

Cabe gave her an apologetic shrug when she glanced back at him.

By the time he reached the two women, Jenna was tapping her toe in tune with the music, swaying slightly with the beat. Midway through the song, Seema excused herself when a young gentleman asked her to dance.

Jenna laughed out loud when the young man twirled Seema onto the dance floor.

"Can I dare to say that you might be finding this enjoyable?" Cabe asked.

Jenna ducked her head but not before he caught the small smile. "It does seem very festive. And the music is very catchy."

He lifted a fresh coconut speared with a straw off one of the tables and reached it out to her.

She shook her head and put a hand on her midsection. "No way. I'm still full from dinner."

He handed her the drink. "Just one sip. You've never tasted coconut water unless you've had it straight from the fruit."

She scanned his face then finally leaned over to take a sip while he held the fruit out to her.

When she lifted her head, a tiny drop glistened at the bottom of her lip. For an insane moment, he wanted to reach out and wipe it away with his finger. Sanity won out and his hand tightened into a fist at his side. He pointed at her mouth instead.

"You just have a little…"

"Oh!" she exclaimed and wiped it away with the back of her hand.

"Well? What do you think? Better than the supermarket bottled kind?"

"It's heavenly. I wish I hadn't eaten so much."

"We'll make sure you get one tomorrow."

He went to take his own sip and her eyes grew wide. He'd shocked her, using the same straw she'd just had her lips on. Surprisingly, he hadn't even thought about it. A boss and his employee could drink from the same straw, couldn't they? Though he'd be hard-pressed to think of any other employee he'd ever done such a thing with. Plus, he had to admit, anyone watching them right now might get a different idea about who exactly they were to each other.

A look around suggested as much. The usual staffers he'd come to know gave them curious glances. He should have announced more widely that he'd be bringing a colleague with him this time around. The last thing he or Jenna needed was a swell of gossip as they were trying to get this project off the ground. If things went as planned, Jenna would spend a lot of time here working with these very people. He didn't want to impact their impression of her before they'd even had a chance to form one.

And he certainly didn't need her to be viewed as the boss's toy.

He was straddling a fine line here. He had to be careful not to step over the edge.

"All right. You win," she said with a small sigh.

"Win?"

"I have to admit, this is quite a party. I'm glad I didn't miss it."

He felt a surge of pleasure clear to his toes. How juvenile, but he was ridiculously happy that she was enjoying herself. Finally. To the point where she felt compelled to admit it.

"I would say I told you so…"

She laughed out loud, a mesmerizing, melodic sound that made him chuckle in return. Something about the sound of her laughter made him want to join in her merriment. "And you essentially just have," she told him.

"Do I appear smug?"

She pinched the fingers of her right hand. "Just a smidge."

"Well, forgive me. But do you know what it took to

get you out here? Worse than negotiating a store lease agreement. It was quite a challenge, I must say."

Her smile widened. "Yet another one that you've met and conquered."

"Was that a compliment? Or a dig? Somewhat hard to tell."

She shrugged, watched as a gaggle of dancing teenagers pranced by them. "Merely a statement."

He took another sip of the coconut drink. "Pity. I was hoping for the former."

"Fishing for compliments, are you?"

"My ego is a fragile thing." He held his hand to his chest with mock melodrama.

That laugh again—he could easily get used to it. "Something tells me you come by compliments quite often," she said.

He took a moment to respond, deciding to throw caution to the wind. "Some compliments mean more than others, given the source."

She sucked in a breath. He wanted to suck the words back as soon as they'd left his lips. Jenna wasn't some new acquaintance; he knew better than to sound even remotely flirtatious. Where had that statement even come from?

They stood side by side now, the party growing ever larger around them, the crowd gradually becoming louder. Cabe waited apprehensively for her response. When she finally did, it wasn't at all what he was expecting.

"I'm sorry," she said.

"Whatever for?"

"My comment was a bit personal. Inappropriately so, I'm afraid."

A jarring sense of disappointment settled in his gut.

Jenna was pulling the curtain of propriety between them. She was right to do so, of course. He was the one being foolish enough to let it bother him.

He turned to face her, though she remained in place and continued to look straight ahead. Definitely uncomfortable. “No need to apologize, Jenna. We’ll be working very closely for quite a while. You can ask me anything. Personal or not. What would you like to know?” Now he’d definitely thrown down the gauntlet. He’d never said those words to anyone else before. What was it about this woman? She was like the smoothest Caribbean rum. Or truth serum.

“What makes you think I have questions about you?”

“There’s nothing you’d like to know?”

Why was he doing this? Why did he want so badly to get her to probe? But he knew the answer. For some bothersome reason he couldn’t explain, he wanted Jenna Townsend to see through his outer demeanor. He wanted her to see the real man beneath the business titles and web articles. For the first time in his life, he wanted a woman to look inside the shell that was Cabe Jordan.

He wanted her to know the truth: that he was nothing more than a fraud.

# CHAPTER FIVE

HOW IN THE world had she gotten here?

Never mind the trip itself. What was she doing here at this boisterous beach party? While Cabe hand-fed her drinks, no less. Of course, she was having fun. But that was hardly the problem.

No, the problem was her reaction to the man here with her. How aware of him she was. They way her heart had pounded in her chest when he'd taken a sip off the same straw she'd used just an instant before.

Now he stood inches from her side, goading her to ask him the questions that had been tumbling around in her head. Right. Like she could ever come out and admit just how curious she was about him. Had he sensed her curiosity? Or was he just used to people being inquisitive about him?

She could swear she felt electricity crackle between them as he waited for her response. Did he feel something also?

She was a fool. Of course he didn't. He was a worldly businessman; conversations like this one certainly amounted to nothing more than small talk for someone like him. And here she was with her heart hammering, falling for his charm.

She shook her head. "I can't think of anything I'd like to ask," she lied.

He looked away but not before she caught the clear flash of disappointment in his eyes. Her heart plunged at his expression and she sucked in a deep breath. She'd clearly let him down with her response.

That was it. She couldn't stay. A few more minutes and she was out of here. She turned to tell him so just as a tall man in a silk maroon shirt and well-fitting white pants smacked a hand on Cabe's shoulder.

"So I see you're back, my friend."

Cabe turned to greet him and the two men shook hands. Cabe's smile didn't quite reach his eyes. Animosity etched his features. She had to wonder if the use of the word "friend" was a bit of a stretch, at least as far as Cabe was concerned.

The man turned to flash her a megawatt smile. "I see you have the most beautiful woman on the island at your side."

Jenna resisted the urge to mock-fan herself. Wow. What a charmer. Cabe's fake smile turned into an all-out frown.

He introduced her while the man lifted her hand and brushed his lips across her knuckles.

"Jenna, this is Maxim Rolff. He's in charge of the on-site casino."

"A true delight to meet you," Maxim said.

Maxim was elegant—tall with dark chestnut hair and a thin mustache that would look silly on most men. On him it looked regal and distinguished. She could easily see him charming vacationers to bet significant amounts of their hard-earned money, particularly the women.

"Nice to meet you," she said with a polite smile.

"Jenna is working on the store opening with me," Cabe told him.

Maxim winked. "Works with you, does she? Glad to hear it."

What was that supposed to mean?

"I hope I can assume that you'll be spending a lot of time on our little island," Maxim said.

"It looks that way."

"Superb. I'd love to show you around the gaming tables while you're here."

Cabe jammed his hands in his pockets. "She'll be pretty busy, Maxim. We have a lot to do."

"Pity. Still, she does need to get to know the resort. And the casino is no small part of it."

"I'd love to check it out sometime," she said and stole a glance at Cabe. His frown had definitely grown. She didn't think he was even trying to hide it. "If timing allows," she added.

Maxim took her hand once more, held it. "We'll make sure of it. Won't we, Cabe?"

"Like I said, we both have a lot to do."

Maxim hadn't torn his gaze off her. "Don't let him work you too hard, my dear. It would be a shame to waste such beauty without fully appreciating it."

Cabe actually snorted. "Are we still talking about the island?" His question had Jenna gasping with surprise.

Maxim laughed. "Maybe. Maybe not. So what is it exactly that you do for Cabe?"

"I'm just assisting him with the opening of the new store."

Cabe stepped closer to her side, their shoulders almost touching. If Jenna didn't know better, she'd think he was trying to slightly push her farther away from Maxim. "Modest to a fault. She's going to be my right hand on this project. By title, she's my regional manager for the New England area."

Maxim lifted an eyebrow in appraisal. "Impressive."

She could feel the heat of Cabe's skin brushing against her shoulder. "Yes, she is."

"You're lucky to have found her," Maxim added.

Jenna stiffened in shock as Cabe threw an arm around her shoulder. "Jenna and I have known each other since we were kids. We grew up in the same town."

Maxim's brows lifted. "Ah, so friends as well as colleagues."

She couldn't come up with anything to say. Cabe's stance was definitely a possessive one. All she could summon was a tight smile.

"I look forward to seeing more of you, Jenna," Maxim said. "And please, if you can steal away from your over-demanding boss, stop by my office. I'll give you the grand tour of all the gaming attractions." He lifted her hand for another kiss before turning to leave.

"Well, that was interesting," she commented as they watched Maxim walk away. Cabe kept his arm on her shoulder for another beat, then dropped it to his side.

"*Interesting* is one word for him."

She had to laugh. "Do I dare ask what other ones you have for him?"

"Sure. Cunning. Sly. He's one to keep an eye on."

"Why do you say that?"

Cabe accepted a bubbling glass of some kind of fizzy punch from a passing waiter. He offered it to her but she shook her head to decline. Taking a swig, he threw another stare at the retreating man's back.

"He's a notorious flirt. As you just witnessed."

"Some people might call that friendly," Jenna countered. "After all, the Caribbean is known for its hospitality. You said so yourself."

"That wasn't friendly. That was shameless. The way he was flirting with you so blatantly. He would have tried to sweep you off your feet if I wasn't here with you."

A silly jolt of pleasure shot through her core. If she didn't know better, she might say Cabe was acting protective. Maybe even jealous.

But that was a ridiculous notion. He clearly simply disliked the man. And he probably didn't want her distracted when she had so much to do.

That was all.

"Come on. Let's go," Cabe said, setting down his drink on a nearby table.

Finally. She was oh, so ready to retire. Her head was spinning. Between jet lag, exhaustion and Cabe's mere proximity, her senses revved on overdrive. Plus, the party had suddenly crowded with dozens of revelers who had somehow shown up all at once when she wasn't paying attention.

But instead of leading her toward their building, Cabe took her by the arm and led her to the middle of the beach. Right toward the dance floor.

"What are you—?"

Her words were cut off when he grabbed her by the waist and pulled her into the crowd. Right into the middle of a conga line. Her knees grew wobbly. She'd never been much of a dancer.

This was a new experience, Jenna thought as she fought to get her bearings. She might have fallen forward on her face if Cabe wasn't holding her. Without any choice, she reached out and held on to the waist of the woman in front of her and tried not to grip too tight. Then she just made her feet move.

"You're not kicking," Cabe said loudly into her ear from behind.

Was he serious? It was all she could do not to stumble into the conga dancer in front of her. With Cabe's fingers splayed across her midsection, holding her. She felt the strength in his hands, his touch warming her flesh through her dress where he held her above her hips. Even in the middle of this large and noisy crowd, his touch felt intimate, private.

Oh, Lord. She had enough trouble keeping her wits around him under the best of circumstances. Now she had to ignore his touch and try to dance at the same time.

"It's one-two-three kick and kick," he told her, shouting above the noise.

This was so not the time for a dance lesson. "I've never done this before," she yelled back over her shoulder.

"It's easy," he said, then laughed when she stumbled yet again. "You can do better than that. You're just not letting yourself."

"I'm trying not to let myself be trampled."

He laughed and she felt his warm breath against the back of her neck. "Don't think too hard. Just relax and let go."

Hysterical laughter bubbled up inside her. Relax, he said. Right.

"I won't let you fall, Jenna."

She believed him. And surprisingly, as soon as he

said the words, some of the tension left her body. Her legs started moving easier, more fluidly. She moved much smoother in the line, not disrupting it nearly as often.

Now that she was no longer horrified, she had to concede that she was actually having fun.

Her respite was short-lived. Just as she was finally synchronized with the other dancers, the music changed. The beat slowed drastically to a smooth, rhythmic reggae tune. Definitely not a conga. Almost everyone around them stopped to find a partner and began to slow-dance.

Jenna's pulse hammered. Sure enough, she turned to find Cabe watching her expectantly. She wanted to turn away, to run from him. But when he lifted his arms and beckoned, she found herself stepping into his embrace instead. He gently wrapped his arms around her, clasping his hands against her lower back.

Then Jenna promptly stepped on his foot. To his credit, Cabe didn't so much as wince. At her mortified gasp, he dipped his head toward hers. "Don't worry. You'll quickly get the hang of this, too. You're a natural."

Jenna's mind barely registered his words. He was so close, she could smell the now familiar sent of sandalwood combined with the sea salt air. The heat from his hands warmed the skin at the small of her back as he swayed with her to the music.

She should pull away, Jenna thought. Thank him politely and then just make her way off the dance floor. She really wasn't being terribly professional at the moment.

As if reading her thoughts, Cabe's hold on her tightened ever so slightly.

"Just relax. You can't dance to a slow song when you're tense," he coaxed.

She wanted to say something, anything. But her mouth had gone dry.

Surprisingly, once again her body reacted to Cabe's words. She felt some of the tension leave her muscles, and the tightness in her shoulders lessened. She leaned into him, let her head rest on his hard chest. She heard his heart beating against her ear, the steady rhythm soothing her down to her soul. She was beyond comfortable in Cabe Jordan's arms. It wasn't that preposterous. She knew Cabe. She'd known him most of her life. They'd grown up within a few short miles of each other, had roamed the same school hallways. And right now, she felt completely safe and secure in his arms.

What was happening to her? Who was this girl, dancing on a silky beach with a wildly handsome, enigmatic man she had no business being attracted to? She'd never behave in such a manner if they were back in Boston.

Or anywhere else on the planet, for that matter.

This wasn't her. Some type of island magic had turned her into someone else. The song ended and Jenna awkwardly stepped out of Cabe's embrace. A foreboding expression shuttered his face, a tic working along his jaw. Her pulse was hammering as well. Before she could think of anything appropriate to say, a beaming Seema ran up to them, holding something out to her.

"Congratulations, Jenna. You won!" Jenna looked down at the object the other woman handed her, three small gold statuettes mounted on a marble base—dancers in a conga line.

A trophy. Jenna had never been rewarded a trophy before.

"You were selected as the best conga dancer at the party," Seema exclaimed, her smile beaming.

Clearly, a sympathy win. Still, Jenna found herself inexplicably pleased.

"Wow. Thanks." She couldn't help the wayward smile that sneaked to her lips. "I've never won anything like this before. And especially not for dancing."

Seema gave her a hug before walking away.

"Nice job," Cabe told her. "Your first time and you get a trophy."

"No doubt it's for *most improved.* Still, this will look great in my office."

He studied her. "You're really excited about it, aren't you?"

She felt the flush creep into her cheeks. "You wouldn't understand. You most certainly have cases and cases full of all the trophies you've won over the years. All the athletic competitions you won."

"There were a few first-place math-club ribbons as well."

Jenna rolled her eyes with amusement. "None for modesty, I'm guessing." She rubbed her finger over one of the small statues. How silly of her to feel so touched—it was just a cheap trophy. One she didn't even really do anything to win. But she was proud of it just the same. "Like I said, you wouldn't understand."

"I'm glad it means something to you, Jenna."

"You're laughing at me. You must be, given all the real awards you've won over the years."

He shook his head. "No, I promise I'm not laughing at you. Trust me, my trophies never meant much. Not to anyone."

Something in the tone of his voice gave Jenna pause.

Cabe took a swig of his drink. "No one ever really saw me win them, after all."

"What are you talking about? The whole school witnessed you win or place most every contest." But as she said the words, an odd thought struck her—Cabe's parents had been noticeably absent at all those events. In fact, now that she really thought about it, she'd be hard-pressed to recall ever seeing James or Tricia at a single school game or play.

Despite the fact that their son had been the star at most of them.

The cursed insomnia plagued him again. Cabe tossed with annoyance onto his side in the king-size bed and noted the time on the bright digital clock. Twelve-thirty. He hadn't slept at all. Nothing unusual about that. But this was the first time it had happened in the Caribbean. Usually the combination of the heat, the long travel time and a packed agenda had him falling asleep before his head hit the pillow.

Not so this time.

Cabe knew the reason. He couldn't help but replay the events of earlier this evening repeatedly in his head: Jenna by his side as he led her through the beach party. The way she swayed to the music. Her delight at the colorful night sky as it burst in fireworks. The way she'd felt in his arms.

He'd behaved utterly unprofessionally.

Especially once Maxim had shown up and expressed a clear interest in her. He'd never been a fan of the overbearing man. But this was the first time he'd actually felt a desire to do him physical harm. And it showed.

Cabe hadn't tried hard enough to hide his animosity.

Then he'd really lost his mind. He'd taken her to the

dance floor. And he hadn't let her go when the music slowed.

It was unacceptable and he couldn't let it happen again. He was treading on thin ice as it was when it came to Jenna Townsend. He couldn't seem to stop acting erratically where she was concerned. He sighed and rubbed a hand down his face.

Outside, the party was still going strong. The band, contracted for up until an hour ago, continued to play. Island time was fluid. They would quit when they felt like it. And people would dance up until they did. The night was muggy and the air conditioner wasn't quite keeping up, none of which helped his insomnia. Shirtless, with just his pajama bottoms on, he reluctantly got out of bed.

He may as well go out onto the balcony for some fresh air. Maybe it would help.

Pulling the screen door open, he stepped into the moonlit night and watched the glitter of the ocean.

Jenna's light was on next door.

Her screen door sat adjacent to his on the same balcony. Though her blinds were shut, it was obvious she was still awake. He could hear her shuffling about. Either she was a night owl or she was having trouble sleeping also.

Well, he wasn't about to ask.

He'd been careless enough with her today. The last thing he wanted to do was knock on her door in the middle of the night.

He heard more muted sounds coming from behind her screen door. What was she doing in there?

Without warning, her screen door flew open and

she stepped outside with a huff. She did a double take when she saw him.

"You're awake," she observed, her eyes wide.

"And so are you."

He leaned over the banister, his arms resting on the railing. He didn't want to think too much about the formfitting tank top she wore or how it offered a tantalizing view of her shoulders, nor the thigh-length boy shorts she had on. Or how they sat low on her hips. Hips he'd had his hands on just a few short hours ago. His fingers tingled at the thought and he shook it off.

"What's keeping you up? The music? The sounds of laughter and partying?"

"None of the above," she answered. "Sorry. You probably wanted some time alone. I'll just go back in."

Damn it. He wanted her to be more comfortable around him. She didn't have to feel like she had to dash inside just because he was out here, too.

"Jenna. We are obviously both having trouble falling asleep. I'm out here to get some fresh air. So are you. There's plenty of it for both of us. We can share our insomnia."

She halted on the threshold and pivoted back. "Okay, then. But I don't have insomnia."

"No? You could have fooled me."

"I can't sleep because I can't stop scratching. My legs in particular are in bad shape."

He glanced down. "Sand fleas."

"Is that what caused the coin-sized itchy welts all over my calves?"

He bit his lip to keep from smiling. It really wasn't funny. "I'm sorry. I should have warned you. Some people are more susceptible to them than others."

"Oh, I appear to be one of the lucky ones."

"Is it bad?"

"I'm ready to scratch my skin off."

He approached her. "Can I take a look?"

Even in the dim lighting of the half-moon, he could see her cheeks redden. "I'm sure it'll be fine. I'll just go soak in the tub or something."

She turned to step away but stopped when he leaned down to her feet. He studied her legs, trying not to notice the toned shapely flesh of her thighs and how they led up to feminine, rounded hips.

Yep, she had several angry-looking bites.

"Soaking won't help," he informed her. "The hot water might actually make it worse."

"Great. Just great."

"But you're in luck."

She gave him a look of disbelief. "Um. How so?"

"Last time I was here I had a couple of bites. Seema gave me something for them. Seemed to work really well."

"Two whole bites, huh? And I'm the lucky one?"

He laughed and motioned for her to come inside his room. "Follow me."

She hesitated. "That's okay, Cabe. I don't want to interrupt your night any longer."

There she went again. Why was she so damn timid around him? Did she think he would bite her, too? Not that the thought hadn't crossed his mind.

"There's no reason to suffer, Jenna. I'll just go get you the stuff."

Without waiting for a response, he turned and walked inside and to his bathroom. She was still waiting outside on the balcony when he returned with a tube of ointment.

He handed it to her. “This works wonders. Put a dime-sized amount on each bite. Here, I’ll help you.”

She looked mortified at the thought. “I can do it.”

“Fine.”

Taking the tube, she went to work on the numerous spots, some already on the verge of breaking open.

“It stings at first,” he warned just as she let out a cry of “Ow!”

“Sorry.”

Several moments later, she handed the tube back to him. “Thanks again.”

He sensed her hesitation. “Is there something else?”

She looked away, off to the side. “No. Good night.”

He reached out and took her by the arm to stop her as she turned on her heel.

“Jenna, what is it?”

She closed her eyes and let out a deep breath. “I feel one just below my shoulder blade. It’s very itchy.”

“I see. You can’t reach it.”

She sighed. “I’ve been trying to scratch it all night.”

“To no avail?”

“I wouldn’t ask but—”

“It’s okay.” He gently turned her around and lifted her ponytail up. Apparently she even slept with her hair in a cursed bow. He fought the urge to untie the ribbon and release her thick curls.

*Focus.* Sure enough, right above her tank’s line, she had a nasty-looking bite immediately to the bottom of her left shoulder blade.

“That one’s a mosquito bite,” he told her. “It appears all sorts of things are attracted to you.”

*Damn.* Why in the world had he said that? An awkward silence fell between them before she finally broke it.

"I can't even reach it to scratch it."

"That's because you're not double-jointed." He laughed but she didn't respond. "I can't see how you're going to locate that one let alone reach it. Here, let me."

Before she could argue, he uncapped the tube and began to apply the ointment.

His breath caught as he touched her. Her skin felt warm beneath his fingers. He found himself leaning in closer. The aroma of her hair teased him, a hint of strawberries and a subtle feminine scent that was distinctly her own.

"Jenna." He whispered behind her ear, unable to help himself. His arm moved of its own accord to reach around her middle. She stiffened for the briefest of moments but then went totally lax against him. Her back against his bare chest. She felt like heaven and he knew he shouldn't be doing this. Shouldn't be holding her like this or touching her even. Hadn't he just vowed as much? But he couldn't seem to let her go. All he could do was repeat her name.

As if on cue, the clouds shifted and erased the faint moonlight they'd been bathed in. Only the dim artificial beams from the party lights in the distance afforded them any hint of respite from the dark.

"You were lying earlier, weren't you?" he found himself asking foolishly. "When you said you weren't curious about me. That you had no questions to ask."

He felt her exhale a long, deep breath. Several moments passed before she replied. "Yes," she finally admitted on a whisper.

She turned her head and his gaze fell to her lips.

What would she taste like? He wanted desperately to find out.

"So do it now. Just ask me."

"I don't know, Cabe. It feels too much like gossip."

"It's okay, Jenna. We're having a conversation. That's very different."

He felt her shrug. "I can't help but see it that way. Your family has always been a source of gossip. So elevated, so unattainable."

He'd help her. "And you want to know if any of the rumors are true?"

She exhaled under his arms. "There were too many rumors to keep track of. It was more the general sense of the villagers talking as they stared at the castle."

He let out an ironic chuckle, though he felt anything but amused at the moment.

She made no effort to turn around and face him. Thankfully. Talking was so much easier this way, with her in his arms, both of them staring off at the dark shadow of the ocean in the distance.

"It was far from a castle."

His words had some kind of impact on her. She stiffened as he said it, suddenly tried to pull away. He instinctively held on to her, didn't let her leave his arms. "What?" he asked, taken aback at her reaction.

"Says the crown prince."

He'd offended her. How could he explain it to her? Did he even want to? That what she grew up seeing was a facade. A well-crafted, expertly framed image of the perfect family. The reality had been so very different.

"It wasn't quite a fairy tale, Jenna. Please believe that." At her silence, he added, "You don't, do you?"

"You said on the beach that your trophies never

meant anything. Are you trying to tell me your life was anything less than idyllic? How so? You're going to have to explain it to me. Because it sure looked that way to me and anyone else in that town."

The skepticism in her voice rang clear and loud. He swallowed, tried to gather the words.

"You know what?" Jenna said. "Never mind. Forget I asked. I only did because you told me to."

"I know. And I meant it. I'm trying to answer in as truthful a way as possible." He took a deep breath. It was true. Something about her, maybe her strength or her openness, made him want to confide in her in a way he hadn't done with anyone else. Maybe it was the way she'd looked at him after they'd danced together on the beach. He wanted to open up more of him for her to see.

"We were supposed to appear that way," he began. "It's what we wanted everyone to see when they looked at us. Do you understand?"

She shook her head slowly, her soft silky hair skimming the stubble on his chin. "I'm afraid I don't."

"From the outside, we projected the image of the perfect little family."

"But inside the castle walls?" she prompted.

*Cold.* It was the first word that came to mind. Followed by *distant* and *unfeeling.* "It's hard to explain."

Her spine stiffened slightly. "Cabe, are you saying that Tricia and James were…?" She paused to take a deep breath. "That they didn't treat you well?"

Damn. She'd just jumped to the absolute wrong conclusion, that he'd been abused somehow. Physically or emotionally. That was also far from the truth. The truth sat somewhere in between.

He was really making a mess of this whole conversation. First he'd come off as the clichéd poor little rich boy. Now he'd led her to believe he'd been harmed by his very own parents. He should end this. He should just drop the whole thing and bid her a hasty good-night. But having her in his arms felt like some sort of balm. It felt right, her pressed up against him, numbing his senses. Dulling the pain.

If he stopped now, if he let her go and walked away, he'd never make his way back.

Not with Jenna. Not with anyone.

He'd never again find a way to open up about the darkness that hung over his perfect life like a heavy curtain, casting all sorts of shadows.

So he took a deep breath and just let it go. "I'm not a real Jordan, Jenna. I'm not really James and Tricia's son." The words hung thick in the air between them. Another layer pulled away from the fantasy.

What he didn't say was that his very existence was a result of his parents' greatest tragedy.

Jenna stilled. Trying to absorb what he'd just told her, no doubt. He couldn't blame her. He knew no one at school ever suspected. James and Tricia were that good at hiding the reality. And so was he.

He finally turned her around to face him, grateful for the darkness that hid what his expression must have held. "I was adopted by James and Tricia as an infant."

She lifted a shaking hand toward his chin. He resisted the urge to turn into it. "I didn't know," she offered.

"You weren't supposed to know. No one is. We moved into town when I was a preschooler. Started the business right after."

"It doesn't make you any less their son."

How many times had he heard that over the years from James and Tricia themselves? Just words. He'd always seen the truth in their eyes. The harsh reality: if they hadn't tragically lost their real son, they wouldn't have even known Cabe existed.

"Thank you for that. But it does."

She sighed, hesitated before she spoke again. "Did it bother you so terribly? Because you never showed it."

He shrugged. "The fact that I was adopted? No, that's not what bothered me."

"Other things?"

"Like I said. It's hard to explain."

"I know your father has always been very proud of you. Everyone in town knows that."

"I worked hard and made sure of it," he said. He'd tried so hard to earn their affection. He'd studied longer, played harder. Everything in his teenage power to make himself what he thought they wanted in a son. None of it was ever enough. "Still, there were those ever so rare times when I caught him staring at me," he told her.

"Staring how?"

"It's not important."

"Please tell me."

He let out a small laugh. "I don't know. He just had this look on his face, you know. A look that made me wonder and think about the reality." He'd spent his whole life trying to erase that look off his father's face. But no amount of achievement had done it so far. Nor had any of it erased the chronic, haunting sadness in his mother's eyes.

"What reality?"

The one that had shaped him since that fateful day when he'd turned fifteen, Cabe thought. That was the day the mystery fell into place just as the whole world around him crumbled. He wanted the knowledge of it off his chest, once and for all. His very heart told him that this was the moment, the chance he thought he'd never get. The woman in his arms was the key to lightening the burden. They'd grown up in such different ways but she'd be the one to understand somehow. Jenna would know what he meant when he told her that he'd been given everything he could have wanted as a child and teen. Except for one minor omission: genuine, honest parental affection.

He sucked in a breath and choked out the words. "That I would never have been their son if they'd had the choice."

"Oh, Cabe. But they did choose you," she said, her voice gentle and soothing. The situation was almost surreal, the way he was opening up to Jenna Townsend on a dark balcony in the middle of the night. Finally having the words out in the open combined with the heady way she said his name sent a surge of pure longing through him. Instinctively, he pulled her closer against him. She let out a soft moan and his gaze fell to her lips. What would they taste like? He dipped his head to find out. A mere brush of his lips against hers. Hardly a kiss at all. But it was enough to rock him straight through to his core. She sighed against his mouth and he wanted more, needed to taste her fully. He pulled her closer so that he could plunge into those lips deeper.

The band outside suddenly stopped playing and a loud cheer erupted, shattering the moment in a fast instant. The effect was like a splash of cold water. Cabe reflexively dropped his arms and for a moment they both stood frozen.

What in heaven's name was he doing?

He ran a hand through his hair. "Jenna, I shouldn't—"

Her sharp gasp cut him off. She stepped away as if struck by lightning. He almost reached for her but some small speck of sanity stopped him.

Without a word, she turned on her heel then fled into her room. He could only watch as she closed the screen door and pulled the curtain closed. In more ways than one. Her light went out an instant later.

Leaving Cabe in the dark shaking with need. And wondering what the hell he'd been thinking.

What in the world had she been thinking? She should have just turned right around and gone back into her room the second she saw Cabe out on that balcony. She'd tried but not hard enough. But then she'd never have known.

Jenna lay in bed and listened to the chirping of the birds outside as the darkness of dawn slowly evolved into a bright sunny morning.

She hadn't slept a wink.

In a couple of short hours, she was supposed to meet Cabe for a working breakfast meeting. Calmly and professionally. She had no idea how she would pull it off. They had to address what had happened between them and everything he'd revealed.

He'd certainly dropped a bombshell on her. Cabe was not the Jordans' biological son. And he seemed very affected by it.

There had to be more to the story. For instance, why had the three of them kept the truth so under wraps? And for that matter, Cabe may have been adopted but he still seemed to have led a charmed life. But the man she'd encountered last night seemed very different than the impression she'd always had of him as the high-achieving, handsome playboy.

His words echoed in her head. *It was supposed to look idyllic from the outside.*

He'd been drinking last night. It wasn't any kind of excuse but it was more than what she'd had. She'd been stone-cold sober while practically melting into his arms. Oh, Lord. He'd kissed her. Well, almost. He'd touched his lips to hers and would have gone further before Jenna had found some semblance of sanity. The memory of it quickened her pulse and that just made her madder at herself.

The kiss didn't mean anything. It couldn't have. She would blame this magical location, being so far from home in such an enchanting place. So far removed from reality.

Even if Cabe was attracted to her, which he seemed to be last night, it wasn't anything to dwell on. She wasn't the type of woman Cabe Jordan was ever going to be interested in long term. They belonged on two different spheres.

Still, what he'd revealed about himself last night led her to the age-old saying: appearances could be deceiving. There was clearly more to her boss than the image she'd held for all these years. As much as Jenna had wanted to pry and get to the bottom of it all, she'd resisted. It clearly cost him to reveal as much as he had. Cabe would tell her the rest when he was ready. She would be there, available for him when he needed her.

*But he pushed you away at the end.*

There was that. She tossed aside the covers and got out of bed.

She was contemplating it all still two hours later after showering and getting dressed when she heard Cabe's knock.

She took a deep, fortifying breath before opening the door to greet him.

"Good morning." He didn't mean it. He looked miserable and he clearly had slept about as much as she had. Still, even with the dark circles he was utterly, heart-shatteringly handsome in his stone-gray suit and crystal-blue tie. Her mind automatically shifted to the way he'd felt last night, hard and firm against her back. She could still smell the hint of his sandalwood scent, could still feel the way his breath had felt against her cheek. The firmness of his lips as they'd touched hers.

*Stop it.*

She stepped aside to let him in. He didn't move though, which surprised her. Then she saw the look on his face. Regret. He thought the whole balcony encounter was a big fiasco. A mistake. He'd probably been kicking himself all night for divulging his lifelong secret. To someone like her, no less.

"Are you ready to go?" he asked.

Jenna blinked. That was all he was going to say to her?

No hint of the gentle, open man from last night could be detected this morning. The one who'd bared his soul to her. Well, what had she expected? That he'd sweep her in his arms the moment he saw her, overwhelmed at the sight of her and all that they'd shared in the darkness?

"Do you need another minute?" he asked, glancing at his watch.

Jenna gave her head a shake. "Um, no. Let me just grab my things."

She forced a smile upon returning to the doorway. "I'm ready."

He silently turned and made his way down the stairs. Jenna stared in stunned silence before following. Now what? Did she dare say something? The awkward silence was downright unbearable. Cabe seemed in no hurry to break it. Perhaps she'd only imagined last night. Maybe it had only been a crazy dream.

No.

It had been real. She had the bug bites to prove it.

Blasted bugs. They were the reason all this was happening. If only she'd taken a moment to peer outside last night before she'd jumped out on the balcony. She would have never gone out if she'd known Cabe was there. Her legs had been itchy and stinging but no amount of balm was worth the discomfort and awkwardness of this moment.

Instinctively, she reached down and rubbed the biggest bite on the top of her thigh.

"Did the ointment not work for you?" Cabe asked, his tone brusque.

"It did. It worked great. Thank you."

"Don't mention it."

The double meaning was clear. Cabe wasn't going to bring up anything that had happened on that balcony. Nor did he want her to. The tight set of his jaw left no question about it.

Also no question that he deeply regretted it all. A brick settled in Jenna's chest. Such foolishness on her part not to see this coming. Cabe had succumbed to a moment of weakness last night. Nothing more. She'd just conveniently been there. He'd been tired, probably missing the companionship he usually had on these trips.

"I'll get you some more of it later. We have a lot to do today. We can't have you distracted. Not by itchy bites, not by anything."

Her composure almost faltered and she gritted her teeth. Subtle, he wasn't.

"I hardly feel them," she threw out. Two could play at this game.

He didn't bother to look at her. "Good."

Her eyes stung. She tried to convince herself that it was the bright early-morning sun. It was easier than facing the truth.

Just as well they'd be busy all day. The busier the better. The less time she had to think and dwell on senseless emotion, the better off she would be.

She just had to hope her highly honed focusing skills didn't let her down. It wouldn't be easy given that she'd be spending the day side by side with Cabe. After a night where she'd done nothing but toss and turn and think about him and what they'd shared.

All of which Cabe was telling her to forget.

# CHAPTER SIX

CABE WANTED TO hit something. An hour spent in the resort's gym at the break of dawn followed by a two-mile jog along the beach had done nothing to ebb his agitation or his anger at himself.

Jenna knew the truth. There was no turning back on that now. At some point he had to acknowledge it. Just not now.

Of all the asinine, idiotic—

"Is something wrong?" Jenna asked him as they reached the podium where the maître d' greeted them with a smile.

He realized he'd cursed out loud. "I was just saying, this is the main dining area of the resort. Vacationers can eat here at any time of day."

She studied him with clear doubt. "Oh, really? Is that what you were saying?"

He didn't respond as they were seated. Their table sat poolside and faced the beach, affording them a perfect view of a clear and sunny horizon. A waiter immediately greeted them and poured steaming hot coffee into two porcelain cups. A moment later, he brought out a tray of assorted pastries and platters of eggs and crispy potatoes.

They went to work right away, going over the numerous to-dos that would lead to the opening of the new store. Jenna impressed him repeatedly with her knowledge and insight. Not to mention her ability to offer solutions to matters that would have taken him twice as long to figure out by himself. Though he had numerous people working on the endeavor both in New York and on the island, he found it invaluable to have another mind just to help him with the sheer volume of details involved. He couldn't have chosen better than Jenna.

They made quite a team.

A team he couldn't risk jeopardizing again by doing anything foolish or reckless. The way he had last night. What had he done? How impulsive of him, how uncharacteristic. An unbidden image of her leaning back against him invaded his mind. He shoved it out of his head.

An hour and a half later, when the dishes had been cleared and the coffee carafe was empty, Cabe felt more in control about the opening than he had in weeks. They both had clear agendas—with phone calls to make and emails to send out.

To her credit, Jenna was staying mum about last night and giving him time to bring up the matter himself if he chose to. She apparently could tell that he was in no mood to deal with the fallout of his revelations. Once Jenna took her last sip of coffee, he stood and pulled out her chair. "Follow me. We can head to the business center and get some work done there before our meeting with the resort's retail manager this afternoon."

She had her hair up again this morning, this time in some kind of tight bun. But it was no match for the Caribbean's morning heat and humidity. A few tendrils had escaped their confines, forming wispy curls around her temples. The few short hours of daylight she'd spent here yesterday had somehow already resulted in a hint of red color across her cheeks and on the bridge of her nose. The effect was a subtle beauty that no amount of store-bought makeup could have achieved.

He stopped short. Not this again. What the devil was he doing? He had no business noticing the added color on her cheeks. Or anything about her looks, for that matter.

He couldn't even blame it on punch this time.

"Do you need to stop at your room for anything?" he asked. "It's on the way."

"No. I have everything I need."

Several children frolicked in the pool while their moms relaxed on lounge chairs reading magazines or the latest bestseller. A squealing wet toddler darted past them toward the kiddie sprinklers with his father fast on his heels. The man caught the child in a hug and carried him the rest of the way, despite the toddler's squirmy efforts to be let down.

They reached the concrete path where the resort grounds met the sandy beach. They hadn't gone far when Cabe realized Jenna had stopped. He turned to find her staring off to the side, her hand cupped over her face to shield her eyes from the blare of the sun.

"Jenna?"

He followed her line of vision to where a young local girl sat, a variety of handcrafted items set up on display on a folding table in front of her. The resort was pretty accommodating about locals who tried to sell various wares on the property. This one had gotten here relatively early.

"Do you know what she's selling?" Jenna asked.

"Looks mostly like beaded jewelry of some sort. Maybe some leather items."

"She looks very young."

He had to agree. The girl couldn't be more than thirteen or so.

"Shouldn't she be in school?" Jenna asked.

"They're pretty relaxed about school here sometimes." She hadn't torn her gaze away from the girl. "Fridays are a good day to set up shop on the beach. A lot of tourists are either coming or going. Those arriving have their wallets still conveniently in their pockets. And the ones departing are often looking to buy last-minute souvenirs."

"I see."

"She probably had to choose between going to school or helping to feed her family for the week."

Jenna seemed torn and took a hesitant step in the girl's direction. Cabe doubted she even realized having done so. "I know we have a lot to do…" she began.

"Would you like to go take a look at the items?" he asked, unnecessarily as the answer was obvious.

He led the way without waiting for a response. "Let's go." She was fast on his heels.

The young girl's eyes lit up as they approached. Two well-dressed interested tourists was always a welcome sight.

"May I take a look?" Jenna asked.

She trailed her hand along the items and picked one up, some kind of leather necklace with colorful beads.

"This one would look so pretty with your hair color," the girl stated with a Creole accent.

"It's beautiful."

Not wasting a second, she came around the table and hung the necklace around Jenna's neck, then held up a mirror.

She turned to Cabe. "You should buy it. For your lady."

Jenna corrected her right away. "Oh, no. He's not… He won't be buying it."

The girl's face fell but she wasn't ready to quit. "You look amazing wearing it, miss." She held the mirror up higher. "See how pretty."

"I know," Jenna blurted out then blushed. "I mean, I like it. I will buy it myself."

She glanced down at the table. "Actually, I think I'll buy everything on this tray."

The girl's eyes grew wide. "Did you just say you want all of this?"

Jenna nodded and smiled. "Yes, please. I'll take that tray, everything on it."

Cabe looked down. The tray consisted of at least twenty items. Mostly necklaces made of beads. A few bracelets made of braided rubber bands. Was one of those a dog leash? Jenna didn't even care what she was buying.

That was probably more than the girl typically sold in a month. Maybe even six months.

"And a couple of those slippers," Jenna added, pointing to a pile of rubber flip-flops under the table. She hadn't even asked the price. Or size.

The girl still hadn't recovered. She stood staring at them both with a stunned expression. "You are joking? Yes?"

Jenna vehemently shook her head. "No. No joking.

I'll come right back with my wallet." She turned to him. "Cabe, will you wait here? I'll be right back."

Before she could turn around, Cabe stopped her with a hand on her arm. "Stay here." He pulled out his wallet, yanked out several bills and handed them to the girl. "We'll take the whole table."

The girl audibly gasped, hesitantly taking the bills, as if Cabe might change his mind any second. Then she sprang toward Jenna, wrapping her in a big, tight hug. "Thank you. Thank you both. So very much."

She pocketed the bills and pulled out several large plastic bags, filling them with the items off her table.

Jenna turned to him with her mouth agape. "What? Why? I could have paid for the things I wanted."

"Consider it a business expense."

"How in the world would such purchases be considered a business expense?"

"Well, for one thing, they're handcrafted jewelry pieces. We're in the jewelry business. Who knows? Maybe it will give us ideas about trends and designs." Not bad for an off-the-cuff response. He was pretty impressed with himself for coming up with that one on the spot.

She pursed her lips. "You didn't need to do that. It was totally unnecessary."

He took the bags the still-grinning girl handed to them and motioned for Jenna to go forward. He could hear the young girl humming a happy Marley tune as she folded up her empty table.

"It wasn't as if you actually *wanted* any of it," he argued. "You were just trying to help the child. You can't deny that."

She lifted her chin. "As a matter of fact, I was buying souvenirs for the personnel in the Boston regional office."

"Is that so? You were going to buy the whole tray."

"My staff works hard. They deserve to be rewarded for it."

"Well, now you can reward the whole building."

"Be that as it may, you didn't have to step in and cover it all for me."

He didn't break his stride. The truth of it was, he could tell Jenna was moved by the girl's plight. And he'd merely reacted to the look in Jenna's eyes when she'd looked at the girl. Then he'd actually felt a sense of shame about all the times he'd seen that very same child set up on the beach and never thought to help her out by buying anything. When he compared that to Jenna's reaction, what did that say about him?

He'd been brought up better than that.

"Are you angry?" he asked Jenna when she'd stayed silent for several steps.

She took a deep breath. "I don't know."

Her honesty gave him pause. The females in his life usually decided right away when they were cross with him and they made sure to let him know.

He sighed. "Don't be. All that matters is we made that girl's life just a little easier. You can't argue with that."

She rubbed a hand over her eyes. "I guess not. I guess I should be thanking you instead. What you did was very generous."

"She has you to thank."

"You purchased her entire table!"

"You're the only reason we went over to her table in the first place."

Jenna looked away with a small shrug. "I wish I could do more for her. She so reminds me of—" She caught herself before she went any further with the statement. He knew what she'd been about to say. The girl reminded Jenna of herself. The Townsend kids hadn't exactly had an easy time growing up, a fact the whole town had been aware of. He wondered how many times during their adolescence Jenna and her brother had struggled to get by. How often had Jenna spent her paycheck on groceries rather than the frivolous knick-knacks most teenage girls spent their money on?

They'd reached a somewhat empty area of the beachfront. Only a handful of suntanning tourists dotted the sand and a couple of kids building a simple yet muddy sandcastle. He'd deliberately taken her this route, hoping it would settle her thoughts.

She'd had quite the forty-eight hours.

"Who knows?" he added. "Maybe once the store is opened, we'll have her or other vendors set up a booth or something inside. We'll do the high-end stuff while displaying the local ware."

She suddenly stopped in her tracks and turned to him, forcing him to stop as well. "You would do that?"

"Why not? Don't you think it's a good idea?"

She smiled up at him then. A true smile unlike he'd seen from her before. And a strange feeling unfolded in his chest, one he couldn't name.

"I think it's the most wonderful idea."

"We could establish a whole program around it. Local craft jewelry being sold along our expensive deluxe pieces." Wow, he was getting really good at coming up with all sorts of ideas right on the spot, completely off the top of his head. He had no one but Jenna to thank for it.

She touched his forearm, clearly pleased. "Oh, Cabe. I think that could really work."

"Of course it will work. And it will please the local authorities. It's a win-win." He stopped to face her. "As a matter of fact, I think you may have helped with our zoning issues. The local brass always appreciate when any new business expands community ties."

Her eyes grew wide. "But I didn't do anything. You came up with the idea yourself. You're the one who can implement it."

None of it would have even occurred to him if she hadn't been by his side. "Not so. My project manager can also implement it. I might put her in charge of the program entirely. If she's interested."

The mild touch on his arm turned to an all-out grip. "Of course I'd be interested. I know firsthand how opportunities like that can make a monumental impact on someone's life." She literally bit down on her lip after she'd said the words.

"Is that right, Jenna?"

She looked off at the horizon, her eyes growing distant and pensive. Several moments passed in silence and Cabe didn't think she would answer. Finally, she took a deep breath. "When you said she was probably out there so that she could feed her family…"

"Yes?"

She clearly struggled to find the right words. "There were plenty of nights when my brother and I didn't eat," she confessed. "Especially during the summers when there was no school lunch to fall back on. I felt responsible when he was hungry."

So unfair, Cabe thought. Jenna had been forced to parent not only herself but also her older brother. "You were just a kid yourself."

"But he was the confused teenage boy. He looked to me for answers. Who else was there? Things got better as I grew older. Once I could start working, I made sure we both had at least one square meal a day. The elderly store owner on the corner of Falmouth and Main, down the street from our apartment, he offered me my first job. He knew I needed it. I never forgot that. Or his kindness. That man made all the difference in our lives."

"What about your mother?"

Her lips formed a grim smile. "My mother wasn't around much."

"Still. She must have had some source of income."

Jenna didn't tear her gaze off the horizon. "She mostly lived off her boyfriends. In between men, she had odd jobs. Waitressing on and off. Cleaning offices here and there. Nothing really stuck. And she had other ideas about what to do with the little income she did earn."

"Others must have helped you along the way." He sincerely hoped so. Or what did that say about the town he'd grown up in?

"Of course they did. But once I started to earn it, then it wasn't charity. It was accomplishment."

He felt the breath leave his lungs in a whoosh. Even at such a young age, Jenna Townsend had valued her pride. While he'd been out pursuing tennis trophies and merit ribbons to prove himself to his parents, she'd been fighting for survival. And she hadn't even done it for selfish reasons. She'd done it for her brother. To make sure they ate.

He didn't know what to say to her. His own struggles in life seemed to pale in comparison. Cabe had never wanted for anything. Not for anything materialistic, anyway. Sure, he'd spent most of his hours alone, his parents completely absent or completely disconnected if they were around. But the thought of going hungry was an absolute foreign concept.

"You've achieved a lot, Jenna. You're a successful, accomplished businesswoman."

A false and bitter laugh escaped her lips. "I had no choice. I had to work harder and be smarter than everyone else. I promised myself I would never be like her."

No wonder she was so driven, so rigid. Like that young vendor, Jenna had been carrying around a heavy burden since she was barely a teen. It all made sense now. Her inability to relax, her workaholic tendencies. All to outrun a legacy she'd already left so far behind. Yet somehow, it still chased her.

He and Jenna Townsend had a lot in common.

Jenna swiveled around in a large leather chair in one of the cubicles in the business center where she and Cabe had been working for the past two hours. Well, she'd been trying to work, anyway. She hadn't really gotten as much done as she would have liked. The scene from this morning kept playing over and over in her head.

Cabe hadn't even thought twice about offering that lovely girl whatever he'd had in his wallet. Sure, he could afford it. But not every wealthy man would have done the same thing. And his idea to have crafters set up in the store, that would be a true way to give back to this wonderful community she'd already grown so fond of in her short time here. Not only had he helped the girl with her immediate concern, he'd figured out a way to help her long term. All in all, a very monumental gesture.

So why did she feel so unsettled? She'd been tense and uneasy since the whole encounter. Something about the way Cabe had stepped in, taken charge of the situation, and gone above and beyond what she had intended.

It had impressed her. His kind gesture had impressed her.

And she didn't like it.

She didn't need any kind of white-knight hero to take over for her in such a situation. Hadn't that been exactly the kind of thing that would have impressed someone like her mother? Amanda loved it when the men she was with took care of things for her. Especially if the gesture involved a display of wealth.

But Cabe's actions had been all about kindness. Then he'd gone further to come up with an idea about how to continue the kindness on a broader scale.

It would be utterly selfish of Jenna to be cross with him. After all, it wasn't the use of his money that had impressed her, it was the use of his heart, his generosity. He had helped that girl more than Jenna would have been able to. So now she was an annoying bundle of frustration, anxiety and anger. Not to mention confused.

She'd spent her life ensuring that she could stand on her own two feet, that she didn't need any kind of assistance or guidance from a man the way her mom did. Cabe's take-charge personality was now blurring that previously solid image of herself she'd worked so hard to achieve.

Yep. Cabe Jordan was totally, overwhelmingly confusing her. The man was a complete enigma, impossible to comprehend. He'd opened up to her about a monumental part of his life—that he'd been adopted. But then he'd refused to even mention it again the next day. Then just when she thought she'd imagined his openness and vulnerability, he'd gone ahead and made the wishes of a needy girl come true right before Jenna's very eyes.

Basically, he'd walked into her office a few short days ago and completely scrambled her senses. She had no idea how to handle him. Nor could she imagine what her life was going to feel like when she went back to it without him in it. Once Cabe returned to Manhattan and she was back in Boston, her life would never be the same again.

But she'd have to accompany him back here to the resort at least once or twice more before the project was completed. Wouldn't she? Not only was she his project manager for the store opening, she'd just been recruited for the local vendor outreach idea.

The thought of returning both excited and terrified her. Her psyche might not be able to handle another trip like this one.

She could not fall for Cabe Jordan. He was absolutely wrong for her. Look how much he'd disrupted her life in the few short days since he'd stepped into it. Who was she kidding, anyway? As if he would even entertain the thought of the two of them in any kind of serious relationship. Haughty models and bright-eyed actresses were far more his style. Technically, he was dating one now.

As if her thoughts had conjured him, he materialized in front of her. His shirtsleeves were rolled up to reveal tan, muscular forearms. The man looked like he'd stepped right out of a male trends magazine. Though that was the kind of thing she did not need to be noticing.

"Late-morning doldrums?" he asked, holding out a sweaty plastic cup of iced tea. "Freshly brewed. Thought you might need a break."

Well, his timing was certainly a point in his favor. She inhaled the scent of the aromatic, lemony brew and felt her senses sharpen before she even took a sip. "Hmm, perfect. Thank you."

"You're welcome. Can't be too long a break though."

"Wow, and you said you weren't a harsh boss."

"Demanding versus harsh. Big difference. We have that meeting with the retail manager."

She turned to check the small bar on top of her laptop screen that read the date and time. "It's not for another two hours. You said we're meeting him right here on-site."

"True, but you might want to change first."

"Change? Why?"

"I meant to mention, Sonny likes to hold his meetings in an open cabana on the beach. You'll be way too warm in that pantsuit."

A business meeting in a beachside cabana. She could really get used to this lifestyle. It did pose a problem, however. All she'd really packed were other suits. Well, except for her tankini in case she had time for a swim in the ocean. That would hardly be appropriate for a meeting, even in this environment.

"Oh, dear." She looked down at her outfit.

"What's wrong?"

"I didn't really pack anything much different than what I'm wearing."

He narrowed his eyes in disbelief. "Really? All you packed are business suits and one sundress?"

He remembered her dress? He didn't seem the type to make note of such things.

She nodded, an embarrassed flush warming up her cheeks. How foolish of her. She didn't even know how to pack for a business trip. "And a swimsuit."

He seemed to think for a minute then turned abruptly. "Okay, let's go."

She knew he was a man used to being in charge and having others jump to fulfill his every demand, but these sudden turns were a bit tough to get used to. "Where exactly are we going? Two hours before our meeting?"

"The adjacent shopping center. I can check the status of the new paneling they're to start putting in today."

"Okay. What will I be doing?"

"You're going to visit the ladies' boutique. There's got to be a couple of outfits you can pick out that are more suitable for an outdoor conference."

She hadn't seen that coming. "You want me to go shopping? Now?" She gestured to the piles of paperwork on the desk and her laptop blinking with several new emails. "I don't have to remind you about all the work that needs to get done. Oh, and we have a meeting very soon."

"Well, I'm not saying you should take all day. Just go pick out a couple of things." He seemed to contemplate her, looked her up and down. "You don't strike me as one of those women who takes forever and tries on a hundred outfits."

She huffed out an exasperated sigh. "No. Of course not." She was never indecisive about clothes. She just couldn't usually afford to buy anything that wasn't marked down and finding adequate, comfortable items on sale took a bit more time. She couldn't be one of those women who shopped indiscriminately.

"Then I don't see a problem. But we're wasting time. Let's go."

"I need to get my purse from the suite."

"Why?"

Was he being deliberately obtuse? "Because you're making me shop."

"Just have them put it on my account."

Jenna halted. Oh, no. Not again. He was oh, so ready to buy things for her. The thought sent an irritated bristle up her spine. After all, this was no way comparable to the way he'd helped that girl on the beach. This was totally different. She wouldn't have it.

"You are not buying me clothes, Cabe."

"No. I'm not."

She was about to breathe a sigh of relief when she paused. Way too easy.

She was right. "I'm ensuring my project assistant has what she needs to be productive and useful at a very important meeting," Cabe said.

Productive and useful! She lifted her chin. "It doesn't take clothes to do that."

Cabe pinched the bridge of his nose and let out a deep sigh. "Why are we arguing about this? You need something to wear. The solution is simple."

"But why do you want to pay for it? I can purchase the outfits myself. You do pay me well." The second half of her statement was true. As far as the first part, well, she was on shaky ground there. She had no idea how expensive this boutique would be. And though she'd rather die than admit it to Cabe, she had to live on a strict budget and justify the spending of every dime. Or she'd never have anything left over for a rainy day after paying off her monthly school loan dues and taking care of all the other responsibilities.

"That's not the point. The point is, I'm asking you to purchase the items. It's not something that you have asked for or even want apparently. Anyway, it's my fault you're unprepared. I should have warned you about needing some casual beach clothes."

Irritation flooded through her. Why did he have to make sense? But his argument did hold some truth. It wasn't like this was her idea. She would have no intention of buying more clothes if he wasn't asking her to.

Cabe obviously saw her softening. He moved quickly to further rally his point. "It's just another asset."

That was also true. If she needed a different laptop or a new tablet, she wouldn't be expected to pay for it herself.

Besides, she had to admit the utter foolishness of walking into a luxury boutique on her budget and expecting to be able to find something. She doubted a place like that would have a sales rack.

Cabe broke through her thoughts. "If it makes you feel better, consider it a loan."

She worked hard not to grit her teeth. "Oh? How so? Will you be wearing the clothes after I'm done with the meeting?"

His mouth twitched. "An interesting solution. But I was thinking more along the lines of donating the items in the company's name to the women's shelter back in Boston."

That gave her pause. Of course, Cabe immediately sensed her hesitation and pounced.

"You know I'm making sense." He drove the point home.

That may be, Jenna thought, but the fear that she was

tumbling down a dangerous slippery slope sent an icy trickle between her shoulder blades.

He stood staring at her, waiting for her response. She forced herself not to look away from his intense stare. His eyes had grown dark. Due to utter irritation, she'd bet. Cabe probably wasn't used to women turning him down when it came to such offers. Or anything else, for that matter.

The dress would go to good use. It wasn't as if she'd be keeping it. A serpent of doubt crawled into her brain. Was she merely justifying the concept? Giving her head a quick shake, Jenna made herself take a mental step back. She hadn't even seen the dress yet and she was already fretting about having to return it. Cabe continued to stare at her.

She folded her arms across her middle. "Fine. I'll go take a look. If, and only if, I find something that I think may work, then I'll put it on your account. And I will guarantee a donation receipt upon our return from the charity."

"I have no doubt you will."

"Fine."

"Fine," he repeated. "Well, that required more of a battle than it should have. You know, most women would jump at the chance of a shopping spree on the house."

"I am not most women."

He let out an exasperated sigh. "Oh, I'll give you that."

"What is that supposed to mean?" she demanded, ready to do battle yet again for some reason.

He held up his arms in surrender. "I'm agreeing with

you. You are definitely not like most of the women I know. Not in the least."

She noticed the slight upward turn of his lips. He was teasing her! And she was falling for it.

She pushed her chair in and stepped away from the desk. "I'm going to take that as a compliment."

He winked at her and her insides quivered like pudding. Not good. Not good at all. A professional, serious Cabe she could handle. She couldn't say the same about this playful one. Or the generous one she'd witnessed on the beach. Or the concerned one who helped put ointment on her bites. Then held her against him as he told her the pressure he'd felt his whole life to be perfect.

Those Cabes were dangerous indeed.

"Go right ahead," he said. "It was meant as one."

As she moved to the door, Jenna had to remind herself that she was irritated.

Cabe reread the same email for the seventh time and found he'd be hard-pressed to recall exactly what it said. He couldn't focus. His mind insisted on wandering to Jenna. No little wonder with her scent still clinging to the air. Things certainly weren't dull when she was around him. This morning alone, she'd managed to have him buy a tableful of island souvenirs and then she'd sparred with him over the simple purchase of a meeting-suitable dress. He hadn't realized how uneventful these trips had been until this time. This trip had so far been one unexpected adventure after another because of her.

Had she found a dress she liked? Was she trying it on even at this moment?

Those thoughts had him wanting to kick himself. Surely, he had better things to do than contemplate the shopping status of a woman who was merely here to help him with a large venture.

He had to admit, however, that he'd be more than a little disappointed if, after all the back and forth about it, she came back empty-handed. It had not been easy to convince Jenna Townsend to accept something he'd offered to purchase for her. He'd done it twice in one morning.

She would have never accepted if it hadn't been presented as a loan. Pledging the dress to charity had finally trumped it for her. Or so he hoped. He couldn't really be certain of anything when it came to her. Why in the world did he find that so enticing?

He understood. Or thought he did. Jenna had fought fiercely her whole life to become and stay independent. He admired her for it. Who would blame her, growing up as she had? Rather than taking even the slightest risk of becoming like her mother, Jenna had worked hard and sacrificed to make a success of herself. And what a tremendous job she'd done.

His email folder dinged at him again, signaling the arrival of ten more urgent messages in his mailbox. He leaned back in his chair and decided it wasn't even worth his effort to open any of them. His attention was too scattered, a first for him, he admitted with a jolt of surprise. Even more surprisingly, he wasn't going to try to fight it. None of his to-dos were going to get done at this rate anyway. He may as well take a walk over to the shopping center.

Something told him yet another adventure awaited over in that part of the isle.

"Will this be on Mr. Jordan's company account or his personal one?"

Jenna paused at the question.

Cabe had a personal account here? At a women's boutique? The answer dawned on Jenna as she handed her purchases to the impeccably dressed saleslady who'd been helping her.

Cabe had traveled here with other women. Apparently, he had treated them to expensive clothing.

Well, she was not like them. Her situation was completely different. She was here to do a job and work hard to make Cabe's life easier as the CEO of Jordan's Fine Jewelry. Big difference. She did not need to depend on a man to buy her things. She was not like her mother. In fact, the outfit she'd found was quite sensible and quite a bit less costly than many of the other items in the store. Though it was still higher than what she could actually afford herself. But she had managed to find a pair of butter-soft leather sandals that had been drastically marked down. Those were going to be her one and only splurge on this trip as a way to treat herself.

"Definitely the corporate account, please."

The woman began to ring her up and Jenna couldn't help but let her eye travel to the gown sitting on display behind the register. A piece of art—that was the only way to describe it. A shimmery gold color that reminded her of the sand on the beach when the sun hit it just so. Draped over the mannequin like someone had sculptured it into place. The straps holding it up appeared impossibly thin and fragile. She imagined that was an optical illusion. Nothing about this dress appeared to have been left to chance.

She made herself look away. It probably cost more than she made in a year. The saleslady noticed.

"Would you like to try it on?"

Jenna blinked. The thought would have never occurred to her. “Oh, no. That’s okay.”

“You should. It would look so exotic on someone with your coloring.”

Jenna shook her head and took a deep breath. “I’m afraid I’m not in the market for something so glamorous.” Especially considering the price would make a nice down payment on a small house.

She smiled. “You’re just trying it on. Come, I’d like to see it on you.” She moved over to the mannequin and gently began removing the dress. “You’ll be doing it for me.”

Jenna gave her head a shake. “How so?”

“It will help break up the day and make my shift go a little quicker.”

Jenna’s heart did a little jump in her chest. Did she dare?

Why not? When would she ever get an opportunity to have an haute couture item actually on her body? She’d probably never even get a chance to set eyes on such a lavish garment again. What could be the harm in indulging in a little fantasy just this once?

And just like that, Jenna found herself in the dressing room, the dress hanging like a golden waterfall off a small garment hook. Her fingers trembled as she handled the silky, delicate material. Light as air and smooth, as though she were somehow holding liquid within her hands. Carefully, she put the gown over her head and gently tugged it down over her shoulders. She closed her eyes as it fell into place.

For several moments, she simply allowed herself to revel in the smooth texture of the material against her skin. Soft and airy, it must have been made from the finest silk.

When she dared a look in the mirror, her breath caught. It was like looking at a different person. A Jenna Townsend she hardly recognized stared back at her. One who belonged in a whole other universe. More magical.

She ran a hand down her midsection and couldn't resist doing a small little spin. The dress twirled around her like a light, airy cloud. Reaching up, she released the complicated clip that held her hair in place and shook out her curls. Giddiness wasn't usually a part of her personality but she felt that way now. She looked good. Better than good. If she had to say so herself, Cinderella had nothing over her in this dress.

She could have been a picture straight out of the pages of an international fashion magazine. Maybe even on the cover. Puckering her lips, she struck a pose in the mirror. Just like those haughty, glamorous runway models. The ones Cabe was always being linked to and seen with. The idea made her smile. It was silly, she knew, but her heart thudded in her chest at the vision staring back at her from the glass. Who would have thought that a girl from the fringes of South Boston could have pulled off a garment like the one she had on? It was such a far cry from the last formal gown she'd worn. The one she'd scraped and saved for close to a year in order to purchase secondhand for her high school prom. The one she'd stood out like a sore thumb in because it was clearly out of style and clearly used.

If only her former classmates could see her now. Suddenly she wished it with all her heart. Memories of the snickering and sideways glances she'd endured that night came crashing down upon her. No one had said anything, but their knowing, condescending stares communicated it all. She wouldn't let those memories mar this moment.

They wouldn't believe their eyes if they caught a look at her now. She hardly believed her own. Maybe a sneaky invisible little fairy had sprinkled some pixie dust her way and she had entered some kind of delicious alternate universe. And maybe, just maybe, she actually belonged there.

"Are you going to come out so that we may see it?" the saleslady asked from behind the fitting room door, pulling her out of her fanciful thoughts.

"Just one moment." Jenna inhaled deep and straightened to her full length. Such a dress demanded the utmost proper posture. Lifting her chin, she yanked aside the curtain and stepped out of the dressing room then executed a flamboyant, exaggerated bow.

And nearly dropped to the floor when she realized the saleslady hadn't been talking about a figurative "we."

Cabe stood less than three feet away.

# CHAPTER SEVEN

CABE FOUND HE could do nothing but stare. He couldn't recall any moment in his life when he'd felt so completely frozen. No words came to his head, no thoughts he could formulate.

His mind zeroed in on one thing and one thing only: Jenna Townsend sheathed in a dress that hugged her so well, all he could do was imagine taking it off her.

She was something out of a portrait. An unearthly goddess who could command an army of men to live or die for her. At the moment, he himself would do anything she bade. The unusual color of the dress matched the golden specks in her hazel eyes. The effect was mesmerizing. He had to remind himself to breathe.

"Cabe." She spoke his name on a whisper. It sounded like a verbal caress beckoning him. How would it sound if she were to cry it out in pleasure?

His jaw clenched tight. He couldn't think of a thing to say. Here he was, the CEO of a highly successful private company who had to make multimillion-dollar decisions every day. And he'd been struck dumb by a woman in a dress.

She subconsciously ran a hand over her hair. Heaven help him. Her hair. A heavy cascade of dark, flowing curls curtained over her shoulders. He'd feared he'd never see it down. He'd tried to picture the way she would look if she ever saw fit to release it in his presence. But his imagination hadn't nearly done the image justice. Heat raced along his skin. He had to fist his hands at his sides in order to keep from reaching out and running his fingers through the lush, silky strands. His mind may have gone numb but his body knew exactly what it wanted to do.

He swallowed, clenched and unclenched his hands in a strained effort to keep from reaching for her.

She was saying something. He had to force himself to focus. "…just for fun. I obviously had no intention of trying to buy this."

"A shame." The words came out hoarse, strained even to his own ears.

She narrowed her eyes, and an expression of confusion settled over her features. What didn't she understand? Couldn't she see the effect she was having on him? Not just right at this moment but ever since he'd first laid eyes on her in Boston. He'd never behaved so irrationally. She'd dumped food on him and instead of firing her on the spot he'd promoted her! She teared up watching strangers get married. She attempted to buy a tray full of baubles she didn't need, pretending she wanted every piece. She had an amazing head for business.

And looking at her now took his breath away.

*Damn.* This was bad. This was very, very bad. He had lost all control. It was totally unacceptable. He didn't have time for this. His vast experience with women consisted of taking them to a few social gatherings followed by explosive breakups due to his lack of willingness to move things along to the next level. It had suited him just fine. Until now. Now he found himself thinking all sorts of thoughts about the future that he had no business entertaining.

Well, he had to grasp at some kind of sanity. He had too much to do.

Everything in his life was planned out, controlled. That was the only way to avoid regrets and mistakes. He wouldn't allow himself either of those luxuries. He didn't deserve to.

None of his plans included the kind of complications that would result from any kind of fling with a woman like Jenna Townsend.

He knew the best course of action would be to pivot on his heel right now and just hustle right back out of the store.

He couldn't be what she deserved.

Cabe didn't have time for any kind of a real relationship. He had to spend his time and every ounce of his energy proving himself worthy of the Jordan name. What kind of mate or partner would that make him? A lousy one.

The lady standing before him deserved so much more than he could give.

It was settled. He'd made his decision. From now on, he would make sure the relationship between the two of them remained strictly professional. He would keep her at arm's length during the day, and he would make sure to stay off the cursed balcony at night. No more mistakes. He had to promise himself that. He had to guarantee it. All he had to do right now was turn around and leave.

So the next words out of his mouth surprised him indeed. "Come here, Jenna."

* * *

Oh, boy.

Jenna took a hesitant step forward. The look on Cabe's face was impossible to read. Was he cross with her? All she'd done was try a dress on. She'd tried to explain she didn't actually intend to buy it.

That idea was preposterous.

He couldn't think she would buy such an extravagant item on the company's account. So what was with the look he currently had on his face? His jaw was tight, his eyes hard, his brows furrowed close together. She couldn't venture a guess what he was thinking. Then again, she'd be hard-pressed to guess what Cabe thought at any given moment.

"I said, come here."

She'd tried to ignore that command, hoping she hadn't heard him right. Her breath caught in her throat, and her limbs didn't seem to want to move. She'd never really seen him angry. Maybe he was about to chew her out and didn't want to do it too loudly. The other woman had made herself scarce. That couldn't be a good sign.

She took a hesitant step forward. "The salesclerk said she wanted to see it on me. I honestly wouldn't even consider actually…"

The words died on her lips as he moved with sudden swiftness, breaching the distance between them. His hand reached out and for one insane moment she thought she might reach for him as well. A bolt of electricity shot through her chest. The room seemed to shrink, to just the small patch of space where the two of them stood.

She felt a rough yet gentle finger trail along her shoulder, up toward her collarbone. There was no way to even try to hide the shudder his touch elicited. Cabe leaned closer, his lips a mere hair's width away from her ear.

She read clear, utter desire on his face.

When he spoke, his breath felt like a subtle caress over the skin on her neck. Her stomach did a flip, the feeling one got when just about to fall but caught herself just in time. Or someone else caught her.

"You need to take this off." Barely a whisper, his command sent a shiver of excitement down her spine.

This couldn't really be happening. She'd obviously fallen down some kind of rabbit hole. Cabe Jordan was not standing in the middle of a chic dress shop with her, telling her to undress.

She swallowed the hard lump that had formed in her throat and licked her suddenly dry lips. "Like I said, it was just in fun."

"Jenna?"

"Yes?"

"We have to go."

"Go?"

Every inch of him was tense, his jaw clenched, his hands fisted at his sides. He looked like he wanted to throw her over his shoulder. The thought had her cheeks burning. She thought of the way he'd almost kissed her and wondered if he would do it again. Heaven help her, she wanted him to. Very much.

"We have to go," he repeated through gritted teeth. "Or we'll be late for our meeting."

If Jenna thought their walk this morning to breakfast had been awkward, their stroll after leaving the shopping center was downright torturous. The fierce blare of the late-afternoon sun didn't help. They passed a lazy-strung hammock slung between palm trees and all Jenna wanted to do was collapse in it for a while. And try not to replay the scene in the dress shop over and over in her head. The way the touch of Cabe's finger had sent a tingling rush over every inch of her skin. She couldn't think about any of that. Instead, she had to somehow focus on a business meeting.

Next to her, Cabe cleared his throat. "That was a smart choice."

She had no idea what he could be referring to. Her brain seemed to have ceased functioning.

"The dress," Cabe added.

What? Was he seriously going to bring it up?

"I mean, you know, the one you have on. Right now. Not that other one." He pointed at her. "This one."

Oh. She could only nod in his direction.

"I don't mean to say that other gown wasn't flattering." He rubbed a hand over his forehead and cursed under his breath.

"It's okay, Cabe. I know what you mean."

He let out a long sigh, his frustration palpable. She fully understood. Life, and this trip, would be so much easier if they had a smooth, uncomplicated relationship. "That makes one of us."

"You're saying this dress I'm wearing now works well for an important meeting that's being held in a casual, outdoor atmosphere."

"Yes. That's exactly what I'm saying. The light color works well in this heat."

"Thank you."

"You're welcome." He hesitated. "I like your shoes, too," he said after a beat, somewhat wryly.

Jenna glanced down at the strappy, low-heel leather

sandals she had on. She'd bought them somewhat impulsively, using her own money, of course. Her navy, thick pumps were not handling well in all this sand. Despite the awkwardness between them, she felt downright giddy that Cabe had noticed.

How schoolgirlish of her.

He suddenly stopped and turned to her. "Jenna, listen—"

Oh, no. No way. He was not going to do this to her. He was not going to try to discuss the dress shop fiasco. Did he want to totally scramble her brain before this meeting?

She didn't break her stride, forcing him to resume walking and catch up.

"So tell me about Sonny," she asked, before he could finish his sentence. Cabe got the hint and followed the change of topic.

Thank heavens for small blessings.

"Sonny is in charge of the retail establishments in the resort's shopping center. He can help us with the latest zoning issue." They turned a corner on the path and Cabe pointed to the distance. "There he is now."

Jenna looked up to see a stout, thick man sitting at a picnic table at a cabana, pounding away at a laptop. Introductions were made when they approached and the three of them wasted no time before getting to the business at hand.

Jenna even managed to focus on taking notes rather than the magnetic pull of the man sitting next to her. No small miracle after this morning and last night.

At the conclusion of the meeting two hours later, she was actually pretty impressed with herself. She'd held her own and even made some useful suggestions.

Now she just had to get through the rest of the day.

After Sonny left, she looked up to find Cabe staring at her. Like a specimen he couldn't understand. She suddenly felt a nervous hitch in the middle of her chest. Perhaps her performance in front of the retail manager hadn't gonc as well as she'd thoughl. Had she done or said something wrong?

"Sonny seems very efficient," she commented, by way of fishing.

"You impressed him." Cabe's answer surprised her. The other man had shown no outward signs of any such thing. In fact, he'd been very matter-of-fact throughout the whole two hours.

"Why do you say that?"

"I've dealt with him quite a bit over the past several months. Trust me, you impressed him."

Jenna swallowed. "I was just trying to get all the details covered."

"You did well."

Her heart thudded at his words. It was one thing to impress Sonny, but to hear Cabe was pleased with her performance sent a lightning bolt of pleasure through her core.

"You're truly one of a kind, Jenna Townsend."

She looked up at him then and realized instantly that this was one of those moments she would never recover from. She was lost—lost in Cabe's steady blue gaze, transfixed by the silky smooth sound of his voice. She'd never find her way again.

She grasped for some kind of response but none would come to her lips. Several seconds went by—she couldn't guess how long. Suddenly, the unmistakable sound of a camera shutter snapped her out of her daze and broke the spell.

"A quick photo, Mr. Jordan." She hadn't even noticed the photographer approach them, holding a large camera to his face and wearing a colorful shirt with the resort logo.

Cabe held his hand up to hold off any further picture taking. "Maybe later." Gently taking Jenna by the elbow, he led her away from the cabana.

Jenna had to remind herself to breathe as they walked away.

"Damn it," Cabe bit out, sparing a glance behind him.

"You don't like your picture taken?"

"Not particularly."

"He's just doing his job."

"Let's hope so," Cabe bit out.

"What do you mean? Isn't he just one of the resort photographers?"

Cabe kept walking, apparently trying to gain as much distance between them and the camera. "Yes, but sometimes my photo doesn't merely end up in a souvenir frame for me to purchase."

"Where does it end up?"

"Too often it ends up in a tabloid or some tawdry website."

It took a moment but his meaning slowly dawned on her. He wasn't merely upset that his picture had been taken. Cabe was upset that it had been taken *with her*.

"Will Carmen be cross with you?" she blurted out without thinking.

Cabe paused then, just long enough to give her a

confused look. "Carmen? No. I mean, I guess not. I honestly don't know."

She merely nodded as they resumed walking.

"You're not worried about her potential reaction to the photo, then?"

"The thought hadn't even crossed my mind."

That was interesting. Then again, Carmen was probably one of those women so secure with her beauty and attractiveness she probably wouldn't have cared if Cabe had taken a hundred pictures with someone like her. The likes of Jenna Townsend were certainly not enough to elicit any kind of jealous reaction from an international supermodel.

"I thought maybe that's why you wanted to avoid the camera."

His answer was notably matter-of-fact. "Carmen and I broke up. Just before I left Boston."

Jenna nearly stumbled before she recovered her step. She had no business feeling giddy at that bit of news. "I'm sorry to hear that."

Cabe shrugged. "Don't be. It was bound to happen."

"I see."

"Carmen's been pursuing a movie career for as long as I've known her. She finally got her big break this past month. She'll be filming a horror piece. In the Amazon. She asked me to visit her. I said I didn't have that kind of time."

"Oh." Jenna took a deep breath. If Cabe was shaken over the breakup, he certainly had shown no signs of heartbreak. Not that she'd ever expect a man like Cabe Jordan to wear his heart on his sleeve when it came to women. Still, Jenna didn't detect any sense of loss or regret. Well, she had no business speculating on that.

Or hoping the notion to be true. "Then, if you don't mind my asking..."

Cabe finally stopped, took her by the arm and gently turned her to face him. "Spit it out, Jenna."

"Why are you so agitated about the photographer, then?"

She knew she shouldn't have asked. And wanted to kick herself when he answered.

"I really don't want a picture of the two of us plastered all over the gossip sites."

Jenna felt the lump form in her throat and made herself swallow it down. She understood, she really did. She knew whatever was happening between them right now on this resort wasn't reality. Once they were back in the States, they would go back to living their regular lives. She'd return to her boring, repetitive existence back in Boston. And Cabe would return to his exciting life in Manhattan. Why would he want to answer anyone's questions about public photos with his project manager?

He took a different way through the center of the island in order to ensure they'd ditched the photographer. And besides, this route held something Cabe wanted Jenna to see.

He had to catch her as she stepped on the wooden hanging bridge. Or else Jenna was headed for a dramatic face-plant. Cabe didn't realize how fast he'd been walking or how Jenna had made sure to keep up with him. Unfortunately, she'd miscalculated the steadiness of the wobbly bridge and was about to fall over. "Here. I've got you," Cabe said, taking her by the arm and gently pulling her up.

She gave him a look of surprise and gratitude, and

then her gaze fell to the hand that held her arm. Her skin felt smooth and warm under his touch.

She gently pulled her arm free and took hold of the thick rope railing.

"Thanks. Guess I'm still breaking into these new sandals."

"You can always take them off. Feel free to go barefoot, now that our business day is over."

She gave him a small smile that didn't really reach her eyes. "Can we slow down now? I think we lost our tail."

"Sorry. I didn't realize how fast I was walking. Not like the photographer was actually following us."

"Well, we couldn't have risked that now, could we?" Her voice held a hint of annoyance.

He didn't want to be the reason Jenna's picture was pasted all over the internet. He'd grown used to the lack of privacy over the years. But for someone as inexperienced with it as Jenna was, the intrusion could be daunting and upsetting. She'd done nothing to deserve that. Not to mention what his parents would say.

"Like I said, I'd rather not give the tabloids any fodder."

"Got it," Jenna replied. "I am clearly not an ideal photo op."

Her tone was sharp. "Something wrong?" he asked.

She let out a deep sigh. "No. Nothing at all."

He waited a beat but she didn't go on. "Doesn't sound like it's nothing. Is there something you'd like to say?"

Her cheeks suddenly turned pink with annoyance. Maybe even anger.

Which made no sense. All he'd done was try to spare

her the unwanted scrutiny an international photograph would garner. But Jenna remained frustratingly silent.

"You have no idea what kind of attention one lousy picture can elicit," he told her. "I was trying to protect you."

She blinked and her expression softened. "Is that the only reason? That was all for me?"

What in the devil's name was she talking about? Of course it was. "You are clearly a very private person, Jenna. I didn't think you'd appreciate such an intrusion."

He waited as she let that sink in.

"I guess you're right," she said, looking up and finally noticing their surroundings. They had reached the majestic waterfalls at the center of the resort. Surrounded by lush greenery and gray rocks, three high waterfalls dropped close to a hundred feet into a crystal-blue river. A series of rustic wooden bridges like the one they currently stood on webbed throughout the area.

Jenna's expression held wonder and awe, as he knew it would. Their swift jaunt just now had brought a rosy hue to her cheeks, and her lips remained parted. "Wow, this is beautiful."

Breathtaking, Cabe thought. But he wasn't thinking of the scenery. Jenna's skin glistened with the thin sheen of mist that drifted in the air. She looked like a heavenly angel ascended from paradise.

"Why did it bother you so much, Jenna? That I had us run from the photographer?" he prompted. The situation had triggered something in her, something he wanted to get to the bottom of. This was a perfect spot to do it.

Her eyes narrowed on his face. "You were saying how clearly guarded I am."

"Yes?"

She blew out a deep breath, went back to studying the scenery. “I didn’t exactly have an ideal upbringing, Cabe. As you very well know.”

“I know you didn’t have it easy. And I know how much you’ve overcome to get to where you are.”

She sniffed. “I’m Amanda Townsend’s daughter. The town drunk, the desperate single mom who flirted with everyone’s husband.”

“None of that was your fault, Jenna.”

“I know. But it was certainly my responsibility. It fell on me to take care of her when she drank so much she was sick for days. It fell on me to find a way to feed and care for my brother when there was no food or money to be found.”

He ached to hold her, to erase her past and pain somehow. She deserved so much better than what she’d been handed in life. Unlike himself. “You were the caregiver, even though your brother was older.”

She smiled, with genuine affection clear on her face. “We split responsibilities. He’s protected me in myriad ways, too, over the years. A girl tends to get picked on when she’s known as the trashy daughter of the town’s trashy drunk.”

“You and Sam are lucky to have each other.”

He heard her inhale deeply, slowly let the breath out. He’d do anything to bear some of the weight on her shoulders, if only he could.

“I suppose we are. I can’t imagine dealing with Amanda over the years without him. Though sometimes I wish he didn’t have to deal with it at all. That I was a single child, for his sake.” A small laugh escaped her lips. “I used to daydream that someone rich would show up one day and adopt—” She stopped suddenly and cupped her hand over her mouth, as if she could pull back the half-spoken word that hung in the air.

"It's not all it's cracked up to be," he said.

"I'm so sorry," Jenna whispered. "I should have known better than to say something like that."

"It's okay, Jenna. It's a common fantasy among children. Funny thing is, I had the opposite daydream."

"What do you mean?"

"After I found out, I kept having these visions of my real parents appearing at the door one day. To tell me how sorry they were that they ever gave me up. Then they would beg me to forgive them, ask if they could take me back." He grew somber as the memory further surfaced. "Then I would feel terrible. Guilty for hoping to leave James and Tricia when they were so sad." What a silly kid he'd been. Worrying himself sick over a fantasy that had no basis in reality.

"You've been trying to prove yourself for as long as you can remember, haven't you?" she asked in a soft voice.

"I guess I have. It's hard to live up to a ghost."

"A ghost?"

"James and Tricia adopted me after losing their biological son. Unlike you, I may not have had an actual living, breathing sibling. But his presence was always there. Right down to the room my parents never altered after he died." A room he was never allowed to so much as enter.

"They never emptied his room?" Jenna asked, her voice breaking.

"No, never."

"Cabe, there was no way you could have reached them. Nothing you could have done. They were broken and shattered over their loss."

"It's tough for a child to see through all that."

She leaned closer. "You never stopped trying, did you? To make them happy?" She was close enough that he could read her eyes even in the dim light. They held no pity. If anything, she appeared to be looking at him with something resembling admiration. "Cabe, you deserve to be happy."

Her words hammered into his soul. In one simple sentence she'd cut to the very core of him, through to all his childhood insecurities and disappointments.

"Jenna, you amaze me," he told her. He'd never made a truer statement. He thought back to that first day in Boston. It horrified him how insensitive he'd been. He should have realized someone like Jenna, who'd had a lifetime of trying to escape the shadow of her mother's reputation, would take questions about the theft personally.

And just now, with the photographer. She'd thought he was ashamed to be seen with her for the very same reason. Jenna's whole life had been about others judging her based on the actions of her mother. He could be such a careless, thoughtless lout at times.

"This conversation is getting pretty deep," Jenna said quietly in a tone that broke his heart. "Too deep to be having with my boss." She let out a small laugh, clearly forced.

If only she could really see him, not just as a boss, but as a man. A man who wanted to unearth the many layers that were Jenna Townsend. "Do me a favor," Cabe began. "Take a good look around this place. A really good look."

She did as he asked, although not before giving him a confused frown. "It's wondrous. I didn't realize places like this actually existed." Jenna ducked her head shyly, as if embarrassed by what she'd just revealed.

"It's all an illusion."

"What do you mean?"

"That large waterfall in the middle, that was in the original landscape. The other two smaller ones on either side, those were formed by manipulating the cliff side. Just like everything else in this place, it's been painstakingly planned and created. None of it is genuine or the real thing. Just like me," he added, meeting her eyes.

The lines on her forehead deepened. "Cabe, why would you think that?" Maybe she did see the real him after all.

Before he could answer, a strong gust of wind shook the bridge they stood on. Without giving it a thought, Cabe reached to grab her around her middle and pulled her closer, both feeling and hearing her sharp intake of breath. "Sorry, these bridges aren't really meant to stand around on for extended periods of time." He spoke low against her ear.

"Right. They're more for appearances as well."

"It would seem." It was safe to let go now, but he continued to hold her anyway. For some reason, he couldn't seem to stop touching Jenna. He would enjoy it while he could. For now, he was simply happy that she made no attempt to step out of his embrace.

"Why was it me?" he blurted out. Her eyes searched his even as her touch soothed him, comforted him. So he went on. "I wonder about it every day. The mere randomness of it."

"Oh, Cabe." She reached for him then and he felt as if time had stopped. Her soft, delicate fingers found his face then ran gently along his jaw. He reflexively dipped his head into her touch.

"I'm also a made product, Jenna. As artificial and fake as these waterfalls. I'm not an original. I'm not any kind of rarity. I was merely randomly selected, treated and polished to transform into someone else entirely. A lie. A falsehood I've lived every day of my life. It's hard not to feel like a fraud. My parents lost their real son. Their one and only precious child. And somehow I was chosen by some mysterious twist of fate to step in and take the life he was meant to lead."

To his shock, she stepped farther into his embrace. A shiver ran through him at her closeness. He knew one of them should pull away. But, heaven help him, it wasn't going to be him.

Her eyes glistened and it tore at his heart. She remained silent, giving him time to continue if he desired. Apparently, he did. "I have everything. And he's gone. How can my mother and father not resent me for that? They tried so hard not to show it. But I could tell by their indifference. I could see. How in the world would I blame them?"

"You worked hard for all that you have, Cabe," she said. "Everyone knows how much you've done for Jordan's Fine Jewelry. The way it grew once you took over."

"Maybe so. But so much of it was handed to me."

She gave her head a small shake. "You aren't giving yourself any credit. I can't even imagine the company being run by anyone else. You're really good."

"I had to be good." He tightened his grip around her waist, pulled her closer. And she felt so right up against him. "Don't you see?"

"See what?"

"The reality is, I can't squander it. It has to mean something that it was me." He took a deep breath, inhaled the scent of her shampoo. "After all, I'm the Jordan Golden Boy."

She shook her head slowly. "I know who you are. You're Cabe Jordan. A talented and accomplished CEO. You've done so much for your employees. And you're a credit to your parents. Just today you changed the life of a young girl you just happened to see selling cheap jewelry on the beach. You're the kind of man any woman with a pulse would fall head over heels—"

The roaring in his ears kept him from hearing any more. He didn't need to. What he needed was to taste her, to feel her up against him. Inside his very soul. Pulling her even closer, he took her mouth and plunged in. She tasted like heaven, like redemption, like everything he could have hoped for.

He'd never be able to let her go.

This was a fairy tale. She was convinced now. Or it was a sweet, unimaginable dream. Jenna hoped never to wake up. Cabe held her tight against him, his mouth devouring hers. She wrapped her arms around his neck and shifted her hips closer against his, felt the strength of his desire for her. The knowledge made her skin burn. This dazzling, enigmatic man wanted her. She'd seen the longing on his face, and now could feel it in the power of his kiss and in the reaction of his body.

"Jenna," he whispered against her mouth, his voice full of longing. A heady shiver of need ran up her spine. "Tell me. I have to know."

She couldn't think, couldn't seem to breathe. What

was he asking for? She'd give him anything. Her soul, her heart. Anything. So she simply answered yes.

His hands moved down her rib cage, down farther along her hips. Then she felt herself suddenly hoisted off the ground. He lifted her completely off her feet and started to carry her, steady and balanced despite the crooked and wobbly bridge. She couldn't tear her gaze off Cabe's face. His eyes reminded her of the ocean during a violent storm—dark and shadowed. The sound of the crashing water grew fainter and fainter behind them. She couldn't guess where they were going, but would let him take her anywhere. As long as he never stopped holding her.

She wanted so much more. She wanted all of him.

She'd wanted him since the moment he walked into her office. No, she'd wanted him since she'd known him, practically her whole life.

Cabe was the star of her daydreams, her girlhood crush. He'd transformed her life since walking back into it. He'd transformed *her*. She didn't recognize this reckless, careless woman she'd become. Was she really kissing her boss outside in the open, where anyone could walk by? This wasn't like her—this was downright wanton. But she didn't care. All she cared about was having Cabe completely.

He carried her out of the maze of bridges. The sounds of the waterfalls echoed soothingly behind them. An unseen bird chirped a melody in one of the trees above. He clearly knew the island well. The path he took her on was completely deserted. Before she realized, they were somehow in the hallway outside his suite. Cabe managed to unlock the door and bring her into his room, still holding her tight in his embrace. Slowly, he set her down on the thick, plush comforter on the bed.

She was in Cabe Jordan's hotel room as he kissed her and caressed her. The ocean view outside the balcony window looked like a painting created by a master painter. Her desire-fogged mind told her this all had to be some separate fantasy away from the rest of the universe.

And she would pretend it was. She would make believe she was in a universe where Jenna Townsend for once in her life got what she wanted. One where she succumbed to her desires. Just this one time, with this one man. Gently, slowly, he lowered himself to balance on his elbows just above her.

"Jenna?" He said her name as a question, touchingly making sure this was what she wanted.

It was, more than anything. She answered him by slowly undoing the top of her dress. She didn't get a chance to unbutton the rest. Covering her mouth with his once again, Cabe took over, making quick work of the remaining buttons.

There was no doubt in her mind. She wanted him. It was the only thing that mattered in this moment. Jenna knew this was what paradise would feel like.

Cabe confirmed it by taking her straight there.

She'd fallen asleep in his arms.

Cabe ran his fingers through Jenna's soft, thick hair. He sat cradling her with her back against his chest. Outside his window, the ocean shone like a rare glittering jewel in the distance.

Let her sleep, he thought. This moment would be over all too soon. Once they stepped out of this room, reality would set in. Then he would have to examine what had just happened. But not now.

Now he was just going to enjoy the feel of Jenna's languid body against his, savor the sensation of what it had felt like to hold her and love her.

He stroked her hair, breathed in the scent of her tropical shampoo mingled with the salty sea air. Jenna was not like anyone he'd ever known. That she was still helping her mother, even as an adult, didn't surprise him. This amazing, dynamic woman in his arms was the type of person who'd never turn away from anyone who needed her. Didn't she realize how special that made her?

Thinking of what she must have endured as a child made him want to throw something. Or punch the headrest behind him. She really was extraordinary. Jenna had prospered and shone into adulthood despite the genetic cards she'd been dealt. She'd worked hard and earned it all. Unlike those who'd had everything handed to them. Unlike him.

Suddenly, he felt lacking, inadequate. Jenna had accomplished so much in her life despite being given so little. Compared to her struggles, he'd had it so easy. All he had to do was take advantage of all the ample opportunities he'd been awarded.

The memory of the first day of his Boston visit flashed through his mind's eye. Her anger had been vibrant and strong. He'd deserved her ire then. He'd been an utter ass. When he thought about what that must have felt like for her, to have the boss come to town and practically accuse her of being a thief.

*He was her boss, the CEO.* Someone who had a direct say on her career, her very future.

And he'd just made love to her.

A bubble of acid churned in his gut. Damn his impulsiveness.

Jenna wasn't the type to have a meaningless office fling. She had substance, character. With all that she'd been through, she had every right to a bright and fulfilling future. Complete with the rewarding career and a caring steady man who would always be there for the woman in his life.

She deserved the kind of future Cabe would never be able to give her.

For one hazy moment upon awakening, Jenna thought perhaps she had dreamed it all. There wasn't any kind of way the fates would have really allowed it to happen. She had *not* just been intimate with Cabe Jordan.

"Hey there, Sleeping Beauty." His rich baritone served to pull her out of that fallacy very quick. As did the weightlessness in her muscles. Not to mention the warm body she was snuggled against.

Dear heavens. What had she done? How could she have just made love with her *boss*?

Scrambling to gain some sense, she removed herself out of his embrace and stood up off the bed with the top sheet wrapped around her. Cabe sat up at the edge of the mattress and rammed a hand through his hair.

A glance at the window showed the sky had turned a deep, rich purple. The hour had to be approaching early evening. They'd apparently been there awhile. What time was it? She never wore a watch but where was her phone? She had no idea. If she had dropped it on the bridge, she hadn't even done a backup since arriving.

How utterly unprofessional—she didn't even know

where her phone was. But then again, so was sleeping with someone she worked with. Correct that—Cabe was the man she worked *for*. The blood left her brain. She dared a glance in his direction. He was clearly avoiding looking at her.

Cabe cleared his throat. "We should probably go get cleaned up."

"Um, I seem to have misplaced my phone." Great. On top of everything else, she had to admit to misplacing company property.

They both saw it at the same time, resting on the carpet near the leg of the bed. Disastrously, they both bent to reach for it, bumping heads.

This had to be the most awkward moment of her life. She had no idea how to process it. There were no excuses but she'd just felt so off balance on the bridge by the waterfall, literally and figuratively. Cabe's anguished face coupled with the way he'd opened up to her. And the location. It was all a perfect storm of overstimulation and she'd just snapped. She'd given in to her aching desire to be close to him. In every way.

Straightening, she took a deep breath. "Cabe, I—"

He held a hand up to stop her. "Let's just both get cleaned up. I, for one, could use a long hot shower before dressing for dinner."

Jenna winced. He'd effectively just dismissed her. There had to be a large sinkhole or underground cave on this island she could go crawl in. Or better yet, she could run into the ocean and dive into a large wave, just swim out into the open sea. It couldn't be any worse. She already felt like she was drowning.

"Probably a good idea." She forced out her agreement and grabbed her phone off the floor.

And her blood went cold again. Her screen was lit up with text messages. Most of them from home. Her mother. She could think of no good reason for Amanda to be trying to reach her here. The messages could only mean one thing: Amanda was in some kind of trouble.

# CHAPTER EIGHT

CABE JORDAN HAD made love to her—there was no way to focus on anything else.

Jenna lathered up the rich mango gel soap and let the soothing water of the shower wash over her still-tingling skin.

She could still feel his touch. Every word he'd whispered in her ear still echoed in her head. Every second of what they'd shared would be ingrained in her memory for the rest of her life. She'd never forget the way he'd felt, the things he'd said to her. It would all torture her for the rest of her life. Stifling a sob, Jenna turned off the water and grabbed the thick Turkish robe hanging from the shower door, wrapping it around herself and stepping out of the stall. Cabe had said he would wait for her in his room while she got cleaned up. She had no idea what she would say to him. He couldn't possibly know how torn she felt right now.

How in the world could she have let things get so far between them? And what in heaven's name was she to do now?

The beeping of her cell phone interrupted her thoughts again. Two more texts came in, and several missed calls registered.

Not now…not just yet.

She just couldn't tackle any of it now, not on top of everything else she had to grapple with. Call her a coward, but despite knowing that she should just answer the phone and find out what was happening back in Boston, her nerves just couldn't handle anything else at the moment. First she had to gain back some of her equilibrium before she faced Cabe. She would deal with Amanda's newest crisis when she regained some semblance of sanity and strength. A couple of hours more when she was half a world away certainly couldn't make any sort of difference anyway.

With shaky hands, Jenna gripped the phone and pressed the reset button until her finger hurt. When the device finally powered off, she sank down onto the love seat against the wall of her room. Her knees had suddenly gone weak.

What a fool she'd been. Forgetting about her reality for even a few moments of guilty pleasure. Pretending she could escape who she truly was. Her truth had even found her here, on this beautiful island paradise.

She could never be anything to someone like Cabe Jordan.

She had too much baggage, too much of a responsibility, the likes of which he'd never be able to relate to. An alcoholic mother who was repeatedly in and out of jail. Dear God, Amanda may even need bailing out right at this very moment. Or perhaps she'd been evicted again and couldn't get ahold of Jenna's brother nor find the spare key to her apartment that Jenna had given her.

Cabe was worried about a reporter simply posting a picture of the two of them. She shuddered to think how he would feel about being tied to a woman whose mother had such a sordid past. The press would have a field day with Amanda's history.

Well, there was nothing Jenna could do about it now, being hundreds of miles away on a Caribbean island.

Jenna took a deep breath and forced herself up. First thing first, Cabe awaited her. She had to shake off the self-pity and get dressed. They planned to get an early dinner at a seaside tavern and then head over to the casino. As far as she knew, none of those plans had changed.

How was she going to face him? Just a couple of short hours ago they'd been as close and as intimate as any two people could be. But next time she faced him, things had to be different. She had no one but herself to blame. She'd let her guard down, let herself forget who she was and where she belonged on the hierarchy of life.

Somehow, she had to rectify all that. What had happened between them this afternoon could never happen again. She had to make sure of it, even though it was breaking her heart into a million jagged pieces.

Pieces that would never be put back together no matter how hard she tried.

Jenna refused to meet him in the eye.

For the life of him, Cabe couldn't figure out what to say to break the ice. Should he apologize? Or would that just make things even more awkward? One thing was certain—the silence was becoming unbearable.

He cleared his throat, decided to go with something mundane, just to start. "I hope you're hungry. This place has quite an extensive buffet. Everything from seafood to the finest Kobe steak."

Again, she didn't face him, barely turned her head. "Sounds good."

Cabe stifled a groan of irritation. He deserved this; he'd done it to himself. Jenna clearly wanted to take back what had happened between them. He could guess why. They were completely wrong for each other. He'd never be able to give her the kind of things she deserved from a man.

Jenna needed someone with substance, a man who could give her a future. She'd grown up with enough instability. She didn't need any in her adulthood.

Between his nonstop workdays and his lifestyle, Cabe couldn't pretend to be that man. Hell, he barely stayed in the same city for more than two weeks at a time. She was smart enough to see that. A future with him wouldn't be much of a future at all. Not for someone who had as much going for her as Jenna did.

He should never have touched her, never so much as let himself stroke a hair on her head.

He had no excuse, only the fact that once again he'd proved what a weak person he was. His resistance had completely crumbled when she'd cupped his face and uttered soothing words no one had ever said to him before, her voice full of concern.

He would have to find a way to apologize. If not with words, then with some kind of way that would make all this up to her.

The soft music of a steel-drum band started up behind them on the beach as the maître d' greeted them. It took all of Cabe's will not to touch her as they were being led to their table. He wanted so badly to place his hand at the small of her back, feel the heat of her skin beneath his touch.

He cursed under his breath. To anyone in the dining area, they appeared to be the perfect picture of a well-suited couple enjoying each other's company while on vacation.

He would never have that. Not with Jenna. Not with anyone. How silly of him to believe that even for a moment he could. He'd long lost his appetite. Jenna hardly looked interested in food either. But it appeared they were both willing to go through the pretense.

But she surprised him when the waiter appeared. Instead of her usual water or iced tea, she asked for a glass of wine. He lifted an eyebrow in question after the man had left. "Looking for something a bit stronger this evening?"

She ducked her head when answering. "I'm afraid there isn't anything strong enough."

Cabe indulged in a deep sigh. Enough was enough. "Jenna, I think it's time we faced this head-on. Something happened between us. Something major."

She ducked her head. "I know that."

Unable to help himself, he reached for her hand across the table. At her flinch, he hastily pulled it back.

He just didn't learn, did he? Always taking too much, offering too little in return.

The tension between them hung thick and palpable.

"Maybe we should just cancel the visit to the casino," Cabe suggested, pulling his hand back. In an act of self-preservation, Jenna had jumped when he'd reached for her. As much as she might long for it, she lost all her resolve when he touched her. "I don't think either of us is really in the right frame of mind," he added. "Maxim will have to understand."

Great. Another work obligation that was being impacted because of her. She shook her head. "It's okay. That won't be necessary."

Try as she might, Cabe saw through her attempt to act professional. He rammed his fingers through his hair. "Jenna, please. Just say something. Tell me what's going on in your head."

Her eyes stung. There was really no good way to begin. "Oh, Cabe. We both know there's really only one thing to say."

He lifted an eyebrow. "And that is?"

"It's all wrong, what's happened between us."

He sucked in a breath, looked away. "Trust me when I say I didn't see it coming, either, the way I suddenly feel about you."

She shook her head, held her hands up. The lump in her throat made it hard to speak but she pushed through it. "That's what I mean. You can't do that."

"Do what?"

"I can't hear about how you feel about me. Nor think about how I feel about you. I can't do this, any of this. This project is too important to me. My job is too important. I can't believe I jeopardized everything by sleeping with my boss." A deep shudder shook her through her core. Her heart felt like it was splitting down the middle. And there was nothing she could do.

"Who says you jeopardized anything?"

"It's the truth. My reputation means everything to me."

"And it's still intact."

She shook her head. "Maybe for now. But everything I've worked for, none of it will matter if people find out I was intimate with the boss on a business trip!"

"It's not as scandalous as it sounds."

How she wished he was right, that things could be different between them. That she could somehow actually be sitting here and enjoying a moonlit dinner by the ocean with the man she— She gave her head a shake. That word kept popping up. And she had to stop even thinking it. Imagine, she'd practically said it out loud to Cabe at the waterfall earlier. What did it matter if she knew she was in love with him, that perhaps she'd always been in love with him? The cold slap of reality was all that mattered now.

"Jenna, I never meant to put you in such a position. It just kind of happened. I'm not sure what I can do to make it up to you, but I promise you I will. I'll think of some way."

The blood left her brain. "Oh, my God. You're not suggesting that I get some kind of reward because of what happened between us! Like some kind of—"

He jolted in his seat. "No! Of course not. I just mean— I don't know what I meant. Just that I hate what's happening, what you're feeling right now."

Suddenly it was too much. The events of the afternoon, the mystery texts and phone calls. This whole conversation. She just had to get away. Without a thought as to how it would look, she rose from her seat and dropped her napkin onto the table. "Excuse me."

Cabe stood as well. "Jenna, wait."

She didn't. The waiter gave them both a curious look but Jenna didn't care. She needed to get away. Cabe was fast on her heels. Part of her wished he would stop chasing her. But another foolish part would be crushed if he let her just run off into the night.

He kept on. She heard him calling her name behind her, felt a sharp pang of guilt for ignoring him. But she couldn't bring herself to stop, couldn't let Cabe see the tears in her eyes, the anguish that had to be written all over her face.

Her nerves couldn't handle the conversation that would ensue if he caught up to her. She'd fallen for him. Cabe was a known playboy who had a new woman on his arm more often than the moon changed phases. She knew she could never be anything more than a flippant affair for him. And yet she'd still gone and risked her professional career.

For a few moments of pleasure, she'd risked everything.

She figured it would just be a matter of time before he found her, and she was right. When he did, she was sitting on a large boulder on the edge of the beach, her toes submerged in the sand. She didn't look up at him as he approached.

"Hey there," he ventured.

"Hey."

"Mind if I sit?"

She didn't respond but shifted slightly to make room for him on the big rock. And instantly regretted it. Hardly a hair separated them, and his warmth seeped through her skin. And brought back unwanted memories of this afternoon, the absolute last thing she needed to be thinking about.

"I keep saying the wrong thing to you," he told her, looking straight ahead. She'd inadvertently run toward the casino. They could see its bright and colorful lights in the distance across the water.

"It's not you," she answered.

He grunted. "I beg to differ."

"We both seem to be stumbling here." She was just so embarrassed. And downright disappointed in herself.

"So…maybe we just move forward, acknowledge that even the best of us make mistakes?"

The word made her cringe, but he was right. "I guess we don't have much choice."

They sat in awkward silence, for how long Jenna couldn't guess. Cabe's sigh finally broke through it. "Well. There it is. That's the grand Paraiso Casino," he said, nodding his head in its direction.

She followed his gaze across the water. Even from this distance she could tell she had no business there. The place was completely out of her league. A steady stream of sports cars and luxury sedans pulled up the circular driveway. Those cars cost more than she'd hope to make in several years. Much more.

The people emerging out of those cars looked elegant and regal. Men in tuxedos and women in gowns. She looked down at her simple outfit. She'd been resourceful, finding a fitted black blouse in the boutique this afternoon to match one of her slim business suit skirts. At the time, she'd felt great pride for coming up with the idea and making it work. Now she felt like a lowly pauper who'd thought she could sneak into the prince's ball.

Which was exactly who she was.

"I've never been to a casino before," she admitted.

"Really? There are quite a few in New England. You haven't even been to any of those?"

She shrugged. "I'm not much of a gambler."

"Well, if you'd like, I could show you how to play some of the tables."

"No, thanks. Gambling's not really a habit I want to

pick up." She wouldn't bother to explain that her aversion to gambling was due to another one of her mother's failings. How many times had Amanda skirted her parental duties to go spend time on the slots? How many times had she gambled away money they could have desperately used for food or rent?

"I understand," Cabe told her. And somehow, she knew he did, that he grasped exactly what she was referring to. That was part of the problem. She felt as if Cabe understood her better than anyone else ever had. It was one of the reasons she'd forsaken all sanity earlier and let herself become intimate with him.

"Well, you get to tour one right now," he said and clapped his hands in mock excitement. "I guess I better get you over there before Maxim sends out a search party for us. We're already late."

Great. So now she could add tardiness to her list of professional missteps on this trip. She suppressed a groan of irony. In the overall scheme of things, being late to meet her casino tour guide was relatively trivial.

"We'll be taking a boat there," Cabe added.

"A boat?"

He nodded in the building's direction. "The casino is on its own little island, across the water. I'll drop you off."

"You won't be joining us?"

He shrugged. "He only mentioned you specifically."

"He did?"

"Uh-huh. And I guess you shouldn't keep him waiting."

She should be relieved, Jenna thought. But instead a dull disappointment settled in her chest. She didn't want to spend the evening with Maxim. She wanted to spend it with the man right next to her. Laughing with him, enjoying the warm tropical air. But this was for the best. It would give her some time to sort out her thoughts, settle her nerves. Things she had no hope of doing with Cabe anywhere nearby. It made sense. So why did she want to cry? To beg him to stay by her side? She bit her lip to stop herself from doing so.

They made it to a dock where a small open-air boat waited. A smiling captain took her hand and helped her on board. It appeared no other passengers were embarking for this go-around.

At her quizzical look Cabe responded, “All the avid gamblers are already at the tables. We’re a little late to the party.”

Only it wasn’t going to be a party at all. Not if Cabe wasn’t going to be there with her. The boat revved up and started a steady path across the water. The breeze suddenly picked up and made her shiver. Without a word, Cabe slipped off his suit jacket and draped it over her shoulders. The warmth of his body against the fabric cocooned her skin. She resisted the urge to snuggle deeply into it. “Thank you.”

“It can get chilly on the water. I should have warned you.”

Her heart ached as she thought of the picture they must have made. Alone on a boat on their way to a glamorous casino, his jacket draped over her shoulders to keep her warm. She wanted so much to make believe the idyllic picture could be reality.

But how could it given who she was and where she came from? How soon would someone like Cabe start noticing similarities between herself and the woman who at this very moment was still texting her? Because that needy woman would always text. Amanda would never be out of her life. And Cabe didn't need that kind of lowbrow drama in his.

Jenna knew better. Some things were simply not meant to be.

Maxim stood waiting for them as they disembarked. He greeted her with a warm smile and a barely-there nod to Cabe. Cabe offered a small grunt in response. Any other time, she might have found the competitive aura between the two men humorous and maybe even flattering. But not right now. She had too much on her mind. Too much to deal with. Her pocketbook buzzed yet again with another message on her phone.

Maxim stood staring at her. Cabe looked at her expectantly. One of them had obviously just asked her a question.

Jenna forced a smile and nodded, hoping it was an adequate response to whatever may have just been posed to her. Cabe's eyes grew wide. And clouded with something else she couldn't name. Hurt? By contrast, Maxim's grin had grown twofold. Oh, dear, what had she just agreed to?

"I guess I'll leave you two to yourselves, then," Cabe said then turned away. Her heart plummeted. Apparently, she'd just agreed to being alone with Maxim, essentially sending Cabe away. The exact opposite of what she really wanted. For one insane moment, Jenna wanted to yell at him to stop, to run after him and just explain everything. That she was oh, so wrong for him. That she had too much baggage. She'd never be the type of woman Cabe Jordan needed to have on his arm at his swanky social functions and his family gatherings.

She wanted to tell him all that. And then beg him to want her anyway.

But Maxim was speaking to her. She'd better listen this time. Who knew what she would agree to next without meaning to? Besides, Cabe had already walked several feet away. How foolish would it look to chase after him like a silly twit?

"Let's go find you a drink, my dear," Maxim offered. "Then we'll get the tour started." Dear heavens. The last thing she needed tonight was another drink.

What she needed, down to her soul, was to have Cabe back by her side. He was her anchor, a tether in this alien world full of riches and excess. Maxim was nice enough, every inch the attentive gentleman. Any single woman with a pulse would be thrilled to have him as her very own personal guide for the evening. Just not Jenna.

To top it off, she might have just hurt Cabe. She'd certainly be hurt if he'd dismissed her the same way. To spend time with another man, no less. Professional or not.

Meanwhile, her phone kept buzzing, buzzing, buzzing… Jenna cursed Amanda under her breath. She'd been cursing her all night. What did her mother want? Maybe ignoring her hadn't been the wisest decision, because now she could hardly think of anything else. What fresh hell had Amanda created for them all this time?

They'd made it to the entrance of the grand casino when Maxim turned to her. "Are you all right, dear?" he asked, concern etched in his face. "You look a little pale."

Jenna gave her head a shake and placed her hand on her midsection. "I'm afraid something I've eaten doesn't seem to be agreeing with me." It wasn't exactly a lie. "I'm not used to such rich food, as delicious as everything is."

Maxim gave her a sympathetic nod and pointed behind her. "The ladies' restroom is down that hallway. Take your time."

She gave him a grateful smile and turned on her heel. When she got there, the restroom was blessedly empty. Taking a breath to steady her nerves, she fished her phone out of her small purse. Without giving herself a chance to change her mind, she pulled up her brother's contact file and clicked on it.

It was time to face the piper. And the harsh reality that was her life.

He answered on the first ring. "Hey, sis."

"Sam, what's going on back in Boston? Amanda's calling and texting me relentlessly."

Sam sighed deeply before he spoke. "It's bad, Jen. You should probably sit down."

*Oh, no.* Jenna leaned back against the tiled wall. "Just tell me."

By the time he finished, Jenna really was going to be sick. According to Sam, the person who'd robbed Jordan's Fine Jewelry, committing the crime that had started Jenna on this whole journey, had been discovered.

That person was her mother.

She'd barely said three words to him last night as he walked her back to her hotel room. Cabe shuffled the papers on the table in the conference room and glanced at the door for the umpteenth time. Jenna hadn't made her way in yet. They'd agreed to meet here in the morning and get some work done. She still had a few minutes but he couldn't help but be impatient. There were things he needed to say to her. Questions he needed to ask.

He hadn't played his cards right yesterday. When Maxim had asked her if she needed Cabe to come along with them, he should have interjected right then and there. He should have said something along the lines of *Of course I'm going with her*. It just hadn't occurred to him that she might actually decline his company on Maxim's silly little tour.

He pinched the bridge of his nose and reclined in the plush leather chair. He stared at the door again, willing it to open and for Jenna to walk in. He checked his phone again. No messages from her. It wasn't that she was late, just that she was usually early to every meeting.

He wanted to see her, first to make sure she was all right. And secondly to finally clear the air between them. They had to start behaving like adults about what had happened between them. They were attracted to each other and they'd acted on it. He wanted to reassure her that it wouldn't happen again. She didn't need to be so skittish around him. He couldn't wait to explain that to her. In fact, if she didn't come in within the next couple of minutes, he would walk back to their villa and go knock on her door.

But then she did walk in, and with one look at her face his resolve faded like a punctured balloon. Her eyes were red-rimmed and puffy, the tip of her nose crimson. Her cheeks held a light sheen. There was no question in his mind—Jenna Townsend had been crying, probably for most of the night.

*Maxim.* That son of a bitch! But they'd left Maxim

at the casino last night and walked back to their suite together. So what had happened?

He watched as she pulled out her laptop and took a seat across from him, a tight smile plastered on her face. “Good morning. Where would you like to start?”

Was she serious? Did she honestly think they were going to simply get to work like it was a typical morning?

She blinked when he didn’t answer. “If we could get started, there’s something I need to tell you as soon as we’re finished.”

Yeah, no kidding. He leaned toward her over the table. “Maybe you should just tell me now.”

She shook her head. “No. It can wait. We should get some work done first.”

Right. As if that was even a possibility in the state she was in. Not to mention his own. “Jenna. I insist.”

She looked down, picked at her fingernail. Several beats passed in silence. As much as he wanted to, he couldn’t push her. She clearly struggled to blurt out whatever her news was.

When she looked back up at him, the fake smile was back in place. “Please, Cabe. We need to get through these to-dos.”

He nodded once. “We have plenty of time.”

“That’s just it—” She took a deep breath, but apparently couldn’t make herself continue.

“What?” he prodded.

Her mouth opened. Then shut again. He waited for her to say something, anything. Nothing but more silence.

That was it. He’d had it. A man could only muster so much patience in the face of so much left unsaid. Cabe pushed out of his seat, slamming his pen on the table in frustration. The action startled her and she clamped a hand to her mouth.

"Jenna, I'm trying to understand what's happening here. Can you help me do that?"

To his horror, her eyes filled. What had he said to cause that?

"Are you crying?" he asked, his tone harsher than it probably should have been. He was just at such a loss about what to say or do. His arms ached to hold her, to tell her everything would be all right. But he had no doubt in his mind that any such gesture of comfort or physical closeness would be shunned.

Suddenly, she stood. "I'm leaving in a couple of hours, Cabe."

He couldn't have heard her right. Surely, whatever was upsetting her couldn't be that pressing. "You're leaving? Why in the world are you leaving? Our jet doesn't even return for another two days."

"I understand that," she told him. "I've booked a seat on a commercial flight."

"Why would you do that?"

"Because I'm dropping this project. I can no longer work on it. In fact, I can no longer work for *you*."

He couldn't have heard her right. Was she that regretful about their relationship? "Listen, Jenna. What happened between us will not happen again."

She shook her head, her cheeks growing a fiery red. "That's only part of it, Cabe."

"I get that I crossed a line."

Anguish flooded her eyes. "No. It's just—there's something you should know."

"I'm listening."

She sucked in a breath before answering. "You're going to get a call soon from your security personnel. Or maybe it will be Boston PD who notifies you first."

Cabe blinked. "Come again?"

Whatever he'd been expecting, it hadn't been anything along these lines. And then he remembered. "Does this have anything to do with the stolen bracelet?"

She nodded, swallowed hard. "I'm afraid so."

"Jenna, what's going on?"

Her face visibly crumbled and she held a hand to her midsection. In that instant, Cabe wanted nothing more than to hold her and find a way to alleviate her anguish. Clearly, Jenna thought she was at fault somehow for whatever had happened. Maybe she'd left the jewelry case unlocked and the thief had gotten to the jewelry that way. That certainly wouldn't be grounds for her dismissal. She had to know he didn't care. Everyone made mistakes. No bracelet, no matter how costly or valuable, was worth the pain she was clearly burdening herself with right now.

But he kept himself in check, stood firm where he was. It wouldn't do either of them any good to interrupt her. She had to continue. Had to get this over with. "See, there was a reason your security head suspected me."

He could have sworn the room spun around him. "What exactly are you saying? Did you have something to do with the theft after all? Just tell me, Jenna." Could she really have been that cunning? Kept it from him all this time?

He just needed her to come clean. He needed her to be straight with him.

"Cabe, I'm so sorry. I didn't know. It was my mother."

"Your mother? I don't understand. I thought they

were investigating the security guard on duty that night?"

She pursed her lips, her eyes full of tears. "They are. He stole it with her help. Apparently, she'd been studying my routine. Knew where I kept my keys and told him everything. She gave him hints about what my passcode might be. She also told him to strike while I was away at that conference." She took another steadying breath. "He pretended to be interested in her in order to get her help."

His mouth had gone dry, which didn't matter. He couldn't seem to find any words anyway. Questions pummeled at him like a jackhammer in his brain.

"You have to believe I didn't know," she continued, her lip quivering. "I only just found out last night."

"Of course I believe you. I know you're not capable of being that duplicitous."

Jenna's shoulders visibly relaxed. "Thank you."

"I wish you'd just told me, instead of all the dramatics." He sighed, eyed the manila folder on his desk. All that would have to wait now. "I guess we should wrap up here. Then we can fly back together and deal with all this. I'll call the jet back today. We'll meet with Corporate Security as soon as we land."

Her eyes grew wide at his words. "Didn't you hear anything I said? My very own mother stole from you."

"I heard every word."

"She used me to do it."

"That's right. She used you. Am I missing something?"

"You said it yourself, Cabe. I didn't even know what she was up to."

"And none of that has anything to do with your competence. Or how valuable you are to this company." *To me*, he added silently.

"Nevertheless..." She looked away before adding, "There's no way I can continue to work for Jordan's Fine Jewelry as if none of this ever happened."

"You're not thinking this through, Jenna."

"I can't stay, Cabe." Her voice was low, pleading.

"What you really mean is that you *won't* stay," he corrected her. "The choice is yours to make. Yours alone."

She held up her hands. "That's what you're saying now. But this is just going to get uglier. You're going to end up regretting the day you hired me, that you had anything to do with Amanda Townsend's daughter."

He studied her, decided to call her bluff. "That's not what any of this is about."

"What does that mean?"

"It means that the real issue here is that you're blaming yourself. You're covering for Amanda. And as far as I can tell, you've been doing that your whole life."

She lifted her chin. "All that may be true. But it doesn't change anything."

"And that's the sad part. It doesn't change a thing. How long are you going to let Amanda's shortcomings impact your life?"

Suddenly, her eyes grew darker. She stepped closer to him, jabbed a finger in the air toward his chest. "You don't get to lecture me about this. You don't have any kind of cred when it comes to family dynamics."

The air crackled around them, the words hovering menacingly in the air. Jenna sucked in a breath, seemingly surprised by what she'd said.

He could only respond with silence. What was there

to say? She wasn't wrong. He certainly couldn't confront her about the real reason he was so frustrated and angry about her decision. There was so much more at play here than Jenna's response to Amanda's crime.

The harsh reality was that she was running. From him. Here he was, offering to stand by her. To help her through this. And her response was to slam the door in his face, to totally shut him down.

It didn't even occur to her to turn to him, to trust him.

What did that say about him?

The silence prevailed until Jenna finally turned on her heel. "Goodbye, Cabe. I'll contact you in Boston via an attorney."

Well, that had gone well. Jenna adjusted her seat belt and tried to settle into the too-tight space. Just her luck, she had been seated between a heavyset gentleman and an overpacked older lady with a purse larger than she was. But when had luck ever been on her side?

The tears threatened to flow again and she fought them back. What good had crying ever done? She had to gather her wits about her and figure out what to do. First she needed an attorney. One who would no doubt take all her life savings. But she couldn't risk any less—her life depended on it.

Bad enough Amanda had devised the theft, but in true maddening form, she was now bragging about it. All over town. So much so that word had eventually gotten back to her brother, who was trying to convince Amanda to turn herself in. Before the authorities figured it all out and she had the book thrown at her. That was why Amanda had been trying to get hold of her so desperately. She wanted to get Jenna to try to convince her brother to back off.

The man next to her started to snore. A baby wailed from somewhere in the back. This was a far cry from the private jet she'd arrived on. That was another lifetime ago. Back when she was still a professional with a career. She'd still had a future, maybe even a shot at happiness. Someone the likes of no other than Cabe Jordan had actually been attracted to. Jenna closed her eyes and tried to pretend that none of it had ever happened. That she was back to that first day on the jet with Cabe.

She remembered the look of shocked disappointment on his face when she'd told him about her leaving.

*Snap out of it.* She had to get that image out of her mind. She also had to forget about how he had looked at her that day near the waterfall. Like she was the only one who could have brought that smile to his face. Like she was the only woman for him.

There was no doubt that the next time he saw her, he would have nothing but disdain in his eyes. Jenna's stomach churned and it had nothing to do with the plane taking off. The things she'd said to him. Why couldn't she learn to control her mouth? He'd only been trying to help.

But she'd had to show him that he couldn't help her. There would be no white-knight scenario for Jenna Townsend. Cabe had his own demons. She wouldn't burden him with her own. He didn't know it now, but she was doing him a favor. Soon, he would realize it.

The sooner the better. For his sake.

Jenna surveyed the mess that was her mom's apartment. Take-out containers littered the floor, and empty beer bottles sat turned sideways on every flat surface. Various puddles of unknown liquids spotted the ground. And what in heaven's name was that smell?

She certainly wasn't in paradise any longer. In fact, Jenna would be hard-pressed to prove she hadn't imagined the whole Paraiso Resort and her time on it.

No, this was more like the depths of Hades. And she had her mother to thank for it.

She walked down the hall to the bedroom. Hard to believe, but there was an even bigger mess in here. An empty pizza box sat at her feet. Half-eaten bags of chips and candy cluttered most every surface. And of course, more assorted bottles lay strewn about the floor. She'd only been out of town a few days.

Looking for a priceless bracelet in this mess would be like looking for the proverbial needle in a haystack. Not that it was likely to be here. But she had to make sure.

Jenna felt the tears burn her eyes and a welt form in her throat. Why had she thought she could escape this? This was her life—this depressing, dirty town house and the woman who lived here, the burden of whose care fell solely on Jenna's shoulders. How could she have let herself forget that? How could she have let herself get close to anyone? Let alone someone like Cabe.

Her lips tingled as she remembered their kiss in the conference room. Such a mistake, she should have never let it happen. She thought she could let herself indulge, just one last time before he found out who Jenna Townsend really was. But then again, he'd always known. Everyone did.

Suddenly it was all too much. Her legs grew weak and she perched herself on the edge of Amanda's bed.

Several moments passed as she just sat there. Jenna felt nothing but shame. Even her anger had left her. All she held in her soul was a gnawing, hollow sense of shame.

"Hey, thought I might find you here." Her brother's voice startled her; she hadn't heard him come in.

She hurriedly wiped the moisture off her cheeks then turned and stepped over the garbage piles to give him a hug. "I just got here. Thought I'd look for the bracelet. Just in case."

Her brother let out a low whistle. "I doubt it's here, sis."

"It couldn't hurt to look, right?"

"Guess not."

But hours later, they were both ready to admit defeat. Despite having turned the mess in the apartment upside down, they couldn't find the bracelet anywhere. In fact, the place held nothing of value whatsoever. At least her mother's thievery had been a one-and-done affair.

Sam gave her shoulder a reassuring squeeze. "We'll fix this, Jen. I swear I won't let you fall because of her latest stunt."

She managed a weak smile. "I'm not so sure this time's going to be fixable, Sam. Even if people believe I had no part in the theft, my reputation is ruined. What retail establishment is ever going to hire me again? I'm too much of a risk."

She choked as she said the last word. She was no longer employed with her dream company. She'd never be with Cabe again, not in any way. Reaching behind her, she found the edge of the bed once more. Her legs just weren't going to hold her up.

"Don't say that," Sam insisted. "We'll make them believe you. We'll make her." He pointed an accusatory finger at the empty bed, as if Amanda were still in it. "She'll explain what she did. Tell them that you had nothing to do with it."

"Who do you think is going to take her word for it?"

"Jen, we'll make them see the truth."

As usual, her mother had wreaked complete havoc in her children's lives.

"I have to go," she told her brother.

"Where are you going?"

"To find Amanda. I have to try to make at least part of this right." She turned on her heel and walked out the door before Sam could see the fresh round of tears.

Not that she really could make any of it right in any way. Not with the Jordans. And certainly not with Cabe. An anguished cry tore from her throat and she dropped down to sit on Amanda's cold stone stoop.

She thought about the way Cabe had smiled at her at the beach party as he'd sipped from the straw that she'd just used. The way his eyes had traveled over her that day in the boutique when she'd worn the designer gown. Now she wished she'd never gone to that party with him. She should have never set foot in that boutique.

Because it was all a fairy tale that she'd been living these past few days. One she now had to give up. It would have been so much easier on her heart never to have lived it at all.

# CHAPTER NINE

SO SHE WANTED to see him.

Cabe set his office phone back down on the top of the mahogany desk, resisting the urge to listen to Jenna's message once more just to hear her voice. She'd left it at two o'clock in the morning. Apparently, neither of them had gotten much sleep last night. Hell, he hadn't gotten much sleep at all since he'd seen her last. He'd barely been able to think straight. Now she was requesting "time on his schedule" the same day he'd arrived back in Boston. That was exactly how she'd phrased it. So formal. So straightforward. As if nothing had ever happened between them. It would serve her right if he ignored her. Make her come to him.

He sighed. Of course he wouldn't do that. Instead, he typed out a text to her cell phone.

I have time right now. My office.

It took less than five minutes before he heard her knock on his door. He fixed his cuff links and stood. Maybe he'd finally get some answers. She opened the door and he motioned for her to come in. He lost his breath when she did.

So beautiful. The severe ponytail was back, as tight as he'd ever seen it. Her navy pin-striped suit—all business. Dark circles smudged her eyes. She looked utterly beat. And still, she was the most beautiful woman he'd ever laid eyes on. Insanity nearly took over his better judgment and he almost went to her. All he wanted to do right now was pull her into his arms, absorb her warmth, kiss those beckoning lips that so haunted his dreams. He wanted to tell her that everything would be all right, that he would see to it.

Instead, he tightened his fists at his sides.

She stopped in her tracks several feet away from him then took a deep breath. Definitely hesitant. Cabe perched himself on the edge of his desk, motioned to the chair opposite him. "Can I get you anything?" he asked, just to get some kind of conversation going before sitting down.

She shook her head. "No, thank you. And I'd rather do this standing, if you don't mind."

Well, now he felt awkward as he'd already sat. But standing again would look silly. Wouldn't it? Damn it, she was the only woman in the world who could get him so riled. He made million-dollar decisions on a daily basis. But around her he didn't even know whether to sit or stand, for heaven's sake.

"It won't take long," she added.

He simply nodded for her to continue.

"I just wanted to return this." She stepped over and dropped something shiny and bright onto the desk in front of him.

The bracelet.

"How?"

"We found the thief, Sam and I. Convinced him to

hand it over. The authorities are on their way to arrest him now." She pointed to the object that had caused so much havoc in their lives. "I assure you, it's the real piece."

Cabe could only stare. "I don't understand."

"It's simple. I made my mother tell me where your sneaky security guard could be found. Then Sam and I had a heart-to-heart with him."

He didn't like the sound of this, not at all. "Let me get this straight. You and your brother searched out and approached a known thug. Just to retrieve a stolen bracelet. Putting your very life at risk in the process."

She narrowed her eyes on him. "Hardly. We just convinced him it was only a matter of time before the cops came for him. He was almost relieved to dispose of it. Couldn't even fence the thing on the street. Too valuable. He didn't have those kinds of connections. Lord knows Amanda doesn't."

Cabe's heart pounded with anger. To think she had jeopardized her personal safety. For some bauble he honestly couldn't have cared less about.

"At least Jordan's has the piece back," Jenna said.

How could she be so flippant about this? "Look. You didn't need to risk your safety by retrieving it. We had the matter under control." That was a lie. Cabe hadn't even thought about the cursed bracelet since the day Jenna had left his office. He'd done absolutely nothing about its theft. Not even so much as to call Jordan's Security and give them an update. That bracelet had only caused one headache after another. But she didn't need to know that. When he thought of the danger she put herself in, he wanted to grab her by the shoulders and shake her.

Then he wanted to kiss her until she finally started to see some sense.

"I know it doesn't really solve anything," she said, apologetically.

No, it didn't. Not at all. Which made it all the worse. "What the hell are you trying to prove here, Jenna?"

Ire flashed in her eyes. "I wasn't trying to prove anything. Merely rectifying a mistake I made."

Cabe wanted to throw something. "There you go again. *You* didn't make a mistake. You did nothing wrong. *Amanda*, your mother, stole from the store." He emphasized the name, hoping it would drive his point home.

No such luck. Her back stiffened before she spoke. "My mother was targeted by a charming con artist because of where I worked."

"Are you apologizing for where you chose to be employed?"

She actually stomped her foot. "I'm not apologizing at all. Not for getting the bracelet back. I'm merely returning it."

"Which you did by risking your own safety, going after a known thief. Can you not even see the danger you put yourself in?"

"I've been dealing with people like that thief since I can remember. My mother didn't exactly have high standards when it came to her boyfriends."

"How long are you going to let her run your life, Jenna? You quit your job because of her, you foolishly went and got the bracelet back to make up for her mistake. When are you going to realize that you have your own worth? Beyond the stain of your mother's reputation?"

She gasped. "I made my own decisions."

He actually laughed. "Do you really think that? You just keep trying to prove yourself."

Her jaw dropped. "Did you just accuse me of trying to prove myself to atone for who my mother is?"

"Don't you?"

She snorted a small laugh. "You have no idea how hypocritical that is."

The one word struck like a dart in his brain. "Hypocritical?"

"You really don't see it, do you? You've done nothing but reach for and achieve goal after goal, just to prove yourself worthy of the Jordan name. The whole world can see you're a credit to your parents. Everyone except you!" She threw her hands in the air. "It's almost as if… Oh, never mind!"

Cabe crossed his arms over his chest. "No, please. Continue. I'd really like to hear this."

"It's as if you have to ensure James and Tricia don't ever regret adopting you. Like you have to continually find ways to earn their love, only to come up short time and time again."

The room grew dark around him; he felt the muscles in his neck tighten to the point of pain. Jenna had no idea what she was talking about. Why in the world had he ever thought she might be someone who could understand? He'd been a fool to ever confide in her about his parentage.

"Thank you for bringing back the bracelet. Now, if you don't mind, I have a lot of work to do. On top of my regular workload, I no longer have any assistance with the Caribbean expansion."

Jenna flinched, his words finding their target. So be it. "That's it?" she asked incredulously.

"Yes. It is. I believe we've both said all there is to say to each other."

She shook her head and turned to the door, slamming it hard on her way out.

Cabe paced the length of the room and tried to get his pulse in check. It didn't help. All the confusion and frustration of the past two days formed into a barreling rage inside his chest. He turned with a vicious curse and landed a swift, hard kick to the parlor table in the center of his office. It landed with a thud so loud it must have resonated to the floor below. But he barely heard the noise over the roaring in his ears.

Cabe's administrative assistant knocked on his door again. This was probably the fourth or fifth time this morning. She'd been doing that, checking in on him, ever since the incident a few days back when he'd kicked the table over and caused such a loud ruckus. Apparently she wasn't buying Cabe's story that he'd tripped and toppled it accidentally. The interruptions were getting annoying. Not that he'd actually been focusing enough to get anything done. He hadn't been able to focus on anything since Jenna had left his office three days ago.

"Betty. I really am fine," he began. "You don't have to—" He stopped when he realized there was someone in the reception area behind her.

"Actually, Mr. Jordan. Your father is here to see you."

Cabe put down the spreadsheet he held in his hand. James was here? Now what? Then it occurred to him—

his parents had no doubt heard about Jenna leaving their employ.

Cabe had some explaining to do.

Standing, he nodded at her. "Show him in."

James entered wearing jeans and a blue checked shirt, no tie. His father had a sharp head for business, but had never been interested in dressing the part.

"Father. I've been meaning to set up a time to talk to you. And Tricia."

"I figured I'd come by while you were in town. I probably should have called first."

Did he always have to sound so overly polite with him? "It's technically your company."

His father pulled out the chair opposite the desk and sat. "You run it. Although that's what I came to talk to you about. I hear we may be losing a valuable member of the Jordan team."

He should have seen this coming, Cabe thought. Very little happened within the business that James wasn't swiftly made aware of. He made it a point to know everything that went on with the company he started, regardless of who actually ran it.

"Jenna Townsend was on location to help me with the Caribbean expansion when things got a little… complicated."

"So I gathered. Was there more than one complication? In addition to the missing jewelry?"

At Cabe's puzzled expression, James continued. "Your reputation as a ladies' man somewhat precedes you, son. Jenna's a very attractive woman."

Cabe grunted. Despite ditching the photographer back at the island, it looked like the gossip mill still churned out its story.

"I'll squelch the rumors. This isn't a long-term concern."

James held up a hand. "That's not why I'm asking, not because of the business."

"It's not?"

James shook his head. "Your mom and I, we've known Jenna since she was a little girl. She hasn't had the easiest life."

Cabe barely suppressed a groan. "Don't I know it?"

His father's eyebrows lifted. "She confided in you?"

He hadn't really thought about it that way, but now that his father mentioned it… "I guess she did."

"That's surprising. She tends to keep that stuff about her family close to her chest."

"We had a few opportunities to talk." He looked his father square in the eye. "I sort of confided in her, too. I know we don't normally talk about it with anyone, but I told her the truth."

"The truth?"

"That I'm not really your son."

His father sucked in a breath. "Is that how you put it? When you told her?"

"More or less."

"That's how you see yourself, then. As not really my son."

How in the world had this conversation veered in this direction? They were supposed to be talking about Jenna and what it would mean to their business if she left the company.

"It's not like I don't realize how lucky I am. I owe everything to you and Tricia."

James nodded slowly. "You're not really my son and you owe us for bringing you up."

Well, when he phrased it that way… But, as off-putting as it sounded, it was essentially the truth.

"As parents, you did everything you could," Cabe reassured him.

"If that's the impression you have of us, we clearly needed to do more." He looked off to the side, summoning the words. "Listen, Cabe, your mother and I probably should have waited before adopting another baby. Tricia couldn't handle her grief, and I wasn't strong enough to help her. I was barely containing my own. But that doesn't mean you weren't wanted. Or loved."

James may as well have sucker punched him. A lump formed at the base of Cabe's throat. "Thank you for saying that."

"I should have said it years ago. And more." He swallowed visibly. "But I never found the right times. And frankly, I never found the courage. Until now. Better late than never, right?" James chuckled, thought it sounded false and the smile didn't reach his eyes.

"Truth be told," his father went on, "not only have you earned our respect repeatedly over the years, you've been a constant source of both joy and love in our lives, more so than we could have hoped that first day we brought you home. And I'm ashamed to admit that I didn't tell you that or show you nearly as often as I should have."

Or at all, Cabe thought. James's words were beyond unexpected. He'd never so much as uttered an affectionate word to him over the years.

The James Jordan sitting opposite him right now bore little resemblance to the distant and distracted man Cabe had grown up with.

Was Cabe mistaken or were his father's eyes actually shimmering with moisture? James was the strongest man he had ever known. Never once in his life had he seen him so much as shed a tear. He'd just appeared perpetually sad.

When James spoke again, his voice was thick. "You are and have always been my son."

Cabe had to remind himself to breathe.

The words hung powerfully in the air. Both men stared uncomfortably at each other for several moments. For the life of him, Cabe couldn't come up with a single thing to say.

Finally, James cleared his throat. "Now, where exactly do we stand with Jenna?"

Cabe blinked at the sudden question. His father was clearly ready to change the subject. Pushing his hair off his forehead, Cabe searched for a way to answer. How to describe where he stood with Jenna? "She's unlike anyone I've ever met. She's got an incomparable business sense, yet she's sensitive and so aware of the needs of others. She can be infuriatingly stubborn but somehow knows when to compromise. She can make me angry as a hornet one minute, and then make me laugh the next. I've never been with anyone like her."

"I see." James studied the carpet, didn't look up when he asked the next question. "Does she know?"

"Know what?"

His father looked at him as if he should be wearing a dunce cap. Maybe he was right. But he was still trying to process the overwhelming conversation of a few minutes ago. "I mean, did you ever actually come out and tell her any of this?"

"Uh. No."

James shifted in his chair, uncomfortable again.

"Listen, Cabe. Your mother and I haven't exactly been the most open or, God forgive me, the most willing, when it came to demonstrating affection. I've known that in my gut. But I guess what we just talked about drove it all home."

Another shocking admission. His father was making all sorts of confessions here.

"Maybe we're not the best examples to follow."

Cabe hadn't realized that he'd been following anyone's example. But he had to acknowledge James's point. In his last few conversations with Jenna, he'd been totally focused on her complete willingness to set aside her own needs for the sake of her family. He'd been trying to point out to her how wrong that was.

It was Cabe who was wrong; James had just shown him that. No, that wasn't correct. Jenna had been the one to show him. James had merely just confirmed her point.

Up until today, Cabe had been too blind to see what was so clear all along. He'd always had the love of his parents. They really did value and cherish him. They just had no idea how to show it.

At least Jenna had the courage to accept the family she had and to love them anyway. She was right to call him a hypocrite.

"What I'm trying to say is," James continued, "you've been a fighter your whole life. This is something worth fighting for. Jenna's not the type of woman you want to lose once you have her."

Clearly, James was no longer referring to the company.

# CHAPTER TEN

JENNA TENSED WHEN her doorbell rang. She just couldn't bring herself to entertain the possibility that it might be the police. She had no clue what she would say to them if they were already here for her. Though it would have to count for something that the bracelet had been returned. Taking a fortifying breath, she yanked open her door. Then did a double take when she saw who her visitor was.

"Cabe? I thought you would have returned to Manhattan by now."

"Not yet. I had some agenda items to finish."

Her heart plummeted. He was here on some kind of business.

"I wanted to come by and tell you that you can relax. No one's going to press charges against your mother."

Could she have heard that right? "I don't understand."

"Roger, my head of security, is former Boston PD. He's still got a lot of connections. He'll make sure the authorities know you had nothing to do with the robbery. And he can put in a word on your mom's behalf, make sure she gets a break. They'll be easier to convince now that the item is back in its rightful place. And because she's seeking help for her addictions."

Jenna's relief almost had her knees buckling beneath her. That was an unexpected turn. She didn't want to look a gift horse in the mouth but the development begged a question. "But why would your security head do that?"

"Because I asked him to."

He had? Her mouth fell open. "I don't know what to say. Except that I can't thank you enough. Really, Cabe, that was above and beyond. You don't know how much I appreciate it."

But it still didn't explain why he was here, at her door. He could have called with the info. Or had his secretary do it even.

He surprised her further by asking, "Can I come in?"

Stepping aside, she motioned him inside and shut the door. His eyes grew wide when he saw her packed airline bag against the wall.

"Are you going somewhere?"

She nodded. "I have some interviews lined up. Out of state."

His lips thinned into a slim line. "I apologize. I should have called first."

Suddenly he was serious, matter-of-fact. His mouth didn't hold a hint of a smile. Still, all she could think about was how good it was to see him, just to have him in the same room. It didn't seem possible that fate had given her a chance to see him one more time. Taking a moment to study his face, she thought how haggard he looked now. Dark circles framed his weary bloodshot eyes. He clearly had not bothered to shave this morning.

"It's okay," she assured him. "I have some time." Though the truth was she'd actually be cutting it really close if she delayed any longer, barely giving herself enough time to get to the airport and check in. But she couldn't bear to send him away just yet. She missed him! She'd been walking around zombielike these past few days, barely able to function, the features of Cabe's face etched in her mind. The feel of his touch imprinted onto her skin. "Can I get you anything? Coffee?"

"Sure, that'd be great."

Jenna went to the still-warm coffeepot, half full. She was glad she hadn't had a chance to empty and rinse the carafe. When she returned, Cabe was sitting on her sofa, with her sketchbook lying open on the coffee table in front of him. He pointed to the page she'd been working on. "These are really good. Did you do them?"

She ducked her head at the compliment. "I try some designing in my spare time. Mostly necklaces."

He picked up the book and studied it. "I had no idea you designed jewelry."

Jenna set the coffee cup down, hoping he didn't notice the trembling in her hands. This conversation was so awkward. All she wanted to do was wrap her arms around his neck and feel his lips on hers. Instead, she was racking her brain trying to come up with what to say next.

"I don't know if it's any good," she replied with genuine doubt. No one had ever actually seen any of her sketches until now.

"You're full of surprises, Jenna."

Another awkward pause settled between them.

He inhaled a deep breath. "Jenna, you're unlike any

woman I've ever met. You design jewelry. You have an amazing head for business. You charm everyone you meet. And you've done an amazing job of managing your severely troubled parent while raising yourself and a brother." He stood to face her, ran a finger down her cheek. A hot tingle ran up her spine at his touch, and the smell of his aftershave teased her senses. "You're one of the bravest people I know, man or woman."

Whoa. Jenna gave her head a shake. "Brave? How in the world am I brave in any way?"

"You really don't see it, do you? The way you put your mom first, despite what it's cost you. That takes the kind of rare courage few people possess. You actually confronted a known criminal to rectify what she'd done." He visibly shuddered. "Please don't do anything like that ever again, by the way."

She sniffled on a laugh. "I won't—I promise."

He motioned toward her suitcase. "I know I have no right—but cancel those interviews. Say you'll stay, Jenna."

"You want me to stay at Jordan's Fine Jewelry?"

Cabe shook his head. "Not exactly."

She swallowed down the hope that had blossomed in her chest. How foolish of her. Of course she'd misunderstood him. Until she heard his next words.

"I want more than that. I want you to stay with *me*."

He grasped her hand in his. Jenna couldn't seem to make her brain work. Thoughts scrambled around in her head like fallen leaves during a windstorm. It was hard enough to wrap her mind around the fact that he was here, in her home. She couldn't process what he was telling her. It was simply too good to be true. "Cabe, what are you saying?"

"I'm saying that watching you walk out of my office that day nearly broke me. I haven't been able to sleep. I keep thinking about the way you felt in my arms, the way we were together on the island. I can't lose that, Jenna." He inhaled deeply. "I know I have a lot to work on. To make myself the kind of man you deserve. I just need you to be patient."

That settled it. She'd obviously awoken to some alternate reality. The world had turned upside down. Cabe Jordan was pleading with her to be patient with him. Asking her to understand that he would work hard to become the right man for her.

"I know it's a lot to ask," Cabe continued. "You've obviously had the patience of a saint over the years. You've raised yourself and your brother on your own, made sure your mother didn't completely self-destruct. It's unfair to ask you to extend yourself any more for my sake."

Tears sprang into her eyes. She reached for him, clasped his unshaven chin in her hand. "As far as courage goes, you have it in spades, Cabe Jordan."

It was his turn to look shocked. So she explained, "You've done your utter best all your life to try and make your parents happy. Even knowing that it may never be enough. That's the definition of loyalty. Of bravery. You're everything anyone could ever hope for in a son."

He turned his face in her cupped palm, exactly as he had that day at the waterfall. "Then why? Why did you feel the need to leave at first?"

She choked down on a sob. "How can you ask that? I could barely face you. By then you meant so much to me. How was I supposed to ask you to accept the fact that my own mother had stolen from you?"

"You beautiful, silly fool. You have no idea how you impressed me."

She was definitely hearing things. "Impressed you?"

He nodded. "You could have surrendered Amanda to the authorities. Then gone back to your job and lived your life. No one would have blamed you for doing so. Instead, you quit the job you loved and hired an attorney for her. You might not realize what kind of a person that makes you, but I do."

"Is that really how you see me?"

"It's exactly how I see you. I just didn't know how to tell you any of that."

Just those simple words, and somehow the steel bands around her heart snapped open. Cabe didn't judge her on who her mother was or where she came from. He saw her strengths and judged her on her actions. He saw Jenna for who she was.

Maybe he could help her see it, too.

He pulled her to him then, kissing her deeply and holding her tight against his frame. "Besides, by then I'd already fallen in love with you. You could have asked me anything."

Her heart had not only just sprung free but Jenna was certain it would burst any moment now. "You love me?" she stammered, her mind on the verge of going numb.

He didn't need to use any words when he answered her.

"You look beautiful, Jenna."

Jenna turned away from the boutique mirror to face

the two ladies helping her get ready. "Do you really think so, Seema?"

Seema beamed back at her. "Yes. That dress may as well have been made for you." She walked over to give Jenna a tight squeeze around the shoulders. Martine, the saleswoman who had encouraged her to fatefully try on this very dress all those weeks ago, gave her a conspiratorial wink.

A low rumble of thunder sounded through the walls from outside. The forecast this morning called for a major storm far off the coast. No doubt she and Cabe would be saying their vows under a cloudy sky with sprinkles of rain. None of it mattered or could make so much as a dent in her joy. She could weather any storm with Cabe by her side.

As she turned back to her reflection in the mirror, Jenna's heart did a little jump at the sight. Was that really her staring back from the glass? Jenna had known the moment Cabe asked her to marry him that this would be her bridal gown.

She also knew there was no other place on earth she'd rather have her wedding than here, at the Paraiso Resort.

And no other man she wanted to spend the rest of her life with.

Cabe was in the process of admiring his bride and marveling at his luck when his father surprised him by standing up. His parents were seated at the closest table to the wedding dais, along with Seema and Jenna's brother. Jenna's mom remained in Boston, getting the rehabilitation treatment she so desperately needed. That had been part of the deal when the Jordans agreed not to press charges.

His father picked up his wineglass and raised it, clearing his throat to get everyone's attention. A toast. The roar of chatter gradually diminished as their guests noticed.

Cabe inhaled and braced himself. He honestly had no idea what his father might say; it hadn't even occurred to him to ask his father to speak. No doubt his speech would be all about the growth of Jordan Enterprises under Cabe's leadership. Or something.

He was wrong. In fact, his dad surprised him and didn't even mention business.

James took a deep breath and began. "I'm not sure if I can find the word to adequately express what I want to say. But here goes," James said and smiled in a way that didn't quite reach his eyes. He turned toward the wedding guests. "My son has managed to do so much in his life. He's been a terrific son and he's achieved more into his thirties than most men do in a lifetime. And now he's managed to snare himself a wife as accomplished and beautiful as Jenna."

Cabe heard Jenna gasp in surprise as she reached for his hand and gave it a gentle squeeze. He in turn clung to her fingers.

His father went on. "You've done so much for yourself, Cabe. All on your own. We should have been there for you more than we were. For that, I can only ask your forgiveness." James looked him straight in the eye as he said the last word.

Cabe could only stare frozen, unable to come up with anything appropriate to say or do. He stole a glance at his mother and immediately realized there'd be no help from that corner—she was definitely crying. An awkward silence ensued.

James took a deep breath, opened his mouth to presumably say more, but then suddenly shut it again. He looked to the ground, clearly struggling to find the wherewithal to continue.

Jenna's hand slowly released his. He felt the loss of her touch immediately. But then she did something so simple yet so powerful, it reaffirmed why he'd fallen head over heels in love with her in the first place. She stood and slowly started to clap. It wasn't long before the rest of their guests joined her. The look of gratitude and relief on his father's face said it all. No, not his father, Cabe corrected himself. His dad. James held the expression of a man who'd just been rescued from drowning.

And they had Cabe's new bride to thank for it.

Once the applause died down and everyone had lowered their glasses, Jenna looked up to find Cabe holding out his hand to her.

She stood and he took her by the waist, led her to the dance floor. As they swayed to the rhythmic reggae song, he leaned over to whisper in her ear. "I love you, Mrs. Jordan."

The words, coupled with the magic of the moment, brought tears of happiness to her eyes. "And I've always loved you, Mr. Jordan."

He laughed and it sent pure pleasure through her whole body, down to her toes. "If only I'd known. Think of all the time we've wasted."

"It was your fault for never asking me to prom."

He affectionately nipped at her ear. "Perhaps. But you know, *you* could have asked me."

"Hmm. You're right. We'll just have to find a way to make up for lost time," she teased.

He brushed his lips against hers. "I can't wait to start."

Jenna knew they already had.

* * * * *

# HER HOLIDAY MIRACLE

JOANNA NEIL

## CHAPTER ONE

AT LAST. REBECCA GAVE a soft sigh of relief as a sixty-foot-long catamaran smoothly eased into position alongside the dock. The sound of calypso music came from on board, floating on the air waves towards her, and her spirits lifted in an instant. She'd been patiently standing in the queue for some time, wilting in the heat despite her light camisole top and loose cotton skirt, but now there was an end in sight. She would soon be on the last part of her journey to the beautiful Caribbean island of St Marie-Rose.

Just up ahead of her a man straightened as the boat approached. She'd noticed him earlier—in fact there was no way she could have missed him. He had midnight-black hair and sculpted, lightly tanned features, and he stood out from the crowd—tall, muscular, supremely fit-looking, wearing pale chinos and a white T-shirt that outlined broad shoulders and well-muscled biceps. He'd been looking around, taking in his surroundings. Presently, though, he seemed preoccupied, deep in thought, not at all like the others who lined the quayside.

Perhaps he felt her glance resting on him just then, because he half turned towards her and looked directly at her, his dark gaze meshing with hers for a heart-stopping instant. His eyes widened and his glance moved over her, taking in her slender yet curvaceous figure, the long copper-coloured hair that tumbled past her shoulders in a mass of unruly curls. All at once he seemed stunned, as though he couldn't take his eyes off her.

Heat swept along her cheekbones and she looked away, embarrassed for her own part to have been caught staring. Somehow she hadn't seemed able to help herself…there was just something about him… He probably wasn't a tourist, she decided. There was nothing of the loose-limbed, laid-back sunseeker about him.

Actually, much the same could be said of her right now. She didn't feel at all touristy. After being cooped up in an aeroplane for almost a dozen hours, followed by a short taxi ride to this port, she was more than ready for the last leg of her journey. At least she hoped this was the last leg. It was already late afternoon, and she really wanted to arrive at the house before nightfall. With any luck her sister, Emma, would be there to greet her. She smiled, a thrill of excitement running through her at the prospect—it would be so good to see Emma again.

Up to now, though, nothing had gone quite to plan—instead of flying directly to the island she'd found herself stranded here, on the verdant, equally lovely tropical island of Martinique, waiting for a ferry to take her across the sparkling blue sea to her final destination.

The people in the queue began to move slowly forward. 'Ah, looks like we're boarding at last,' someone said behind her. 'Finally!'

It was a male voice. She turned to glance at him. He was a young man—in his mid-twenties, she guessed, much the same as herself. She was twenty-six. He had blond hair and blue eyes, and a ready smile. Dressed for the heat, he wore three-quarter-length shorts and a T-shirt. Clearly he was in a good mood—most likely returning with his friends from a day trip to Martinique. The three young men with him were chatting to one another, lively and exuberant.

He returned her gaze and waved a hand towards the boat. 'Shall we? I'm William, by the way. William Tempest.'

He looked at her questioningly and she responded in a soft voice, 'Rebecca… Rebecca Flynn…most people call me Becky.'

'Hi, Becky. We should be able to get some refreshments on board. Perhaps I could buy you a drink? I'm not hitting on you,' he hastened to explain. 'Well, maybe I would in different circumstances. It's just that I noticed earlier you were looking a bit fed up and I thought maybe you could do with something to cool you down and perk you up—perhaps an iced juice of some sort—they do a good orange and mango mix?'

'Do they?' So he'd noticed her wilting. What was it that had given her away? Was it her hot cheeks or the way her curls clung damply to her temples? She should have taken the time to pin her hair back while she was on the plane.

She'd no experience of the facilities on board ferries in the Caribbean, but now she moistened her lips with the tip of her tongue in anticipation.

'A cold drink sounds wonderful. I'd like that.' She added as an afterthought, 'This whole thing is a bit of an adventure for me.'

'Are you here on holiday?'

'Sort of. More of an extended break, shall we say? Things were getting me down back home and I needed to get away.'

'Really? I'm sorry. I feel a bit that way, too. I've had a break-up with my girlfriend…it was really hard to take. It was a while ago, and I keep trying to put it all behind me, but it's difficult.'

'Yes. I know how that feels.'

Together, chatting amiably, they walked the short distance along the quay to the boarding ramp and stepped on to the deck of the boat.

It was strange… She didn't know him from Adam, but she liked him instantly, in a platonic, unthreatening kind of way. All her usual English reserve seemed to be disappearing fast—melting away in the tropical sunshine.

Perhaps it was the heady atmosphere of the Caribbean beginning to exert its hold on her—or maybe the energetic beat of the music coming from the boat was serving to loosen her up. Whatever the reason, she'd throw all her inhibitions away right now for the chance of downing a long, cold glass of something. Anything.

William looked around. 'Where do you want to sit? Would you like to be under cover, or do you want to look out over the sea?'

'Both, I think.' She smiled. 'I've been stuck on a plane for several hours, so it will be great to move around and feel the fresh air for a bit.'

He nodded, his mouth curving. 'Sounds great. We

can get to know one another—it'll take about an hour to get to St Marie-Rose.'

He was friendly and open with her, and as they chatted Rebecca was startled to find herself responding readily, a bit like a flower opening up to the sun. Why did she feel so at odds with herself about that? He'd already told her that he was getting over a broken relationship. Would it hurt to talk some more and maybe confide in him in return? He was easygoing and sociable and that was what she needed right now.

'So what's been getting you down?' he asked.

'Oh, a few things… I was ill, and my boyfriend decided that he couldn't handle it.'

'Ouch! That's a tough one. It must have been difficult for you.'

'Yes…'

It had been a few months since her relationship with Drew had disintegrated, and what had happened over that time had certainly taken its toll of her… Complications after her appendicitis had added to her problems and left her feeling low, and Drew had been less than supportive. After her appendix had burst, peritonitis had almost killed her, with the poisons in her bloodstream keeping her in the hospital's Intensive Care Unit for a couple of weeks.

But her problems hadn't ended there. The doctors told her she might be infertile because of the scar tissue from those complications, and that was when Drew had decided to bow out. She had been devastated, overwhelmed by everything that had happened to her. How could she cope with the possibility of never having children? That question haunted her still.

It had all been a bit of a struggle. She desperately

needed a change of scene—a chance to put herself back together again. Wasn't it time she tried to relax and let her hair down? It could hardly matter what happened here, what she decided to tell William—he was only going to be around for a short time, after all.

She found a seat on one of the benches under the awning and put her bags down on the floor by her feet while he went to fetch the drinks. Padded bench seats were arranged along the deck, facing a central four-sided counter where dusky-skinned youths were busy cutting up all manner of fruits—oranges, melons, passion fruit, limes. There were a couple of urns available for hot drinks, along with juice dispensers and water coolers. She glanced around. There were even potted palms placed at discreet intervals on deck, all adding to the holiday atmosphere.

The man she'd seen earlier had gone to stand by the rail, looking out over the sea. He braced himself, leaning back against a stanchion, as the boat's engine started up. He glanced her way, watching as William came towards her with a tall glass of iced juice. She couldn't tell what the man was thinking. His gaze was smoke-dark—brooding, almost. As though he was disturbed to see her with another man. That couldn't be so, though, could it?

For some reason he bothered her. Perhaps it was because in some way—maybe in the way he stood apart from the others—he reminded her of Drew. Though her ex had never possessed those bone-melting good looks, or that way of looking at the world as if it was his to command.

'Don't worry about him.' William must have seen

her cautious glance, and now, as she accepted the drink he handed her, she looked at him quizzically.

'I won't. Do you know him?'

He nodded. 'He's my cousin. He's been over to Martinique on business—I think he probably wants some space to mull things over.'

'Oh, I see… I think.' She frowned and tried to put the man out of her mind, turning her attention to William and chatting to him about nothing in particular.

He was good company. He was fun and he made her chuckle, and at one point he even pulled her to her feet and had her dancing with him to the hot, rhythmic music that spilled out from the loudspeakers overhead.

Other passengers were already moving to the beat, and from time to time William's friends came to join them. She laughed with them and exchanged banter, simply enjoying the freedom of letting herself go for a while. Her hair tumbled this way and that over her bare shoulders and her skirt gently swirled around her thighs as she sashayed to the beat of steel drums. She hadn't felt this unrestrained in a long time.

The music stopped for a moment as the latest song came to an end and she stood still, attuning herself to the rhythm of the boat as it crested the waves.

'Shall we go and stand by the deck rail for a while?' William suggested, and she nodded, going with him and turning her face to the cooling breeze as the boat ploughed through the waves.

Standing with her by the rail, he put an arm around her shoulders to point out dolphins in the distance, playing in the clear, crystal water.

She felt a prickling at the back of her neck and looked around, suddenly distracted. The man at the rail flicked a glance in her direction, inclining his head in acknowledgement, his eyes narrowed against the glare of the sun. Was he still intent on watching her? Or was it William he was keeping an eye on?

William spoke to her, cutting into her thoughts. 'Perhaps we might see each other again—hang around together from time to time? Don't get me wrong—I know you're not looking for a relationship and neither am I—but we do have something in common. We've both been hurt and we could be friends, maybe?'

'Yes, I'd like that.' It would be good to have a friend out here.

She looked out over the blue water once more. The island of St Marie-Rose was drawing closer, its green-clad mountains beckoning, while picturesque white-painted houses nestled among the trees on the hillsides—a perfect invitation to visit.

'Whereabouts are you staying?' he asked.

'Tamarind Bay. My sister's renting a house there… well, nothing quite so grand as a *house*—it's more of a cabin, really. She was lucky to get it—it's quite secluded, apparently, near to a small private marina. The owner of the property is a friend.'

He frowned. 'That's the opposite direction from me. We're all staying at a rental place in the north of the island. Still…' He brightened. 'It's not too far away. It's not that big an island. You could go from one end to the other in two or three hours.' He smiled. 'There aren't that many bars and nightclubs in Tamarind Bay. I'm sure I'll manage to find you again. Maybe I could have your phone number? I could help cheer you up.' He made a wry face. 'Heck—we could cheer each other up.'

She nodded and smiled in response, but she wasn't about to commit to anything. She wasn't averse to having fun—in fact it would be great—but above all she'd come out here to spend time with Emma.

The catamaran moved into place alongside the dock at St Marie-Rose just a few minutes later and they readied themselves to disembark. Ahead of them, William's cousin was among the first to leave the boat.

William helped her with her bags as they negotiated the steps to the quay. She paused for a moment to look around, feeling a deep sense of satisfaction as she took in the curve of the bay, with its wide strip of golden sand and palms that tilted towards the sun, their green fronds drifting gently in the light breeze.

'Are you going to be okay getting to your sister's place?' William asked as they stood among the melee of disembarking passengers. 'Tamarind Bay's about an hour's drive south from here.' He seemed concerned, anxious to stay with her, but also aware of his friends waiting for him a short distance away. 'I could find you a taxi. Better still, I could ask my cousin—'

'No, please don't do that,' she said hurriedly. 'Don't worry about me. I'll be absolutely fine. Go and join your mates. Enjoy the rest of your holiday.'

'Okay…' He frowned. 'I suppose so…if you're sure?'

'I am.'

Reluctantly he walked away, and she looked around to see if there were any cabs left for hire. A man thrust a leaflet into her hands—an advertisement for sea trips to the local islands—and she glanced at it briefly. In the meantime passengers were still getting off the ferry, descending upon every waiting vehicle.

'I help you, lady—yes?' A dark-skinned, athletic-looking young man came to stand beside Becky on the dock. 'You need help with your bags?'

'No…no, thank you.' Becky gave him a tentative smile. She'd been warned by the tour company about hustlers, and though he seemed innocent enough she was cautious. Perhaps he had a car somewhere, but from his manner she seriously doubted he was a legitimate cab driver. 'I'll be fine. I'm sure I can manage.'

Unfortunately, her suitcase was still back at the airport, but she had her hand luggage with her—a hold-all and a roomy bag.

He shook his head. 'You give me money—I take your bags for you.' He bent down and started to grasp the handles of her overnight bag.

'No, no…please don't do that… I can manage,' she said again, but he wasn't listening.

'I take care of it for you,' he said.

'No—I'd rather you didn't do that.'

She tried to reach for her bag but he was too quick for her, deftly swinging it away from her into the air. She sucked in a sharp breath. How on earth was she going to deal with him? Should she kick up a fuss? Call Security? Where *was* Security around here?

Even as the thoughts darted through her head the man she'd seen earlier stepped forward. He moved so fast she blinked in surprise, watching as he came up to the stranger, gripped the handles of her bag firmly and wrenched them from him. Rebecca was stunned. He was lithe and supple, his body honed to perfection. It was simply amazing to watch him in action.

His steel-grey gaze cut through the young man like

a lance. 'She told you that she didn't want your help. Now *I'm* telling you—leave her alone.'

It was clear he meant business. It was there in the clipped tone of his voice and in the firm thrust of his taut, angular jaw. Even Rebecca was in awe of him, and she was an innocent bystander.

'Okay. Okay.' The young man held up his hands in submission, backing off. 'I didn't mean any harm. I'm going.' He looked wary, taken completely aback by the opposition that seemed to have erupted out of nowhere.

Her rescuer watched him leave. 'He won't bother you any more,' he said.

'No. I see that.' She sent him a grateful glance, her green eyes drinking him in. The youth was hurrying away along the quayside, anxious to stay out of trouble. 'Thank you. I wasn't sure whether there were any security people around here. They didn't seem necessary. Everything looked so peaceful.'

His mouth made a wry curve. 'It is—usually. But anywhere you go you might find people who want to supplement their income any way they can.'

'I suppose so.' She used the leaflet to fan her cheeks against the heat. How did he manage to look so cool and in control? He must be used to the conditions out here.

'I'm Cade, by the way,' he said. 'I'm William's cousin. He may have mentioned me.'

He held out a hand to her and she slipped her palm briefly into his. His grasp was firm and reassuringly strong.

'Rebecca,' she answered. 'Yes, he did. Thanks again for your help.'

'You're welcome.' He gave her a thoughtful look. 'I couldn't help overhearing some of your conversation with William on board. You said you were staying at Tamarind Bay—that's roughly where I'm headed. Near there, anyway. I have a place in the hills above the bay. I could give you a lift, if you like?'

'Um…that's okay, thanks. I don't mind waiting for a taxi. I don't want to put you out.' She didn't know him, after all, so why would she trust her safety to him?

'You could be in for a long wait…' His glance shifted over her. 'To be frank, a woman on her own—a beautiful young woman at that—could invite unwanted attention…as you've already discovered.' He reached into the pocket of his chinos and showed her a business card. 'Perhaps this will help to put your mind at ease.'

*Dr Cade Byfield*, she read. *Emergency Medicine Physician, Mountview Hospital, St Marie-Rose.*

'People know me around here,' he said. 'I make the trip to and from Martinique on a regular basis. Ask the officials at the end of the dock if you need reassurance.'

That sounded reasonable enough. She'd seen one of them acknowledge him with a nod a short time ago. 'A doctor?' she said quietly. 'So you live out here?'

He nodded. 'I have done for the last few years, anyway. I'm from Florida, originally, but my parents settled on the island some years ago.' He glanced at her questioningly. 'And you?'

'I'm English—from a busy town in Hertfordshire.'

'Ah, I thought I recognised the accent.' He smiled fleetingly and waved a hand in the direction of the harbour wall. 'My car's parked over there. Shall we go? I promise you, you'll be safe with me.'

'Okay.' As she nodded he placed the palm of his hand in the small of her back, sending small whorls of sensation eddying through her spine. She tried not to think about the touch of his warm, strong fingers on her body as she walked with him.

'We could have done with your help as a doctor on the plane coming over here,' she murmured as they set off along the quayside.

'Really? Why is that?'

'We had to divert to Martinique to drop off a man who was taken ill. He was sitting in the seat across the aisle from me when he collapsed. He looked dreadful—pale and waxy. The pilot had to radio for help and they made sure they had an ambulance waiting for him at the airport.'

He frowned. 'It must have been serious if they had to do that. What was wrong with him? Do you know?'

She nodded. 'He complained of chest pain radiating to his ears and gums, and then he lost consciousness. I felt for a pulse but there wasn't one.'

He sent her a quick, concerned look. 'Sounds like a heart attack. What happened?'

She pulled a face. 'There was general panic all around me for a moment or two. Then I started chest compressions while a flight attendant rushed to get a portable defibrillator. We managed to shock his heart and establish a rhythm and restored blood flow to his vital organs.' Her mouth flattened. 'I thought he was going to be all right, but then things went wrong again and his heart went into an irregular rhythm and stopped for a second time.'

Cade sucked in his breath. 'He was obviously in a very bad way—that must have been scary for you.'

'It *was* worrying,' she admitted. 'But I'm a doctor, too, so I suppose the training kicked in. They had adrenaline on board in the aircraft's medical kit, so I gave him intravenous doses until he started to recover.'

His eyes widened with interest. 'Are you an emergency doctor?'

'No. My specialty's paediatrics.'

'So, do you work in a hospital or general practice?'

By now they were approaching his car—a dark metallic red sports utility vehicle. It managed to look both sleek and sturdy at the same time, and she guessed it would be capable of managing most types of terrain.

She said quietly, 'I was working in a neonatal unit, but actually I'm taking a break from medicine right now.' How could she bear to go into work every day and be surrounded by babies, knowing she might never hold one of her own? It was like a pain deep inside her. 'At least I thought I was taking a break until I stepped on the plane. My plans certainly went wrong after that.'

He opened the passenger door for her and ushered her inside. He was frowning again. 'Obviously you weren't heading for Martinique at the outset. Wouldn't it have been easier to fly the rest of the way from there instead of getting the ferry?'

'Probably.' She was thankful he hadn't asked about her reasons for having a break from her career, but maybe he assumed she was just taking a holiday. 'There wasn't another flight until tomorrow morning,' she explained. 'Once we stopped at Martinique the flight crew had worked their allotted hours, apparently. I didn't want to mess about. I wanted to get here on time to be with my sister—and my luggage had already been taken off the plane.' She pulled a face. 'I'm not quite sure where it is at the moment… en route to Barbados, I think. I've filled in all the appropriate forms, so hopefully I'll be reunited with it at some point.'

'You've had an eventful journey.' He slid into the driver's seat and switched on the engine. 'Let's hope things go smoothly for you from now on.'

'Yes, we should look on the bright side, shouldn't we?' She leaned back against the luxurious upholstery and felt the cool waft of a delicate breeze fan her cheeks as the air-conditioning kicked in. 'Oh, that feels good.'

He gave her a sideways glance. 'How long are you planning on staying over here?'

'Three months to begin with—maybe longer, but if so I might need to find work of some sort. I'm not in a hurry to do that yet—I suppose I'm looking for a change of direction. I may even decide to go home when the three months is up. I just want to spend time with Emma—my sister. She's over here on a temporary contract with the nursing directorate.' She frowned. 'She messaged me a short time ago when I was on the boat, to say she'd been called out on a job—some last-minute thing that cropped up. I'm just hoping she'll be back before too long.'

His cool, thoughtful gaze swept over her before he turned his attention back to the road ahead. 'Talking of jobs, it seems a bit strange for you to be taking time out so early in your career. You're very fortunate if you can afford to do that. A lot of people would envy you.'

She winced inwardly. Was that a veiled criticism? After seeing her on the boat, getting on so well with his cousin, he probably thought she was a bored rich girl looking for thrills.

'Perhaps they might. You're right—it's good to have enough money to be able to choose—but I don't see myself as "fortunate", really,' she countered. 'My parents died when I was twelve. They left money in trust for me and my sister, so we're both comfortably off, but I'd much rather they were still around. We were brought up by an aunt and uncle. They've been good to us, but they had their own two little girls to care for. It can't have been easy for them.'

'No, I expect not. I'm sorry.' He studied her briefly. 'Does it bother you, leaving them behind to come here?'

'Oh, yes—I'll miss them all…especially my cousins. But we're all older now, going our separate ways.' She was pensive for a moment or two, lost in thought. 'I suppose we were lucky that there was no rivalry or resentment bubbling away in the background because we were taking up the love and attention that should have been reserved for family. In fact we get on very well with one another. My aunt and uncle did a good job.'

'Four youngsters must have made for quite a lively household?'

'Yes, it was a bit rumbustious at times. We had a lot of fun…holidays and family picnics and generally hanging out together.'

'I never had that experience.' There was a slight thread of regret in his voice. 'I was an only child—that's probably what makes me value my cousin's friendship all the more. We're very close—a bit like brothers.'

She sent him a curious glance. 'Really? I didn't get that impression. You kept to yourself on the ferry and didn't really have any contact with him—he said you'd been to Martinique on business and needed some space.'

'That's right. I had to go over there to talk to some clients—I have a plantation in the hills, a few miles from Tamarind Bay, so I make the journey to Martinique on a fairly regular basis to see people about supplies and exports and so on.'

'Wow!' She smiled. 'I'm impressed…a plantation owner…that's inspiring.'

'Not so much.' His mouth made a wry twist. 'I took it over a couple of years ago, when it was completely run down, and I'm learning a few lessons on the way. It's taking a lot of effort to get it going once more, but we've made a reasonable start, I think.'

'It sounds as though you have a busy life.' She wanted to know more about the plantation, but he hadn't yet commented about leaving his cousin to his own devices. Why had he done that if they were so close? 'You said, "We've made a reasonable start"—is William part of that? Where does he fit in? If you're so close, I don't understand why you didn't want to talk to him on the boat?'

'He works for me, but he's on holiday at the moment. As for when we were on the boat—he was with his friends and I didn't want to intrude…more especially since he seemed to be very taken with *you*. In fact, I'd say he was smitten…so much so that I doubt he'd have thanked me for getting in the way.'

She looked at him in mock surprise. 'Smitten? We'd only just met!' Why would he have reached that conclusion? Was he jealous of the attention William had been giving her? Of course he hadn't heard the bulk of their conversation, or he would have known they were just going to be friends. William liked her, but he was still getting over the break-up with his girlfriend and wasn't making any romantic overtures. 'You're reading too much into the situation.'

'I don't think so.' Again, that wry smile. His glance drifted over her, taking in her slender curves, the way her camisole top nipped in at the waist and her skirt draped itself over the swell of her hips. 'What chance did he have against a flame-haired beauty with emerald-green eyes and a come-hither smile? He was done for the moment he looked at you.' He pulled a face. 'Heaven knows—*I* was done for.'

She stifled an uncertain laugh. Did he really feel that way about her? And that was the second time he'd commented on her looks. 'Well, thanks for the compliment… I think…' He made her sound like some kind of Delilah… 'But if it really was as you say, do you imagine he'd have some sort of a problem getting involved with me? I couldn't help feeling you were keeping a weather eye on him.'

'I was, to be honest.'

She blinked, startled by his frank admission. 'You were?'

He frowned. 'I was…most of the time. At least I was trying to, when I wasn't distracted by thinking about you. There's something about you—a vulnerability that I sensed, maybe. I suppose it must have brought out the protective instinct in me.' He sighed and gave his head a shake, as though he was trying to pull himself together. 'Perhaps William feels it, too. Either way, I don't want to see him land in hot water. My aunt asked me to watch out for him over the next few months. He may not look it, but he's vulnerable, too, right now. He's easily led and he's been hurt in the past.'

'Haven't we all?' She said it under her breath, but he gave her a quick, sharp glance before concentrating on negotiating a twisty bend in the road.

Rebecca gazed out of the window, watching the landscape unfold in all its glory. It was easier than trying to fathom him out. She sensed there was a lot more to Cade Byfield than she'd learned so far. He was attracted to her, but he was fighting it, and at the same time she had a sneaking feeling he didn't trust her around his cousin. She wasn't at all sure why.

Not that it mattered. Did she even trust *herself* right now? She was here to chill out, to get over the breakdown of her relationship with Drew and the turmoil that had caused...and hopefully to recover from the aftermath of the illness that had thrown her life into disarray these last few months.

The road wound its way through forested slopes, and their journey of discovery helped to take her mind off things. Beneath the thick canopy of trees she glimpsed the occasional flight of a colourful parrot or a yellow-chested peewee, and on the ground, which was thickly covered with broad-spanning ferns, she caught sight of small green lizards darting through the undergrowth. There were wild flowers hidden among the foliage along the route—waxy lilac anthuriums and the pretty scarlet rosettes of bromeliads peeking out here and there. It was beautiful, and all new to her.

'You said you often go to Martinique on business?' she murmured, turning her attention back to Cade. 'Wouldn't it be quicker and easier for *you* to fly?'

He nodded. 'That's true. But I like having the chance to unwind on board the ferry. It gives me time to clear my head and maybe get things into perspective. In a place like this you don't always want to be rushing about. I get plenty of that in my job at the hospital.'

He pointed out the pristine waters of a yachting harbour as they rounded a curve in the road. 'We must be getting fairly close to where you'll be staying, I think.'

'Oh…' She gave a small gasp of delight as she looked out over the hillside and down into the rocky cove. 'It's so lovely. It's perfection.' Beyond the shoreline, outlined beneath the deep blue of the sea, she saw the turquoise ridge of a coral reef. 'It's even better than the way Emma described it to me.'

'Yes, it's an exquisite island—a beautiful place to live…and work. I've travelled the world, but I always love to come back here.' He negotiated a winding road down to the scattering of houses that made up the small hamlet. 'Yours is the cabin, you said?'

'Yes… I think I can see it amongst the trees. Emma sent me pictures of it.'

Excitement bubbled up inside her as she caught sight of a timber-clad house with white-framed windows and a white-painted wooden balustrade enclosing a wide veranda. The sun was setting on the horizon, casting a golden glow over the hills as they drew up in front of the house. Everything looked tranquil and untouched by the outside world. She sat for a moment, taking it all in. She could be happy here. She felt it deep inside. Surely this was a place of healing, where she could mend her body and her spirit?

'Presumably your sister would have been expecting you earlier? How will you get into the property if she's not here now?'

She frowned. 'It's been a couple of hours since her text message—I would have thought she'd be home by now. But she said she would leave a key in a safe place where I'd be sure to find it.' She laughed softly. 'Knowing Emma, that probably means it could be under a rock marked *"Key is here"*.'

He laughed with her. 'I dare say the locals are all on good terms with your sister. You can rest easy. We don't get a lot of crime out here.'

He parked the car in front of the cabin a few minutes later. It was set against a backcloth of leafy trees and dense shrubbery, its location completely private, and everything smelled fresh and open to nature.

Cade waited while Rebecca knocked on the door. When there was no answer she stifled her disappointment and went in search of the key.

'It was hidden in a box under the veranda,' she told him. 'Would you like to come in for a drink of some sort? I expect there'll be juice in the fridge—or coffee?'

'Thanks. I'll have a coffee, if you have the makings. I'll see you settled in and then I should be on my way. I have to get over to the plantation to meet up with my estate manager.'

'You work late out here?'

He nodded. 'Occasionally. Sometimes it's necessary if problems crop up. My manager wants to see me about getting a new truck—the one we have at the moment keeps breaking down. He lives in a cottage on the plantation, so it's not as if he'll be put out too much. I need to get it sorted.'

All this on top of his work as a doctor? He obviously believed in keeping busy. She stepped on to the veranda and unlocked the front door. 'Come in.'

'Thanks.'

They both took a moment to look around. The living room was simply furnished, with a polished light oak floor, a couple of settees and a coffee table, and opened out into a light and airy kitchen-diner at one end. The units there were cream-coloured, with pale oak worktops that were easy on the eye. Two sets of French doors led from the kitchen and the living room out on to the veranda that swept around the building, giving a view through the trees of the delightful cove below.

'I'll just see if Emma has any coffee.' Rebecca checked the cupboards, then set out porcelain mugs on the oak table while she waited for the kettle to boil. There was a note from Emma propped up against the sugar bowl. 'She doesn't know when she'll be back,' Rebecca said, quickly scanning it. 'She says the landlord will stop by tomorrow morning to sort out a problem with the window shutters.'

She frowned. It definitely sounded as though she would not be back tonight.

'Ah, I might have known it—Emma's left some food for supper,' she murmured, continuing to read and then going to rummage in the fridge. 'We might as well help ourselves…there's plenty for both of us, from the looks of things. Spiced chicken drumsticks and salad, with savoury rice.' She turned to him. 'How does that sound?'

He pulled in a breath. 'Too tempting to refuse,' he admitted with a grin. 'It seems to be quite a while since I had lunch.'

'Mmm…me, too,' she agreed, taking dishes and platters from the fridge. She frowned. 'I wish I knew how long she was going to be. I was so looking forward to seeing her again.'

'Is she older than you or younger?' he asked as they sat down to eat a minute or so later.

'Older by just a year. But for all that she's always sort of looked after me…kept me on the straight and narrow, so to speak—our cousins, too. They're three or four years younger than us.' She waved a hand over the food she had set out. 'Help yourself.'

She'd always looked to Emma for guidance over the years. Perhaps Emma would know how she could get over her illness and the break-up with Drew and restore her self-confidence once more. When her consultant had said she might have difficulty in having children because of scar tissue blocking her fallopian tubes it had come as a devastating blow. Rebecca had withdrawn into herself for a while and shut out the outside world. She hadn't wanted to face up to anything for some time.

As for now… A recklessness seemed to have taken her over. She'd left her job, left the country, put everything behind her. And she'd met a handsome young man on the ferry coming over here—not to mention the fact that now she was sharing a meal with a perfect stranger in the privacy of a secluded cabin. Had she lost her senses? Perhaps she was hell bent on self-destruction. She didn't want to take anyone down with her, but was she headed that way? Emma would surely put her right.

She shook the thoughts from her mind. Better to think of something completely different. 'What kind of plantation do you have?' she asked now. 'What do you grow there?'

Cade had been watching her, she realised, clearly curious about her introspection, but now he followed her lead and answered readily. 'Cocoa—everything depends on producing a good crop.'

'You said it had been run down—why would that happen?'

'Because of disease in the plants, the weather—hurricane winds, tropical storms—and low prices. A lot of people out here gave up on cocoa and turned to banana-growing instead. It must have seemed like the better option.'

'But you think you can make a go of it where others have failed?'

He nodded. 'I'll certainly have a good try.' He finished off his chicken and wiped his hands on a paper serviette. 'That was delicious.'

She inclined her head briefly. 'Emma's always been a good cook.'

They talked some more about food in general, and his hopes for the plantation, and then her phone rang, cutting in on their conversation.

'Perhaps it's Emma. I should answer it,' she said quickly.

'Of course. Please—go ahead.'

She stood up and walked across the kitchen to take

the call. It wasn't Emma, though, and a swift wave of disappointment washed over her.

'Hi, Becky…it's William. I'm just checking that you managed to get to your sister's all right. I was concerned about you. I hated leaving you alone at the harbour.'

'Oh, hi, William. Yes, I did, thanks. You didn't need to worry about me. I'm fine.' Out of the corner of her vision she saw Cade brace himself slightly. His head went back a fraction.

'That's good. Listen, I'm coming over to the bay tomorrow evening. Maybe we could go for a drink together?'

'I'd like that… It depends what my sister's doing, though. She isn't here right now.'

'She could come with us.'

She thought about it. 'Okay, then. Yes, we could do that. It sounds good. I'll let you know if anything changes.'

'Great. I'll meet you in Selwyn's Bar at around eight o'clock?'

'Selwyn's Bar? Yes. Eight o'clock, then. I'll look forward to it.' She was smiling as she said it, and when she cut the call she turned to look at Cade once more. 'That was your cousin,' she said unnecessarily. 'He was just checking to see that I got here all right.'

'So I gathered.' He stood up, his features guarded. 'You'll be seeing him again, from the sound of things?'

'Looks like it.' She sent him a quick, challenging look. He seemed tense. 'Do you have a problem with that?'

'Not really… Maybe…' He shrugged awkwardly. 'Like I said, I don't want to see him get hurt. He's just come out of a bad relationship and he's vulnerable right now. I know it doesn't seem that way...'

'Surely he's old enough to take care of himself?'

'You'd think so, wouldn't you? But some people take a while longer than others.'

'He seemed fine to me.' Her green eyes flashed. 'Anyway, why do you imagine I'm likely to be such a problem for him?'

'Are you *kidding*?' His mouth made a crooked shape as his glance drifted over her. 'The way you look, I suspect you'd be a problem for a saint,' he said, with feeling. 'My cousin stands no chance at all.'

A wave of heat ran through her cheeks. 'Well, I'm flattered you imagine I have such powers...'

He smiled. 'I suppose I want you to go easy on him. I sense you just want to have a good time and enjoy your stay here—and there's absolutely nothing wrong with that.' His dark eyes glinted. 'I'd be only too happy to help you do that. As for William—he's here for the duration, while you'll be moving on in a short time. I can't help thinking that if you and he get together I'll be left to pick up the pieces again.'

'I'm sure you and your aunt are being overly concerned... I've never thought of myself as a heart-breaker.' Still, something in her prompted her to say, 'Anyway, you could always come with us to the bar.' Even as the words left her lips she wondered what on earth she was thinking. 'He suggested my sister might want to come along,' she added, 'so you could join us and make up a foursome.'

'I'd like that,' he said. 'I'll look forward to it—I'll come and pick you up.' His smoky gaze rested on her once more. 'It's a great pity William saw you first,' he said softly. 'I'd be more than ready for the challenge.'

She looked at him directly, her green glance unwavering. 'I've said before that we're just going to be friends...but even if that wasn't the case I'm not some prize to be won.'

'Like I said, I have his interests at heart. I won't stand by and see him hurt.'

She wasn't sure whether that was a threat or a promise.

He left soon after that, and she watched him drive away. She ought to be feeling relaxed, at peace with herself, but instead she felt a sense of nervous anticipation—a vague worry starting up inside her. What was she doing, getting involved with Cade and his cousin? Hadn't she been through enough turmoil—and could William really get hurt because of *her*?

Her mouth made a crooked twist. She doubted Cade was the kind of man who would let that happen. She frowned. Perhaps that was what bothered her. What did he have in mind? Somehow she suspected a man like him would leave nothing to chance. Wasn't that why he'd been waiting around on the dock after William had left?

# CHAPTER TWO

'I WAS SO worried when you didn't come back here last night.' Rebecca watched her sister search through the clothes in her wardrobe. 'Does it happen very often—that you don't manage to get home?'

'Sometimes—it depends on the circumstances.' Emma held up a pale green dress that had an off-the-shoulder neckline and a skater skirt. 'How about this one? It'll go beautifully with your eyes.'

'Oh, that looks great. Thanks. I'll try it on.'

They were getting ready for their night out at Selwyn's Bar, and as most of Rebecca's clothes were still in her suitcase, travelling between airports, she was having to rely on Emma to help her out. Luckily they were of a similar shape and size.

'So what happened last night?'

'We had to go to a rural area up in the hills.' Emma frowned. 'A couple of people have gone down with headaches and fever, and we're not quite sure yet what we're dealing with. We looked after them, made them comfortable, and sent blood samples and so on to the hospital. We shan't know what's wrong with them until we get the results back in a couple of days.'

'So you'll be going back there?'

Emma nodded. 'I have to wait for a call from the chief nursing officer. They'll send a Jeep to take me back to the village.'

The girls finished dressing, and Rebecca added a final touch of blusher to her cheeks just as a rapping noise sounded on the cabin's front door. Her stomach muscles tensed. That would be Cade, of course. He was a few minutes early and she didn't feel at all ready for him. She hadn't had time to compose herself, but she didn't know why that bothered her. Why was she nervous about meeting up with him again?

'I'll get it.'

Her sister left the room and Rebecca took a moment to quickly check her hair in the bedroom mirror. She'd pinned it up for the evening, doing her best to tame the unruly curls, though a few spiralling tendrils had escaped to frame her face. Satisfied that she looked okay, she smoothed down the dress. The silky material skimmed her hips lovingly and fell in soft folds almost to her knees.

Emma was already opening the door, greeting Cade with a cheerful, 'Hi, there. You must be the man Becky's been telling me about. Come in.' There was a pause as he entered the cabin. Then, 'She says you have a plantation up in the hills?' Emma said. 'That is *so* exciting! I've never met an estate owner before—or seen a cocoa plantation.'

'You should come and visit, then,' Cade answered cheerfully. 'I'd love to show you and Rebecca around—you could come tomorrow, if you like?'

'That sounds great.'

'Good. It's a date, then. Late afternoon would be

best for me—I could pick you both up after I leave the hospital.'

'You have to work at the weekend?'

'I do, unfortunately.'

He hadn't wasted any time in issuing the invitation, had he?

His deep voice sent ripples of tingling sensation coursing along Rebecca's spine. She tried to shake it off. How did he manage to have this effect on her? She wasn't looking for any kind of involvement or attachment, yet he'd figured constantly in her thoughts ever since she'd watched him drive away the evening before. It was disturbing. Hanging out with William would be one thing—his cousin was a different matter entirely. With Cade she sensed danger at every turn... Her nervous system had gone into overdrive and was sending out vigorous warning signals that she would ignore at her peril.

'Hello again.' She took a deep breath as she walked into the room, and knew a perverse sense of gratification as she saw Cade's grey eyes widen in appreciation.

He said nothing for a second or two, but then his dark gaze swept over both girls and he commented softly, 'It's clear to see that you're sisters. You have the same high cheekbones and perfect jawline. You both look lovely.'

'Why, thank you!' Emma laughingly touched his arm, her long chestnut hair fleetingly brushing his shoulder as she moved in close to him.

She was wearing a simply styled blue dress with thin shoulder straps, leaving her arms bare. As for

Cade, he looked cool and immaculate in a freshly laundered shirt and pale-coloured trousers.

'Just give me a minute to get my bag,' Emma said, 'and we can be on our way. I've been to Selwyn's Bar before,' she confided. 'I love it there.'

Cade led the way to his car a few minutes later and saw them seated comfortably. Rebecca chose to sit in the back seat alongside Emma. It didn't feel as though they'd had much time to talk, since Emma hadn't arrived home until mid-afternoon, and she doubted they'd have much chance to confide in one another this evening. It was good to be together again, though.

'How long have you been working out here, Emma?' Cade asked as he turned the car on to the coast road.

'A couple of months. I'm having a great time out here. The work hasn't been too difficult up to now—mostly we've been running health clinics and visiting the more remote villages. We've been giving vaccinations and checking out the under-fives to make sure they're okay.'

He glanced in the rearview mirror. 'Is that the sort of thing *you* might want to do, Rebecca—work with the under-fives, I mean? Not now, obviously, but maybe later? You talked about wanting a change of direction.'

Rebecca's face paled at the unexpected question. 'Um… I'm not sure. It's something I'd have to think about.'

'I suppose in neonatal your work was much more specialised?'

'Yes. Some of the babies were very ill. They might

have been born prematurely, or they had heart defects or lung complaints and so on.'

'Is that why you stopped doing the job—because it was too harrowing?'

She swallowed hard. 'In a way, yes.'

She didn't want to talk about this. Delving into the different aspects of her work was far too painful, and it brought up a host of reminders she would rather ignore. It had been so hard going back to work after her illness. She hadn't been able to bear to hold those tiny babies in her arms when she might never have one of her own. She hadn't realised how badly she had been affected until she'd cradled those sweet, frail infants.

Beside her, Emma shifted closer in a silent gesture of support. 'Sometimes it's good to do something different for a while—to explore other opportunities. But for the moment Becky's taking time out to recharge her batteries. She's worked really hard over the last few years, qualifying as a doctor and taking her specialist exams. She hasn't really had much time for herself and she's well overdue for an extended holiday.'

'Of course. I understand.'

Seeing the reflection of his dark eyes in the rear-view mirror, Rebecca knew he didn't understand at all. How could he? As far as he was concerned she was young, energetic, on the cusp of life—why would she need to take time out? But she wasn't going to explain her circumstances to someone she'd only just met. And talking about it was upsetting.

She hadn't been able to discuss things much with Drew, because his negative, unhelpful reaction had made matters worse. Whatever future they might have contemplated had been wiped out when he'd realised there was a possibility she might not be able to have children. She'd been devastated by his response to her predicament.

As for now, she wondered if any man she met might respond in the same way? She couldn't even think about her situation without feeling shaky and unhappy. It was too soon…the emotional wound ran too deep and was still too raw.

'They do marvellous mojitos at Selwyn's,' Emma said brightly, changing the subject. 'You'll like them, Becky. They make them with white rum, fresh limes and a sprig of mint. *Yum.*'

'Sounds good.' Rebecca made an effort to pull herself together. She glanced at Cade once more. 'What do you like to drink, Cade?'

'I like rum, too—it's the national drink out here in the islands—but mostly I drink lager. Maybe I'll have a rum cocktail this evening, but after that I'll stick with non-alcoholic lager because I'm on the early shift tomorrow at the hospital… And, of course, I'm driving.'

'Ah…you drew the short straw.' Emma chuckled sympathetically. 'They serve food at Selwyn's, so you could always try soaking up the rum with a tenderloin steak or some such.'

He smiled. 'I might do that.'

William was waiting for them, greeting all three of them with enthusiasm when they stepped on to the boardwalk leading to Selwyn's Bar a few minutes later. The bar was made of wooden decking and built over a shallow tidal strait where mangroves emerged in a dense tangle of arching roots from the flood plain left by the ebb and flow of salt water. There was lush greenery all around, and the sounds of the forest mingled with the lively music coming from speakers positioned under the solid awning. Tables covered in white cloths were set out alongside the balustrade, so that customers could sit and eat and look out over the water.

William was smiling, wearing a T-shirt and knee-length cut-off shorts. 'Hey, it's great to see you again,' he said, giving Rebecca a quick hug and nodding amiably to his cousin. 'And this must be Emma…' He turned to Emma. 'Hi, there. Becky told me you're a nurse? It must be a whole new experience for you to come out here and work in the Caribbean. How are you finding it?'

'It's great…' Emma said. 'It's very different to what I've known before, back in the UK, but it's really good—most of the time. Some things can be a bit frustrating—like equipment shortages or breakdowns—and of course everything tends to move at a slower pace.'

He nodded. 'I know what you mean. Food stores can run out of staples like bread and milk, if you don't get there early in the day, and the Internet can go down when you're in the middle of something.'

'And if your truck breaks down you might have to wait for a part to be sent over from one of the other islands,' Cade put in, with feeling. 'That's happened to us more than once.' He smiled and led them over to the bar. 'I'll get the drinks in. Mojitos, was it?'

'That would be lovely.' Rebecca glanced at him. 'So, did you talk with your estate manager about getting a new truck?'

'I did. It'll take a while to sort out, but things will start to run a lot more smoothly for us once it arrives.'

They took their drinks to a table by the rail and the four of them chatted while they looked at menus and decided what they wanted to eat.

'We could share a seafood and chicken platter?' Cade suggested after a minute or two, and they all agreed. It sounded appetising…saffron rice with grilled spiced chicken and mixed seafood.

Rebecca looked out over the water and watched graceful white egrets searching for titbits in the shallows. In the distance, where the mangroves gave way to tall dogwood trees, she saw a blue-and-gold macaw spread its wings and take flight.

She smiled. 'I love it here,' she said softly. 'It's so restful.'

'It's good to see you looking relaxed,' William commented. 'You were a bit stressed after your journey yesterday.'

Smiling, she said, 'Well, twelve hours on a plane and then finding they've lost your luggage can do that to you.'

Cade lifted a dark brow. 'Have your cases still not caught up with you yet?'

'Not yet. I rang the airport this morning, to check, but nothing doing so far. They don't seem to have any idea where they might be.' Rebecca's mouth curved a fraction. 'It pays to have a sister who'll share her clothes with you.'

'Yeah, I guess so.' He leaned towards her and added quietly, so that only she could hear, 'If that's Emma's dress it certainly suits you…and it fits like a glove.'

Warm colour flooded her cheeks. 'Thanks.'

William was still thinking about the boat journey. 'Actually, I thought there was more to it than lost luggage...there were a few moments when you were off guard and you went a bit quiet.'

'I was fine,' she said. 'I'm still fine. Who could be stressed in a place like this?'

He grinned. 'You're probably right.'

Rebecca sent him a fleeting, thoughtful glance. Was it possible William was more perceptive than she'd given him credit for? Maybe through his own experiences William understood deep down how it was to be out of sync with everything around him and his general air of good humour was something of an effort for him.

She was conscious all the time, though, of Cade's watchful gaze. He still wasn't happy about her getting to know William to any great extent—she could feel it in her bones—and he'd even managed to arrange the seating at the table so that his cousin was placed next to Emma and sitting diagonally across from Rebecca. Of course that could have come about in the natural course of events—maybe she was reading too much into things.

Cade said now, 'Perhaps you were quiet because you were thinking about that man on the plane—the one who was taken ill?'

'Yes, that was probably it.'

William and Emma listened interestedly as she quickly recounted what had happened.

'That must have been so worrying.' Emma frowned. 'I wonder how he's doing?'

'His condition's stable,' Rebecca said. 'I phoned the hospital this morning. Apparently he's been assessed, and they've made the decision to do heart bypass surgery tomorrow.'

'That must have cheered you up—to know that you enabled that to happen.' Cade smiled. 'It's good that you followed up on him—I was wondering how he was doing, too.'

'From the way the nurse spoke, I'm sure he'll be fine. I think he's in good hands.'

William was momentarily subdued. 'I'm surrounded by medics,' he said, in a voice tinged with awe. 'What *I* do is nothing in comparison.'

'You shouldn't feel that way,' Emma said. 'We all have something to offer.' She studied him briefly. 'You work on Cade's plantation, don't you? What do you do there?'

'I help out in all areas—getting to know the job from the bottom up, so to speak. Cade thinks that's the best way for me to start.'

He told them about his role in ordering new seedlings and supervising the planting.

'When we took over the plantation there were a number of mature trees that were viable—a lot of them are ready for harvesting now,' Cade put in. 'They have to be at least three years old before they produce pods—five years is best for a good crop—but we want to plant seedlings every year to ensure quality and continuity. You'll be able to see what we're doing when you come and take a look around tomorrow.'

'I'll look forward to that,' Rebecca said.

Emma nodded. 'Me, too… Provided I'm not called away to work.' She pulled a face. 'I'd arranged to take a few days off, with Rebecca coming over, but we're not sure if there's some kind of outbreak happening up in the hills.'

A waitress brought their food over to the table and they spent the next hour or so talking about this and that while sampling the delicious dishes on offer. Rebecca ate shrimp sautéed with peppers and onions in a spicy ginger and lime sauce, along with crab cake and rice accompanied by a tasty green salad. Dessert was a delicious concoction of caramelised pineapple with a drizzle of lime, vanilla and rum syrup, and a scoop of ice cream.

'Mmm…that was heavenly,' Rebecca murmured, pushing away her plate when she had eaten her fill. She laid a hand on her stomach. 'I don't think I'll be able to eat another morsel for at least a week!'

William laughed. 'Let's hope it's not as long as that. I was thinking of tempting you with my own recipe for melt-in-the-mouth chocolate tart when you come over to the plantation tomorrow.'

'Oh…chocolate…you've found my weak spot—stay away from me!' She laughed with him. 'So you're planning on being there, too? That's great. But what about your friends on holiday in the north of the island? I thought you would want to be with them?'

'They're going back to Miami,' he said, his mouth turning down a fraction at the corners. 'To go on with their university courses or work commitments. I met them over there, when I was studying food and agricultural sciences, and we stayed in touch after I finished my course. But my vacation ends today, and I'm due back home tomorrow—so, yes, with any luck I'll see you there. I live in one of the cottages on the plantation.'

'That's handy.'

'Yes.' He leaned towards her and spoke confidentially. 'It's rent-free, courtesy of my cousin, so I'm more than happy. I owe him—though he's very dismissive of his generosity.'

Rebecca returned his smile. Cade couldn't hear what they were saying, but all the while she felt his brooding gaze resting on her. He obviously felt great responsibility towards his cousin. She understood his concerns, at least in part, but outwardly William was fun and that was what she needed right now. She responded to his lively, engaging manner, but it wasn't as if she was setting out to capture his heart.

Emma was in a playful mood, too, unwinding after her busy time at work, and was more than ready to let her hair down. She teased William and laughed with Cade.

Both girls drank mojitos, and then at Cade's persuasion Rebecca tried another cocktail, made up of dark rum, lemon juice, grenadine syrup and Angostura bitters. The evening passed quickly and in a bit of a haze after that. She was enjoying herself, but the others had to prepare for work the next day, and so all too soon their night out came to an end.

'I'll drop by the cabin around three-thirty tomorrow, if that's okay?' Cade said as he delivered the girls safely home.

The moon was a silvery orb, glimmering through the branches of the trees, casting shadows all around and highlighting the night-scented jasmine. The heady fragrance of the white flowers lingered on the air.

'Yes, that should be all right. All being well, we'll be ready and waiting.' Emma waved him off as he slid back into the driver's seat of his car and disappeared into the night.

Things didn't turn out quite as they'd expected, though. Rebecca was disappointed when, early the next afternoon, Emma received a text message calling her out to work. Several more people had gone down with the mystery illness in the village high up in the hills, and the nurse in charge wanted extra staff on hand to be available to deal with the ailing patients. They were very ill, apparently, with high temperatures and headaches.

'We think it's some kind of bacterial infection,' Emma told Rebecca. 'We'll probably have to give antibiotics as a precautionary measure.'

'Shall I go with you?' Rebecca asked. 'It sounds as though you could do with some help.'

Emma shook her head. 'No, Becky,' she said firmly. 'You've not long recovered from an illness yourself—you might still be under par and we don't want to risk you going down with anything. Anyway, I doubt the nursing director will allow it.'

'But what about the risk to yourself?' Rebecca was worried, instantly on the alert. 'What if it's typhoid fever? I heard a whisper that there have been sporadic outbreaks on a couple of the other islands.'

Emma shrugged. 'I've had all my vaccinations, so I should be okay. We take precautions, anyway, with gloves and masks where we think it's necessary.'

Rebecca was still anxious, though she stayed quiet, not wanting to upset her sister. The typhoid vaccination wasn't always a hundred per cent reliable—you still had to be careful not to eat or drink contaminated food or water. 'You'll keep in touch, won't you? Phone me and let me know what's happening?'

'Of course I will.' Emma gave Rebecca a hug and then glanced at her watch. 'The Jeep will be here to pick me up in half an hour,' she said. She pulled a face. 'It's such a shame—I was really looking forward to seeing the plantation. You'll have to tell me all about it.'

Rebecca frowned. 'I might ring and cancel…but I'm sure Cade will invite us another time. He and William both seemed keen for us to visit.'

'They did, didn't they?' Emma smiled. 'William's so sweet. He has such an innocent, boyish look about him. He was telling me how much his mother loves chocolate—but she's as thin as a rake, apparently. She's really pleased about him working on the plantation. He's had a bad time lately, from the sound of things…and now his father has been taken ill.'

She hurried away to her bedroom to start packing a few things into a holdall.

Rebecca followed her. She wondered aloud what was wrong with William's father, but Emma wasn't sure.

'Some sort of virus, I think,' she said. 'They're still trying to figure it out, but it seems to be affecting his heart. It's very worrying, by all accounts.'

No wonder Cade was being protective towards his cousin. It sounded as though he had a lot on his plate right now.

Rebecca searched through one of the cupboards. 'I'll give you a hand. Do you need fresh towels—moisturiser and so on?'

'Yes, thanks.'

Emma left for the village a short time later, and Rebecca tried in vain to phone Cade. Each time she tried she received the unavailable tone. Then, some half an hour later, he knocked on the cabin door.

'Oh, hi,' Rebecca said, trying not to let herself be distracted by his flawlessly turned out appearance. He was wearing a crisply laundered shirt, a pale blue silk tie, and dark trousers that emphasised the tautness of his flat stomach and his powerful, long legs. 'I'm afraid Emma isn't here—she was called away to work. I tried to ring you to cancel, but your phone seemed to be switched off.'

He nodded, frowning. 'I was driving. I tend to switch the car phone off if I'm not on call. Some of the roads in the hills can be tricky—very winding and steep—so I like to give them my full attention, especially if there's been heavy rain or a storm.' He sent her a questioning look. 'I'm sorry she isn't here, but there's no reason for you not to come along, is there?'

'Uh…no…if that's all right with you?' Her brows drew together. 'I know Emma's disappointed to be missing out.'

'It's okay—she can come another time. We'll arrange something. It's no problem.'

She brightened. 'All right, then, if you're sure.' It felt strange to be going without Emma, but since he'd taken the trouble to come out of his way to fetch her, she didn't want to argue the point. 'I'll just get a light jacket.'

A moment later she slipped the jacket on over her T-shirt, then checked her jeans pocket for her key and cash card, transferring them to a small bag. 'I'm ready,' she said at last.

'Good. I told my manager to expect us just after four. His wife's arranging afternoon tea on the terrace for us.'

'Afternoon tea?' She smiled, giving him a quick glance as she slid into the passenger seat beside him. 'It sounds lovely—but isn't that a very English tradition?'

He smiled. 'It is, but I hoped you might like it. I could certainly do with something—I've been on duty since seven this morning and I'm starving. It isn't always easy to stop and grab something to eat and drink when you're coping with emergencies.'

'No, it isn't.' She recalled her time as a junior doctor, working long hours and fitting in breaks wherever possible. 'Have you been very busy today, then?'

She frowned. He looked clean and fresh after his exertions, but maybe he'd managed to shower and change at the hospital. Come to think of it, his black hair *was* faintly glistening with moisture.

'We have… The usual variety of patients, with chest pains, viruses, bleeding…' He glanced at her, his mouth twisting faintly as he started on the road up into the hills. 'Even though this is the Caribbean, and we have lots of tourists around, enjoying the beaches and water sports quite safely, people still get ill—people who live and work here.'

'I never thought otherwise.' Perhaps he'd mistaken her frown for a look of disbelief that there could ever be trouble in Paradise.

'No?' He didn't say any more, concentrating his attention on the winding road that led ever upwards.

As she gazed out of the window Rebecca saw the cloud-covered peaks of the mountains rising majestically in the distance. The landscape was awe-inspiring, vibrant and rugged.

They arrived at the plantation a few minutes later, and Rebecca looked around in wonder at this dark green jewel set in the midst of the rainforest. All around her were cacao trees, standing about twenty feet high, with glossy green leaves as big as her hand. The tree bark was covered with mosses and lichens, and small, delicate orchids peeped out from crevices here and there. Large pink fruit pods hung from the branches, ready to be harvested.

Set amongst these trees were other, taller ones. She recognised banana and coconut palms. She looked at them, a little puzzled, wondering what they were doing here in the middle of a cocoa plantation.

Interpreting her glance, Cade said, 'They provide shade for the cacao—otherwise the hot sun would shrivel them. The cocoa trees are quite fragile, especially when they're young, so they need protection. I planted these trees when I first took over the plantation so that I could shield the young plants. They grew very quickly.'

'Ah, I see.' The banana leaves were huge, spreading shade, and the nearby coconut palms added extra security.

'Up ahead they're harvesting the pods—we can go and watch for a while, if you want?'

'I'd like that—thanks.'

She went with him to an area where workers moved among the more mature trees, hooking the pods from the branches with long-handled implements. The pods fell to the ground, where young men and women with machetes cut them open and removed the white beans from inside. They dropped the large seeds into clean metal buckets.

'They'll empty the beans into wooden boxes and cover them with banana leaves to keep in the heat,' Cade told her. 'We let them ferment for a few days before drying them, so that the colour and flavour can develop.'

'It's fascinating,' she said simply. 'I'd no idea the beans were white to begin with.'

His mobile phone pinged and he took it from his pocket and glanced at a text message on the screen. 'If you're interested I can show you more of the process,' he said, 'but maybe we should go and have tea first. It's all ready and waiting for us at the house, apparently.'

'Okay.' She smiled and started to walk with him towards the white-painted building in the distance. 'Is William there? I was expecting to see him this afternoon.'

A muscle flicked briefly in his jaw. 'Actually, no… Perhaps I should have mentioned it earlier… I'm afraid William won't be back until much later today—he's gone to a neighbouring island to organise the transportation of our new truck. Things will go a lot quicker for us if he takes charge of it, I think.'

She shot him a quick, penetrating glance. 'You sent him to do that today?'

He nodded. 'The dealer called this morning. It seemed to me like a good opportunity to follow up on things right away.'

He sounded nonchalant, though she suspected he was covering his actions. The truth was he hadn't wanted her spending more time around his cousin.

'Really?' She eyed him doubtfully.

Had it been so necessary for William to go this afternoon? Wouldn't a phone call have been enough to set things in motion? She frowned. It wasn't up to her to interfere, or tell him his business, but she was suddenly on edge, wary of Cade's motives. Did he think she was such a bad influence?

'It's a shame he isn't here,' she said. 'I know he was looking forward to seeing Emma and me today.'

His dark eyes glinted in a way that only confirmed her suspicions. He'd deliberately sent his cousin on this errand.

'I'm sure he was, but I dare say there'll be other opportunities for you to get together.'

He laid a hand lightly in the small of her back, and with that gentle possessive touch it dawned on her that maybe he wanted to keep her all to himself. His dark gaze moved over her and a small ripple of panic ran through her—a feeling of nervousness mingled with a strange sadness. She couldn't get involved with anyone, could she? Any relationships she had from now on would have to be light-hearted, fleeting—nothing of any great significance. She didn't want to risk getting the same reaction she'd had from Drew. Once had been quite enough.

They'd arrived at the plantation house by now, and were standing in front of wide veranda steps. It was a beautiful house, built of stone to withstand the ravages of Caribbean storms, and meant to last a lifetime. There were lots of glass doors opening out on to the decking, giving her a glimpse of a light and airy interior.

Just then a woman came hurrying from the house. She was in her mid-forties, Rebecca guessed, with neat brown hair cut into a silky layered bob, and hazel eyes that were filled with anxiety.

'Cade—there's been an accident in the east section. One of the lads has hurt his hand—a machete cut. Don says it's bleeding quite badly.'

'Thanks, Harriet,' he said, looking worried. 'I'll go and get my medical bag.' He glanced at Rebecca as he moved towards the house. 'I'm afraid I'll have to go and deal with this right away. Will you stay here and let Harriet look after you? I'll be back as soon as I can.'

'It's all right. I understand—you have to go, of course.'

All her instincts as a doctor kicked in as soon as she realised that this was an emergency. If the cut had gone deep the boy would need stitches at the very least. If there had been major damage to the muscles and tendons of his hand he might require an operation in order to save the function. There was also the possibility that Cade might need help with administering an anaesthetic…

Deep down, she knew she didn't have a choice. 'Perhaps I should go with you to see him?'

He didn't argue the point. 'Are you sure you want to do that?' He raised questioning dark brows, and when she nodded said, 'Thanks. We'll take the runabout.' He pointed to an open-sided vehicle parked on the drive. 'It'll get us there in a few minutes.'

He went into the house and came out a minute later with a large immediate care response pack.

She was impressed. 'It looks as though you're very well prepared for any eventuality,' she commented, as they climbed aboard the four-seater golf buggy and set off.

He nodded. 'I always keep a medical kit in the car, too. I'm on call outside the hospital sometimes, so I need to be ready for anything.'

'I can understand that.' A worrying thought occurred to her. 'Does this sort of thing happen often here on the plantation?'

'No, not at all. We're really careful to show our workers the correct way of going on, but I suppose it's inevitable that accidents happen from time to time. The aim is to keep them to a minimum.' He frowned. 'One way I've changed things is by paying everyone a proper wage, instead of giving payment for how much they produce. It seems to be working out for the better so far.'

They arrived at the east section a short time later, and he jumped down from the runabout and hurried over to where a small crowd of native workers had gathered. There were murmurs of concern, people talking all at once, but as soon as Cade appeared the group quietened and opened up to give him access to his patient.

He knelt down beside the injured boy, a lad of about seventeen years old. He was holding his hand to stem the blood flow, his face etched with pain. He was pale and in shock.

'Let me see, Thomas.' Cade examined the wound—a deep cut across the back of the hand between the thumb and first finger. 'Can you move your fingers? Open and close your hand for me?'

After examining him carefully, Cade gave an almost imperceptible nod.

'I think you're fortunate—there's been no major damage. You've lost quite a bit of blood, and obviously you're in shock. I think we'll need to clean up the wound and put in a few stitches.' He studied the boy thoughtfully. 'I could take you to the hospital, or we could do it back at the house. What would you prefer?'

'Will you do it here...please?'

'Okay.' Cade rummaged in his medical bag and brought out a pack of sterile dressings. 'I'm going to put a pad over the wound to stem the bleeding and then cover it with a dressing. Once we get you to the house we'll clean it up properly and put some sutures in place.'

All the while he was speaking, he was working efficiently to protect the injured hand.

'Okay, let's get you into the runabout.' He signalled to two of the workers to help get the boy settled in the back of the buggy. 'How did you come to hurt yourself, Thomas, do you know?'

Thomas shook his head. 'It happened so suddenly... I was cutting open a pod with my machete and I saw something out of the corner of my eye—it might have been a small lizard, running through the undergrowth.'

'Hmm...that's a difficult one. These things happen sometimes, but you need to try to keep your attention on the blade at all times.' Cade frowned. 'Maybe we should issue everyone with leather gloves?'

'Too hot, boss,' one of the workers said. 'No one would want to wear them.'

'Well, we'll have to think of something—maybe we can find gloves that have air holes... I don't want any more accidents if I can help it.' He glanced at the other worker once more. 'Benjamin, will you make sure Thomas's parents know what's happened? Tell them he'll be okay.'

'I will, boss.'

Cade nodded, and saw the boy settled into the buggy while Rebecca slid into the seat beside the patient, making sure that he was securely strapped in and that his arm was supported in a comfortable position.

Back at the house, Cade helped Thomas through the front door and into a room that seemed to serve as a clinic. Rebecca looked around, taking in the clean lines, the treatment couch laid with fresh tissue roll, the glass-fronted cupboards stocked with all kinds of medical supplies. In one corner there was a sink unit with stainless-steel taps and dispensers for soap and paper towels.

'Sit down here, Thomas. Let me adjust the backrest for you.' Cade settled the boy on the couch and then went over to the sink to wash his hands.

Rebecca joined him there. 'Do you want me to help anaesthetise the hand?' she asked, and he nodded.

'Thanks. We'll use lidocaine, and then clean the wound with sterile water. He'll need several stitches to hold it in place.'

She worked with him to tend the boy's injured hand, and when Cade had finished applying the sutures she covered the wound with a sterile dressing, fixing it in place with tape.

'I'll give you some antibiotics, Thomas,' Cade said, 'so that you don't get an infection. It's important to keep the wound clean, okay? I'll need to see you back here in a week's time, to check that everything's healing as it should.' He looked at the boy carefully. 'Are you okay with that?'

Thomas nodded. 'Yes, thanks.' He was still pale, but at least he appeared to be recovering from the initial shock of the accident.

'Mrs Chalmers will give you tea and something to eat in the kitchen,' Cade said, helping him to get down from the couch. 'Take your time—your father will be along in a while to take you home, but there's no rush.'

Thomas smiled. 'Thanks, Dr Byfield. I'm sorry to be so much trouble.'

'You're no trouble, Thomas. I don't like to see anyone injured—especially on my property. I want you to take extra-special care from now on.'

'I will. Thanks again.'

Cade took him along to the kitchen—a large, superbly equipped room with doors that opened out on to a wide area of the veranda. A table and chairs were set out there, and Harriet Chalmers was waiting with reviving tea, home-baked scones and fruit preserves.

Thomas's father arrived just as the boy began to tuck in, using his good hand, and Cade spoke to the man for a few minutes, inviting him to sit down and eat with his son before turning his attention back to Rebecca.

'We'll leave them to it,' he said. 'Harriet's set out some sandwiches for us in the breakfast room—through here.'

He led the way from the kitchen to a small room, surrounded on two sides by floor-to-ceiling glass doors. It was simply furnished, with a white table and chairs, and a white-painted dresser displaying plates and dishes that added a pleasing splash of colour. Here and there were green ferns, extending their delicate fronds to bring a touch of the outside into the room.

An arrangement of pale yellow orchids on the breakfast table caught Rebecca's attention and she gave a small gasp of delight. 'Aren't they beautiful?' she said, smiling. 'This room is lovely. It's so cool and fresh and restful.'

'I'm glad you like it.' Cade returned the smile and pulled out a chair for her. 'Harriet fetches the flowers from the garden. She looks after the house for me and prepares food—she thinks I'll starve if I'm left to my own devices.' He thought about that for a moment or two, a small line furrowing his brow. 'Actually, she's probably right about that. I've never been any good at cooking—apart from eggs or pancakes.'

'You're lucky to have her, then.'

She looked at the array of food that had been set out. There were perfectly cut triangular-shaped sandwiches arranged on a platter, decorated with a crisp-looking side salad. Alongside that were skillets filled with chicken kebabs made with peppers and mushroom, bowls with savoury rice, and a mango salsa dip.

'Oh, what I would give for someone to cook for *me*! Beyond price!'

They ate the food, drank hot tea and talked about Cade's hopes for the plantation.

'Did you start all this with William in mind?' she asked after a while. 'It must have seemed relevant that he was studying food and agricultural science at university.'

He nodded. 'That did come into it,' he admitted. 'But my father was always interested in growing food, so I suppose I developed an interest along the way.'

'What does he do? Does he have some sort of farm or plantation? Or work on one?' She wondered why he didn't work with his father if they shared the same passions.

'He lives back in Florida now, and works on one of the teams doing restoration work in the Everglades. His interests have changed over the years.'

His tone was faintly cynical and she immediately picked up on that. Was there some kind of problem between him and his father?

'Do you see much of him? It must be difficult for you…working at the hospital *and* running the plantation.'

'We keep in touch. I see him at least once a month—but when he and my mother split up my priority was to make sure *she* was all right.'

'Oh, I'm sorry. I didn't realise—does your mother live on the island?'

'She does.' He smiled. 'She was part of the inspiration behind the cocoa plantation—she and her sister… William's mother. They're both hugely interested in how it will turn out. She lives fairly close—just a mile or so away—so I see her often.'

'That's good. Family's important.'

'Yes. You tend to find that out when you don't have it—as you know. I guess we've both lost out, though in different ways.' He sent her a penetrating glance. 'It must be disruptive for you, with Emma being called away? All your plans for doing stuff together must have been put on hold for the time being?'

'Yes.' Her mouth flattened. 'It's a bit of a blow, but it can't be helped. I'll probably take the time to go and look around the island. From what William told me there are lots of places to see, beaches to lie on, markets to visit. I'd like to see the other islands at some point, but I suppose I've plenty of time to do that with Emma.'

'Well, yes, from the sound of things you'll be here for a few months, so there should be plenty of opportunity for you to explore.' He looked at her oddly. 'I guess it's great to get the chance to take time out from your career.' He frowned. 'Though from what I saw this afternoon when you helped with Thomas, the way you talked to him, and from what happened on your plane over here, you're a highly skilled, competent physician. It seems strange that you've put it all on hold to come halfway around the world.'

'Does it?' She picked up her cup and drank slowly. 'You're quite right—people don't often get the chance to do that, do they? Maybe I'm just taking advantage of my special circumstances and making the most of things.' She spoke nonchalantly, as though it didn't matter one way or the other, but as she viewed him over the rim of her cup she knew he didn't accept her answer.

'Did something happen, back in Hertfordshire?' he asked. 'Something that sent you on the run?'

She hesitated for a second or two. Then, 'Nothing that I want to talk about,' she said flatly.

He pulled in a quick breath. 'I'm sorry. I shouldn't have pried.'

'It's okay.' She glanced at her watch. 'It's getting late. Perhaps I should call for a taxi to take me home. I've taken up enough of your time.'

'Not at all… I have to stay here to supervise the workers, but I'll arrange for Benjamin to take you home. I'm glad you came along this afternoon. Maybe we could meet up for a drink this evening?'

She shook her head. 'I'm sorry, but I'm afraid I've already made plans.'

He frowned. 'With William?'

'With a friend of Emma's.'

'Oh, I see.' He relaxed a little. 'Is she one of Emma's nursing colleagues?'

'No—actually, he's Emma's landlord. He dropped by earlier today, to check that everything was okay with the property, and after we'd talked for a bit he asked me out. I thought, why not? Since Emma isn't going to be around.' She paused momentarily, sensing Cade's sudden tension in the bracing of his shoulders and the narrowing of his eyes. She sent him a quick glance from under her lashes. 'I suppose that only confirms your opinion of me as some kind of good-time girl?'

He returned her gaze with penetrating scrutiny. 'Oh, I don't know about that, Rebecca. You seem to be intent on enjoying your stay out here in the Caribbean—good luck to you in that. I'd be only too glad to help you make the most of your stay on the island in any way I can.' He frowned. 'I can't help thinking, though, that there's a whole lot more to you than meets the eye… I guess I'll just have to bide my time and look forward to getting to know you better.'

## CHAPTER THREE

REBECCA LISTENED TO the wind howling about the cabin and shivered unconsciously. Already it had whipped up trouble and blown down a fencepost. It could be that a freak tropical storm was threatening but, whatever the situation, she had to go outside and fix the post before the whole fence collapsed.

The weather had changed overnight, and she wasn't sure what to make of it. It was definitely a bit scary… though she doubted she'd be worried about it if Cade were there with her. Somehow with him around she was fairly certain she would feel safe and secure. But he wasn't here. Nor was he likely to be.

She hadn't known what to make of his comments the other night. She'd tried to keep her feelings hidden deep inside herself, but it looked as though he'd guessed she was holding something back.

Now, as she went outside, she wondered what made him tick. He was obviously a perceptive, ambitious, intelligent man, who cared deeply for the people around him. He even knew the names of all his workers—that had surprised her, because she'd seen for herself that there were a good many of them employed on the plantation, but in a moment alone with the housekeeper

Harriet had confirmed he knew every one. From other things he'd said, he knew their families, too, and about their hopes and their worries.

She straightened the wooden post in the ground and hit it squarely with a mallet she'd found in the outhouse, but her efforts didn't appear to be having much impact. It still remained stubbornly loose and tipped over to one side.

'Try holding the mallet further back along the handle. It'll give you more leverage.'

Startled, she looked up to see Cade standing by the wide-spreading fig tree. Its glossy leaves lifted fitfully in the breeze and sent dappled shade over the garden. 'Cade,' she said in surprise. 'Hello.'

He looked incredibly good, dressed in a dark, beautifully tailored suit, his jacket open to reveal a pale blue shirt and deeper blue tie.

'I didn't hear you arrive. Is everything okay? I wasn't expecting to see you.' Her copper curls flicked about her face and she pushed them away with the back of her hand.

'I was coming home from the hospital and I thought I'd drop by to see how you were doing. I've been on call or I'd have come sooner. It's been a couple of days since you were up at the plantation, hasn't it?'

'Yes… Though I saw William yesterday. He's been keeping me up to date with things. He said he'd brought the truck over and everything is going well with the harvesting—and that Thomas wants to be back at work but you think he should wait until the stitches are removed.'

She wielded the mallet once more and this time the post sank a few centimetres into the ground. It was still not enough, though, and she stared at it in frustration. She wasn't making much headway. The wind had done a good job in dislodging the post and tipping over the fence—even now it was buffeting around her, promising mayhem.

He reached for the mallet. 'May I?' he said, and she nodded, handing it over. He hammered the post effortlessly into place with a couple of hefty swings. 'Shouldn't your landlord be doing these repairs for you?' he asked, attempting to straighten the rest of the fence slats and fixing them to the main post with the nails she handed to him.

She shrugged, causing her loose-fitting top to slide downwards, leaving a shoulder bare. 'It was hardly worth fetching him out for such a minor thing—though I'm sure he would have obliged if necessary.'

His glance moved over the smooth expanse of creamy flesh exposed inadvertently and her cheeks flushed with heat.

'I've no doubt you're right,' he said, 'but I hope he fixed the window shutters for you—there's a storm brewing and you'll need to be able to batten things down.'

'Yes, he did. It was something simple—a couple of rivets missing. It wasn't worth bringing a workman in to do it, he said. He did the repair himself.'

'I'm glad that's sorted. That's partly why I came over here—to make sure you were all right and prepared for the weather.' He hammered a nail home and then studied her thoughtfully. 'So how did your date with him go?'

'It went well, actually,' she said brightly.

It was somehow good to know that Cade cared

about her enough to check that she was okay...but perhaps she ought to remain cautious in her dealings with him. It might be just as well if he realised she wasn't confining her attention to William, considering he seemed to have such a problem with that—even though 'that' was just friendship! She wasn't sure what she wanted in the love department any more...

'He's surprisingly young for a landlord—in his early thirties,' she said. 'But I guess it's a family-run enterprise. His parents are in business over here, dealing in property. He showed me round some of the houses they own and then took me to a nightclub in a resort along the coast. We had a great time.'

His eyes narrowed. He didn't seem too happy with her answer. 'Are you going to be seeing him again?'

'Possibly.' She'd enjoyed her evening with him, and they'd met up for coffee the next day, but when he would have taken things further she'd held back, doubts creeping in. He was keen, but she wasn't ready for that level of involvement. 'We exchanged phone numbers, but I'm a bit cautious about making too many arrangements until I know when Emma's going to be coming back. I don't want her returning to an empty house.'

'I suppose that's understandable.' His shoulders relaxed a bit. 'Have you heard anything from her? William told me you were getting anxious. She's been gone for a couple of days now, hasn't she? Though that's probably to be expected if there's an outbreak of some sort?'

Finishing up, and checking the fence was secure, he returned the mallet to her.

'Thanks.' She nodded agreement. 'I think there

must be something wrong with the phones—a problem with the signal up there in the hills, or some such. She promised she would call me, but perhaps there was a local storm. Otherwise I'm sure she would have been in touch. It's a bit of a worry.' She put the mallet into the storage shed and padlocked the door. 'Shall we go into the house?'

'Good idea—we definitely need to get out of this wind. I just need to fetch something from my car—I have your luggage in the boot, courtesy of the airline authorities.'

She stared at him, her eyes widening in astonishment. 'You *do*?'

He nodded. 'I gave them a call and chased things up, since you weren't having much success… William mentioned it still hadn't turned up. I hope that's all right with you? My handling things? I've had more dealings with people out here…'

'All right? *Definitely* it's all right. You tracked it down? Oh, that's wonderful! I was beginning to think it was gone for ever! How on earth did you manage it?'

He made a crooked smile. 'It was a process of elimination—tracing the route it was most likely to have followed, starting with the trip to Barbados, then back to Martinique. It did a bit of a detour along the way, but I got them to forward it here.'

'Bless you for that. Oh, *wow*!' She wanted to hug him, but contented herself with touching his arm in a brief show of gratitude. They walked around to the front of the house and she watched as he lifted her cases from his SUV. 'Bring them inside, will you? Thanks. Oh, it's *so* good to have them back!'

'I thought you'd be pleased.' He looked around as

he stepped into the cabin. 'Where do you want them? In your bedroom?'

'Yes, please—it's through here.' She showed him the way to the second bedroom.

He glanced at the neatly made bed with its mosquito net drapes and then at the desk with her laptop computer set up in a corner of the room. There were doors leading on to the veranda.

'Your sister did well to find this place,' he said, placing the cases at the end of the bed. 'It seems to have everything going for it.' He straightened and looked around properly.

He was very tall, very muscular—an overwhelming male presence in the confines of the small room.

'It does.' She moved to the door, suddenly very much aware of him and a little uncomfortable to be standing in a bedroom with him. 'Come through to the kitchen. I'll make us some coffee.'

'That would be great, thanks.' He went with her and helped set out mugs, cream and sugar on the table, while she added freshly ground coffee to the filter machine and searched for cookies in the cupboard.

'These are made with cinnamon,' she said, opening a packet and sliding them on to a plate, pushing it towards him. 'I found them in the bakery in the village. Help yourself. They're delicious.'

'Thanks.' He took off his jacket, draping it over the back of a chair, and waited while she poured coffee. Then he sat down with her at the table.

'Do you really think there's a storm coming?' she asked. She sipped the hot liquid.

'I'd say it's practically on top of us,' he said. 'It's already affected the south part of the island and it's moving towards us all the time. The wind's building up and it won't be too long before the rain starts.'

She bit her lip. 'Perhaps I shouldn't be keeping you here—you still have to drive up into the hills. I'm not sure what to expect, but from what I've been hearing on the radio these things are a lot more powerful than the storms we get back in England.'

'Are you worried about that?'

'I'm not sure. I suppose so… It's the not knowing that's the worry.'

'I could stay with you—we can see it out together?'

He glanced at her and she gave an almost imperceptible nod, relief flooding through her.

'Would you? I think that would make me feel much better.'

'Of course.' He drank his coffee and then headed purposefully towards the door. 'First thing to do is to close the shutters,' he said. 'It'll make things dark in here, so you might want to put on the lights and check if you have any candles.'

'Do you think the power might fail?'

'It could do. It often happens—lines come down… services get disrupted. You get used to it after a while. The water sometimes goes off as well, so it might be useful to fill some containers as a precaution.'

He went outside and started closing the shutters. As he'd said, it became dark in the house once the doors and windows were blacked out, and he finished the task only just in time as the first drops of rain started to fall. It very soon became pounding, torrential rain.

She looked outside as he came back in through the kitchen door and the sky was ominously dark, with storm clouds gathered overhead. He shut the door behind him and she busied herself pouring more coffee and listening to the reports on the radio.

'They say it's heading north towards the other islands,' she said. 'I hope Emma and her colleagues are okay.'

He frowned. 'I expect they'll be fine away from the coast. Situated here, by the sea, we're probably bearing the brunt of it.'

Thunder boomed overhead, shaking the cabin, and her eyes widened in dismay. She tried to ignore the tumult outside, talking to him about anything and everything—about the beautiful Caribbean islands and beach barbecues, the colourful wildlife that lived in the trees around the cabin—and he told her about his work at the hospital, how he'd come to medicine through his interest in the work of the doctors back in Florida, where he'd grown up.

As the day wore on flashes like strobe lightning sparked through the gaps in the shutters and the wind screamed around the cabin. This was nothing like the mild storms she'd experienced back home. This was violent, booming, nature at its most destructive.

'It'll be okay. It sounds worse than it really is.'

'If you say so. It's been going on for hours.' She went over to the stove. She needed to keep busy. 'It's getting late,' she said. 'I could make us some soup, and there are some crusty rolls and butter we can have with it.'

'That sounds great.'

Another thunderclap shook the cabin and there was an almighty rumble overhead, followed by a shrill clattering on the roof. She jumped slightly and felt the colour drain from her face. It seemed as though the very fabric of the house was being torn apart.

Cade came over to her and put his arms around her, holding her close. 'We'll be all right,' he reassured her. 'It was probably just a few loose shingles on the roof. This place is solidly built.'

She nodded, knowing he was doing his best to comfort her. It was soothing, having him draw her to him this way. He wasn't at all bothered by the hurricane force that hurled itself in a fury around the building. That knowledge in itself was calming, and she leaned into him, gaining strength from him, glad of the steady thud of his heartbeat beneath her breast. His powerful body shielded her, offered protection while the storm raged around them. She was ashamed of herself for needing that comforting gesture, but all the time she was thankful that he steadfastly held her.

Even so, there was another inherent danger in being in close proximity to him in this way. She was becoming far too aware of him—of his strength, his lithe, supple body, the way the lightest touch of his hands evoked a tingling response.

'I think I'll be okay now,' she said after a while. She couldn't let him go on supporting her this way. It was too intimate, too tempting to stay here, locked in his embrace. If this carried on she might want to make a habit of it—and that wouldn't do at all, would it?

'Are you sure?' He looked at her, his gaze smoke-dark as he tried to read what was in her mind. 'I promise you I'm quite happy to go on holding you for as long as you like.'

Heat flickered in his grey eyes and a half-smile pulled at the corners of his mouth. She was feverishly conscious of the warmth of his body, the taut muscles of his thighs pressuring hers, of the way his long body offered refuge.

'I'm sure. I'll be fine.' She couldn't allow herself to respond to his mischievous invitation. Instead she carefully began to ease herself away from him, and in the end he reluctantly let her go. 'I'll… I'll see to the soup,' she said.

He watched her as she worked. 'Did you have a boyfriend back in Hertfordshire?' he asked. 'I can't imagine a girl like you not being scooped up by some determined man. Have you left someone behind—someone who's nursing a broken heart, maybe?'

She gave a small choked laugh at that. Even now it brought a lump to her throat to think about Drew. She didn't have feelings for him any more, but the hurt and associated fall-out from their relationship still lingered.

'There was someone, but it didn't work out,' she said. 'You could say I've decided to move on.'

'Ah.' He was silent for a moment, his glance drifting over her. 'I thought there had to be something like that.'

She stirred the soup and set out bowls on the table. 'What about you?' she asked. 'You have everything going for you, but I don't see a woman around.'

His mouth flattened a little. 'Perhaps I've learned to be cautious over the years. Women tend to come with their own agendas, I've found… They want marriage, wealth, status—all perfectly reasonable ambitions, but no good if they come at the expense of true, basic human feelings.'

'So you've been hurt? Someone let you down?' She

said it in a matter-of-fact way, glancing at him as she served up the hot vegetable broth. 'Just because you've had one or two bad experiences it doesn't necessarily mean that *all* women think along those lines.'

He shrugged. 'Maybe not.'

He wasn't convinced of that, obviously. 'Is that why you're so concerned about William—you think he might be hurt in a similar way?'

'In part. He fell for someone, but she led him a bit of a dance and cheated on him. He was heartbroken. Then his father was taken ill, and he became the main breadwinner in his household, and things became too much for him for a while.'

She frowned. 'And now?'

'Now he seems to be coping well enough. My uncle's in hospital, being treated for a virus that has affected his heart muscle. They had to sell the house to fund the medical bills, and now they live in a property on the plantation. It's made me all the more anxious to make a success of things, so that I can give them a livelihood. William will become a partner one day, and maybe my uncle, too.'

So there was more than his own land-owning expectations resting on the venture. 'I'm sorry for what you're all going through.' She sucked in a breath. 'Is your uncle going to be all right?'

He pulled a face. 'We hope so. The doctors are giving him supportive treatment, along with a low-salt diet, and they're making sure he gets plenty of rest. It all depends on how serious the damage is and whether his heart can recover from it.'

'I'd no idea it was so bad. William manages to hide his feelings well, doesn't he?'

'He does.'

They sat at the kitchen table, savouring the food, and by mutual unspoken agreement changed the subject, talking about how the storm might affect the plantation.

'It's possible we could lose a few trees,' he said. 'But the main harvest is in, and in general the crop and the houses are protected, so things may not be too bad. The biggest worry is the road network. Rivers tend to swell and flood, and you often find that debris is swept along in their path.' His phone bleeped but he ignored it, going on with his soup.

'I imagine the authorities are used to dealing with—' She broke off as another thunderclap exploded in the distance and all the lights went out. 'Oh, no… there goes the power.'

He stood up and went over to the worktop, where she'd set out hurricane lamps and candles. 'Good—these are battery-operated,' he said, bringing one of the lamps over to the table. It gave out a decent light, so they were able to finish their meal in relative comfort.

When she started to clear the table a little while later she was suddenly aware of the gentle splash of water droplets dampening her hair and her clothes. 'Oh, dear…' She glanced upwards, searching for the source, and discovered a dark patch of moisture spreading across the ceiling.

'I guess I was right about the shingles on the roof,' Cade said, making a wry face. 'There must be a tear in the roofing felt. I'd better do a quick check on the rest of the house.'

He took one of the hurricane lamps with him and

went from room to room, searching for more seepage. Rebecca went with him, dismayed to see similar patches of water forming on her bedroom ceiling.

'I'll do what I can to stop the leaks temporarily,' Cade said, 'but your landlord will have to get things fixed as soon as he gets the chance.'

'I'll let him know. Is there anything I can do to help?'

'You could see if there are any sheets of polythene or something similar that I can use to mask the tears,' he suggested.

'Will bin liners do?'

'They'll be fine. I could do with some tape, as well.'

She searched in one of the kitchen drawers and pulled out a roll of plastic liners, handing them to him. 'I think we have some PVC tape in a toolbox in the loft. I'll get it for you—the loft access is in the hallway. There's a pull-down ladder.'

'Okay, leave it with me.'

She didn't leave him. Instead she stood at the foot of the ladder and held a second lamp to give him more light as he accessed the roof space. It took several minutes for him to locate the leaks and fix the waterproof sheeting in place, but finally he came back down the ladder to her.

'That should hold things until you can get a permanent repair done,' he said, walking back with her into the kitchen. 'At least the storm's beginning to move on…it's heading further up the coast, I imagine. We've had the worst of it here, I think.'

His mobile phone was on the table, flashing to show that another message had been received.

'Do you need to answer that text message?' she asked. 'It might be important.'

'Yes, you're right. Perhaps I should. I'm not on call right now, but given the circumstances…' He glanced at his phone and read the message on screen, then winced. 'It's the hospital—they texted earlier—there's been an influx of patients injured in the storm and they're putting out a general call for any medics available to go and help.'

'So you'll be going back there? Will it be safe for you to drive?' She was worried for him, but knew instinctively that he wouldn't be comfortable staying here with her when there were patients who needed him.

'I expect so—I don't really have a choice. I have to go and help out.' He frowned. 'I don't want to leave you here,' he said. 'If the storm doubles back for any reason that roof could be totally destroyed. I'd feel much happier if you were to come and stay up at the plantation house until things are sorted here.'

She shook her head. 'Thanks for the offer, but I can't go anywhere—what would I do about Emma?' She wasn't thinking clearly, was concerned for her sister, worried about leaving the cabin, and anxious because she knew she ought to go and help out in the emergency. 'I haven't been able to get in touch with her. She won't know what's happening. Anyway, I'm sure I'll be all right staying here now that the roof leaks have been sorted.'

'No, you won't,' he said firmly. 'That's only a temporary fix.' He reached for her, grasping her arms in a gentle but firm hold. 'You can leave a note for Emma to tell her where you are. Apart from the risk of the roof giving out, the power is still down. At least up at the plantation house we have a generator for when the electricity cuts out. Emma will be fine, I'm sure. The phones are probably temporarily out where she is—I expect you'll be able to talk to her soon enough.'

'I don't know…' Her brow furrowed. 'I need to see her…make sure she's all right. It isn't like her not to keep in touch. I need to go up to the village and try to find her.'

'But not right now—in the middle of a storm.' He tugged her close to him. 'Think about it, Rebecca… You can't stay here, and you won't be able to get in touch with your sister until things calm down a bit. You have to come with me—let me take care of you.'

She shook her head. 'I don't need you to tell me what to do, Cade. I'll be perfectly all right here now that the storm's moving on. I can look after myself.'

'Sure, you can… But there's no way I'm going to leave you here alone. These storms are fickle. You don't know what might happen.' He looked down at her, his eyes sparking with determination. 'You can't stay here. I won't let you.'

'Oh, really?' She raised her brows. 'I don't see that you have a choice. It's *my* decision to make, not yours.'

'Is it? Maybe I can persuade you otherwise…'

Before she had time to realise his intention he swooped, claiming her mouth in a fierce, possessive kiss that caused the blood to course through her body in an overwhelming tide of heat. Her lips parted beneath the sensual onslaught and she clung to him as her limbs responded by trembling under the passionate intensity of his embrace.

It was like nothing she'd ever experienced before.

His kisses made her feverish with desire, the touch of his hands turned her flesh to fire as they shaped her curves, leaving her desperate for more. It was so unexpected—such a coaxing, tantalising raid on her defences. Her resistance crumbled. She wanted to stay here, locked in his arms, having him hold her, with his long, hard body pressuring hers and promising heaven on earth.

But these moments of bliss came to an abrupt halt as an almighty crash rocked the wall of the cabin. She froze, shocked into stillness by the noise and the sheer terror of wondering what might have happened.

'The storm—' she said. 'The wall—surely it's strong enough to stand up to the storm? Something must have happened outside—some damage—'

'It's probably a tree that's come down.' Reluctantly, he released her, then went to the kitchen door and looked out. 'I was right,' he said, closing the door abruptly. 'The wind must have weakened it and finally it collapsed. We need to get out of here, Rebecca. You know what I'm saying makes sense, don't you?'

She nodded. 'Yes, okay. I suppose so.' Even *she* couldn't argue if trees were crashing down around them. Who could tell if the cabin wall would give way at some point? There were trees surrounding the house.

'I'll get your cases and load them into the car.' He started towards the bedroom. 'Is there anything else you need to take with you?'

'No, I don't think so.'

'You'll need a jacket—the wind's dying down, but it's still raining out there.' He pulled his own jacket from the back of the chair and shrugged it on.

She nodded. She could hear the rain, still frantic, hitting the roof shingles and spattering against the door and the shutters. 'Okay. I'll get it. But maybe we should head for the hospital—I'm a medic… I could help.'

'I'd rather you didn't—for whatever reason, you've turned your back on medicine for a while. Besides, you're not familiar with the terrain out here…the way things operate…and anyway I'd feel better if I knew you were safe up at the plantation house. It will be one less worry for me.'

She frowned. 'I'm sure I could make myself useful in some way.'

Perhaps the people up at the plantation would need help of some sort. If he didn't want her working alongside him, at least she could offer support where it was needed.

They hurried out to the car a minute or so later and he stacked her luggage in the boot, alongside his medical bag and equipment. She took a moment to take a quick glance around. Most of the garden had withstood the brunt of the storm, but a couple of trees had succumbed to the elements, which had left several branches twisted and torn. One of them had split along the length of its trunk and fallen against the cabin wall.

Cade set out along the road to the plantation. It was disturbing to see the destruction in some places along the way. Crops were ruined, plantains and banana trees had been brought down. Fields were flooded where rivers had overflowed, and landslides had caused devastation. In one part the road was blocked by an accumulation of detritus that Cade had to toss to one side so that they could continue their journey.

She slid out of the car and went to stand at his side. 'There's no need for both of us to get wet,' he said, but she helped him move the debris despite his protests.

They set off once again, driving ever higher into the hills, and soon came to a small settlement. A dozen or so houses were clustered in what in any other circumstances would have been a breathtakingly lovely part of the island, where several waterfalls cascaded into a blue lake.

'Look—over there…' Rebecca pointed to what looked like an abandoned car, slewed at an angle where a slip road veered off to the west and formed a narrow bridge over a stream. 'Something's wrong. We should stop and take a look.'

He nodded, edging his SUV on to the slip road and following it as far as he could do so safely. Further on the road's surface disappeared under a tangle of broken concrete and stone. The bridge had collapsed and water flowed all around, swamping the saloon car that had apparently been heading towards the village in the distance. As the bridge had collapsed the car must have been hurled into the water, and now it was tilted precariously on one side, lifted up at its front end by a grassy mound.

As they moved closer Rebecca pulled a swift intake of air into her lungs. 'There are people still in the car,' she said urgently. 'We have to help them.'

Cade brought the car to a standstill on a dry stretch of the road above the level of the water. He was already getting out of the SUV as she spoke, and grabbing his medical bag from the boot before heading towards the car. Rebecca followed, gasping as the cold water swirled around her denim-clad legs and slowed her progress.

She waded forward, peering into the stranded vehicle. There were signs of movement inside. A youngish man—the driver—was slumped to one side, leaning towards the passenger seat, a trickle of blood running down his temple. Beside him a woman was apparently unconscious. The back of the car was under water.

Rebecca pulled at the doors but they were jammed solid. 'They must have locked automatically, somehow.'

'I'll get a wrench,' Cade said. 'We'll have to smash the side windows.'

He ran back to his vehicle and returned a moment later to swing the wrench at the glass. It gave way, shattering into a thousand pieces, and quickly Cade cleared a gap so that he could reach in and release the door catch.

The man began to come round. 'What's happening?' he said. Then, as his thoughts became more focussed, he added, 'The bridge—'

'You've been in an accident,' Cade told him. 'You've banged your head. Are you hurt anywhere else?'

'Just a headache,' the man answered. Then suddenly, 'My wife—Jane—' He looked around. 'I think she's bleeding.' He was dazed and shocked, not thinking clearly.

Cade helped the man out of the car and, seeing that he was going to take care of him, Rebecca slid into the driver's seat so that she could tend to the passenger. The woman's airway was clear, she was breathing fitfully and there was a faint, erratic pulse. After a while, she stirred, and Rebecca gave a swift sigh of relief.

'Jane,' she said urgently, 'are you in pain at all?'

'It…hurts…to breathe,' the woman said. 'My chest…hurts.'

Rebecca quickly checked her over. 'I think you've broken some of your ribs, Jane,' she said. 'Don't worry. We'll get you to hospital.'

'My baby…?' The woman frowned. 'Is my baby all right?'

'Your baby?' Rebecca echoed. 'Are you pregnant?'

'No…no…my *baby*…' She tried to twist around, gasping in pain at the effort, and with dawning horror Rebecca realised that she was looking at the back seat. It was completely submerged in water.

'Oh, no…'

She started to slide out of the driver's seat, but Cade was already on his way. The man must have told him about the infant because he looked shocked to the core, determination written in the clenched set of his jaw as he wrenched open the back door of the car.

'There's a child seat,' he said. 'I just need to feel for the release catch.'

It seemed like an age to Rebecca that he struggled to locate and press the buttons that would free the seat, but it must have been only seconds. He lifted the baby seat out of the water and she gasped as she saw the limp, lifeless form of the child fastened in there, her head lolling backwards, golden curls plastered wetly to her deathly white forehead.

'No, no…no… This can't be happening.' Rebecca was out of the car now, trying desperately to get to the baby, her legs hampered by the strong current of the water that eddied all around her.

'I have her,' Cade said briskly. 'I'll take care of her. See to the woman.'

It was like a cold slap across the face, bringing her to her senses.

'See to the woman. Get her out of the car. Get her and the man out of danger.'

She did as he said, moving like an automaton, but all the while her mind was on the child. She wanted to be with her, looking after her. The child was about a year old, with pale, chubby cheeks, and there was a bluish tinge to her rosebud mouth. Rebecca's heart squeezed in anguish. It wasn't fair. It wasn't right. Things like this should never happen.

She led the man and his wife to safety and sat them down on a grassy hillock set back from the water. The man was showing signs of concussion, the woman coping with the effects of the broken ribs that hampered her breathing. They were supposedly the lucky ones…if you could call losing a child anything remotely to do with luck.

She felt sick, her lungs heaving with the effort of holding back her emotions. 'I'll get something to cover you,' she said, aware that both the survivors might go into deep shock at any time. 'Stay there.'

'But my little girl—' The woman called out in desperation.

'We'll take care of her. I'll be back in a minute.'

Cade was working on the child. He'd taken her out of the car seat and laid her flat on her back on the ground near to his SUV. He was giving chest compressions. She heard the whispered rhythm of his voice as he accompanied his actions by counting the number of times he pressed down on the infant's chest with two fingers.

'Twenty-eight, twenty-nine, thirty…' Two breaths into the baby's mouth. Then he started the chest compressions again. 'One, two, three, four…'

Rebecca searched in the boot of his car and opened up his medical bag. Her hands were shaking, but she managed to find two carefully folded foil blankets. She didn't dare think any more about what was going on with the child. It was heartbreaking to witness Cade's efforts.

'Twelve…thirteen…fourteen…'

He was doing everything he could for the baby. Was it too late? How long had she been underwater? She couldn't bear to dwell on it.

'I'll phone the hospital to tell them to expect us,' she told him, and he nodded, not stopping for a second, keeping up the compressions in perfect rhythmic timing.

'Twenty-nine…thirty.' Two breaths.

Hurrying back to the parents, she wrapped the heat-retaining blankets around them and gave them what comfort she could. They were desperate to be with their child, but both were dazed and injured and in no fit state to go anywhere without help just then.

Moving away so that they couldn't hear, she phoned the hospital and told the emergency team that they were bringing in an infant, suspected drowning, an adult with broken ribs, query internal injuries, and a man with concussion from a head injury.

She looked over to where Cade was working on the infant and heard a choking sound. Hurrying back to him, she saw that he was lying her down in the recovery position on her left side. She had vomited.

'Is she breathing?' she asked in a strained voice, hardly daring to believe it was possible.

'Yes,' he said simply. 'She suddenly choked and coughed up water from her lungs. Will you get the oxygen and an infant mask for me from the medical pack?'

'Of course.'

Going quickly to the back of his car, she searched the emergency response kit once more. A tear trickled down her cheek and she dashed it away.

'We don't know how long she was without oxygen, do we?' she asked, handing him the equipment he needed. There was the awful possibility that the little girl could have suffered brain damage… 'But the water was cold…'

'Yes, that will have helped.'

The cold water would have the effect of stimulating the diving reflex in a young child, slowing the heartrate and constricting the peripheral arteries, so that oxygenated blood was diverted to the heart and brain where it was most needed. There was a chance she would be all right.

She watched for a moment as he gave the baby oxygen through the small face mask. Then she said, 'I should go and talk to the parents. I'll start to get them into your car.'

He nodded. 'I'll feel happier if you sit in the back with the mother and the baby—the father can go in front with me.'

'Okay.'

He looked at her, studying her thoughtfully, a frown creasing his brow. 'Are you all right?'

The question startled her for a second or two. Of course she was distraught—seeing the baby in that condition had totally unnerved her. But she realised that she had subconsciously laid a hand over her abdomen. Perhaps it was meant to be a protective hand, laid over her womb—over that place which might never hold a child.

Sometimes she thought she felt pain where the adhesions left by her former illness had marred her fallopian tubes, but it might be a purely psychological reaction. It would be so much worse to give birth to a child, to nurture it and then to lose it in such a dreadful manner as these parents had almost experienced—might yet still experience.

'Yes, I'm okay. I'm just anxious to get this family to safety.' She looked at him, full of respect and awe for what he had achieved. The baby wasn't out of danger yet by a long way, but her lips had begun to pink up a little and her cheeks were less pale than before. 'You did a wonderful thing just now. I'm so overwhelmed by how you responded. You were so calm, so determined.'

'You would have done the same thing. As I recall you were ready to leave the adults to come and help the child… It was instinctive once you knew the parents weren't in immediate danger.'

She reached for another, smaller foil blanket from his pack. 'We should try to warm her—take off her wet clothes and wrap her in the blanket,' she said. 'She needs to be in the hospital.'

'Yes, we'll do that. And we'll be on our way in a

minute or two. I just want to make sure she's stable before we set off. Her heartrate is a bit erratic at the moment, but it will probably settle once she's less chilled.'

They worked together to get everyone settled in his SUV. Reunited with her baby, the mother laid a gentle hand on the child, needing a connection of some sort despite the discomfort of her own injuries.

'Her name's Annie,' she said. 'She's my angel.'

Rebecca sat on the other side of the child, holding the oxygen mask in place and making sure that she was still breathing. The infant's pulse was slow—a protective reflex, no doubt—but once she was in the hospital the emergency team would do everything they could to resuscitate her. There was always the danger of pneumonia after a near drowning. The lungs had been flooded with water and there would be constant worry about the after-effects.

The journey seemed interminable, but in fact it only took around three quarters of an hour. Cade drove as swiftly as he dared, negotiating bends in the road and checking all the time for trees that might have come down along the way. Twice they had to get out and move fallen branches from the road.

Eventually, though, they arrived at the hospital and handed over their charges to the waiting team of doctors and nurses. Annie was whisked away to the resuscitation room and her parents were taken to Radiology for X-rays.

'I could take you home,' Cade said, 'but I expect you'll want to wait for news of how Annie's doing?'

'Yes, please… I'd rather wait. I don't think I could settle, otherwise.'

He nodded. 'Me, too. We'll go to my office. They'll come and find us when they have some information.'

'Okay.' She went with him along the corridor, not fully aware of how she'd arrived there, just putting one foot in front of another. The last hour had been traumatic. The child's parents must be feeling as though they were caught up in a nightmare.

He showed her into his office—a light, comfortably furnished room with a polished wooden desk to one side and a couple of upholstered chairs for visitors. There was also a two-seater couch against one wall. He shut the door and she stared blankly around her, not really taking anything in.

'You probably want to go and help your colleagues with all their other patients,' she said quietly, trying to gather her thoughts. 'I'll just stay here for a while and get myself together, if that's all right?'

'I'll stay until I know you're okay,' Cade said. 'I wondered if it all might be too much for you.' He came over to her and wrapped his arms around her. 'You're too emotionally involved with your patients, aren't you? Is that why you gave up on your job?'

'I don't… I can't talk about it,' she said huskily. 'Please don't ask me. I can't even think straight right now. I just—I just need to know that little girl is going to be all right.'

'I know.' He held her tight, as though he would give her his strength and the will to go on. 'I feel the same way. I'm worried about her, but I'm concerned about *you*, too, Rebecca. I want to help you any way I can. You can trust me… I need you to know that.'

She didn't answer him. She closed her eyes and pressed her cheek against his shirt-front, wishing that things could be different… It would be such a relief to know that she could put her faith in someone—know that it would all come out all right in the end. But deep down she knew that wasn't going to happen.

Cade was a good man, but he couldn't turn her life around, and he had his own problems and aspirations to deal with.

# CHAPTER FOUR

REBECCA WENT WITH Cade over to the couch, where he sat down beside her. He'd managed to find some fresh clothes for them to change into—clean scrubs, the outfits made up of the loose-fitting trousers and shirts that were used by the medical staff in the Emergency Unit—and now that she was at least dry she was beginning to feel a little better.

He laid an arm around her shoulders in a gesture that seemed entirely natural and right, and she was content for the moment to sit and talk to him and try to regain her emotional strength.

Her reaction to the events of the day had unnerved her. She had always thought of herself as decisive and independent, but over the course of the last few months she felt as though the stuffing had been knocked out of her. Somehow Cade must have picked up on that.

'How are you feeling now?' he asked. 'That was traumatic, wasn't it?'

She nodded. 'I'm okay. It was difficult for both of us. Are *you* all right? It must have been so much worse for you…trying to save the little girl…not knowing if she would breathe again.'

'I just did what had to be done. You don't really

think about it, do you, when you're faced with something like that? Like you said about that man on the plane—you follow your instincts, go with the training.'

'Yes, I suppose so… But it was awesome, what you did. You kept going. You didn't give up for a second. I'm so proud of you.'

'I'm a doctor,' he said simply. 'That's the reason I took up medicine…to save lives and help where I can.' He looked at her, lifting a hand to gently ease back the fiery curls that fell across her temple. 'I was worried about you, Rebecca. You were upset and anxious for the baby, but there was more to it than that, wasn't there? Something was troubling you deep down inside, at your very core—I wish you would talk to me about it, tell me what's wrong. Is it something to do with the reason you gave up your job back home? Did you lose a patient…a child in your care?'

She didn't answer him directly. It hurt too much to tell him the truth about her situation, and perhaps she was afraid it would change the way he felt about her.

'It happens sometimes…occasionally,' she said. 'You lose a patient despite everyone's best efforts. You do everything you can but there's nothing you can do if your best is not enough. There are times when medical science doesn't provide the answer.'

A knock at the door interrupted her and she tensed, brought back with a jolt to the reality of where they were. Cade eased himself away from her and instantly she felt the loss of his warm body and his gentle support. It was a wrench, losing the comfort of his embrace. She'd wanted to stay like that, wrapped up in his arms.

'Hi, Cade.' The consultant in charge of baby Annie's care came into the room. 'I only have a minute or two—things are hectic out there.'

'Hi, James.' Cade introduced Rebecca to his friend and colleague, who acknowledged her with a smile.

'I'm very pleased to meet you. Cade said you were the one who pointed out the car and saw that the family was in trouble.' James became serious. 'I came to let you know that we're doing everything we can to warm the baby. I've just been to talk to the parents, to try to reassure them, but it will be some time before we see any definite change in her condition.' He winced. 'She's lucky to be alive.'

Cade nodded, getting to his feet and going over to a worktop at the side of the room to switch on a coffee machine. 'We thought she'd already gone when we found her. It was a shock for both of us.' He set out mugs on the counter. 'Do you have time to grab a coffee?'

'Just a quick one, thanks. I can imagine how you must have felt. But, as I said, we're doing all we can. We're giving her warmed oxygen and an infusion of warmed intravenous fluids, so her core temperature should begin to rise gradually. We'll just have to hope there are no complications—and at the same time be prepared for them. There are often setbacks in these cases, unfortunately.'

Rebecca shuddered inwardly. She didn't want to dwell on that. All her hopes rested on the baby making a complete recovery.

They drank coffee and he updated them on the condition of the infant's parents. 'Mrs Tennyson has three fractured ribs, and her husband is suffering from concussion—as you suspected. They've both been given painkillers, and we'll keep them under observation for a while to make sure there are no other problems. Of course they're not going anywhere for some time—they're at Annie's bedside.'

'It sounds as though they're in good hands,' Rebecca commented, 'even though you must have a lot more patients than usual to look after. I noticed all the people milling about in the waiting room and in the corridors.' She'd seen men and women nursing injuries to arms and legs, and children with a number of bad cuts and grazes. 'It must be a difficult time for you.'

'You're right—it is. We've put out a call for more doctors—it's been difficult for some to get in, though, given the condition of the roads.'

'Well, *I'm* here,' Cade said. 'I can help.'

'Me, too.' Rebecca said, and saw the surprise on his colleague's face. 'I'm a doctor,' she explained, 'though my specialty's not emergency. If you can get me clearance, I'm happy to help out wherever I'm needed.'

She would rather do that than wait around, wondering what was happening with the baby.

'That's great news.' James's face lit up with enthusiasm. 'I can sort that out for you right away if you're sure you want to do that? We need as many medics as we can get.' Then he frowned. 'Do you have any training in obstetrics? We have a woman being brought in by ambulance—she went into labour several hours ago but only called for the ambulance when the contractions started to get more frequent. It's her first child. We're trying to get hold of an obstetrician to attend her as soon as she gets here, but they're swamped in Maternity.'

He looked at her hopefully.

'We really need someone to attend her as soon as possible. The paramedics are looking after her just now, but from what they've said when they radioed in it looks as though it might be a difficult birth.'

She felt the blood drain from her face, and her stomach lurched at the mention of obstetrics, but she nodded. 'I did a specialist course before going on to do my neonatal training. I'll go and see her, if you want.'

Cade sent her a narrow-eyed look and she braced herself. He must be wondering why she'd paled, but she hoped he wouldn't ask. When she'd volunteered she'd had in mind that she would be working with trauma patients—not mothers and babies—but she would do this despite her reservations. She didn't see that she had any choice. She couldn't stand by and do nothing when there was chaos and suffering all around her, could she?

'Bless you for that. She should be here any minute—I'll take you to the admissions ward now…and I'll get my secretary to sort out the necessary paperwork for you to sign.'

'Okay.' She pulled in a deep breath. 'Lead the way.'

They all walked along the corridor to the main area of the Emergency Unit, and James was pointing out the list of patients waiting to be seen when a nurse came up to them.

'We've had a call from the paramedics bringing Mrs Nelson in. Their vehicle has been hit by a tree—no one's hurt, but they're stuck out there. They're about a ten-minute drive away from the hospital. The birth's imminent, and it looks like a breech presentation.'

'Thanks, Greta.' James remained calm. 'Tell them

I'll get someone out there to them.' He glanced at Rebecca. 'Are you up for it?'

'Yes—I guess so. But I'll need transport to get out to them.' She frowned. 'I don't know how easy it will be to get a taxi with conditions as they are.'

'I'll take you,' Cade said briskly, stepping forward. 'If it's a breech birth it may be better to have two of us present. I'll get directions—from the sound of things we should leave right away.'

'Okay.'

She went with him to the car park, keeping her head down against the wind that buffeted around them. The rain here was a steady downpour that quickly soaked through her jacket, but she ignored it, thinking ahead to the woman in the ambulance. A breech birth meant that the baby was not in the usual head-down position. Usually it would be best to deliver the infant by caesarean section—an operation that was the safest option for mother and baby. That was not going to be possible in these circumstances, when the woman's labour was far advanced.

'We'll be there in a few minutes.' Cade drove carefully to where the ambulance was stranded. 'Are you sure you're up for this?' he asked. 'I didn't want to say anything in front of James, but I saw your reaction when he said it was a case for an obstetrician. I can take over if it's going to be a problem for you.'

'I wouldn't have offered if I wasn't up to it,' she said briskly. 'I'll be fine.'

'Okay. This is it, I think,' Cade said in a while.

They saw the ambulance on a straight stretch of a road that was lined with trees, and even in the darkness of late evening it was clear to see the devastation that had been caused to the side of the vehicle when a papaya tree had crashed down on to it. It was a miracle no one inside had been hurt, but no doubt a good deal of the equipment had been damaged.

The emergency services had been called out to deal with the accident, but so many similar incidents were taking up their resources that it would be some time before help arrived.

Rebecca slid out of the car and hurried to find her patient. The woman was being tended by the paramedics—a man and a woman—who stood to one side as Rebecca entered the ambulance.

'Hi, I'm Jimena,' the woman paramedic said. She was tall, with curly black hair, and she looked strong and capable. 'We're *really* glad you could make it out here to us—aren't we, Kenzie?' She looked at her patient for confirmation.

Kenzie Nelson nodded. Beads of sweat had broken out on the young woman's brow and Rebecca guessed she was in pain from her contractions and under stress after the accident.

Jimena continued, 'We've been giving her gas and air, but it isn't really helping with the pain. Contractions are regular—every five minutes—she's six centimetres dilated, and her waters have broken.'

'It sounds as if things are well under way,' Rebecca said with an encouraging smile. She introduced herself and Cade, and then told Kenzie, 'I could give you an injection of pethidine into your thigh, if you like? That should help relieve the pain, but it might make you feel a bit sleepy.'

'Thanks, that would be good.'

'Okay.'

Rebecca prepared for the procedure, cleaning her hands with antiseptic solution and pulling on surgical gloves, leaving Cade to gather together the rest of the equipment and the medication she would need. She examined the pregnant woman, checking her blood pressure and observing the contractions, as well as monitoring the foetal heartbeat. She made sure that Kenzie had understood that the baby would be delivered with either its bottom or its feet first. Apparently she didn't know the sex of the baby she was expecting.

'Everything seems fine,' she said, at last, hoping to reassure her patient. For herself, she had to prepare mentally for what lay ahead. Breech births could be tricky, and most doctors would prefer to deliver them in the safety of a hospital theatre.

She turned to the paramedics. 'Would you go on giving gas and air as she needs it? And perhaps one of you could see to it that we have suction apparatus to hand?'

'Will do.' They both nodded and the other paramedic, who was also the driver—Marcus—said he would keep in touch with the hospital by radio.

'Thanks.' She glanced at Cade. 'Perhaps you could monitor her vital signs and keep an eye on the baby's condition?'

'Of course.' Cade was already preparing the woman, cleaning an area of skin on her thigh, ready for Rebecca to give the injection. 'It'll take a few minutes before you feel the effects of the pethidine,' he told Kenzie, 'but it's a good pain-reliever.'

It wasn't long before Kenzie's contractions became stronger, and soon they were coming at faster intervals. 'She's fully dilated,' Rebecca said. 'I can see the baby's bottom. I may need to do an episiotomy—a small cut,' she told Kenzie, 'to make it easier to deliver the baby. I'll anaesthetise the area first, so you won't feel it.'

She waited awhile, letting nature take its course, and then, as more of the infant's rear end came into view, presenting at a sideways angle, she carefully turned the baby so that its back was facing upwards—the safest position for delivery.

'I'm going to very gently insert a finger, so that I can bring down the baby's leg on the right side,' she told the woman. 'Are you okay?'

'I think so. I just want this to be over.'

'I can imagine… It shouldn't be too long now. You're doing really well.'

Rebecca concentrated on delivering the first leg, and then adjusted the baby's position once more to enable her to bring down the left leg more easily. It was a delicate manoeuvre, and she held her breath as she performed it, taking care not to cause any damage to either mother or baby.

'That's good,' Cade said, smiling his relief. 'Both legs are out safely,' he told the mother. 'Oh, and it's a boy!'

Kenzie gave a soft gasp of delight. 'A *boy*! That's what my husband was hoping for.'

'We'll let nature take its course for a while,' Rebecca said quietly.

Gradually more of the baby's body descended, until she could see an elbow peeping out. Two more careful manoeuvres and gentle turning motions helped bring down the infant's arms one by one. She let out a slow breath. Feeling her way, she placed her middle finger at the back of the baby's head and supported its body underneath with her forearm, placing two fingers either side of his nose. Then she slowly tilted the infant so that his head could be delivered fully.

Exposed to the air, he let out a protesting cry and Rebecca felt a lump forming in her throat. He was safe. He was perfect.

Quickly Cade suctioned the baby's nose and mouth and wrapped him in a blanket. Then he laid him in his mother's arms, smiling at her blissful expression. Kenzie was exhausted, but all the pain and difficulties of the last few hours receded in an instant as she held her newborn infant for the first time.

Rebecca watched Kenzie and her baby, a joyous picture of unity, and despite her happiness for them felt unbidden pain suddenly tug at her heart. Would she ever hold her own baby in her arms that way? How certain could the doctors be that it would never happen? Was it hopeless? They'd told her the scans weren't good—that her ovaries might be affected by scar tissue, too. It was a nightmare situation.

She'd debated the possibility of having surgery at some point in the future, but Drew hadn't been prepared to await the outcome. 'I'm sorry,' he'd said. 'I know it's not your fault but… I can't do this…'

He'd wanted perfection, and he had made her feel as if she was somehow defective. It made her wonder if all men would react in the same way…

She blinked, as though that would blot out the image before her, and made a determined effort to pull herself together. Perhaps, as Emma had said, events were still too raw in her mind. It had been several months since the break-up now, but she was still at a low ebb healthwise, and that had made things seem far worse.

Cade glanced at her. His pleasure at the birth was undimmed, but now his gaze was curious. He knew something was troubling her, but she ignored his unspoken question and brought her attention back to her patient.

'I can give you an injection to help the placenta come away,' she told Kenzie, and the new mother nodded. She was too absorbed in her baby to care very much either way, Rebecca guessed.

She gave her the injection, again in her thigh, and waited for a minute or two before clamping the cord. Delaying the clamping gave the baby a better initial blood supply from the placenta—one that was full of nutrients, especially iron.

Cade continued to monitor the baby's condition, but it looked as though the infant was fine. Once the placenta had come away, and the episiotomy cut had been stitched, Jimena stepped in to see to the mother, and Rebecca moved back to give her room.

The other paramedic, Marcus, had been talking on the radio for the last few minutes, keeping in touch with the hospital and the ambulance service, and now they all chuckled as he announced, 'Backup's arrived.'

He climbed down from the vehicle to go and greet the new ambulance crew. 'Sorry we took so long,' his colleague said. 'How are things going?'

'Mother and baby are both doing well.'

Rebecca cleaned up and then stepped down from the ambulance, conscious of Cade following close by. She gave a report on the mother's condition, and Cade did the same for the baby.

'He's a little cold,' he said, 'so he'll need to be warmed.'

'We'll make sure of it. Don't worry.'

'Thanks.'

They said their goodbyes and then walked quickly back to Cade's SUV.

'You did a great job back there,' he said as he set the car in motion. 'You were fantastic every step of the way.'

'Thanks. I'm just glad that things worked out all right.'

Darkness was all around them as they drove back along the country lanes towards the town, but it looked as though the rain was finally beginning to ease off. She settled back against the luxurious upholstery and closed her eyes briefly.

'Are you okay?' he asked. 'I thought something was bothering you, back there in the ambulance. Do you want to talk about it? I wish you would let me help you.'

'No. It's all right. I'm fine—really. It's just been a difficult day, that's all.'

It was the truth. The day had seemed endless already—full of worries, problems and complications—and they still had to go back to the hospital and wait for news of baby Annie.

'And I'm still worried about Emma.' She fished her phone out of her pocket and tried calling her sister once more. 'I keep trying to get in touch with her,' she told Cade.

He must have guessed she was prevaricating, not wanting to talk about her other worries, but he said nothing more about it, driving on and concentrating on watching the road while she dialled and waited. And waited.

'Is she still not answering?' he asked.

'No.' She frowned. 'It's not like her not to phone me. I'm sure something's wrong.'

'As I said, the phone network may be down—or she may be busy, or sleeping. It's getting late now, you know.'

'Yes, perhaps you're right. But if I don't hear from her soon I think I'll have to go and find her…to make sure she's okay.'

She settled back in her seat once more, trying to calm herself and get some rest before they arrived back at the hospital. After a while her phone burbled and she checked the caller information.

'It's William,' she said.

'Ah.' He sent her a fleeting sideways glance, his brows drawing together. 'He probably wants to meet up with you again.'

'Yes, maybe…' She answered the call and chatted with William for a while, asking him about his work day and about his father's illness. In turn, he asked about Emma.

'I still haven't been able to get in touch with her,' she told him. 'I shan't feel happy until I know she's okay.'

'I know how you feel,' William said, with more emotion in his voice than she'd expected. 'I'm worried about her, too. But it's probably nothing—just a problem with the phone signal in the village.'

'You're probably right,' she said. It was strange William was so worried about Emma, given that they didn't really know each other that well. Emma had that effect on people, though. She was friendly and caring and everyone seemed to like her.

'I could finish work at the plantation early tomorrow afternoon,' he said. 'Take you out to cheer you up. Maybe we could go to the beach once the storm clears up.'

'Bless you—you're an angel,' she said, smiling. 'It sounds wonderful. I'd like that.'

'Me, too,' he murmured.

She cut the call a minute or so later. Cade was frowning.

'Sounds as though you and William will be getting together again?' he said, and she nodded.

'He's promised to take me to the beach,' she said.

'Oh, I see.' He said it as though that bothered him. 'You and he get on really well together, don't you?'

'Well, we're friends. We have a lot in common with one another.'

'Hmm…'

She sensed that he was battling with feelings of jealousy. The way he had kissed her during the storm had been so full of raw passion and command, and yet he clearly felt unsure about what it had meant. As did she. It had played on her mind—and her senses—ever since. And no matter how much she insisted that she and William were just friends, it was clear his worries persisted.

His frown had deepened, and to divert his train of thought she said, 'He says his father is now being given corticosteroid medication to reduce the inflammation around his heart, and they've given him a different kind of tablet to regulate his heart rhythm.'

'Let's hope that will help things improve.'

He was quiet the rest of the way to the hospital, and she wondered if he was thinking about his uncle. It *was* a worrying situation.

Things were no better in Accident and Emergency.

'Annie's showing signs of pulmonary oedema,' said James, when they met up with the consultant once more in the Emergency Unit. 'It can happen, I'm afraid—as I'm sure you know—even several hours after being rescued from near drowning. We think a patient is doing okay, and then they suffer a downturn.'

Pulmonary oedema meant that there was fluid in the lung tissue, causing the infant to have difficulty breathing. It was what Rebecca had been dreading.

'Presumably you're giving her a diuretic to try to remove the water?' she said.

'Of course… Along with medication to stabilise her heart rhythm and regulate her blood pressure.' He laid a hand lightly on her shoulder. 'Believe me, we're doing everything we can for her.'

'I know… I'm sorry… I'm not doubting you…' She hesitated. 'Perhaps I should go and see to some of the other patients on your list? I need to keep busy.'

'All right. If you're sure.' James nodded. 'If you don't mind, I need to get on—so I'll leave it to Cade to show you the ropes.' He left them, hurrying away to see to the list of people who were waiting.

Cade frowned, studying her closely. 'Don't you think you've had enough for one day? It's very late—I could take you home. I've already rung Harriet to ask her to get a guest room ready for you. She'll have some supper put by for us, too.'

She shook her head. 'I don't want to go anywhere until I know Annie's all right.'

'Okay…' he said doubtfully. 'But if it gets too much for you there's always the couch in my office. If you need anything at all, you must let me know.'

She glanced at him. 'I will—but you don't need to worry about me, you know. I'll be fine. You're the one who needs to take time out and get your head down for a few hours—you came to the cabin to see me after being on call. To be honest, I don't know how you're managing to keep going.'

He gave a crooked smile. 'Years of practice,' he said, 'along with supreme body fitness, of course… From my regular workouts, great energy levels, vitality, suppleness…' He was struggling to keep a straight face.

'Yeah, yeah…' She laughed and waved him away. There were patients waiting to be seen.

But she couldn't help but eye him surreptitiously as he walked away. He certainly was in good shape—lithe and supple, in top form. She was glad she wasn't his patient—he'd make any woman's heart race just by being in the same room with her.

They worked for a couple of hours into the night, seeing to patients who had been injured in the storm and coming across one another briefly as they compared notes or when he signed her treatment records.

'Shall we go and look in on Annie?' he suggested. 'Her parents are with her doctors at the moment, so there'll just be nurses with her.'

She nodded. 'Have you heard anything? Has James said any more about how she's doing?'

'He says she seems to be responding to the treatment.'

Encouraged, she went with him to the observation ward, where the baby lay in a cot, surrounded by monitors that showed her temperature, respiration rate, heartrate, blood pressure and blood oxygen level. She was sleeping, her pale cheeks showing small patches of pink colour.

'Her vital signs are coming up to something near normal,' she said, relief washing over her. 'She's going to survive—do we know if she's all right neurologically?'

Cade glanced through the baby's file. 'Apparently she recognises her parents, and she's responded to them. Things are looking good.'

'Thank heaven. That's so wonderful to know.' She gave a heartfelt sigh. 'It's been a nightmare. It feels like the whole day's been one long trauma.'

As a doctor, she was used to dealing with situations like these, but somehow over these last few months her emotional safety net had been shredded.

He must have read the self-doubt in her eyes, because he reached out to comfort her. 'Not much of a holiday for you, eh?' He laid an arm gently on her shoulder. 'Time to go home, I think. We could both do with some sleep. You'll feel a whole lot better in the morning.'

'I expect so.'

'I'm sure of it.'

He drove to the plantation, following the winding road up into the hills. The rain had slowed to a drizzle and the wind was dying down—the storm had lasted a relatively short time, by all accounts, but it had been bad enough to bring down bridges, flood roads and cause landslides that had created havoc.

'I'll phone my landlord first thing in the morning,' she said. 'I expect he'll want to organise repairs straight away.'

'It could take several days for him to fix things, you know. Tradesmen will be in demand all over the island.' He sent her a sideways glance, as though to gauge her reaction. 'It could mean you staying at the plantation house for around a week…possibly longer.'

'Oh, I see.' She frowned. 'I suppose I don't have many alternatives… So if you're all right with that…?'

'I'm more than happy for you to stay with me.'

The plantation house was lit by a lantern in the porch, and security lights sparked into life on the veranda as they came up the drive. Cade parked the car and showed her into the hallway, leaving her to look around while he went back to fetch her cases from the boot. It was a two-storey building, with a wide staircase leading from the central hallway to the upper floor.

'I'll show you to your guest room,' he said, hefting the cases as if they were lightweight. 'It's an en-suite room, so you'll have your own bathroom, and there's plenty of wardrobe space.'

He led the way to the room, setting her luggage down on the floor beside a double bed, and then showed her around.

'There are doors that open out on to the upper veranda,' he said. 'I think you'll love the view from here when you see it in the morning.'

'It's a lovely room,' she said, taking time to look around. There were voile drapes at the windows and beautiful silk covers on the bed to match the pale upholstery of the chairs and the dressing-table stool.

A built-in dressing table and wardrobes took up the whole length of one wall.

'Harriet said she's left us some supper—cold cuts of meat and salad, with fruit for dessert. We could have it downstairs, in the kitchen, or I could bring a tray up here and you can help yourself whenever you're ready?'

'That's really thoughtful of you—and of Harriet. Thank you. I think I'd like a tray up here, if that's okay?'

'Of course.'

He came over to her and placed his hands lightly on her shoulders. If he was disappointed that she wasn't going to share the meal with him, he managed to hide it. There was just the faintest flicker of a shadow in his dark eyes as he looked at her. Perhaps he accepted that they were both tired after a difficult and draining day.

'You can have whatever you want. You did so well today…and I know it was hard for you. I'm not sure what went wrong for you in your job back home in England, but I sense you have a huge problem, working in obstetrics, don't you? I felt it in your reactions—but I know you don't want to talk about it…it's okay. I understand.'

He kissed her gently on the forehead, a kiss as light as thistledown, and she looked up at him in bemused wonder.

'What was that for?' she asked softly, and he gave a faint shrug.

'I just felt you needed it right now,' he said, 'and I want you to know that I'm here for you.' He straightened and reluctantly let her go. 'I'll leave you to get ready for bed and I'll bring supper up here for you.

Don't worry if you're in the shower. I'll leave a tray on the table.'

'Thanks,' she murmured.

It seemed that she was in his debt yet again. He'd rescued her at the harbour on that first afternoon and he'd come to her aid today when the storm had damaged the shingles on the cabin roof. Now this.

She smiled tentatively as he turned to leave the room, but she was welling up with emotion inside. How had it happened that she had started to feel such tenderness and affection towards him? It was gratitude, surely, for everything he'd done for her…? But, no…it was more than that…much, much more.

It had been all too easy for her to grow attached to him, to want to have him close by. It was reassuring to know that he was only a heartbeat away.

She'd been so tempted to invite him to stay with her…and he would have accepted in an instant, she knew. From the way he had kissed her earlier, and the tension in his body as he'd held her just now, she could tell he was also struggling to hold back.

But that would have led to all sorts of complications. It wouldn't do for her to fall for him, would it? That could bring about all kinds of heartache. It would be unbearable to love him and have it all go wrong when he learned that she was so terribly flawed.

## CHAPTER FIVE

'HI, THERE.' CADE LOOKED across the room as Rebecca came into the kitchen the next morning. His eyes glinted approval, his gaze resting on her for a fraction longer than was necessary, taking in the curving lines of the pencil-slim skirt that hugged her hips and the sleeveless top with spaghetti straps that revealed a smooth expanse of golden skin.

The toaster pinged and he jumped slightly, distracted and disorientated for a second or two. Rebecca went over to him. It was somehow gratifying to know that she had such an effect on him.

He was obviously trying to multitask, toasting English muffins and whisking up what looked like a Hollandaise sauce at the same time. As she approached him she saw there were a couple of eggs gently poaching in a pan of hot water on the hob.

'Did you have a good night?' he asked.

'I did—thank you. I fell asleep as soon as my head touched the pillow. And you were right about the view from the French doors—it's fantastic.' She'd stepped on to the balcony first thing this morning and seen the rainforest laid out in front of her, sloping down the hillside, and in the distance the bay had been a vivid blue.

'I'm glad you took the time to look.' He smiled. 'I thought I would make eggs Benedict for breakfast… is that all right with you?'

'Oh, that sounds wonderful. I'm starving. It must be the fresh air that's giving me an appetite. You wouldn't know there had been a storm here, would you? Everything just looks as though it's been washed clean.'

He nodded. 'We get these storms from time to time, and after a downpour everything springs to life—plants and trees green up and flowers open.'

'It's beautiful.'

Sunlight streamed in through the tall windows and a warm breeze drifted in through the open glass doors. Out on the veranda she saw that a table had been laid with a white damask cloth, and there was a jug filled with fresh juice, along with two glasses.

Cade slid the hot buttered muffins on to plates that were warm from the oven and topped them with slices of smoked salmon. Then he added the lightly poached eggs, drizzled smooth Hollandaise sauce over the top and sprinkled chopped chives over that.

'Mmm…it looks and smells delicious.'

'Good…that's what I was aiming for. Let's eat outside, shall we?'

He led the way to the veranda, carrying the food on a tray that also contained a coffee pot and porcelain mugs. The aroma of freshly brewed coffee drifted on the air and Rebecca followed it as though mesmerised.

'This is heavenly,' she said as they sat down to eat. 'It must be the best way to start the day.'

This part of the veranda looked out over the garden,

a wonderful landscape of fruit trees—lemon, tamarind and pineapple among them—and there were palms that surrounded an immaculate lawn area. Showy purple bougainvillaea and scarlet kalanchoe brought colour to the borders, along with sweet-scented pink and yellow frangipani. The delicate fragrance drifted over to them on soft air currents. In one corner of the garden there was a lily pond bordered by masses of bright pink sedum.

'I'm glad you like it. I was keen to get the plantation underway, but the house and garden were my next priority. We're fortunate out here that everything is so lush. Plants grow very quickly, so it just takes a bit of landscaping and a gardener who can keep on top of things to make it all come together. I love sitting out here in the mornings before work. It's tranquil, and it helps to set me up for the day.'

'I can see why it would do that.' She savoured the taste of the smooth sauce and runny egg yolk on her tongue and sighed with satisfaction. 'This food is wonderful—I thought you said you couldn't cook?'

He shrugged, making a crooked smile. 'Let's say my repertoire is limited. I can manage a few egg recipes, pizza and maybe toss a pancake, so you wouldn't go hungry if you were relying on me. That's about my limit, though.'

'Perhaps you've never had much time to spend in the kitchen?'

'That's true—especially in the last couple of years, with my work on the plantation and the house.' He looked around. 'As I said, this place was pretty much run down and in need of some tender loving care when

I took over. It's taken a while, but I think I finally have things on track.'

He poured coffee for her and she added cream and sugar. She said, 'From what I've seen so far it's a big house. It must have taken some doing to get it right. The kitchen is absolutely lovely. You have very good taste.'

He smiled. 'Thanks. I've always preferred light-coloured units, with display cabinets and plenty of glass shelving. And of course the central island unit is very useful.' He swallowed some coffee and then added, 'I'll show you around the rest of the house if you like?'

'That would be great, thank you—if you have the time. Do you have to go to work at the hospital today?'

'I'm on call this morning, and at some point I'll have to go in to deal with some paperwork. After that I have a couple of days' leave due to me—I'd planned to use it to finish off overseeing the building of my new fermentation sheds…though perhaps that's something William could get involved in.'

They finished breakfast a few minutes later and set off on their tour of the house.

The living room was long and wide, with three sets of French doors opening on to the veranda. They had been flung open to allow the warm air to circulate. The room was furnished along pale, uncluttered lines, with pale oak flooring and a corner sofa with matching armchairs. The coffee table was made of pale green-coloured glass, and that same green colour was reflected in the ferns placed at intervals around the room. Outside, beyond the veranda, there was more greenery, with graceful palm trees and yuccas and climbing philodendrons.

They went upstairs and he showed her several bedrooms, each with its own bathroom. They were all exquisitely furnished with stylish fabrics and restful colour schemes. Each room had doors opening out on to the wide balcony.

'This is breathtaking,' she said, looking around in wonder. 'The whole house is beautiful.' Her mouth curved as a thought struck her. 'I've no idea how you're going to fill all these rooms, though. Maybe you plan to have a lot of visitors?'

He smiled. 'I do have visitors, from time to time, but you're right, of course. It *is* a big house—but that's one of the things that drew me to buy this particular property.'

He leaned against one of the French doors in the main bedroom, looking out from the balcony over the forest and the curve of the bay in the distance.

'I like everything about it, and I'm hoping that perhaps one day I'll have a family of my own to fill it. It's not something I dwell on, or that I'm specifically planning, but it's there in the back of my mind—something to aim for. I didn't much like being an only child, but my parents' marriage broke up so there were never going to be any brothers or sisters. I want something different from that for my own future.'

She met his gaze as steadily as she could, with an equilibrium she didn't quite feel. 'Family's important to you,' she commented. Unaccountably, her heart was sinking. She should have known it was foolish to get to know and like him…to have deeper feelings for him. She was hurting already, and a heavy ache was starting up deep inside her. 'It's something that's been missing from your life.'

He nodded, moving away from the balcony and back into the bedroom. 'I suppose so. I haven't really analysed my feelings as such, but in the back of my mind I think I bought this house with the idea that it would be a happy family home one day.'

They went out into the hallway. She said slowly, 'Of course that would depend on you meeting the right woman. You *did* say you'd had some problems with that…'

He laughed. 'Well, yes. Perhaps I've been unlucky in the women I've dated so far.' He stopped on the landing, by the balustrade, his gaze meshing with hers. 'That could change, though. Who knows what life holds in store? After all, here I am with an incredibly beautiful girl—someone who's thoughtful, sweet-natured and caring—it's the stuff that dreams are made of.'

He moved closer, reaching for her, his hand resting on her waist, drawing her to him and folding her into his arms. He kissed her—a tender, coaxing, sweetly gentle kiss that stirred her senses and made her pulses rocket out of control. His hand stroked warmly along the curve of her spine, bringing her even closer to him so that her breasts were softly crushed against his chest and their thighs tangled.

The breath caught in her throat. For a moment—for a heartbeat in time—she almost gave in to her deepest desires and leaned into him. Then she came to her senses and reluctantly, with a feeling of angst rising inside her, put a hand on his chest to ward him off.

She couldn't get involved with him. No matter how much she wanted to...she couldn't...

'It might not be,' she said softly.

He was teasing her, surely, and she batted away the notion of him wanting her before it had time to take hold. When he'd kissed her and held her back at the cabin, emotions had been running high. It didn't have to mean anything...did it?

'I'm not looking for a relationship, Cade,' she said flatly. 'I've been there, done that, and it all went very badly wrong for me. I don't think I want to dip my toe in that water again for quite some time.'

'Are you quite sure about that?' His eyes darkened and his hand gently stroked the rounded contour of her hip. 'Perhaps I could persuade you to change your mind?'

'Oh, I wouldn't bank on it,' she said, with a jauntiness she didn't feel. 'You know me—I'm here for a holiday...to have fun and take life as it comes. No strings attached, so to speak.'

She stepped back, moving away from him. It was too much of a temptation, being close to him this way, feeling the warm touch of his hand on her body. It made her want what she couldn't have, and she felt a sudden desperate need to escape. She turned around and started to go back down the stairs, conscious all the while that he was following her.

'And doing that will involve William, I suppose? *I* don't figure anywhere in the equation, do I?' His expression was taut, a muscle flicking briefly in his jaw. 'You want to be with *him*.'

It felt as though she was on a course of self-destruction, but she plunged on. 'Well, he did see me first—

and he did offer to take me down to the beach this afternoon. I'm quite looking forward to that.'

It was cruel—a harsh way to treat him, perhaps—but wasn't this better than hurting him even more deeply in the long run? He wouldn't want her if he knew the truth about her, and she couldn't bring herself to tell him right now. Perhaps saying it out loud to a man she cared about would make it inevitable—the desperately dreadful aftermath of her illness. She didn't want to admit the finality of it even to herself.

He stared at her in an arrested fashion, thrown by her flippant reply. She might have slapped him, judging by the way he'd reacted. It seemed he was about to say something in response but his phone beeped and he hesitated, a soft, unspoken curse hovering on his lips.

'I should take this—it might be the hospital,' he said.

She nodded and he quickly checked the text message that had come up on screen.

She glanced at him after he'd put the phone back in his pocket. 'Was it the hospital?' she asked.

'No, but it's a call-out.'

Rebecca frowned. 'I'm sorry. You must go, of course.'

He braced himself, straightening his shoulders. 'I don't want to leave you stranded here,' he said. 'If you want to go out and about anywhere, I can arrange for Benjamin to drive you.'

'No.' She shook her head. 'There's no need for that. I'll have to sort out some form of transport while I'm on the island. I can't rely on you and William all the while. I'll see if I can rent a car.'

He was thoughtful for a second or two. 'Actually, it's just occurred to me,' he said. 'I have a four-wheel drive car you could use. It's a few years old, but it's been maintained well and it will get you around reliably. My uncle uses it sometimes, when he works on the plantation, but he's not up to driving at the moment. It's yours if you want it—until he's back on his feet again.'

'Oh…really? Thank you.'

She looked at him, a smile curving her lips. She didn't deserve his kindness. He was doing this for her despite their recent altercation, though she suspected part of his motive for making the offer was to make her less reliant on William… His cousin was more than willing to help her out, and Cade clearly wanted to nip that in the bud.

'That's settled, then,' he murmured. 'We have insurance to cover us for any driver, so there's no problem there.'

'You're being very good to me,' she said. 'And I do appreciate it, you know? It'll give me the chance to explore the island.' And maybe she could even go and look for Emma. That was her first priority.

He studied her, his brows drawing together. 'You're welcome. I should have thought of it before. The car's just sitting around in the garage at the moment…it'll be ideal for you to get around.' He seemed a touch hesitant as he added, 'It's probably best to avoid going up into the hills, though—especially right now. Road conditions will be tricky after the storm.'

He looked at her musingly for a moment or two longer, trying to gauge her thoughts, and she tried to put on an air of innocence. After all, he hadn't really been able to read her mind…had he?

'Have *you* driven up there?' she asked. 'Into the hills?'

He nodded. 'There are hairpin turns and in places there are sheer rock faces on either side of you, with vertical drops. It's not a drive for the faint-hearted.'

'Oh, I see.' She frowned, thinking about that.

She wasn't normally of a nervous disposition, but she balked at taking to roads where she wouldn't see a hedgerow or houses or at least something fairly solid on either side of her. But she hadn't heard from Emma for a few days now, and she was concerned about her. Something was wrong—she was sure of it… And, no matter that Cade had warned her against it, she would have to go in search of her sister sooner or later.

'It will be good to have a means of getting about, anyway. Thanks again.'

A frown cut into his brow but he simply said, 'We could go and take a look at the car right now, if you like?' He glanced at his watch. 'I have to go out to look at one of my workers who's been taken ill—the text message was from Harriet, to tell me about it. We could take the car for a spin over to his house if you want to get used to it.'

'Sounds like a great idea.'

She went with him to the garage—which turned out to be an old stable block at the back of the house. It had been renovated, and now accommodated a number of vehicles—including the new truck.

Cade stowed his medical bag in the boot of a smart silver-coloured vehicle and then handed her the keys. 'Okay, you're in charge. I'll give you directions on how to get there. Agwe lives in a village some six or seven miles away from here. It's a tourist area, where people go to fish in the river, and when he isn't working on the plantation he helps out with the catch. They run competitions and weigh the fish. Unfortunately his village was hit by the storm several hours before we were. There are flood waters all around.'

'Do you think we'll be able to get through to his home?'

'It should be possible. The bridge held up, and his house is on higher ground.'

'Okay.' She started the car, pleased when the engine fired into life straight away. 'What's wrong with him—do you know?'

He shook his head. 'The message was a bit vague. Flu-like symptoms, muscle pains, headache…'

'Do you treat *all* of your workers when they're ill?' She turned the car on to the road leading away from the plantation and set off towards the south of the island.

'I usually try to do what I can for them. Medical bills can be an unwanted expense—their insurance premiums might be affected by any claims they make—so if it's at all possible I'll help out. It's part of the package they get, working for me. So far things have worked out all right.'

The car handled well, she discovered, and once she was used to the gears and the instrumentation, things went smoothly. They reached Agwe's village only a few minutes later.

'Thank you so much for coming,' his wife said. She was a middle-aged woman, with springy black hair and dark hazel eyes. 'Come in…come in.' She ushered them into a small cottage. 'I'm really worried about him. I thought maybe he needed to go to the hospital—but he won't listen to me. He says he doesn't want to be a burden to anyone.'

'He's not a burden, Marisha,' Cade said. 'Has his condition worsened in the last few hours?'

She nodded. 'Yes, I think it has. He's feverish. He's not well at all.' She led the way to the bedroom. 'He was taken ill yesterday. We thought it was just a virus, and it would pass, but he seems to have gone downhill since then.'

At Marisha's invitation Rebecca went with Cade into Agwe's bedroom. The woman hovered in the doorway.

Her husband was lying in bed, beads of perspiration breaking out on his forehead. 'Hi, Agwe,' Cade said, going over to him. 'I'm sorry to hear you're not well.'

Agwe mumbled a response. 'My wife shouldn't have bothered you. I'll be fine.'

'You don't *look* fine,' Cade answered. 'I'd like to examine you to see if I can help, if that's all right?'

Agwe nodded wearily, clearly unwell, and Cade started by taking his temperature and running a stethoscope over his chest. He checked his pulse and blood pressure.

'You're running a fever, and your heartrate is very fast,' he said after a while. 'Added to that, your blood pressure is low, and you say you're having problems with your waterworks—it seems as though you've picked up an infection of some sort.'

He looked at a graze on the man's hand.

'It's just a thought, but have you been handling fish from the river recently?'

'Yeah…a few days ago. I caught my hand on a fishing hook.' Agwe frowned. 'Why?' He was becoming breathless and finding it difficult to speak. 'Is it important?'

'I'm trying to work out what we're dealing with,' Cade answered. 'There are a number of possibilities… but there have been one or two cases of Weil's disease admitted to the hospital recently, and your symptoms are similar. It's a bacterial infection that can be caught in various ways—through contact with contaminated water or soil, for instance. That graze of yours would have been an ideal entry point. I really think the best place for you is the hospital, Agwe.'

Agwe's wife said worriedly, 'So you think he has this disease?'

Cade nodded. 'It's very possible.' He turned back to Agwe. 'We need to get you to hospital so that they can do some tests and put you on intravenous antibiotics. I'm going to give you tablets to take right now, to start the treatment straight away.'

Agwe looked as though he was about to protest, but his wife stopped him with a look. 'Dr Byfield says you need to be in hospital, so that's where you're going. No argument.'

Cade smiled at the interchange and glanced at Rebecca. 'Are you up for driving there? It'll be quicker than waiting for an ambulance. I'll ring ahead to tell them to expect us.'

She nodded. 'Yes, I can do that—if you can make him comfortable in the back of the car.'

She knew Cade was worried about the possibility of kidney failure. Weil's disease could be very dangerous, and treatment should be started as soon as possible if there was to be a successful outcome.

They set off a few minutes later and Rebecca covered the distance in short time, thankful that the main roads had been cleared of debris. It hadn't taken her long to get used to the car, and she really appreciated Cade's offer to let her borrow it.

Once they reached the hospital Cade handed his patient over to the emergency team. The man's wife stayed with her husband, going to sit by his bedside.

'We'll bring in the renal consultant,' the doctor in charge of the team told Cade. 'I think you're probably right about the diagnosis—we'll start him on intravenous therapy straight away. He may need corticosteroids, too. Thanks for bringing him in.'

'I was glad to help.'

Cade left Agwe in capable hands and went over to Rebecca, who was waiting to one side.

'I have to stay and sort out my paperwork,' he told her. 'It'll take me some time, so you might want to take the car and get back to your holiday. I can make my own arrangements for getting back home. I'm sure someone here will drop me off later.'

'I don't mind waiting,' she said, but he shook his head.

'You've already done more than enough to help out. Besides, I think I ought to stay around here for a while, to see how Agwe's doing and talk to his wife. She's upset, and could probably do with knowing a bit more about what's likely to happen to him. He'll be in hospital for a few weeks, I expect.' He ran a hand down her arm in an unexpectedly tender gesture. 'This is your holiday. Go and enjoy it.'

'Are you sure you don't want me to stay?'

She frowned, uncertain about leaving him. Then it struck her that clearly he was no longer concerned about her seeing William this afternoon, and perversely that troubled her. Had she been all too successful in pushing him away from her? Wasn't it for the best? Then why did she feel so dreadful? Her stomach clenched in despair.

'I'm positive,' he said. 'Perhaps I'll see you at the house for dinner later this evening?'

She nodded, not willing to answer him outright. Now that she had a car at her disposal she only really had one thing in mind—as soon as possible she would go in search of her sister. She didn't want to involve Cade in what she was planning, because this was her problem to resolve on her own. Perhaps she was worrying unnecessarily, but she wouldn't rest until she was certain all was well.

She drove back to the plantation, stopping off to buy a few supplies, but hurrying because William would be arriving to take her to the beach in a short time. She thought about calling to put him off, but she didn't want to disappoint him. He was anxious about his father, and maybe some time at the beach would be good for him.

'Hey, it's good to see you, Becky!'

William arrived just as she'd finished packing a holdall with the things she thought she might need for a trek up into the hills. The storm might have caused problems up there—she didn't know what to expect—so she'd included a change of clothes, fresh water, food supplies… She put as much as she could cram in her backpack, together with medication she'd bought from the local pharmacy. She wanted to be prepared in case Emma was ill, or had been cut off by the storm. She couldn't imagine what had happened up there in the village, but if she'd been able Emma would have been in touch by now, she was sure.

William glanced at the holdall she'd left in a corner of the kitchen. 'Are you planning on leaving us?' he asked. 'I thought you were staying on the plantation for a few days.'

'That's the general idea,' she said, smiling, hoping to throw him off track. She hadn't expected him to notice the bag. 'That's just a few things I've scrambled together in case I decide to go exploring.' It wasn't exactly a lie, was it? Although she had filled a backpack, too… 'There's such a lot of the island I haven't seen—including your beach…'

He laughed, taking the hint. 'Come on, then. It's perfect out there just now. The tide's out, and there's a soft, warm breeze.'

'Sounds idyllic. I'll just put this holdall up in my room and then we'll be off.'

They spent a couple of hours by the sea, alternating between splashing in the calm waters and lying on the sand and soaking up the sun. William went over to one of the tilting palm trees that grew along the shoreline and shimmied up the trunk to get to the coconuts. He picked one and brought it over to her, cracking it open on a rock and handing it to her so that she could drink the juice.

'Mmm…wonderful…' she murmured. 'I'm having the greatest time.'

'Me, too.' He was quiet for a moment or two. 'I bet Emma would love it here. She said how much she likes to spend time on the beaches around here. Have you any idea how long she was planning on staying up at the village?'

She shook her head. 'None at all. She didn't say.'

'I suppose her colleagues would have let you know if anything was wrong?'

'Yes, I'd have thought so.'

Only she hadn't been able to contact any of them. It was disturbing. There *was* the possibility that a phone signal wasn't available up there, but she couldn't help wondering if her sister had been taken ill or been involved in an accident of some sort.

William dropped her off at the plantation house and apologised for having to leave her so soon. 'Cade asked me to check on the new fermentation buildings,' he said, 'to make sure the workmen are doing everything according to the plans—and then I need to go with my mother to visit my father in hospital. He's on this new medication and we're hoping it's going to help him get better.'

'Good luck,' she told him. 'I hope things start picking up for him soon.'

After he'd gone she made a swift check to see if there was anything else she needed to take with her on her journey up into the hills. She quickly changed into jeans and a T-shirt and then downloaded a map from the Internet and printed it out. She hurried—she was anxious to get away before Cade returned from the hospital.

At last, she was ready. There were still about three hours left before sunset—surely it wouldn't take her more than an hour to make the drive up to the village? There would still be plenty of daylight to make the journey there *and* back, if need be.

She set off, driving carefully along a road that turned out to be exactly as Cade had predicted. It became progressively steeper as time went by, and there were potholes left by the recent storm, so she bumped and clattered and worried about the car's suspension. It was an all-terrain vehicle, though, so that shouldn't be a problem.

The landscape she passed through was awe-inspiring. She caught glimpses of mango and avocado trees being grown on small farms, and as she climbed higher into the hills saw slopes that were thickly forested with tall chataignier and spiky breadfruit trees. Vines grew everywhere, winding around tree trunks and climbing upwards towards the sunlight. As Cade had said, the tropical vegetation on the island was lush, thriving in the warm, humid atmosphere.

She drove on, and the road became more narrow and winding, with deep chasms falling away to one side. She slowed the car, alarmed by the increasingly craggy landscape and the towering cliffs that had been battered by the recent storm. As she went further, she saw there were landslips, where soil and rubble and other debris had accumulated in falls down the rock face. It looked precarious—as though it might tumble on to the road at any moment.

Rounding a tight bend, she held her breath as she negotiated the difficult turn—and then gasped as she saw what lay up ahead. A large portion of the cliff had been undermined by rainwater and the softer sedimentary rock had sheered away from the volcanic grey basalt beneath. It had fallen across the road in a mass of boulders, tree roots, branches and rotting leaves.

She stopped the car and sat for a moment, debating what she should do. There was no way she could risk taking the car beyond this point, but she'd come too far to go back—she would have to go the rest of the way on foot.

She parked the car in as safe a place as she could find, as far off the road as possible, just in case anyone else might be as reckless as she and try to venture up further into what was virtually a small mountain. They would need room to turn around. Perhaps this was why Emma hadn't come home. The road was blocked.

Rebecca pulled on her backpack, took her holdall from the boot of the car and set off along the road. Even up here it was hot, and without the benefit of the car's air-conditioning she was wiping beads of perspiration from her face within half an hour. She sat down to rest on a flat outcrop of rock at the side of the road and gazed around her. She caught the green flash of a parrot's wings as it flew among the branches of the mountain cabbage palms. If only she could fly…

How much further was it to the village? According to the map it was only some twenty miles from the plantation, and she must have covered a good deal of the journey by now, surely? Perhaps she'd miscalculated somewhere… The sun was already getting low in the sky and she'd still not come across the small settlement of houses she was expecting to see.

Perhaps she ought to call someone and report that the road was blocked? She checked her phone, but there was no signal. She'd not really expected it to work up here, but it was a bit daunting to find that she was totally isolated, with darkness coming on. Had she been completely foolhardy to start out on this expedition?

She stood up and started on the road uphill once more. Cade would certainly have something to say about her actions when she finally returned to the plantation house. Her thoughts lingered on him. She felt strangely empty inside, with a feeling of unaccustomed loneliness washing through her. She missed him and wanted to be with him.

A soft sigh escaped her. He would have left the hospital some time ago. Was he wondering why she wasn't around to have dinner with him? Guilt ran through her. He'd been nothing but good to her and she'd pushed him away.

Lost in thought, she trundled on—until, bizarrely, from out of nowhere she heard someone calling to her.

'Hey, Rebecca! Wait…wait up…' The words cracked across the air like a whiplash.

She froze in her tracks, hearing that familiar deep voice coming out of the wilderness. It couldn't be Cade—could it? Was she hallucinating? Had she conjured him up out of pure wishful thinking?

Slowly, as though in a trance, she turned around and looked back at the road. Giant tree ferns covered the hillside, verdant among a stand of tall Caribbean pine. Then her glance settled on a lone figure and her heart leapt in her chest.

She shook her head briefly. This wasn't real. She was imagining he was there, surely? But, no, he was standing in the road, tall and broad-shouldered, his hefty medical pack slung over his back.

'Rebecca…thank heaven I've found you.' Cade walked briskly up to her, studying her from under dark brows. Putting his medical kit down on the ground beside him, he reached for her, his hands circling her bare arms. 'Are you okay? You don't look quite right.'

'It…it must be the shock of seeing you,' she answered huskily. 'I thought I was alone out here. How did you know where to find me?'

He gave a short, harsh laugh. 'It wasn't too difficult. I had the feeling you'd come after Emma. I guessed she'd been on your mind ever since she came up here. So when I got back to the house and you weren't there I rang William. He said you weren't still with him, but he told me you'd packed a holdall and taken it up to your room, so I went to check. It wasn't there, and it was fairly easy to guess the rest.' His mouth tightened. 'You've no idea how worried I've been.'

'There was no need for you to worry,' she protested. 'And you didn't need to follow me out here. This is my problem—not yours. I didn't want to involve anyone else.'

His eyes glittered, skating over her. 'Can't you imagine how concerned I was when I realised you'd taken it into your head to come up here?' He shook his head, tugging her close to him. 'How could I let you do this on your own? You've no idea what you might come up against. I've been so worried about you. This is a dangerous road and you're not used to the car.' His voice was edgy and tinged with impatience.

She looked into his smoke-dark eyes, trying to

gauge the depth of his emotions. She was feeling overwhelmed. He'd actually come after her—had cared enough to make sure that she was safe—but he seemed to be rigid with tension.

'You're angry with me?'

'Angry? No. Not angry. Frustrated…concerned… It's getting late, and there's no way we can go back down that road in the dark. There could be another landslide at any moment and we need to be on the lookout for it.' He wrapped his arms around her. 'Rebecca, I was so afraid something might have happened to you…that you might be hurt…'

'But I'm fine—'

'You're *not* fine.' His tone was clipped. 'You're a pain in the neck, going off like that without a word. Anything could have happened.' He drew her up against him, holding her tightly, his whole body pressuring hers. 'I wish I didn't feel this way about you—but I can't help myself—'

He bent his head to hers and kissed her on the mouth, crushing her lips with intense passion—as though he couldn't get enough of her, as though he would rid himself of the demons that were driving him.

Her soft curves meshed with the hardness of his chest and her legs collided with the taut, powerful muscles of his thighs. A wave of heat ran through her from head to toe. She ought to be putting up some kind of a protest, she knew, even as she kissed him in return and lifted her arms to let her fingers caress the silky hair at his nape.

She was so glad that he was here, that he'd bothered to come after her. She'd been fully prepared to do this on her own, but now that he was with her she felt as though she could move mountains. He filled her with strength. Together, they could do anything…

Her body melted into his in an involuntary movement of longing, of deep, instinctive yearning. A soft moan rumbled in her throat. She wanted to run her hands all over him—over his arms, his chest—wanted to tell him how much she needed him, how glad she was that he was here with her.

His lips left a trail of kisses over her mouth, her cheek, her throat, and his hands made sweeping forays over her curves.

'I need you,' he said, the words hot against her cheek, and she felt her body tremble in response.

A soft, shuddery sigh escaped her. What was she doing? What was she thinking? How could she go down that road again? Falling for a man who would turn his back on her as soon as he learned the truth about her?

'I can't,' she whispered. 'I should never have let this happen.'

The breath caught in his throat and he stared down at her, his gaze hot with desire. 'Don't do this to me,' he said, his voice roughened. 'You kiss me as though you want me every bit as much as I want you, and then you change your mind and call a halt. You can't behave that way. You're driving me crazy.'

'I'm sorry.' She stared up at him, tears in her eyes. 'I'm *sorry.*'

He gave a ragged sigh and appeared to be making an effort to pull himself together. Slowly he put her away from him, holding her at arm's length.

'Okay,' he said. 'Explain it to me. You want to have fun. No strings attached. I can do that. I'm willing to give it a try. What's the problem?'

'It won't work,' she said, her chest heaving. 'Not with you and me. Not like that. It just won't work.'

He stared at her, trying to fathom what was going on in her head. 'Sooner or later,' he said, 'you're going to have to talk to me and tell me what's going on with you. Right now, I don't understand what makes you tick. But I *will* find out, Rebecca. That's a promise.'

# CHAPTER SIX

'We need to find the village before nightfall.' Cade's tone was clipped, decisive.

'Yes. I'm not sure exactly how far it is.'

Rebecca sent him a swift glance as she picked up her holdall. Just a few moments ago he'd been holding her in his arms but now he was remote from her, as though he was steeling himself to keep a distance between them—at least physically.

He looked at the setting sun and lifted up his medical pack—it was a very large immediate-response kit, designed to provide every available means of helping patients in the dangerous time before they could reach a hospital.

'It looks as though you came prepared for trouble,' she said.

He nodded. 'I thought it was best to be on the safe side.'

She frowned as they set off once more along the road. 'But I thought you believed I was worrying unnecessarily?'

'No, that's not true. I didn't say that. I didn't want to upset you by agreeing that your sister might be having problems. There was no point in making you any more anxious than you already were.'

'But if I'd known you *agreed* she might be in difficulty I might have been persuaded to come up here earlier.' She sucked in a breath, upset by the waste of time. He knew this country and its idiosyncrasies far better than she did.

'You could hardly have come up here while the storm was raging. We couldn't even have got rescue helicopters in the air to check things out. Besides, as I recall we had our hands full—with a baby rescue and a breech delivery.'

'I suppose so,' she acknowledged, giving it some thought. His logic was unassailable.

They trudged up the hill, rounding a bend in the road. A tarmacked path led off to the east, and they turned in that direction.

'It can't be far now,' she said, cheering up a bit. 'That's the landmark I was searching for. I knew there was a place where a side road turned towards the village.'

In the distance the land rose still higher, the slopes covered with luxuriant rainforest, broken only by the cascade of waterfalls that cut into the rock face and pooled far below into a wide lake. Just here a river tumbled down the hillside in a torrent fed by the recent rains. As Rebecca and Cade went further along the path it soon became clear that there had been a lot of flood damage up there.

'The path's been broken up by the water and the boulders that have been washed down,' Cade remarked. 'It'll be impossible to get supply trucks through here.'

Ahead of them they could see the outline of some painted wooden houses set out in a clearing.

The ground was now soft and muddy underfoot, and Rebecca stopped for a moment to pull a pair of boots from her backpack. She was wearing jeans and a T-shirt, and now she put on a light jacket. A light breeze had sprung up and she was beginning to feel apprehensive, not knowing what they might find when they reached the settlement.

'At least we should soon have some answers,' Cade said, glancing at her as they set off once more. 'It looks as though this place has been cut off by flood water—it's beginning to recede now, but from the state of the houses it must have been pretty bad while it lasted.'

He was right. It appeared most of the houses had been submerged up to a foot from the ground. There were dirty marks left on the houses' framework, from where the water had risen and then gradually started to ebb away.

'I expected to see more movement,' Rebecca commented. 'People going about the business of clearing up. Everything's so quiet…it's like a ghost town.'

'It's odd, definitely,' he agreed. 'Perhaps the families moved out of the lower-lying houses into those on higher ground—out of the path of the water. There's some kind of communal building and a few dwellings over there that should have missed the worst of the damage.'

They headed towards the communal building—a large wooden structure. The entrance door swung open when Cade pushed it, and soon they were standing inside a long, wide room.

'This must be the school,' Rebecca murmured.

Desks had been pushed to one side to make space, and chairs were stacked neatly against the wall. Instead of being used as a place of learning, the hall had been turned into a hospital, with half a dozen beds arranged in a row, facing the windows. Three children lay in bed, covered by mosquito nets, whilst adults sat quietly next to them, reading or talking to one another in low voices. They looked up as the newcomers walked in, surveying them with tired interest. Two further beds contained adults who were sleeping.

Rebecca and Cade introduced themselves to the people in the room. 'We're here to help—any way we can,' Cade said.

A door at the end of the room opened, and Rebecca drew in a sharp breath when she saw Emma walk in. She was pushing a medicine trolley, obviously trying to go about her work as usual, but Rebecca was shocked by the change in her sister. The vital, energetic and bright young woman who'd been laughing and joking at Selwyn's Bar had disappeared completely, and in her place was someone who looked ill and drawn. She was very pale and looked intensely weary, walking stiffly as though she was in pain.

Emma glanced across the room and saw the visitors. Relief seemed to wash over her. 'Oh, *Becky*,' she said in a choked voice. 'I *knew* you would come. I knew if anyone could get through it would be you.'

Rebecca went over to her sister and hugged her. 'What are you doing up and about? You don't look well,' she said. 'Why aren't the other nurses looking after you?'

Emma shook her head. 'There's no one else here—only the people you see in this room. When the floods came we had to evacuate as many people as we could to the next village.' She paused to get her breath. 'I said I would stay behind and take care of the patients. They were going to come back for me—but I think the villages must have been cut off from one another. They never came.'

She reached for a chair and sat down, suddenly losing strength.

'How long have you been feeling ill, Emma?' Cade asked.

'A few hours. It came on quickly. I'm tired, I suppose. I've been working through the night, looking after the patients.'

He frowned. 'From the state you're in, I think it's a lot more than tiredness. Do you have the same symptoms as the others?'

'No.' She tried to shake her head and cried out, wincing as pain shot through her. She held her hand to her neck and rubbed gently. 'The children have spotted tick fever. They're beginning to recover—I've been giving them antibiotics. They're due for another dose now…the adults, too.'

She started to get up to go to them but Cade gently pushed her back down.

'We'll see to all that. You need to rest. We have to find out what's wrong with you.'

'But it's time for their meal.' Emma's brow creased with anxiety. 'I've got to find something for them, but there's not much left—we're just about out of food.'

She drew in a shaky breath and shivered a little, wrapping her arms around herself for warmth.

'I've scrambled together what I could find, but the storehouse was flooded and everything was ruined. I don't know what we're going to do. The power's out, and the water pipe gave way on the first day—since then we've been managing with bottled water.'

She sank back in exhaustion.

'I've a couple of canisters of water and some food supplies in my holdall,' Rebecca told her. 'It's only protein bars and chocolate, and some nuts, but it's all high-energy stuff. It should keep everyone going for a while, at least.'

'And more help should be on its way before too long,' Cade put in.

Rebecca sent him a quizzical look. 'How can that be?'

'I have a friend who works with the air rescue service,' he explained. 'I called him from the hospital this afternoon and he said he would take the first opportunity to fly over the area and see if anyone was stranded. He said they were busy with other rescues, so he might not be able to do anything today, but he'll try tomorrow. We need to get something up on to a roof to show him there's a problem—something he'll be able to see in the daylight.'

Her eyes widened. 'So you've been thinking all along that there might be an emergency situation? You were never going to leave things to chance?'

'That's right.'

She frowned. 'You didn't tell me.'

'I wasn't sure I'd be able to reach him, or if he'd be able to help. I would have told you if you'd been at the house when I came home.'

'I'm so glad you managed to get in touch with him.' She smiled at Cade and then said quietly, 'What should we put up on the roof?'

He thought for a moment, and then asked Emma, 'Are there any paint supplies around here? All the houses are painted, so I'm assuming there might be.'

'Yes. In the store room.'

'Good. I'll paint a large SOS on the roof.' He shot Rebecca a quick glance. 'Can I have a word with you? We need to sort out how we're going to organise things.'

She nodded, then turned to Emma. 'Stay here and rest. I'll come back and check you over in a minute—see if we can make you more comfortable. We'll see to everything so you don't need to worry… I'm assuming there are treatment charts for all the patients?'

'Yes, of course.'

Natural light was still coming in through the windows, but Emma closed her eyes as though it was too bright for her.

'My head really hurts,' she said. 'I'm so glad you're here, Becky.'

Rebecca laid a hand on her shoulder. 'So am I. Get some rest. I'll be back before you know it.'

She went with Cade to stand a short distance away.

'I'm afraid your sister is very ill,' he said in a low voice. 'Whatever it is that's wrong with her, she needs treatment right away.'

She nodded. 'I know. I'm really worried about her—*and* about the other patients. We need to get things sorted quickly.'

'Okay. I'll do a medicine round and then see what food we have—if we hear a helicopter I'll go outside and wave my arms or something.'

'Thanks, Cade.'

She laid a hand on his arm in an affectionate gesture, but he stiffened at her touch and she gazed at him, disturbed by his reaction. She'd really hurt him in her rejection of him earlier.

He seemed to brace himself, and she took her hand away from him.

Taking a quick breath to steady herself, she said, 'Thanks for telling your friend about this. When I came out here I didn't know if I should be worried or not—whether I'd be able to handle things by myself. I'm so glad you decided to come after me.'

'I would never have left you to do this on your own. I'd already made up my mind to find out what was going on up here.' He frowned, studying her briefly, taking in her uncertain expression. 'Any time you have a problem I'll help you any way I can. I'll *always* help you—with anything.'

'Thank you,' she said softly.

She wished that could be true. How would he respond if she confided in him? If she told him that her illness had left her damaged, that she couldn't let herself fall in love with him? He wanted children, and that was something she couldn't promise him. She couldn't allow him to get involved with her, because in the end he would discover her deepest imperfection and then he would turn away from her—just as Drew had done.

She didn't think she could bear that. And nor could she cope with having an affair with him—a temporary fling—because already she cared too much for him. It would hurt too badly when it came to an end. Was it already too late? Had she already fallen in love with him? Why did this hurt so much?

'All right,' he said, straightening, ready to move

on. 'Let's get on with this. Go to your sister—take my medical kit with you.'

'Thanks, I will.'

Rebecca hurried back to Emma. 'Where have you been sleeping?' she asked. 'I think we should get you to bed.'

'In the back room.' Emma started to get up, swaying a little and leaning on Rebecca for support. 'Oh… I feel really sick. I've been vomiting a lot. I can't seem to keep anything down.'

'I'll help you. Don't worry about it.' She waited with Emma while she was being sick in the bathroom, and then helped her into bed. 'I'll do a quick examination,' she told her.

Emma's hands and feet were cold, she discovered, but it was fairly clear she was running a fever. Things weren't looking good. Rebecca already had a horrible suspicion about what they were dealing with, but she put on a calm, reassuring front as she checked her sister over.

A few minutes later she packed away Cade's stethoscope and blood pressure machine and spoke gently, attempting to explain what she thought was wrong with her.

'Your blood pressure's low and your breathing and heartrate are quite fast,' she said. 'I'm pretty sure you have an infection—a bacterial infection—so I want to get you started on an intravenous antibiotic right away. I'm going to give you dexamethasone at the same time, to prevent any inflammation.'

Emma lay back against her pillows. 'You don't need to wrap it up in cotton wool for me, Becky,' she said, her breath coming in short bursts. 'I'm a nurse. I'm pretty sure I know what's wrong with me… It's meningitis, isn't it?'

Rebecca sighed softly and nodded. 'I think so. We won't know for certain until we get you to hospital and they do some tests, but we can't afford to take any chances. Luckily Cade has the medication we need in his kit, so we can start you on the treatment right away. All you need to do is try to get some sleep. I'll give you something for the headache.'

'Thanks, Becky.' Emma closed her eyes. 'It's so good to have you here…'

Rebecca stayed with her until she was sure she'd done everything she could, and then went in search of Cade.

She found him playing a card game—Snap—with one of the children, a boy of around five years old, who was sitting up in bed, recovering from his illness. They were laughing, because the boy was winning and Cade was pretending to be put out by it.

'We'll play again later,' he told the boy, and stood up, leaving the child's mother to collect the cards and find a storybook to entertain him.

'Okay. I'll win again,' the boy said with a wide smile.

Cade chuckled and came over to Rebecca. His mood immediately became serious. 'How is she?' he asked.

'She's sleeping right now. I've put her on an IV drip and I'm giving her oxygen, but we need to get her to hospital as soon as possible.'

'Meningitis?' he guessed, and she nodded.

'I think so.'

The danger lay in the swelling of the protective membranes around the brain. This was causing Emma's bad headache, and if it became worse she might start having seizures. Then there was the awful worry about blood poisoning. That could cause all kinds of problems. Rebecca didn't even want to think about that.

'How are the other patients?' she asked.

'They're generally not too bad. It's a farming community, so the youngsters were exposed to tick bites from the goats their parents herd. They're being given doxycycline to combat the infection. There are two five-year-old boys who are well on the way to recovery. The little girl is three years old—there's still some swelling on her leg, where she was bitten by a tick, and she's a bit fretful, having nightmares—they're part of the way the illness presents.'

'Really? I've never come across this kind of tick fever before.'

'Well, along with a high temperature and a rash, sufferers get bad headaches and muscle pain. The rash doesn't itch—which is a blessing, I suppose.' He looked over to the beds where the adults slept. 'Those two are suffering from chest infections. They're on oxygen and antibiotic therapy, as well.'

'It sounds as though everything's under control—what about the food situation? Did you manage to put a meal together?'

He pulled a face. 'After a fashion. I'll show you the facilities.' He walked with her towards a small kitchen at the back of the building and pushed open the door. 'There's no electricity, so I've had to make do with very little. I thought we'd better save the protein bars for tomorrow.'

She nodded, glancing around. The room was utilitarian, with a deep sink, a cooker and a fridge—neither of which were working—and a counter for food preparation.

'Let's hope your friend gets here with a rescue team before too long. Heaven knows what we'll do if we have to stay here for any length of time.' She gave a shuddery breath, thinking of Emma.

He laid an arm around her shoulders. 'I'm sure we'll find a way to cope, whatever the situation. You had the foresight to bring provisions—I brought a medical kit. We make a good team, you and I, don't you think?'

'Yes, we do.' She pulled herself together. With him by her side she could move mountains. 'Do you want me to help you with painting the SOS? Maybe we need to do more than one?'

'No, I'll do it in a few minutes—before it gets dark. But first I should get you something to eat. I bet you haven't had anything since breakfast, have you?'

'Um…no, actually…' She hadn't even thought about eating until now. Maybe she'd been too stressed. 'I'm not really hungry—and anyway I need to stay with Emma.' Anxiety rose up inside her once again. 'I should get back to her.'

'That's okay. You can do that. I'll bring some food to you in there…see if I can tempt you with cold left-over rice and tinned peas.'

'Oh—stop…such a gourmet meal—how can I resist?' She gave a broken laugh in spite of her anxieties and he smiled.

'That's better—we'll get through this together… you'll see.' He looked into her eyes. They were damp with unshed tears and he said softly, 'I think you need a hug…would that be all right?'

She nodded wordlessly and he folded her against him, kissing her lightly on her forehead. 'We're doing everything we can for her—for all of them,' he said. 'You're doing fine—you're a great doctor and a good person to have around in a crisis.' He stroked her back, his hands gliding over her in a tender gesture. 'I can't think what your ex was thinking of, letting you slip away from him. Whatever happened between you must have destroyed your faith in men.'

'It wasn't Drew's fault—not really,' she said huskily. 'Things just didn't work out for us. He's a decent man, but things went wrong. I was ill—appendicitis—and there were complications. I ended up in intensive care for a while.' She sighed. 'He didn't handle my illness very well. I think I realised then that he wasn't the right man for me, but perhaps there were signs before that…we were opposites in quite a few ways. He could be quick-tempered and impatient, whereas I tend to be a bit more laid-back. With hindsight, I think we would have gone our separate ways before too long anyway.'

'I'm sorry. It sounds as though you cared for him very much and that finishing with him has had a bad effect on you. But it would be a pity if you're going to let it put you off all relationships.'

'Maybe.' She straightened. Talking about Drew was bringing back memories of things she would far sooner forget. 'I think I should go to Emma.'

'Yes. All right.' He let her go, easing his long body away from her. 'I'll fix some food for you and then see to the SOS. Don't worry about the patients. I'll look after them.'

'Okay.'

She stayed with Emma through the night, and by morning was thankful that her condition didn't seem to have worsened too much. She was sleeping a lot, and complaining still of a bad headache, but at least the vomiting had stopped. As ill as she was, she'd even managed to let Rebecca know how concerned she was to find out how her patients were getting on.

'I'm going to look in on them now,' Rebecca told her. 'I'll be back in a few minutes.'

When she went into the main room she saw that Cade was sitting with the three-year-old, wrapping a blood pressure cuff around her teddy bear's arm. The child watched him, utterly absorbed in what he was doing.

'Well, I think Teddy might be feeling a bit better this morning,' he said. 'I'm wondering if he might even like to try a cookie?'

The infant nodded cautiously. 'I'll give it to him… can I?'

'Yes, all right…if you want to… But you might have to show him how to nibble at it. What do you think?'

'Yep. I can do that.'

'Okay, then.' He handed her a plate with several cookies. 'Maybe he can eat the whole lot?'

She screwed up her nose. 'Nah.'

'Oh. Well, perhaps you'll have to help him, then?'

She nodded, picking up a biscuit and putting it to her teddy's mouth. Then she took a small bite for herself, tasting the honey and oats and deciding she liked them. Cade smiled, and Rebecca felt a lump form in her throat. He was so good with the little girl, just as he had been with the boy the day before. He would make a wonderful father.

Satisfied that the child was eating, Cade stood up and came over to Rebecca, leaving the infant with her mother to watch over her.

'She hasn't been wanting to eat up to now,' he said, 'but I think from the looks of things she might be feeling a bit better today.'

'That's good news. You were brilliant with her, from what I could see.'

She looked around the room. The two boys were in bed, eating protein bars and doing what looked like simple crossword puzzles set out on sheets of paper.

'I thought they would keep them amused,' Cade said. 'I used to make up crosswords for William when he was little. The five-year-old can read, so he can manage simple words, and the seven-year-old is doing well with slightly harder ones. They were getting bored, but they're not strong enough to be up and about yet. Doing that and colouring pictures seemed like the best option for now.'

'You're full of surprises,' she murmured, helping herself to a few nuts and a protein bar from the selection of food he'd laid out on a table. He was a natural with the children, and they clearly liked him.

'How's Emma doing?' Cade asked.

Her mouth flattened. 'Much the same, I think. I'm worried that there's still a lot of inflammation around her brain. She's a bit confused, which would suggest things haven't improved, but at least the antibiotic seems to be keeping sepsis at bay.'

'That's something to be thankful for.' He poured some water into a glass and sipped slowly. 'We need to get everyone ready for evacuation. If the rescue helicopter arrives we should have things all packed up and set to go.'

'Yes, I've been thinking about that. I've made a start with the medication. Each adult patient should take his own treatment chart, drugs and any equipment like IV lines with him. If there's any problem—like limited numbers of passengers—then the most seriously ill should go first. My sister, the man with pneumonia, and the little girl.'

He nodded. 'With any luck the rescue team will be here some time this morning. I've marked out a landing pad for them, where I thought it would be safest. We'll have to stretcher people over there.'

There was still no phone signal, so they had no means of knowing what to expect, but a couple of hours later they heard the heartening drone of an aircraft overhead.

The helicopter landed shortly after that. Relieved, they hurried to greet the crew.

'How many people do we have?' Cade's friend asked.

'Three children,' Cade said, 'and three adults—all of them sick—and four parents. That's ten people, plus Rebecca. She needs to go with her sister to make sure she's okay on the journey. Can you carry that many?'

'Three little ones and eight adults? Yes, we should be able to manage that.' The man frowned. 'What about yourself?'

'I need to go back down the road to get my car. I'll join you at the hospital later.' He turned to Rebecca.

'I'll send someone to pick up the other car and take it back to the house.'

'Okay. Thanks.' She was anxious to get Emma on to the helicopter, but at the same time worried about Cade making the journey back alone. 'What if there have been more landslides? What will you do?'

He shrugged. 'I'll deal with that as it comes. You can load my medical kit on to the helicopter—you might need it, and it'll make the going quicker for me.' He made a crooked smile. 'If I don't turn up at the hospital in, say, a couple of hours, you can send William to find me with a search team.'

'I'll do that,' she said. 'You're making a joke of it, but I mean it. I didn't like the look of those rock falls on the way here.'

'Go,' he said firmly. 'Don't waste time… You need to get out of here.'

Together they supervised the transfer of all the patients on to the helicopter. Rebecca made sure Emma was secure for the flight, and then sat by her for their journey to the hospital. She was worried about her. Her sister was becoming very sleepy, and showing signs of delirium, and soon after that she deteriorated badly and started to have a seizure.

Alarmed, Rebecca quickly searched in Cade's pack for medication to control the fitting. Any seizures might increase the pressure on Emma's brain and cause her to become even more desperately ill. She had to do everything she could to stabilise her condition fast.

The pilot radioed ahead, so that when they landed on the helipad at the hospital medical teams were waiting to take care of the patients. Emma was whisked away to a treatment room where doctors took over the responsibility for her, doing everything they could to save her life. Rebecca had to stand by helplessly, watching and waiting.

Cade's friend Jamcs was the consultant in charge of her care, and he came to see Rebecca around an hour later. 'We've given her drugs to try to stop the swelling on her brain and prevent any more seizures,' he told her. 'It'll be some time before we know if the treatment's going to work. We've done tests, and now it's up to the lab to tell us if there's any other antibiotic we can use that will combat the infection more effectively.'

'Thanks, James. I know you're doing everything you possibly can.'

He nodded. 'Why don't you go to Cade's office and get a coffee? There's nothing you can do hanging around here. I'll tell Cade to come and find you when he arrives.'

'Okay.'

She went to Cade's office and phoned William to keep him up to date with what was happening before switching on the coffee machine. He was immediately concerned, both for Emma and for his cousin. 'Is he not back yet?'

'Not yet, no.'

The hot brew was reviving. She sat down on the couch and finished her drink, and then leaned her head back against the cushioned upholstery. Last night she'd watched over Emma and had hardly any sleep. She was so tired…

There was a knock on the door and then William walked into the room. 'Rebecca?' He came over to her. 'I had to come as soon as I heard. You must be worried sick.'

'Yes. There's been no more news. It could be several days before we know if she's going to be all right.'

He sat down beside her and wrapped his arms around her. 'I'm so sorry,' he said. 'I went to see her and she looks so pale…so still. I can't believe this has happened to her.'

'I know. It's a shock. But they're doing all they can.' She glanced at him. 'This must be a difficult time for you—I know you like her—and you must be so worried about your father, too. He's at this hospital, isn't he?'

'Yes, I've just come from seeing him. At least he's responding to the new medication, so we're very relieved about that.'

'I'm really pleased for you.'

He nodded. 'Emma will pull through, Becky. She's young and strong—so full of life. You and Cade were there for her, and she has every chance. She *has* to get better.'

'I hope so. I hope she's strong enough to fight it…'

Tears trickled down her cheeks and William drew her close, comforting her. She laid her head wearily against his shoulder.

Cade found them like that a few minutes later. He walked into the room and ran his glance over them in a shocked, steely, hard look that told Rebecca he'd completely misconstrued the situation.

'William.' He looked at his cousin, clearly trying to keep himself under control. 'You obviously came here as soon as you heard?'

'Yes.' William nodded. 'Becky rang me and told me what was happening. I was worried sick.'

'Of course. You two are becoming very close to one another, aren't you? You were bound to be anxious.'

Rebecca frowned, gently disentangling herself from William, and sat up, her spine rigid. 'He was worried about you, too—but you've made it back all right. I'm so glad that you're safe.'

'I'm okay. Actually, I rushed over here because I didn't want you to be on your own at a time like this… but I see I needn't have worried.' His eyes darkened as he surveyed them once more, but he kept his thoughts to himself, going over to the coffee machine.

'Becky's upset about Emma being so ill,' William said. 'I wanted to come and give her some support. I've been to see Emma…she looks very sick.'

Cade nodded. 'James tells me there's no change in her condition. We just have to wait it out.' He glanced at Rebecca. 'It's probably good news that there's been no change. It means she's stable for now.'

'Yes.' Rebecca watched him, taking in the tense lines of his body. He obviously didn't like the fact that William had been holding her—perhaps he thought that she and his cousin might get together at some point, become more serious in their relationship? He clearly didn't believe they were just friends, but this surely wasn't the time to get into a discussion about it? She was too upset about the events of the last few hours.

Emma was her priority right now—she would talk to Cade privately later. She just hoped he would listen to her.

# CHAPTER SEVEN

'EMMA LOOKS A little better today, don't you think?' Rebecca glanced at Cade for confirmation and he nodded.

They'd just left the isolation room where her sister was being treated and were heading for the car park. A week had passed since Emma had been admitted to hospital, and for most of that time she had been in intensive care, sedated, and hooked up to monitors that checked her vital signs. It had been a worrying, nerve-racking time.

'She does. I think the new antibiotic must be working. James will perhaps be able to lessen the sedation soon, now that the inflammation around her brain is subsiding.'

The lab had identified the specific bacteria that were causing the problem, and for the last few days James had been able to combat the infection with a more suitable medication.

'William will be pleased,' she said. 'He's been coming with me to see her whenever he has the chance—he said he was going to see his father anyway, and felt I could do with the support.'

Cade frowned, but nodded. 'My uncle's doing well

now—that's been a huge relief all round. Obviously William's still worried about him—and about Emma, too—so this news will buoy him up a bit.'

'Yes, I wanted to tell him but I couldn't get through on the phone just now.' She frowned. 'Last time I saw him he said he was going to be extra-busy this next week, because you have him overseeing the building work at the plantation.'

'That's right. I want him to make sure the carpenters stick to the drawings.'

'Is it really so important for him to keep an eye on the tradesmen the whole time? William said they all seem very good at what they do.' She studied Cade thoughtfully for a moment or two. 'I can't help thinking you're giving him this work so that he doesn't have time to be with me.'

'Do you blame me? You know how I feel about you, Rebecca…and yet you and William are so close at times.' His jaw clenched. 'You were in his arms that day at the hospital—how do you think that made me feel? It was gut-wrenching.'

'I'm sorry you felt that way.' She touched his arm lightly, in a soothing, coaxing embrace. 'William's just a friend, that's all. He was trying to comfort me.'

'Oh, yes? Is that so?' His eyes were dark with disbelief. 'I don't think William sees it that way.' His mouth made a flat line. 'I've always looked out for him—heaven knows, I want him to be happy—but I can't see him with you without wanting to break things up.'

'There's nothing going on between William and me.'

He gave her a sceptical look. 'Perhaps he just hasn't made his feelings clear to you yet. It's obvious to me that he cares about you. I saw for myself the way you two hooked up on the boat over here, and you've been to the beach together, as well as meeting up at other times and talking on the phone.'

Annoyed, she flashed him a quick dismissive glance. 'This argument is getting us nowhere,' she said tightly. 'I told you. We're just friends. I like him… he makes me laugh—and he's been good to me.'

'I don't think young men and women can have platonic relationships,' he said.

'Really? Well, that's your problem. You'll just have to deal with it the best way you can.'

He grimaced, walking with her through the main doors of the hospital. 'All right. I'll accept that you perhaps can't see what's going on with William… But I know I'm right. He has feelings for you…and I think you are more than fond of him.'

She sucked in a harsh, annoyed breath and he shot her a quick look as they crossed the car park.

'Look, perhaps we should call a truce?' he suggested. 'You've been under a huge strain this past few weeks, with everything that's happened and now your sister being ill. It would be good for you to be able to relax a bit and get some of that Caribbean holiday you came out here to enjoy. Perhaps you'd like to take some time out to have lunch with me?'

She thought about it. 'I'd like that,' she said. 'And a truce sounds good.'

He took her to a delightful restaurant a few miles along the coast. It was built on clean lines—a white stone building with wide terraces, set into the tree-covered hillside overlooking the rugged seashore.

A waiter showed them to a table in the loggia,

which was decorated with tubs of glorious flame-coloured hibiscus. Rebecca sat down and looked around, immediately absorbed by the breathtaking view of the glittering blue sea. There were yachts in the harbour below, bobbing gently on the water, and in the distance she could see white-painted houses with ochre-tiled roofs dotted about the hillside.

'I've spoken to the landlord about the repairs to the cabin,' she said, when the waiter had brought their first course to the table. She dipped her fork into a golden pastry basket and speared a tasty scallop, drizzled with a delicious Chardonnay bisque sauce. 'He says he can't get anyone out to fix the roof yet because all the tradesmen are in demand after the storm. It'll be a few more days at least—I hope you don't mind me staying at the plantation for this length of time?'

He raised dark brows. 'Of course I don't mind. You can stay as long as you like.' He smiled. 'I like having you around.'

She relaxed back in her seat, relieved. 'That's good. I don't want you to feel that I'm taking things for granted.'

'I think you worry too much,' he said. 'You were supposed to be here for a holiday, and so far you've had precious little chance to enjoy it. If I can make life easier for you in any way I will. I could take you out and about, if you want, show you the island?'

'That would be lovely,' she murmured. 'I just need to be sure that Emma's well and truly on the mend. Maybe then I could go out with you?'

'I'll keep you to that,' he said, his mouth curving.

They finished off their starters and the main course

arrived—braised lamb with risotto and roast vegetables served with a Merlot and shallot gravy.

'The food here is wonderful,' Rebecca said. 'Have you been to this restaurant before?'

He nodded. 'A few times. I've entertained suppliers here, and people who've helped me get the plantation on its feet or helped me with work on the house.'

She was relieved he hadn't mentioned bringing any other woman here. Just thinking about it made her stomach tighten.

They talked about the food, and then about the plantation and his workers. Agwe was on the mend, he said. 'He's been fortunate—the illness hasn't done any permanent damage to his kidneys. And Thomas's hand is healing up nicely.'

'I'm pleased for both of them. They're lucky to have an employer who looks after them and takes their welfare so seriously.'

They finished off their meal with a fruit dessert, followed by cups of richly flavoured Columbian coffee accompanied by thin dark chocolate wafers.

'I'm so full,' Rebecca said, rubbing her stomach. 'I haven't eaten such a great meal for ages. That was perfect.'

He paid the bill and they left the restaurant, walking at his suggestion through the botanical gardens that covered the hillside. They passed along a trail where avocados and apricot trees grew in abundance, alongside hanging bird-of-paradise flowers and flamboyant heliconia that attracted the attention of tiny hummingbirds searching for nectar.

It was incredibly peaceful out here, and in the tropical heat of the late afternoon they stood for a while on a small wooden bridge over a large lily pond and watched the parrots flit among the trees. Cade put his arm around her and pointed to where bright pink flamingos paraded at the side of the pool. One female was feeding its youngster—a small bird that was pure white.

'Oh, aren't they beautiful?' she exclaimed softly. 'The chicks are adorable.'

He laughed softly. 'So are you,' he said, hugging her close and dropping a kiss on her startled lips. 'It's great to see you looking happy.'

She looked up at him in wonder, still dazed by the unexpected gentleness of that kiss. Her lips tingled with excitement and her heart leapt, her pulses racing in anticipation that he might do it again. Slowly, bending his head towards her, he obliged, brushing her mouth with his, sending a trail of fire to course through every part of her body.

She wanted more—wanted to have him holding her and running his hands over her, tugging her to him. And even as the thoughts entered her head, he satisfied her inner yearning, tenderly shaping her body with his palms.

She kissed him hungrily, lifting her arms and running her fingers over the corded muscles of his shoulders. 'You've been so good to me…' she whispered. 'Taking care of me, offering me a place to stay… I've never met anyone who's been so generous, so thoughtful.'

'I think the world of you,' he said. 'In fact… I think I've fallen in love with you. I've never felt this way before, nor met anyone quite like you, and ever since

I first met you I've never stopped wanting you.' His voice was husky, ragged. 'If you knew how you make me feel you would take me into your heart and trust me. I would never hurt you—you need to know that.'

It was what she wanted to hear more than anything. She lifted a hand to his face, stroking his cheek, running her fingers lightly along his hard jawline. 'I wish I could be sure of that,' she said quietly. 'I wish I knew how to make things turn out the way I want. I can't. But I do wish things were different.'

He frowned, and she suddenly realised he might have misinterpreted her words.

'You mean you're still not sure about whether you want to keep your options open? If you're only with me because you're grateful for the way I've looked after you—'

'No, it isn't like that—' she interrupted, but she didn't have the chance to talk to him about it any more because suddenly, alerted by footsteps in the distance and chattering voices, they realised that they were no longer alone.

They moved apart as other visitors to the gardens approached, coming out from the arbour and moving towards the pond.

Wordlessly Rebecca and Cade walked to the other side of the bridge and followed a path through the lush undergrowth on the route back to the car park.

When they were alone once again he drew in a deep breath and said, 'I can't help the way I feel about you, Rebecca. I was lost the moment I first saw you.'

'But—'

He put a finger to her lips, stopping the flow of

words. 'There's a barbecue on the beach in a few days' time. I thought you might like to go with me?'

'Yes, that sounds good.' She smiled at him tentatively.

There was little point in arguing with him, in pointing out where his thinking was flawed. And she *wanted* to be with him. Her efforts to keep him at bay all this time had been for nothing, because she had well and truly fallen for him. She had to admit it to herself. He was everything she wanted in a man, but she wasn't sure how it had happened that she'd come to love him.

How could it ever be right for her to be with him—knowing that she might never be able to give him the family he wanted? She wasn't being fair to him, letting this go on, and yet she couldn't bear *not* to be with him.

She had to find a way to sort things out, to come to terms with the kind of future she might have. Was it possible for her ever to be with Cade?

Over the next few days Emma gradually gained strength and was able to sit up in bed. Before too long she was even able to chat without getting too tired.

'You're looking so much better,' Rebecca told her. 'I'm so glad you're on the mend.'

'It's you I have to thank for that,' Emma said, leaning back against her pillows.

'Hmm... I think there's more to it than that,' Rebecca murmured.

She looked at the bedside table, bright with colourful flowers and cards from well-wishers. There was one, she noticed, from William—an especially beautiful embossed card, inscribed with affectionate sentiment.

She looked closely at Emma. Her sister's long chestnut hair had regained some of its sheen and her blue-grey eyes were bright. 'Could that sparkle in your eyes be due to the fact that you've had a handsome young man visiting you every day while you've been here?'

Emma blushed. 'You noticed? It's true—William's been coming to see me every chance he gets. He brings me fruit and flowers, and he's doing everything he can to cheer me up.' She glanced at the bedside locker. 'He brought me those beautiful roses, and there's a note with them that says he's thinking of me always.'

'Well, well…isn't *that* a lovely turn of events? How do you feel about him?'

Emma's cheeks reddened even further. 'I really like him, Becky. He has such a good sense of humour, and we have so much in common. I think we clicked the first time we met.' She studied Rebecca thoughtfully. 'You feel the same way about his cousin, don't you? I've seen the signs, and I'm pretty sure you're in love with Cade?'

'What makes you think that?'

'I saw the way you looked at him when he came to the cabin—*and* when we were at Selwyn's Bar. You were laughing and joking with William, but it was Cade you were watching when you thought no one was looking. And I've seen it when you've both been here to visit me.' Her mouth made a crooked shape. 'To be honest, I don't think men can see beyond their noses.'

Rebecca sighed. That was true enough. Cade

wouldn't listen when she told him she and William were just good friends.

'I don't know what to do, Emma. Yes, it's true—I do love Cade. And I know he feels the same way about me. But there's no future for us, is there? How can I be with him if I can't have children? He says he wants a family, and I can't deny him that. I don't know what to do.'

'There's one thing you can do.' Emma reached for her sister's hand. 'Go for treatment…have surgery to try to open your fallopian tubes.'

Rebecca frowned. 'But the doctors back home weren't keen on that—they said it's not done very often. They told me my best prospect would be to try in vitro fertilisation in the future—and that will depend on my ovaries being unaffected by the scar tissue…which they aren't. Besides, IVF isn't always successful. You hear of people having several courses without a good result.'

'That's a negative way of thinking. You're better than that, Becky. You were always a positive person until this happened to you. If you're worried about IVF you should go and make an appointment at a clinic—talk to someone about having specialised surgery to open up your fallopian tubes and remove any scar tissue that's causing a problem. What's the point of waiting? Not knowing if there is anything you can do about it is making you put your life on hold.'

'I suppose you're right.' Rebecca tried to think things through. 'I'll think about it. It's such a big step, though.' She closed her eyes briefly. 'I think I've been putting it off in case it doesn't work.'

'Don't just think about it. Do it. At least then you'll

know definitely, won't you? And then you'll be in a position to make proper decisions about your future. At the moment you're in limbo.' Emma squeezed her hand. 'Don't waste any more time, Becky. In fact—pass me my handbag from the bedside locker, will you? I did some research when I knew you were coming over to stay for a while. There's a clinic on one of the islands that would be just right for you. I checked into them and they're really good, by all accounts. The surgeons there are really skilled.'

Rebecca did as she asked and Emma fetched a card out of her bag.

'Here. Give them a ring,' she said. 'Do it today. They told me they should be able to fit you in at short notice if you're a private patient.' She frowned. 'And for goodness' sake talk to Cade.'

Rebecca shook her head. 'I can't do it now—not while you're still in hospital. What if they can do it straight away? I would be so worried about you. I'll ring them in a few weeks…when you're up and about.'

'No, no… There's no time like the present. I want you to do it now… I'm feeling so much better. I'm not in danger any more, and with any luck by the time I'm out of here you'll be back from the clinic, so we can spend some time together at the cabin. You might only need an overnight stay in hospital. Rebecca—call them and make an appointment.' She smiled. 'William will be here to keep me company when he's not at the plantation. You don't need to worry about me.'

'I can't. Not now. I need to be here with *you*.'

'Those are just excuses.' Emma pursed her lips determinedly. 'I'll do it for you.' She started to reach for her phone.

'No, don't do that.'

Rebecca looked at the card once more. The clinic was situated on an island nearby—just a ferry ride away. She *could* do it, couldn't she? At least then she would know if things were ever going to be all right for her, wouldn't she?

'Okay,' she sighed. 'I'll do it. I'll give them a call.'

'Good. Put it on speaker phone so I can hear what they say.'

Rebecca dialled the number on the card.

'You're in luck,' the receptionist at the clinic said, when Rebecca had introduced herself and explained the situation. 'We've had a couple of cancellations—one patient has a family crisis to deal with and another has decided to try an alternative treatment—so Mr Solomon has some free time. I can book you in to see him tomorrow, if you like? That will be an initial appointment, and he'll arrange any other details with you when you see him.'

Rebecca shook her head. That was far too soon. 'I wasn't expecting to be seen so quickly,' she said. 'I'm not sure—'

'She'll do it,' Emma said, cutting in on the conversation. 'Make the appointment, please.'

'Madam?'

'Sorry, that's my sister...adding her two pennyworth.' Rebecca took a deep breath. 'Okay, then. Thank you. I'll come in tomorrow. We'll take it from there.'

She cut the call a couple of minutes later and sat quietly for a bit longer, getting over the enormity of what she was doing. She had to think of practicalities. There would be a ferry later today. If she hurried she could throw a few things into her holdall and be on her way. Once she arrived on the island she could think about booking a hotel room near to the clinic.

'I came over to the Caribbean to see you and to ask your advice,' she said, looking at Emma. 'I knew you'd know what I should do.' She gave Emma a hug. 'You're my best big sister,' she said. 'I love you to bits.' Glancing at her once again, she added, 'And now look what I've done—I've tired you out with all this talking. I'm sorry.'

'I'll be fine.' Emma smiled. 'I'm feeling so much better now…and I'm getting up and walking about a bit every day… But they say they want to keep me in for several more days to be certain everything's all right.' She sent her a meaningful look. 'Time enough for you to have the surgery,' she said. 'You can call me from the clinic.'

They talked for a minute or two longer and then Rebecca stood up to leave. 'I'll go and see if I can find Cade,' she said.

She found him in the main area of the Emergency Unit, talking with a man and woman who were standing by the main desk. He had his back to her, but she went up to him and laid a hand lightly on his arm.

'Hi, I've just been up to Emma's room and I thought I'd come down here to see you, if you're not too busy.'

'I'm never to busy to see you,' he said, turning to face her.

He was smiling, obviously in a good mood, and she suddenly recognised the couple with him.

'It's Mr and Mrs Tennyson, isn't it?' she said, her eyes widening.

'That's right. We wanted to come in and thank everyone for looking after us so well…and especially to thank Dr Byfield for saving Annie.'

They both looked well—much better than when she'd seen them last, when Jane Tennyson had been suffering with broken ribs after the car accident and her husband Paul had been concussed from his head injury.

'You seem to be recovering well,' Cade said.

'Oh, yes, we're on the mend,' Jane said happily. 'My ribs are healing, and Paul is just fine. And as for little Annie—she's doing brilliantly.'

'I'm so pleased she's recovered.' Rebecca looked around. 'Where is she? Is she not with you today?'

'Oh, she's here.' Jane smiled broadly. 'The nurses were so happy to see her they whisked her away to show her off to everyone. Here she is now.'

Greta was carrying Annie back to them. The little girl looked the picture of health, and she put her arms out to Cade to be picked up. She moved her fingers impatiently, wanting his attention.

Paul Tennyson chuckled. 'Oh, she can't get enough of you. You're her favourite person today.'

Cade smiled and took Annie into his arms, giving her a cuddle. 'You're a real cherub, aren't you?' he said. He tickled the little girl's tummy and she giggled.

Watching them, Rebecca felt her heart contract with pain. She longed to hold the infant herself, but didn't trust herself not to break down. She wouldn't want to give her back.

'She's gorgeous,' she said, trying to keep a firm lid on her emotions.

Cade was jiggling the little girl gently up and down

and she was laughing, loving the sensation and wanting more.

'Again!' Annie squealed with delight. 'Again.'

'Enough, sweetheart,' Cade said after a minute or two. 'Your mum wants to hold you.' He handed her to her mother and the trio said their goodbyes and went on their way.

He turned to Rebecca. 'We'll go into my office. We're having a quiet time in Emergency just now.' As he led the way he said, 'It was great seeing them now that they're more or less back to normal, wasn't it?'

She nodded, trying to get a grip on herself. He sent her an odd look. 'What is it, Rebecca?' He opened the door to his office and ushered her inside. 'Has something happened? Is there something you want to talk to me about?'

'I… Yes…' She took a deep breath.

She'd wanted to talk to him about them maybe having a future together, but seeing him with the infant had thrown her into a quandary. What if her treatment was unsuccessful? How could she put him though that?

'I've decided to go away for a few days,' she said finally. 'I'm going over to Barbados for a short break.'

His dark brows drew together. 'When are you going? I could perhaps get some time off and go with you.'

'No… I'm going today. I've made up my mind… It was a spur-of-the-moment decision and I'm getting the ferry later this afternoon.'

'I don't understand.' He looked bewildered. 'Why would you leave when your sister's still in the hospital?'

'She's…she's feeling much better now… She thinks

I don't need to worry about her…and she'll have William to keep her company.'

His frown deepened. 'Wait a minute… That's what this is about, isn't it? It's about William. Is he with Emma? I had hoped you were over him—that you might—'

'I've *never* had any romantic feelings for William,' she said, cutting Cade off unexpectedly. 'I told you, I like him as a friend. It's you I want… I love *you*…'

He drew in a sharp breath and she went on hurriedly.

'I didn't mean for it to happen, and I tried to stop it, but it just… It's impossible—I can't love you, Cade. It would be wrong for us. It wouldn't work out.'

'But *why* wouldn't it?' He was bewildered. 'We're so good together, Rebecca. And now that you've told me that you love me, too, what's to stop us?' He drew her to him, kissing her fiercely, as though he couldn't bear to let her go. 'We'd be perfect together.' He murmured the words against her mouth. 'I love you.'

The kiss was her undoing. Her lips softened under the tender onslaught and her whole body quivered as he ran his hands over her, shaping her to him. 'I know your ex let you down,' he said in a roughened voice, 'but don't let him come between us. I love you…you say you love me…what could possibly be wrong?'

An alarm bell started to ring in the Emergency Unit and a nurse's voice came over the speaker system to say that a patient was being brought in by ambulance. Cade stiffened, but didn't let her go.

Rebecca laid a shaky hand on his chest. 'Cade, the truth is you've told me you want a family and I don't think I can give you that. I told you I was ill, and there's a lot of scar tissue…adhesions. My doctors have said they don't think I'll be able to conceive. I don't want to put you through that. It wouldn't be fair to deny you something you've always dreamed of.'

He was staring down at her, a shocked look on his face. 'You can't have children? That's a *terrible* diagnosis. Why on earth didn't you tell me this before?'

Before he'd fallen in love with her?

'I don't know—I'm not sure. It was painful for me and I couldn't face up to it. The time never seemed right. I was too busy trying to stop myself from falling for you.'

'Was that because of how your ex reacted?'

She nodded. 'After I told Drew what the doctors had said he went away for a while to think things through. Then he told me he'd thought long and hard about it but he couldn't stay with me if there was the possibility of my not having children.' Her face crumpled. 'I couldn't bear to have you say that to me. I'm sorry.'

A muscle flicked in his jaw. 'We need to talk about this,' he said. 'It's such a shock…coming out of the blue like this. I'd no idea.' He frowned. 'Look, I have to go and deal with this emergency, but we have to talk some more.' He stared at her, his eyes smoke-dark, flickering with a troubled mixture of pain and anger. 'You should have told me, Rebecca.'

'I know. I'm sorry.'

He left her, reluctantly, to go and deal with the patient who was being brought in, and Rebecca made her way out of the hospital, went back to the plantation.

Once there, she quickly packed a bag and called for a taxi. She wasn't going to use Cade's car any more.

It wouldn't be right. She would have to send for the rest of her things at a later date.

Things were surely over between them. He'd been utterly shocked and dismayed by her revelation, and all the talking in the world wouldn't make things come right. He deserved better. He deserved to find happiness with a woman who could give him the family he wanted. This was her burden to bear. It didn't have to be his.

She hurried out of the house as the taxi driver pulled up outside. 'Where to, miss?' he asked.

'The ferry port,' she said.

She looked back at the house as they drove away and inside she felt as though her heart was breaking.

# CHAPTER EIGHT

Rebecca opened her eyes and looked around the unfamiliar room. For a moment or two she was disorientated and couldn't remember where she was, but then a nurse approached the bedside and smiled.

'Oh, you're back with us! You came round from surgery and then went to sleep for a couple of hours. How are you feeling?'

'I'm okay… I think.'

'Good. It'll take some time for the effects of the anaesthetic to wear off, but you don't need to do anything. Just rest for a while. I'll take your blood pressure.' The nurse wrapped the cuff around Rebecca's upper arm and checked the monitor. 'It's a little low,' she said after a moment or two, 'but that's to be expected after surgery.'

'Do you know anything about how the surgery went?' Still a little groggy, Rebecca struggled to sit up in bed. She was a bit sore from the procedure she'd undergone, and there was a dressing on her tummy where the surgeon had stitched up a small incision.

'Dr Solomon will be in to explain things to you in a little while,' the nurse said. 'You were so fortunate to have him as your surgeon—he's a brilliant man—very skilled at doing tubal surgery.'

'So I've been told.' Perhaps it was the after-effects of the general anaesthetic, but Rebecca was feeling overwhelmed, and above all isolated and lonely. She was on her own in this—but then she'd known that from the beginning, hadn't she?

She tried to put a brave face on things, but the nurse must have guessed how she was feeling, because she said, 'How about a cup of tea? That should help to cheer you up.'

'Thanks. That would be lovely.'

'Oh, and you have a visitor… Are you up to seeing anyone yet?'

'A visitor?' Rebecca echoed.

Who could that be? No one knew she was here except for Emma. She'd phoned her sister yesterday, to tell her that the surgery was being done on a day-patient basis—the doctor had found an operating theatre slot for the day after her first appointment. He'd said that if all was well she would be able to leave hospital about four hours after the procedure.

'Oh, yes. He said he came over on the ferry this morning. Looks like a dark thundercloud, but gorgeous with it. He's been here since you went to theatre, pacing up and down, wearing a hole in the waiting room floor. Mind you…' The nurse grinned. 'He could come and pace *my* floor any time!'

'Cade's here? Dr Byfield?'

'That's the one. That'll be two cups of tea, then, will it?'

Rebecca nodded, still trying to take it in. What was he doing here? How had he known where to find her?

The nurse left the room and a moment later Cade came through the door. He stood by the doorjamb, studying her, not saying a word, his face taut, his expression one of controlled anger.

She swallowed apprehensively. 'I wasn't expecting to see you,' she said in a quiet voice. 'Come in and sit by the bed. How did you know where to find me?'

He strode towards the bed, but ignored her offer of a seat. 'I asked Emma where you'd be. She was surprised you hadn't told me. So was I. I thought we were going to talk. Yet you took off without another word.'

'Okay. Okay, I'm sorry.' She looked at him doubtfully. 'We can talk now, if you want.'

'It's a bit late, isn't it…? A bit overdue? I can't imagine why you would leave like that, without saying anything or telling me where you were going. What were you *thinking*?'

She frowned. 'I don't know, exactly. What's the point in talking if I might not be able to have children? I may have to get used to the idea, but you don't.'

'So you walked out on me? You decided I didn't need to know what was going on—that I wouldn't want any part of it?' His jaw was clenched, his mouth a flat, harsh line. 'I told you I would help you any way I can—that I would always be there for you. Did you think they were just meaningless words?'

She gave a half-hearted shrug. 'People say all sorts of things on the spur of the moment, when nothing much is at stake. Drew promised he'd love me for ever, but that fizzled out a very short time after I became ill.'

'I'm not Drew. It's high time you stopped comparing me to him.'

'But you made it very clear to me that you want children—that you want a large family to make up for what you missed out on in the past. I couldn't be certain of giving you that—what was I supposed to think or do?'

'You should have talked it through with me. Yes, I want a family—but I've fallen in love with you, Rebecca… How can I ignore that? Do you *really* think I'm the kind of man who will reject you because you can't give me everything I want? Do you *really* think I'm that selfish?'

Her shoulders lifted. 'I don't know what to think. Are you going to sit down or not? Did you just come here to quarrel with me?' she queried grumpily. 'Because I can pick a fight with myself—I don't need you to do it for me.'

He laughed—a short, sharp sound that cracked on the air. 'No, I'm sorry.' Finally he pulled up a chair and sat down beside her. 'I came to see how you are…and to make you see that I'm nothing like your ex. I *will* be here for you, Rebecca, no matter what happens.'

She swallowed against the lump that had suddenly formed in her throat. A sheen of tears misted her eyes. 'I never expected that,' she said in a muffled voice. 'I'm so glad you're here, Cade.'

She put out a hand to him and he grasped it reassuringly, enclosing her palm in his long fingers, resting their entwined hands on the bedcovers.

'So how did the surgery go?' he asked.

'I don't know,' she admitted. 'They haven't told me yet. The surgeon will be in later to see me.'

The nurse came in with a tea tray and set it down

on the bedside table. 'There you are. Help yourselves. Mr Solomon will be here soon. He's just talking to another patient.'

'Thanks.'

'You're welcome.' She glanced at the monitor. 'Your heartrate's gone up in the last few minutes.' She waggled an admonishing finger. 'Not good.' Then she glanced at Cade and sighed. 'But hardly surprising, really.' She sniffed and left the room.

Rebecca laughed, and then held on to her tummy, where the stitches were under pressure. 'She thinks you're gorgeous,' she said.

He raised a dark brow. 'Oh? And what do *you* think?'

'I think you're pretty wonderful, all told. I just don't want you to get swell-headed about it.'

'There's not much likelihood of that. I don't have time to be swayed by what people think. I'm a very practical kind of man. I like to know where I stand, make plans and see them through.'

'That can be difficult. Things don't always go to plan.'

'That's true.'

There was a knock on the door and Mr Solomon walked into the room. He was a tall man, dressed in an immaculate dark suit.

'Hello,' he said, smiling. 'It's good to see you sitting up and with a bit more colour in your cheeks. Is it all right if I come in and talk to you about the results of your surgery?'

'Yes, please. Come in. Sit down.'

Cade glanced at her. 'Would you prefer it if I leave? I can wait outside.'

She shook her head. 'No, it's all right. I'd like you to stay.'

Mr Solomon sat down. His expression became serious and Rebecca immediately sensed trouble. She watched him, her shoulders stiff, trying to prepare herself for what was to come. It didn't look good.

'You'll recall we talked about the tests we did yesterday?' he said, and she nodded. 'There were a lot of adhesions around your ovaries and both fallopian tubes, and the hysterosalpingogram showed us that the tubes weren't viable in that state.'

'Yes…' It was almost a whisper.

'As we discussed, with that much scarring it's not always easy to remedy the situation, but we went ahead and did as much as we could.'

'And the result?'

'The good news is that one of your ovaries is now completely clear…'

She sighed with relief. It meant that IVF might be an option at least.

'Also, one of your fallopian tubes was blocked at the uterine end, which was good as far as we were concerned, because it was easier to clear. So, it means that with one fallopian tube and a functional ovary your chances of conceiving a baby are much better than they were before you came to see us.' He frowned. 'There is a possibility, though, that the surgery in itself might cause more scarring. But at the moment I'd say you have a forty to fifty per cent chance of getting pregnant.'

She smiled. That was so much better than no

chance at all. ‘Thank you, Mr Solomon. I’m really grateful for everything you’ve done…and for seeing me so quickly.’

‘I’m glad to have helped…and I had a cancellation so there was no problem getting you into theatre.’ He checked the monitors. ‘We’ll check your blood pressure and temperature again, and when they’re satisfactory, we’ll let you go. The nurse will go through your aftercare instructions with you. Any problems at all—come back to us.’

‘Thanks again, Doctor.’

He left the room and she sat with Cade, waiting for the news to sink in.

‘It isn’t perfect,’ she said. ‘But it’s better than I expected.’

He squeezed her hand. ‘I’m glad for you, Rebecca. You did the right thing, coming here. But you should have told me. You should have trusted me. You should always have faith in me.’

He kissed her gently on the mouth, and then leaned back in his chair as the nurse came back into the room.

‘I need to check your blood pressure again,’ she said, ‘and then we’ll see about sending you home.’

Rebecca left the hospital with Cade a few hours later. They took a taxi to the ferry port and managed to time things just right, with the boat leaving for St Marie-Rose shortly after that.

The crossing was smooth, the sea a tranquil, glassy blue. They sat by the deck rail, looking out at the coastline, sipping ice-cold mango juice and eating cool slices of melon.

‘How do you feel?’ Cade asked. ‘Did they say anything about how long it will take you to recover from the surgery?'

'I'm feeling okay. It shouldn't take too long at all, really. I'll probably be back to normal in a couple of days.'

'That's good. We'll get you settled in back at the house and you can rest up as much as you need. I'll take you to see Emma whenever I can, or I'll arrange for Benjamin to take you there and bring you back.'

'That's good. Thank you… I can't wait to see her.' She frowned. 'I should be with her when she goes home to the cabin. She'll need someone with her for a few weeks while she's convalescing.'

'Erm…and what about *you*? You've just had an operation yourself, so you'll both need some looking after! Why don't you both stay at the plantation house? There's plenty of room, and you'll be a lot more comfortable there, I expect…and Harriet will love being able to cook for more than just me.'

'I'll ask her.' She smiled at him and laid her hand on his. 'Thank you…again.'

A week later she was starting to feel a little better. The small laparoscopy wound was healing up and she had managed to visit Emma earlier in the day. She had been greeted with the news that she was soon going to be able to come home.

'Stay at the plantation house?' Emma had been thrilled by the invitation. 'Oh, wow! That sounds fantastic…and I'll be so much nearer to William, won't I? He says he has a cottage not far from there. Oh, it gets better and better. I can't wait to get out of here.'

Cade had already started to move Emma's things from the cabin to the plantation house. He seemed to like having a house full of people. He'd told Rebecca to pick out a room for her sister and that he'd do whatever she wanted to make her comfortable there.

Now, though, Rebecca was getting ready to go out for the evening with him.

'There's that barbecue on the beach, remember?' he'd said earlier. 'It starts just before sunset and goes on till people start leaving.' He grinned. 'I think it's time for you to have some fun. If you're feeling up to it, of course?'

'Yay!'

She didn't know what to wear, but in the end picked out a colourful sarong that had a thin halter-neck strap and left her shoulders bare. It wrapped around her, nipping in at the waist and gliding over her hips in soft folds, and gave a glimpse of a long tanned thigh as she walked. She'd pinned her hair up, so that curls massed around the back of her head and fell in gentle tendrils to frame her face.

When she had finished dressing she went downstairs, ready to leave as soon as the taxi arrived at the front of the house. Cade had been looking around for his house keys, but when he saw her approach he stopped what he was doing and stared at her, transfixed.

'Oh… Rebecca… Oh…you look stunning.' His dark gaze moved over her as though he was captivated by the vision before him. 'You look so lovely…'

'I'm glad you think so.' She ran a hand over the sarong. 'I wasn't sure what people wear at these parties.'

'Whatever they wear, you'll be the most beautiful girl there. I won't dare let you out of my sight for an instant.'

She laughed and went out with him to the waiting cab. The driver whisked them away, stopping to drop them off at the shore a few minutes later.

They walked on to the sand and watched the setting sun dip slowly on the horizon, casting an arc of gold over the blue sky. Palm fronds waved gently in the light breeze and gradually the sky turned a dusky pink.

Behind them the bartender had opened up his wooden shack and was serving fruity rum punch and piña coladas. At the same time the chef had fired up the barbecue, so that soon the aroma of steak and chicken filled the air. People were soon queuing up to sample tasty titbits.

'Try these jerk chicken wraps,' Cade said, taking her over to where a buffet table had been set out. 'They're delicious.'

She tasted them, along with seafood skewers and spicy roast pork. 'Mmm…mmm…mmm…' she said. 'You're right. Everything tastes wonderful. I *love* Caribbean food. And I definitely want to try those coconut kisses for dessert.'

The musicians struck up a rhythm on their steel drums and people started to dance, swaying in time with the music. Cade led Rebecca on to a flat stretch of sand and for a while they moved together to the sound of calypso and reggae.

As the sky darkened and the moon glittered on the

sea he held her close and kissed her tenderly. 'I love you,' he said. 'Will you marry me?'

'I love you, too,' she said softly, her heart leaping with joy at the unexpected proposal. 'And I want to marry you more than anything in the world.'

He pulled in a quick, shaky breath, his face lighting up in a smile. He lowered his head and kissed her passionately on the mouth. She clung to him, wrapping her arms around him.

'Have you thought this through?' she asked after a while, when they came up for air. 'I've had the surgery, but it isn't a guarantee that everything will be all right.'

'I want to be with you,' he said simply, taking her by the hand and leading her by the water's edge. 'If children come along, that will be wonderful. But if they don't…we could go for adoption or find some other way of satisfying that need.'

He looked at her.

'It's early days, but perhaps you should think about going back to working with children—even if it's only part-time? You have a lot to give, Rebecca. You've had a lot to think about these last few months—this year—but now you have a chance to be happy again. We *both* have that chance.'

'I could be happy with you,' she said. 'Being with you is what I want more than anything.'

He slid his arm around her waist and they walked along the beach, the sound of steel drums floating on the air, the fading light dancing on the water.

'We'll be good together,' he said. 'I feel it inside.

It's as though I've been waiting for you to come along my whole life.'

They stood in the shelter of a coconut palm and he took her in his arms. His kisses filled her with exhilaration and made her body tingle with joyful anticipation.

There was a lifetime of love ahead of them. She knew it.

# EPILOGUE

'REBECCA, THE CATERER wants to know where to put the large fruit basket.'

Cade was frowning and Rebecca smiled. For a man who was so good at dealing with emergencies and handling people, he was being strangely inept when it came to dealing with the intricacies of organising his cousin's wedding.

Of course he'd had more than usual to contend with these last few days, with the plantation house full of guests. Her family had come over to the Caribbean to stay for a few weeks, and his family was here, too.

'Tell her I thought it would look good on the end table,' she said. 'The one at the far end of the marquee.'

'Okay.' He came over to her and placed a hand lightly on her tummy. 'How's the bump doing today? Oh…he's kicking.' His mouth curved and he stayed very still for a while, waiting for his son to move around some more.

'Yes, he is.' She laid her left hand on top of his, the gold wedding band glinting brightly in the sunlight that streamed in through the windows. 'He's been doing that all morning. It must be all the excitement, and I think he's feeling cramped in there…only four more weeks to go.' She sighed, looking down at her large abdomen. 'Trust William and Emma to decide to get married when I'm as big as this—I wanted to wear something special for their big day.'

He placed a gentle kiss on her soft lips. 'You look lovely. And think of it this way—at least our boy will be at his auntie's wedding.'

She laughed. 'Okay, I'll grant you that. But let's hope we get the timing right with the next one.'

He wrapped his arms around her and kissed her tenderly. 'Of course we will. It'll be perfect, I promise you. When our children come along the timing will always be right.'

* * * * *